OXFORD WORLD'S CLASSICS

JOSEPH CONRAD

Typhoon
and Other Tales

Edited with an Introduction and Notes by
CEDRIC WATTS

T0130609

OXFORD
UNIVERSITY PRESS

OXFORD

UNIVERSITY PRESS

Great Clarendon Street, Oxford OX2 6DP

Oxford University Press is a department of the University of Oxford.
It furthers the University's objective of excellence in research, scholarship,
and education by publishing worldwide in

Oxford New York

Auckland Bangkok Buenos Aires Cape Town Chennai
Dar es Salaam Delhi Hong Kong Istanbul Karachi Kolkata
Kuala Lumpur Madrid Melbourne Mexico City Mumbai Nairobi
São Paulo Shanghai Singapore Taipei Tokyo Toronto

Oxford is a registered trade mark of Oxford University Press
in the UK and in certain other countries

Published in the United States
by Oxford University Press Inc., New York

General Editor's Preface, Select Bibliography,
Chronology © Mara Kalnins 2002
Introduction, Note on the Text, Explanatory Notes,
Glossary © Cedric Watts 1986, 2002

The moral rights of the author have been asserted

Database right Oxford University Press (maker)

First published as a World's Classics paperback 1986
Reissued as an Oxford World's Classics paperback 1998
Revised edition 2002
Reissued 2008

British Library Cataloguing in Publication Data

Data available

Library of Congress Cataloging in Publication Data

Data available

ISBN 978-0-19-953903-1

17

Typeset in Ehrhardt
by RefineCatch Limited, Bungay, Suffolk
Printed and bound in Great Britain by Clays Ltd, Elcograf S.p.A.

TYPHOON

AND OTHER TALES

JOSEPH CONRAD was born Józef Teodor Konrad Korzeniowski in the Russian part of Poland in 1857. His parents were punished by the Russians for their Polish nationalist activities and both died while Conrad was still a child. In 1874 he left Poland for France and in 1878 began a career with the British merchant navy. He spent nearly twenty years as a sailor before becoming a full-time novelist. He became a British citizen in 1886 and settled permanently in England after his marriage to Jessie George in 1896.

Conrad is a writer of extreme subtlety and sophistication; works such as *Heart of Darkness*, *Lord Jim*, and *Nostromo* display technical complexities which have established him as one of the first English 'Modernists'. He is also noted for the unprecedented vividness with which he communicates a pessimist's view of man's personal and social destiny in such works as *The Secret Agent*, *Under Western Eyes*, and *Victory*. Despite the immediate critical recognition that they received in his lifetime, Conrad's major novels did not sell well, and he lived in relative poverty until the commercial success of *Chance* (1914) secured for him a wider public and an assured income. In 1923 he visited the United States, to great acclaim, and he was offered a knighthood (which he declined) shortly before his death in 1924. Since then his reputation has steadily grown, and he is now seen as a writer who revolutionized the English novel and was arguably the most important single innovator of the twentieth century.

CEDRIC WATTS is Professor of English at the University of Sussex. His books on Conrad include *Conrad's 'Heart of Darkness': A Critical and Contextual Discussion* (1977), *A Preface to Conrad* (1982, 2nd edn. 1993), *The Deceptive Text* (1984), *Joseph Conrad: A Literary Life* (1989), and *Joseph Conrad* (1994). His other works include *A Preface to Greene* and (with John Sutherland) *Henry V, War Criminal? and Other Shakespeare Puzzles*. He has edited numerous texts by Shakespeare, Hardy, Cunninghame Graham, and Conrad.

MARA KALNINS is the General Editor of the Works of Joseph Conrad in the Oxford World's Classics series. She is a Fellow of Corpus Christi College, Cambridge, and Staff Tutor in Literature, Board of Continuing Education.

OXFORD WORLD'S CLASSICS

*For over 100 years Oxford World's Classics have brought
readers closer to the world's great literature. Now with over 700
titles—from the 4,000-year-old myths of Mesopotamia to the
twentieth century's greatest novels—the series makes available
lesser-known as well as celebrated writing.*

*The pocket-sized hardbacks of the early years contained
introductions by Virginia Woolf, T. S. Eliot, Graham Greene,
and other literary figures which enriched the experience of reading.
Today the series is recognized for its fine scholarship and
reliability in texts that span world literature, drama and poetry,
religion, philosophy and politics. Each edition includes perceptive
commentary and essential background information to meet the
changing needs of readers.*

CONTENTS

GENERAL EDITOR'S PREFACE

Conrad is acknowledged as one of the great writers of the twentieth century, but neither in his lifetime nor after have his works been available in authoritative texts. This was partly because Conrad himself revised his writings at several stages (in manuscript, typescript, and proofs), partly because many of his works appeared in different versions (slightly so in the English and American editions, significantly so in serial and book form), and partly because he himself continued to revise them for subsequent publication. Moreover he was involved in still further revision of the texts when his works were issued in the collected editions of Doubleday and Heinemann in 1921, though the extent of his involvement varied considerably from work to work. Like many authors, he also suffered from the well-meant, but often misguided, editorial efforts of his publishers who not only imposed their own house styling but sometimes changed his grammar, spelling, and punctuation, and even altered whole phrases. The textual history of Conrad's works—the revisions they underwent and their transmission and publication—is therefore an intricate and complicated one. A scholarly edition of the *Letters and Works* is currently being prepared by Cambridge University Press and six volumes of the *Letters* as well as two novels have been published to date.

In the absence of authoritative texts which accurately incorporate Conrad's corrections and revisions and which remove the editorial interference, house styling, and printing errors of his publishers, the base-texts for this new Oxford World's Classics edition must be the British first editions. These editions are important because they are what Conrad originally expected to be published, because they were the texts which first shaped his reputation as a writer, and because they are free of later layers of editorial interference. As late as 1919, when Conrad was correcting copy for a limited Collected Edition, he still affirmed their importance: 'I devote particular care to the text of the English Edition always and it is to be considered the standard one' (letter to Fisher Unwin, 27 May 1919). At the same time, however, they are themselves flawed by numerous misprints and some idiosyncratic house styling. The present edition therefore aims to correct such errors in order to restore Conrad's idiom and distinctive prose style.

In this edition the following emendations have been made silently throughout: (*a*) obvious spelling errors and typesetter's mistakes have been corrected; (*b*) inadvertent omissions have been supplied in the case of incomplete quotation marks, final stops, apostrophes in colloquial contractions (e.g. 'o'clock') and the stop following a title (e.g. 'Mr.'); (*c*) the convention of hyphenating words such as 'to-day', 'to-night', 'good-bye' has been dropped in accordance with modern usage; (*d*) inconsistencies in punctuation inside or outside quotation marks have been standardized and other inconsistencies— such as hyphenated words—have been regularized in accordance with Conrad's most frequent practice in each work; (*e*) paragraphs have been indented throughout in accordance with modern conventions and a few typographical details—such as display capitals, chapter numbers and headings, and running titles—have been regularized. However, where the sense of a phrase has been occluded or where there is a controversial reading or some specific textual difficulty, the editor of each volume will record the editorial emendation and explain the adopted reading briefly in the Note on the Text or in an explanatory note where the reader may also be directed to further reading on the issue.

Each volume has an Introduction which seeks to relate the work to Conrad's life and other writings, to place it in its literary and cultural context, and to offer a cogent argument for its relevance both to his time and ours. Although Conrad is a modern writer, his specialized terminology is not always familiar to contemporary readers nor are the literary, historical, and political allusions always clear. Explanatory notes are therefore supplied but it is assumed that words or expressions found in a good dictionary will not need to be glossed. Appendixes in each volume will also provide material useful to the reader, such as a glossary of nautical or foreign terms, maps, or important additional texts. Conrad's own series of prefaces and Author's Notes (the latter written between 1917 and 1920) are reprinted as an appendix to each volume.

Finally, any work on so major a figure as Conrad must be deeply indebted to the research of many scholars and critics, but I would like to express my gratitude especially to Jacques Berthoud, Jim Boulton, Andrew Brown, Laurence Davies, George Donaldson,

Donald Rude, J. H. Stape, and Cedric Watts for sharing their expertise, and to Judith Luna of Oxford University Press for her unfailing encouragement and advice.

Mara Kalnins

Corpus Christi, Cambridge

ACKNOWLEDGEMENTS

In preparing this edition, books which I found particularly useful were *Tait's Seamanship*, by James Tait, Master Mariner (Glasgow: James Brown & Son, 1902), Gershom Bradford's *A Glossary of Sea Terms* (London: Cassell, 1954), Norman Sherry's *Conrad's Eastern World* (London: Cambridge University Press, 1966), and Paul Kirschner's edition of Conrad's *Typhoon and Other Stories* (London: Penguin, 1990; repr. 1992). I am also grateful for the help generously given by friends and colleagues, particularly Mario Curreli, Laurence Davies, Robert Hampson, Tony Inglis (who navigated me skilfully past Koh-ring), the late Hans van Marle, S. W. Reid, and Alan Sinfield.

Cedric Watts

INTRODUCTION

I

The four tales in this volume illustrate both the diversity and the imaginative integrity of Joseph Conrad's work. They vary in location, situation, tone, texture, and intensity, but they all maintain characteristic Conradian preoccupations—with isolation and inadequate communication, with transient and beleaguered solidarity, and with the ordeal that tests character. Each tale offers a sympathetic view of an individual subjected not only to physical stress but also to prejudice and incomprehension: MacWhirr, the indomitable captain who is regarded as merely 'a stupid man'; Falk, the lonely survivor reviled as a bestial cannibal; Yanko Goorall, the castaway scorned as a pariah; and Leggatt, the intrepid seaman pursued as a murderer.

The earliest of the texts, 'Typhoon', was soon recognized as one of Conrad's finest descriptive sea-pieces. Accounts of a ship's struggle with a storm have long been part of the stock-in-trade of sea-writers, but none of them has surpassed Conrad's description of the *Nan-Shan*'s battle with the typhoon. It is graphic, knowledgeable, dramatic; a wealth of vivid particulars (such as the darkness that 'palpitated down' between the flashes of lightning, or the water—both fresh and salt—swallowed by Jukes) brings the vessel's ordeal intensely to the imagination. In recent decades, literary theory has tended to overvalue the political and undervalue the aesthetic, but to neglect the aesthetic features of 'Typhoon' is to neglect the evocative power of such descriptive passages as this depiction of the ship's battering by the elements:

Her lurches had an appalling helplessness: she pitched as if taking a header into a void, and seemed to find a wall to hit every time. When she rolled she fell on her side headlong, and she would be righted back by such a demolishing blow that Jukes felt her reeling as a clubbed man reels before he collapses. The gale howled and scuffled about gigantically in the darkness, as though the entire world were one black gully.

Nevertheless, as Conrad said when recalling the incident on which the tale was based, the interest [...] was, of course, not the bad weather but the extraordinary complication brought into the ship's life at a moment of exceptional stress by the human element below her deck [...] I felt that to bring out its deeper significance which was quite apparent to me, something other, something more was required; a leading motive that would harmonise all these violent noises, and a point of view that would put all that elemental fury into its proper place.

What was needed of course was Captain MacWhirr.[1]

The tale stresses that MacWhirr is stolid, unimaginative, and unsophisticated; and at first we may be tempted to patronize him as simply a semi-comic character. What the narrative progressively reveals is the peculiar integrity which his thick skin both conceals and preserves. He may not have the intelligence or professionalism to evade the typhoon, but he has the courage to take the ship and her crew through it; he may not understand Jukes's patriotic indignation at serving under a Siamese flag, but, when Jukes is almost paralysed by fear, it is MacWhirr who sustains and encourages him. As Paul Kirschner has observed:

The nationalistic meaning of the flag, apparently invoked to illustrate MacWhirr's obtuseness, is later seen as an alibi for xenophobic jitters, then for downright baseness [by the malicious second mate]. MacWhirr's instinctual 'stupidity' is steadily revalued in moral terms.[2]

Crucially important is MacWhirr's treatment of the so-called 'coolies'. He is astonished when Jukes refers to them as 'passengers'. (Kirschner points out that 'they have not paid to travel on a passenger-ship; they are being shipped home in a cargo vessel and therefore, professionally speaking, they are cargo'.)[3] Jukes, whose apparent sympathy for them proves to be spurious, soon expresses the familiar contemporaneous attitude of racial contempt for these labourers (or 'brutes', as he now calls them). This had been presaged

---

[1] 'Author's Note' to *Typhoon and Other Stories* (London: Heinemann, 1921), p. viii.
[2] Paul Kirschner, 'Introduction' to *Typhoon and Other Stories* (London: Penguin, 1990), p. 6.
[3] Ibid. 7. Relevantly, an authoritative manual of those times, Robert W. Stevens's *On the Stowage of Ships and their Cargoes* (6th edn., London: Longmans, Green, Reader, & Dyer, 1873), 139, has only one entry for 'coolies' (in the list of kinds of *cargo*): 'Many coolies are shipped at Swatow for Havannah; a master should carefully inspect them at the depôt and accept the healthy only; he generally receives a small gratuity for those landed alive and not blind.'

in his unwittingly uncouth attitude to the Chinese interpreter, to whom he behaves in a manner which is 'gruff, as became his racial superiority':

'Savee, John? Breathe—fresh air. Good. Eh? Washee him piecie pants, chow-chow top-side—see, John?'
  With his mouth and hands he made exuberant motions of eating rice and washing clothes; and the Chinaman, who concealed his distrust of this pantomime under a collected demeanour tinged by a gentle and refined melancholy, glanced out of his almond eyes from Jukes to the hatch and back again. 'Velly good,' he murmured, in a disconsolate undertone [. . .]

In this scene of comical irony, the contrast between Jukes's infantile 'pidgin English' and the interpreter's 'gentle and refined melancholy' opens to question the mate's presumption of 'racial superiority'. Later, when the labourers panic and fight during the storm, Jukes's inclination is to ignore them. It is MacWhirr who insists that they be reduced to salutary order; and again, after the typhoon has passed, it is MacWhirr who takes pains to redistribute their money as equitably as possible. As he explains:

'Had to do what's fair, for all—they are only Chinamen. Give them the same chance with ourselves [. . .] Bad enough to be shut up below in a gale [. . .] without being battered to pieces [. . .] Couldn't let that go on in my ship, if I knew she hadn't five minutes to live.'

In that gale-interrupted phrase, 'for all—they are only Chinamen', the predictable concession to commonplace racial prejudice is made; but the emphasis falls on MacWhirr's determination to preserve 'fair play' by treating them as fellow-humans (although they regard the Europeans as 'the white devils'). The same simple integrity that enables MacWhirr to captain the ship through the typhoon obliges him to enforce a humane order. The 'simple' ethic proves eventually, in its implications and consequences, to be more considerate as well as more practical than Jukes's apparently intelligent outlook. When Jukes rushes about, mustering men with rifles, MacWhirr replies with exasperated common sense: 'For God's sake, Mr. Jukes, [. . .] do take away these rifles from the men. Somebody's sure to get hurt before long if you don't.' At the end of a letter to his friend, Jukes says of MacWhirr: 'I think that he got out of it very well for such a stupid man'; and the irony is that the stupidity here is mainly Jukes's, for failing to see that MacWhirr's reticent simplicity has eventually approximated a model of humane practicality.

MacWhirr's wife impatiently skims the letters she receives, unable to imagine the ship's perils or to appreciate her husband's courage. The tale has taught us what she may never learn: of the ordeals faced, in the course of wage-earning, by those whose labours are taken for granted, and of the salutary integrity of obscure and unglamorous individuals whose heroism is not the less for its absence of egoistic eloquence.

It remains for the reader to decide whether Conrad's general presentation of the Chinese labourers is culturally patronizing, given that only a European can master their internecine panic, or plausibly consistent, given the thematic need to dramatize their confusion as a daunting challenge. Similarly, the reader may consider whether the tale's political implications are authoritarian, suggesting that a strong leader is needed to meet the threat of social anarchy, or democratic, given that the thick-skinned mariner from a humble background proves equal to a variety of responsibilities and becomes the mentor of his socially advantaged first mate. There's an appeal to socialists, too, in the sharply realistic depiction of the perils and sufferings of the crew as they earn their wages in one of the riskiest careers. Whatever the verdict, it remains obvious that the imaginative intensity of 'Typhoon' lets moral and political considerations be stormed by the aesthetic, just as the tale's linguistic exuberance tends to render impertinent the grey prose of a critical summary.

II

'Typhoon' was written between September 1900 and January 1901. Almost immediately afterwards, Conrad wrote 'Falk: A Reminiscence', which he finished in May. 'Typhoon' had been based partly on hearsay, partly on personal experience of purgatorial voyages through storms (such as the ordeal of the *Palestine*, which survived a tempest to be destroyed by fire), and partly on Conrad's memory of an actual Captain John McWhir, skipper of the *Highland Forest*, a three-masted iron barque in which Conrad served as first mate in 1887. The only vessel that Conrad himself ever captained at sea was the *Otago*, a beautiful 346-ton sailing ship which was moored at Bangkok when he first joined her.[4] This Siamese location, coupled with the exhilaration and the cares of a first command, proved peculiarly fruitful for Conrad's imagination: the same setting is used for 'Falk', 'The Secret Sharer', and part of *The Shadow-Line*.

'Falk' is a lucid, leisurely, assured, and efficient tale; the narrative and its themes are systematically and adroitly managed. The opening provides fine examples of thematic prolepsis. The 'river-hostelry' on the Thames provides an execrable meal, so that the diners afterwards complain of hunger: the chops

brought forcibly to one's mind the night of ages when the primeval man, evolving the first rudiments of cookery from his dim consciousness, scorched lumps of flesh at a fire of sticks in the company of other good fellows; then, gorged and happy, sat him back among the gnawed bones to tell his artless tales of experience—the tales of hunger and hunt—and of women, perhaps!

What ensues is a tale of extreme hunger, of a man-hunt to the death, and of a woman who is the object of a form of hunting. If the tale's opening ironically juxtaposes the civilized and the primitive ('the night of ages'), the ensuing narrative will allow the primitive to infiltrate, shockingly but victoriously, the bourgeois world. Another theme concerns telling and withholding. The dramatic outcome depends on the overcoming of reticence; but, as Tony Tanner has pointed out, the narrator repeatedly withholds information: Bangkok is not named, nor is the niece; nor is the narrator himself; and from time to time he uses such phrases as 'his name was Tottersen, or something like that', 'I can't tell now', or 'of some sort'.

Conrad is hereby building into his text, albeit on a small scale, deliberate imprecision, a sense of approximation, of dubiety, of the erosion of names and identities, an encroaching inexactness. It is part of the attempt to make his very art*ful* piece reproduce the art*less*ness of the told tale [. . .] In Conrad's case I think the motive is to undermine the illusory finality and exactitude of the written text, to unstabilize its silent impersonal

---

[4] I use the phrase 'captained at sea' because, on the River Congo in September 1890, Conrad briefly served as temporary master of the *Roi des Belges*, a wood-burning paddle-steamer of 15 tons.

unquestionable authority, by reintroducing the hesitations of the speaking voice, the uncertainties and fadings of memory.[5]

Falk's confession, when it eventually comes, is an account of horrific privation, of starvation, homicide, and cannibalism; but often the tale is sunlit, resilient, and affirmative, and the predominant tone is one of gently humorous irony tinged at times with satire. The narrative control is so proficient as to be elegant, though we pay a price for it. There are themes in this story which, elsewhere (as in 'An Outpost of Progress' and 'Heart of Darkness'), Conrad could explore with intensity and searching complexity; here, the urbanity limits the tale's potential. In at least two ways, however, that limitation can be seen as polemical: as a deliberate challenge to expectations. The first way is that material which we might expect Conrad to use as the basis of a sombrely sceptical analysis of human nature and civilized society is here firmly contained within a social comedy which augments the author's tonal range. The second way is that if the reader's reflexive response to the idea of cannibalism is one of revulsion, Conrad mocks that reflex by attributing it to the mediocre Hermann. Conrad asserted that the basic idea of the tale was 'contrast of commonplace sentimentality with the uncorrupted point-of-view of an almost primitive man (Falk himself) who regards the preservation of life as the supreme and moral law'.[6] 'Don't be shocked', says the tale's narrator; and by a variety of devices the text seeks to allay orthodox misgivings: we are invited to understand and condone—even to approve—Falk's action. One device is the appeal to popularized Darwinism—particularly to the aspect of Darwinism summed up in Herbert Spencer's phrase, 'This survival of the fittest'.[7] 'The best man had survived', says the narrator; 'I saw him before me as though preserved for a witness to the mighty truth of an unerring and eternal principle.' Another device is the appeal to Homeric primitivism: the suggestion that Falk is a survival of an elemental heroic type. ('Primitivism' has been influentially discussed

---

[5] Tony Tanner, '"Gnawed Bones" and "Artless Tales": Eating and Narrative in Conrad', in Norman Sherry (ed.), *Joseph Conrad: A Commemoration* (London: Macmillan, 1976); repr. in Keith Carabine (ed.), *Joseph Conrad: Critical Assessments*, vol. ii (Robertsbridge: Helm Information, 1992), 526–42; quotation, pp. 540–1.

[6] Frederick R. Karl and Laurence Davies (eds.), *The Collected Letters of Joseph Conrad* (Cambridge: Cambridge University Press, 1983–   ; hereafter *Letters*), ii. 402; the original is in French (p. 399).

[7] *The Principles of Biology*, vol. i (London: Williams & Norgate, 1864), 444–5.

as 'nostalgia for, or appreciation of, the primitive', rather than as a synonym for 'primitiveness'.[8]) In contrast to Hermann's bourgeois domesticity stands an example of primeval directness, force, and simplicity. On the battle between Falk and the carpenter, the narrator comments: 'both had displayed pitiless resolution, endurance, cunning and courage—all the qualities of classic heroism.' And, in stressing the 'Homeric' aspect of Falk, the narrator makes him seem an appropriate suitor to the statuesque and opulently figured young woman, who has 'a beauty of a rustic and olympian order', resembles 'a nymph of Diana the huntress', and induces 'a strain of pagan piety'. There is, however, some tension in the narrative between the sense that Falk's determination to survive, even by cannibalism, is laudable, and the sense that Falk deserves compassion because he is a man neurotically haunted by the horror of his past experience—an affliction implied by his face-wiping gesture, his ascetic, lined face, and his abhorrence of conventional meat-courses.

Another challenge to delicate susceptibilities (though possibly a hostage to feminists) is the narrator's suggestion that there is a clear relationship between Falk's previous craving for food and his present sexual craving for the young woman:

He was hungry for the girl, terribly hungry, as he had been terribly hungry for food.

Don't be shocked if I declare that in my belief it was the same need, the same pain, the same torture. We are in his case allowed to contemplate the foundation of all the emotions [. . .]

Thus, just as the gourmet's delight in an exquisite meal is a sophistication of a savage's glee at a bloody feast, so 'the infinite gradation in shades and in flavour of our discriminating love' is an evolutionary development of a basic sexual hunger that Falk displays with tragicomic clarity. (Conrad had little to learn from Freud, who in 1912 declared: 'Even today, love, too, is in essence as animal as it ever was':[9] culture may refine and elaborate it, but basically love is appetitive and egoistic.) In the tradition of tragicomedy, the whole tale contains affirmatively what elsewhere—in *The Secret Agent*, for example—would be the stuff of pessimism and nightmare.

---

[8] See Arthur O. Lovejoy and George Boas, *Primitivism and Related Ideas in Antiquity* [1935] (New York: Octagon Books, 1973), 7–11.

[9] Sigmund Freud, *Collected Papers*, vol. iv (London: Hogarth Press, 1925), 215.

III

'Pessimism and nightmare' are terms which might, indeed, sum up the main qualities of 'Amy Foster' (written in May and June 1901), that tale of the shipwrecked emigrant 'cast out mysteriously by the sea to perish in the supreme disaster of loneliness and despair'. It is a sombre story of a pious innocent who, after narrowly surviving a shipwreck, is treated brutally and uncomprehendingly. ('If it hadn't been for the steel cross at Miss Swaffer's belt he would not, he confessed, have known whether he was in a Christian country at all.') If Amy, at least, grants him charity, kindness, and eventually the sanctuary of marriage, the sanctuary is brief: terrified by his incomprehensible demands for water during his fever, she flees from him and leaves him to die.

'Why?' he cried in the penetrating and indignant voice of a man calling to a responsible Maker. A gust of wind and a swish of rain answered.

There is no doubt that, as Bertrand Russell suggested,[10] in this tale Conrad has precipitated some of his own deep fears and anxieties as a Polish exile living in an adopted country, a land where, in rural areas particularly, the inhabitants might have been slow to welcome a stranger who spoke with a marked foreign accent. Russell reflected: 'I have wondered at times how much of [Yanko's] loneliness Conrad had felt among the English and had suppressed by a stern effort of will.' ('I feel myself—strangely growing into a sort of outcast. A mental and moral outcast', Conrad once wrote.[11]) Furthermore, a revealingly unintentional commentary on 'Amy Foster' is provided by Jessie Conrad's recollections of her honeymoon with Joseph in 1896, a vacation during which he was ill with fever:

For a whole week long, the fever ran high and for most of the time J.C. was delirious. To see him lying in the white canopied bed, dark-faced, with gleaming teeth and shining eyes, was sufficiently impressive, but to hear him muttering to himself in a strange tongue (he thinks he must have been speaking Polish)[,] to be unable to penetrate the clouded mind or catch one intelligible word, was for a young inexperienced girl truly awful [. . .][12]

---

[10] *The Autobiography of Bertrand Russell: 1872–1914* (London: Allen & Unwin, 1967), 208–9. The subsequent quotation is from p. 209.

[11] *Letters*, iii. 54.

[12] Jessie Conrad, *Personal Recollections of Joseph Conrad* (London: privately printed, 1924), 25–6.

The personal implications of the tale are evident, but that personal material has been carefully, even dourly, controlled and objectified. Yanko Goorall is no Konrad Korzeniowski but a holy fool, an innocent and ignorant 'Austro-Polish highlander'[13] from 'the eastern range of the Carpathians'; and a variety of material has contributed to the story. Ford Madox Ford, the son of an immigrant from Germany, claimed to have supplied its basis,[14] as his chronicle *The Cinque Ports* contained the following anecdote:

One of the most tragic stories that I remember to have heard was connected with a man who escaped the tender mercies of the ocean to undergo an almost more merciless buffeting ashore. He was one of the crew of a German merchant that was wrecked almost at the foot of the light-house [at Dungeness in Kent]. A moderate swimmer, he was carried by the current to some distance from the scene of the catastrophe. Here he touched the ground. He had nothing, no clothes, no food; he came ashore on a winter's night. In the morning he found himself in the Marsh near Romney. He knocked at doors, tried to make himself understood. The Marsh people thought him either a lunatic or a supernatural visitor. To lonely women in the Marsh cottages he seemed a fearful object. No doubt he was, poor wretch. They warned their menfolk of him, and whenever he was seen he was hounded away and ill-used. He got the name of Mad Jack. Knowing nothing of the country, nothing of the language, he could neither ask the way nor read the names on signposts, and even if he read them, they meant nothing to him. How long this lasted, I do not know; I remember hearing from the village people at the time that a dangerous person was in the neighbourhood. The fear of the cottage folk was real enough. For a fortnight or so hardly one of them would open their doors after nightfall. The police at last got to hear of him, and, after a search of some days, he was found asleep in a pigsty. He had the remains of an old shirt hanging round his neck; and under one arm, an old shoe that he seemed to use as a larder; it contained two old crusts and the raw wing of a chicken. In all the time of his wandering he had not come more than nine miles from the place where he had come ashore.[15]

[13] *Letters*, ii. 401. Yanko evidently comes from the part of southern Poland which was annexed by Austria in 1772, and, in particular, from the mountainous Tatra region.

[14] Ford Madox Ford, *Joseph Conrad: A Personal Remembrance* (London: Duckworth, 1924), 120, 132.

[15] Ford Madox Hueffer (later Ford Madox Ford), *The Cinque Ports: A Historical and Descriptive Record* (Edinburgh: Blackwood, 1900), 163.

The character of Amy Foster was, according to Jessie Conrad, based on that of the Conrads' servant-girl,[16] and the Kentish location was well known to them, since they were then living at Pent Farm, near Hythe.

Other source-material was more literary: a remarkable range of material seems to have contributed to the tale. Andrzej Busza has located 'Amy Foster' within a tradition of Polish works dealing with the sad destiny of the Pole who is persuaded to emigrate.[17] Busza explains that in the late nineteenth century, emigration from Poland to the New World became so considerable that it was regarded as a serious social problem: 'The Polish press came alive to the problem, and a powerful anti-emigration campaign was set in motion.' Various well-known writers depicted the unfortunate emigrant: notably Henryk Sienkiewicz in the novella *Za chlebem* (*After Bread*), Maria Konopnicka in the narrative poem *Pan Balcer w Brazylii* (*Mr Balcer in Brazil*), and Adolf Dygasiński in the novel *Na złamanie karku* (*Head over Heels*). Busza argues that Conrad's tale of Yanko shares numerous features with these three earlier works. Yanko is approached by officials of a foreign agency, as is Wawrzon in Sienkiewicz's novella. Yanko's rail journey resembles that taken by Dygasiński's peasants to Bremerhaven. All four works describe the squalid conditions below decks on the ship, and all depict a storm at sea. Yanko's naïve, bewildered responses to unfamiliar objects and situations have precedents in the other narratives. Predictably, isolation, alienation, and homesickness are themes in all these works.

Nostalgia, the sense of not belonging, and solitude are the forces which finally destroy most of the emigrants. The immediate cause[s] of their deaths are various, but it is homesickness and 'the supreme disaster of loneliness and despair' that deprive them of the will to live. All the stories end tragically.[18]

Other commentators, postulating different sources, further testify to Conrad's literary voracity and tenacity. Jocelyn Baines has seen a parallel between the villagers' response to Yanko Goorall and the

---

[16] Jessie Conrad, *Joseph Conrad as I Knew Him* (London: Heinemann, 1926), 118.

[17] Andrzej Busza, 'Conrad's Polish Literary Background and Some Illustrations of the Influence of Polish Literature on his Work', *Antemurale*, 10 (Rome: Institutum Historicum Polonicum, 1966), 224–8.

[18] Ibid. 227.

treatment of the mysterious Gilliatt in Victor Hugo's *Les Travail-leurs de la mer*, while Yves Hervouet has demonstrated that some descriptive details in the tale are drawn from Flaubert's *Madame Bovary*.[19] Conrad had long studied Maupassant, whose tales offer grimly realistic depictions of tough villagers. English readers will readily relate Conrad's story to the sombre side of the Romantic tradition, particularly to the depictions of rural harshness and suffering in Crabbe's *The Village* and *The Borough*, in some of Wordsworth's *Lyrical Ballads*, and eventually in Hardy's *Tess of the d'Urbervilles* and *Jude the Obscure*. 'Amy Foster' is a classic statement of Conradian pessimism; but, when the narrator describes the Kentish landscape, the tones of elegiac bleakness could be those of Hardy.

With the sun hanging low on its western limit, the expanse of the grass-lands framed in the counter-scarps of the rising ground took on a gorgeous and sombre aspect. A sense of penetrating sadness, like that inspired by a grave strain of music, disengaged itself from the silence of the fields. The men we met walked past, slow, unsmiling, with downcast eyes, as if the melancholy of an over-burdened earth had weighted their feet, bowed their shoulders, borne down their glances.

'Yes,' said the doctor [. . .], 'one would think the earth is under a curse, since of all her children these that cling to her the closest are uncouth in body and as leaden in gait as if their very hearts were loaded with chains.'

This is an eloquent mystification of the drudgery of rural work; yet mystification it remains, with its suggestion that the drudges partake of an enduring and seemingly irremediable 'curse' of 'an over-burdened earth'. To a reader who has travelled through Kent in a blossoming springtime, the tale's selectivity is apparent: those 'chains' are not inevitable. Nevertheless, in its dramatization of the ways in which ignorance and fear can generate national or racial prejudice, 'Amy Foster' imparts an indignation which resists the narrative's presentment of a condition so absolute that only a stoical sigh appears the appropriate response.

---

[19] Jocelyn Baines, *Joseph Conrad: A Critical Biography* (London: Weidenfeld & Nicolson, 1960), 266–7. Yves Hervouet, *The French Face of Joseph Conrad* (Cambridge: Cambridge University Press, 1990), 76–7. Furthermore, Elsa Nettels suggests that a tale by Stephen Crane may have provided hints: see ' "Amy Foster" and Stephen Crane's "The Monster" ', *Conradiana*, 15 (1983), 181–90.

'Amy Foster' remains a bleakly intense precipitation of the elements of isolation and mutual incomprehension which pervade Conrad's work. 'We live, as we dream—alone', says Marlow in 'Heart of Darkness'. 'No two human beings understand each other', asserts Nina in *Almayer's Folly*. In a letter of 1897, Conrad wrote:

Most of my life has been spent between sky and water and now I live so alone that often I fancy myself clinging stupidly to a derelict planet abandoned by its precious crew.[20]

In 'Amy Foster', the isolation of Yanko is given an ominous, fatal quality by the leitmotif or recurrent imagery of the ensnared creature: the man (whose singing voice is 'light and soaring, like a lark's') resembles 'an animal under a net', 'a wild bird caught in a snare', a victim caught in 'a net of fate', 'a wild creature under the net', and 'a bird caught in a snare'. An inaugural irony is that Yanko appears to have been washed ashore on a hen–coop 'with eleven drowned ducks inside'. Furthermore, as has been well observed, the tale

is remarkable for the effects of defamiliarization created through Yanko's sense of the commonplace as frighteningly unfamiliar, with the result that provincial Kent emerges in the form of a Kafkaesque nightmare: 'He could talk to no one, and had no hope of ever understanding anybody. It was as if these had been the faces of people from the other world—dead people [. . .]'[21]

Gail Fraser has noted that in the successive stages of revision, at the manuscript stage and later, Conrad

concentrates chiefly on heightening the opposition between Yanko's perspective and Colebrook's point of view, and on defamiliarizing sights and sounds through imagery and language so that the reader experiences the young peasant's disorientation directly. As a result, in the most successful parts of the story—Yanko's voyage from his native village to the Kentish coast, for example—we are made intensely aware of the loneliness and alienation experienced by all foreigners.[22]

In a period when adventure literature so often depicted British gentlemen venturing into the exotic territory abroad, encountering

---

[20] *Letters*, i. 370.
[21] Owen Knowles and Gene M. Moore, *The Oxford Reader's Companion to Conrad* (Oxford: Oxford University Press, 2000), 12.
[22] Gail Fraser, 'Conrad's Revisions to "Amy Foster"', *Conradiana*, 20 (1988), 192–3.

'savages' and returning victoriously, Conrad shows how England itself could, to a stranger from afar (who is 'a real adventurer at heart'), appear a baffling location of cruelty and barbarism. Certainly, Yanko wins the love of Amy, but that love is eroded by cultural differences and particularly by her hostility to the very language in which he sings to his son, and Yanko's lonely death follows.

The tale's bleakness is, however, mitigated in various respects by the two fictional narrators. The first, the anonymous 'visitor from abroad', certainly takes a gloomy view of the locality, but his phrasing is at times so striking as to give the transformative glow of the surreal to the sombre vista. On the skyline, outlined by the declining red sun, a wagon resembles 'a chariot of giants', while the wagoner's figure is 'projected [. . .] on the background of the Infinite with a heroic uncouthness'; and, as for the field:

The uniform brownness of the harrowed field glowed with a rosy tinge, as though the powdered clods had sweated out in minute pearls of blood the toil of uncounted ploughmen.

(That detail of the 'minute pearls of blood' is vividly acute.) The second narrator, Dr Kennedy, is the one character who endeavours to observe with intelligent understanding; and, in eliciting and communicating so well the plight of Yanko, his voice and personality constitute the main redemptive factor in the narrative.

IV

'The Secret Sharer' was written in December 1909. As Conrad explained, it was based on a famous maritime scandal. In the 'Author's Note' (1920) to *'Twixt Land and Sea*, he said that the 'basic fact of the tale' was an incident aboard the clipper *Cutty Sark* which 'got into newspapers'. This incident, in 1880, was the killing of a black seaman by the *Cutty Sark*'s chief mate, who subsequently escaped but was eventually arrested in London and put on trial for murder. The following extract is from the report in *The Times*, 4 August 1882, p. 4:

John Anderson, 31, seaman, was indicted for the wilful murder of John Francis [. . .]

The accused, it appeared, was chief mate on board a tea clipper called the Cutty Sark, which sailed from the port of London in May, 1880. The deceased, who was a coloured man, shipped as an able seaman, and it was stated that he soon afterwards incurred the displeasure of the prisoner in consequence of his incompetency. About the 9th or 10th of August, 1880, the vessel had just rounded the Cape, and at a quarter to 9 o'clock the prisoner was in command of the watch. The night was dark and dirty, and the watch was occupied in hauling the sail round. The deceased not being competent to perform seaman's duty, had been placed on the forecastle on the look out. The watch on hauling the ropes found that the 'fore lazy tack' was fastened, and the prisoner called out to the deceased to let the tack go. The deceased replied 'Very well,' or, according to the prisoner's version, 'Go to the devil.' Immediately afterwards the deceased let go the lazy tack, but instead of doing so as an able seaman would, he let the end go overboard. The prisoner said, 'The —— has done that out of spite.' The deceased retorted, 'Well, you told me to let it go,' and the prisoner exclaimed, 'I will come on the forecastle and heave you overboard, you nigger.' The deceased replied, 'If you come up here I have the capstan bar waiting for you.' The prisoner then went on to the forecastle and was seen to raise the capstan bar, with which he struck the deceased on the head. The blow knocked the man over the forecastle on to the deck, and he never spoke again. The prisoner said to the watch, 'Did you see that nigger lift the capstan bar to me,' but the men replied that they did not. The prisoner said, 'He will lift no more capstan bars to me, for I have knocked him down,' and he added, 'I have knocked him down like a bullock; he never gave a kick.' The account given by the prisoner was that he did it in self-defence. The captain of the vessel attended to the deceased, but he remained insensible till the following day, when he expired from the injuries he received, and was buried at sea. Before the arrival of the ship at Anger the accused, with the connivance of the captain, made his escape. The vessel proceeded thence to Singapore, and during the passage the captain committed suicide by jumping overboard, having previously dropped into the sea the capstan bar used by the prisoner. At Singapore the matter was reported to a magistrate, who, in due course, instituted an inquiry. The prisoner was arrested in London.

It was stated in cross-examination that the deceased man Francis had on several occasions threatened the prisoner's life, and once he sharpened his knife upon the grindstone for the purpose of carrying his threat into execution.

Mr. EDWARD CLARKE, addressing his Lordship at the close of the case, submitted that the evidence could not sustain the Court charging the prisoner with murder.

Mr. JUSTICE STEPHEN concurred; and

Mr. CLARKE said that, in those circumstances, he could not resist a verdict of manslaughter. The learned counsel addressed the Court in mitigation of punishment, pointing out that the vessel had been undermanned, and that at the time in question the accused had had an important manœuvre to perform with respect to the sail. The deceased behaved in an insolent and 'lubberly' manner, and it was absolutely necessary that the prisoner should assert his authority.

Numerous witnesses were then called on the part of the defence to show that the prisoner bore an excellent character and was a man whose disposition was humane and kindly.

The jury, by his Lordship's direction, then returned a verdict of manslaughter against the accused.

Mr. JUSTICE STEPHEN, in passing sentence, told the prisoner he had considered the case with anxious attention and with very great pain, because the evidence which had been given showed that he was a man of good character generally speaking and of humane disposition. He was happy to be able to give full weight to the evidence in his favour. The deceased had certainly acted in a manner which was calculated to make the prisoner very angry, but it must be clearly understood that the taking of human life by brutal violence, whether on sea or on land, whether the life be that of a black or a white man, was a dreadful crime, and deserving of exemplary punishment. He sentenced the prisoner to seven years' penal servitude.

I have quoted the report at length for several reasons. The first is its reminder that life on board a sailing ship, the harsh life that Conrad knew so well, was no refuge from moral ambiguities and dilemmas but, on the contrary, could present them in particularly dramatic and perplexing forms. (In the reported case, which man was the instigator? Was racial antipathy the main factor? What *exactly* happened on the forecastle? The gaps in the evidence set the imagination speculating.) The second is that this incident proved to be an exceptionally fruitful source for Conrad. The threat presented to a ship's discipline by a recalcitrant black seaman, and the difficulty in disentangling racial prejudice from the assertion of hierarchical power, would be depicted amply in the novel *The Nigger of the 'Narcissus'*. The suicide of a ship's captain, precipitated by his emotional involvement with a lawbreaker, would be treated in *Lord Jim*: in the death of Brierly, an assessor at Jim's trial. (Brierly, it will be recalled, vainly attempted to help Jim escape justice.) The relevance of the *Cutty Sark* case to 'The Secret Sharer' is obvious. Not only does it provide precedent for Leggatt's argument that manslaughter (or possibly murder) might be a justifiable response to a seaman who behaved in 'an insolent and "lubberly" manner', it also makes clear the kind of legal process, and likely outcome, that Leggatt seeks to evade.

Another relevant piece of source-material is revealed in Conrad's *The Mirror of the Sea*. When describing the character of Charles Born, first mate of the *Otago*, Conrad writes:

It so happened that we both loved the little barque very much. And it was just the defect of Mr. B——'s inestimable qualities that he would never persuade himself to believe that the ship was safe in my hands. To begin with, he was more than five years older than myself at a time of life when five years really do count, I being twenty-nine and he thirty-four; then, on our first leaving port (I don't see why I should make a secret of the fact that it was Bangkok), a bit of manœuvring of mine amongst the islands of the Gulf of Siam had given him an unforgettable scare. Ever since then he had nursed in secret a bitter idea of my utter recklessness.[23]

Thus, 'The Secret Sharer' combines some adapted features of the *Cutty Sark* incident with some recalled features of Conrad's captaincy of the *Otago*, and one of its creative motivations is clearly a mixture of psychological compensation and vicarious (imaginative) atonement. If the recollection of the 'unforgettable scare' is accurate, then, at one level, the story says to the Charles Born of memory, 'What you deemed to be reckless manœuvring had a very good reason, though one that I, the young captain, could not reveal to you at the time'; or (to phrase the matter less tendentiously), 'Apparent recklessness may be vindicated by the outcome'.

One outcome is 'The Secret Sharer' itself, authoritatively described as 'Conrad's most famous and frequently anthologized short story'.[24] It has attracted numerous and diverse interpretations. It is lucid, concise, tense, exciting, and enigmatic; and, in its morality, there is a grittily resistant feature which may encourage critics to secrete around it the putative pearl of a smoothing exegesis. If a literary text has evident merit, the critic may be tempted to imply that it also has the astuteness to share his or her moral biases; but the text is under no such flattering obligation. Its merit may lie in its

[23] Joseph Conrad, *The Mirror of the Sea* (London: Methuen, 1906), 26–7.
[24] Knowles and Moore, *Companion to Conrad*, 336.

qualities of articulate intelligence, and its paraphrasable morality may be harsher than the critic would like it to be.

'The Secret Sharer' is a tale which succeeds in being at once satisfyingly straightforward and intriguingly mysterious. After the deceptive calm of the opening, there follows the shock of the unexpected visitant, the suspense entailed by the subsequent endeavour to conceal the fugitive, and the climactic tension generated by the captain's determination to take his ship perilously close to a rocky shore while the fugitive escapes. The narrative is terse and economical, and our interest is engaged by a relay race of questions: Who is the fugitive? How can he be successfully concealed? Will the new captain succeed in mastering the unfamiliar ship while yet helping the lawbreaker? And finally, will the vessel survive the risky manœuvre? Broadly, the central principle of suspense is that the evidence to support a reader's prediction of a successful outcome is almost evenly matched by the evidence to support a prediction of a disastrous outcome. The story is well paced, every detail counts, numerous ironies are generated, and the sense of conspiratorial confinement (and eventually of wilfully perilous navigation) is convincingly evoked.

What makes the tale so intriguing to read and reread, and what makes it so seductive to commentators, is its paradoxical nature. Though the narrative sequence is graphically straightforward, it generates a variety of enigmas, connotations, and problems. As the title indicates, the tale has the resonance of a work which extends the *Doppelgänger* tradition. This literary tradition burgeoned in the Romantic period and continued through the nineteenth century into the twentieth. Representative texts include Poe's 'William Wilson', Dostoevsky's 'The Double', and Stevenson's 'Dr Jekyll and Mr Hyde'. The main convention in such texts is that an uncanny complicity is established between two apparently contrasting characters: their relationship is symbiotic. Sometimes the connection is supernatural, one character being an external manifestation of part of the other. The whispering Mr Wilson represents the conscience of the debauched Mr Wilson, while Mr Hyde represents the depraved clandestine self of the respectable Dr Jekyll. In Conrad's tale, there are various uncanny features: the captain and the fugitive are remarkable similar, in that both are former *Conway* boys, both are young 'gentlemen' who are socially superior to their respective crews, and one seems providentially placed to save the other; furthermore, the captain is immediately sympathetic to the fugitive and has no hesitation in deciding to shelter him. Nevertheless, Conrad's treatment is predominantly secular and realistic: Leggatt is two years younger than the fictional narrator, is rather different in temperament (tougher, more impatient and decisive), and eventually goes his own way, leaving his former protector to an independent career. Albert Guerard's attempt to interpret Leggatt mainly as 'a facet of the unconscious', a repressed part of the hero's psyche,[25] is resisted by the tale's predominant realism, which—Guerard conceded—establishes very fully (by means of the hue and cry, for example) the objective existence of Leggatt. Much more germane is Guerard's observation of a recurrent paradox in Conrad's work, namely: 'a deep commitment to order in society and in the self—doubled by [i.e. accompanied by] incorrigible sympathy for the outlaw, whether existing in society or the self'.[26] 'The Secret Sharer' offers a vivid illustration of this.

Leggatt, the fugitive, has killed a man while striving to set a sail. He believes himself to be entirely justified in his homicidal action, since the sail saved the imperilled ship. The narrator of the tale, that anonymous young captain, promptly endorses Leggatt's view and consequently enables Leggatt to elude the laws of the land and of the sea. An unsavoury moral implication is clearly this: that some men constitute a bold élite with a claim to override long-established moral and legal principles. Such men, it seems, may justifiably commit homicide if the act coincides with the survival of a ship, and the justification is not one which needs to be presented in court. Conrad's 'sympathy with the outlaw' is evident; and the paradox is completed when we see that this outlaw believes that he was a better defender of 'order' on the *Sephora* than her own master.

The bond between the narrator and Leggatt is partly an irrational, instinctive one: they have an immediate, intuitive understanding. It is partly a matter of caste and class: they are both 'officers and gentlemen', middle-class ex-*Conway* trainees, sharing the freemasonry of members of the same rather exclusive school or club. We may recall E. M. Forster's famous pronouncement: 'if I had

---

[25] Albert Guerard, *Conrad the Novelist* (Cambridge, Mass.: Harvard University Press, 1958, repr. 1965), 14–16, 25–6, 42.
[26] Ibid. 58.

to choose between betraying my country and betraying my friend, I
hope I should have the guts to betray my country'.[27] The reference to
Forster is doubly appropriate when we notice that 'The Secret
Sharer' has a mild, muted, homophile aspect. In the narrator, the
sense of intuitive comradeship modulates, very reticently, towards
love: he stares, fascinated, as his 'other self' lies on the bed; and the
long, lingering parting resembles that of lovers: 'Our eyes met;
several seconds elapsed, till, our glances still mingled, I extended my
hand and turned the lamp out.' During their final moments together,
Leggatt seems to think that the young captain is engaging him in
some kind of embrace, which he has to fend off:

We were in the sail-locker, scrambling on our knees over the sails [. . .].
I snatched off my floppy hat and tried hurriedly in the dark to ram it
on my other self. He dodged and fended off silently. I wonder what he
thought had come to me before he understood and silently desisted.
Our hands met gropingly, lingered united in a steady, motionless clasp
for a second [. . .]. No word was breathed by either of us when they
separated.

Furthermore, the narrator's insistence that Leggatt is his complement ('my other self', 'my double', 'the secret sharer of my life'),
particularly in the remark 'I felt less torn in two when I was with
him', may recall to us Aristophanes' explanation of homosexuality:
'Man's original body having been thus cut in two, each half yearned
for the half from which it had been severed.'[28]

   The young captain's truest love, however, is for his ship, whereas
the master of the *Sephora* has committed a kind of maritime infidel-
ity by bringing his wife aboard *his* vessel. The narrator's situation on
his first command has some resemblance to that of a newly-wed
husband when, just at the start of the honeymoon, a fascinating male
visitor arrives and by his presence causes numerous distractions and
problems; but at length the intruder departs, and the delayed
honeymoon can at last begin in earnest, its joys now the more fully to
be savoured. As the narrator puts it:

---

[27] E. M. Forster, *Two Cheers for Democracy* (London: Arnold, 1951), 78.
[28] Plato, *The Symposium*, trans. W. Hamilton (Harmondsworth: Penguin, 1951), 61.
Bruce Harkness's parodic article, 'The Secret of the "The Secret Sharer" Bared'
(in *College English*, 27 (1965), 55–61), alleged that the secret of Conrad's story was
'Hyacinthine' homosexuality; subsequently, the idea was taken seriously by various
commentators.

I did not know her. Would she do it? How was she to be handled?

[. . .] I was alone with her. Nothing! no one in the world should stand now between us, throwing a shadow on the way of silent knowledge and mute affection, the perfect communion of a seaman with his first command.

This is one of several patterned features in the narrative: it begins with the captain's hopes of communion; interruption and distraction follow; and finally communion is restored. A related feature is that while a well-intentioned action by him introduced the initial crisis, another well-intentioned action resolves the final crisis. In order to get to know the ship better, the captain had taken on himself the duty of the first anchor-watch. This disrupted the formal routine of watch-setting, so that the ladder was left alongside instead of being drawn up; and it was this ladder that caused the fugitive to linger at the ship. Near the end of the story, when the fugitive is attempting to escape overboard, the captain impulsively puts his own floppy hat on Leggatt's head (so that it may later shield him from the tropical sun ashore); and the hat, falling into the sea, forms the salutary marker which helps the captain to avert shipwreck. A large irony is that while Leggatt had thought it right to kill a man in order to save a ship and her crew, his protector thinks it right to imperil a ship and her crew in order to save a man.

Insofar as the narrative endorses Leggatt's conduct, it seems to commend a provocatively élitist and ruthless ethic. Other Conradian narratives (notably 'Heart of Darkness' and *Nostromo*) offer contrasting commendations. In 'The Secret Sharer', Conrad has chosen to imagine a strange and lucid challenge to orthodox ideas of law and justice. But it remains an imagining, not a manifesto; it is a fictional narrative, not a testament. There exists no encephalograph or cardiograph which can tell us precisely the extent to which, while we are experiencing a work of morally intelligent fiction, our sense of imaginative escape from real ethical problems is outweighed (if at all) by our sense that searching questions have been directed from the text towards that ethical actuality. The satisfyingly vivid descriptive quality of this tale may make it more seductively escapist or more provocatively challenging. For most readers, the appeal probably lies in its distinctive combination of both effects. 'The Secret Sharer' is a yarn and a rune; it is an imaginative sanctuary which proves to be a baited trap.

V

Conrad has a richly associative and dialectical imagination. One text may resume a discussion begun in a previous text. A recommendation implicit in one work may be challenged in another. Characters, locations, and situations may recur (creating networks of 'transtextualities'), although with variations and modulations.[29] Thus, the rather sinister violin-playing captain of 'Falk' reappears in the novel *The Shadow-Line*. The mate, Burns, is depicted (sometimes anonymously) in 'Falk', *The Shadow-Line*, 'A Smile of Fortune', and in the ostensibly non-fictional, autobiographical work, *The Mirror of the Sea*. The anonymous young captain who is the narrator of 'Falk', and whose ship closely resembles Conrad's *Otago*, appears also to be the narrator of 'The Secret Sharer', *The Shadow-Line*, and 'A Smile of Fortune'; furthermore, he has clear resemblances to the young seafaring Conrad depicted in *The Mirror of the Sea*. Conrad was drawing on the remembered and transformable experiences of a very distinctive life-pattern: that of a Pole who became a British citizen, of a seafarer who was an introspective student of literature and philosophy, and of a Romantic who was also a sceptic. Technically, his transtextualities often constitute a fruitful paradox: they are narratives which arise with the seeming spontaneity and vagrancy of reminiscence, but which are constructed with minute attention to irony, allusion, symbolic ambiguity, and literary precedent. They have the freedom of amply elaborated autobiography, yet the discipline of a highly sophisticated creative imagination. Our sense that Conrad offers a distinctively spacious imaginative realm results not only from the far-flung geographical settings and the topographical vistas of ocean, sky, and countryside, but also from our awareness that his transtextual narratives extend strongly into autobiographical reality and autobiographical image-making as well as into compressed, charged, formalized, and symbolic modes of literary fiction.

The Captain MacWhirr of 'Typhoon' clearly resembles the 'Captain McW——' of *The Mirror of the Sea*, who in turn is based on John McWhir, captain of the barque *Highland Forest*, whom Conrad regarded as a sustaining presence even when he was out of sight. Paul Kirschner has remarked that 'the girl [in 'Falk'], Falk and

---

[29] See Cedric Watts, *The Deceptive Text* (Brighton: Harvester, 1984), ch. 9.

MacWhirr all share the quality of taciturnity, and all are in touch with deep truths'.[30] In 'Typhoon', the evocation of the storm and of the diverse human responses to it invite comparison with those features of *The Nigger of the 'Narcissus'*: in both, as in a controlled imaginative experiment, tests of courage, endurance, solidarity, and honour are applied, with varying results.

In a range of works, Conrad questioned the depth of civilized conduct by considering ways in which, under conditions of stress and isolation from familiar settings, individuals may break taboos and regress to corruption and violence: *An Outcast of the Islands*, 'An Outpost of Progress', and 'Heart of Darkness' provide notable instances. 'Falk', however, treats with unusual compassion the taboo-breaker and even uses his conduct as a basis for criticism of bourgeois conventionality. A recurrent preoccupation of Conrad's is the readiness of observers to misinterpret what they perceive, con-structing self-justifying narratives which may distort or falsify the contrasting reality. Whether in Jukes's incomprehension of MacWhirr or Schomberg's misreading of Falk, the errors of com-placent misinterpretation are incisively exposed. As Conrad says: 'The appearances of this perishable life are deceptive like everything that falls under the judgment of our imperfect senses.'[31]

Misinterpretation is largely responsible for the tragedy of Yanko in 'Amy Foster'. Conrad was frequently acute in depicting the degrees of misunderstanding and alienation within an apparently close relationship, the subtlest example being probably that of the later stages of the marriage of Mr and Mrs Gould in *Nostromo*. A rather neglected instance is provided by Alvan Hervey's failing rela-tionship with his wife in 'The Return', while a fiercely sombre instance is the disintegration of the Verloc family in *The Secret Agent*.

Finally, 'The Secret Sharer' can be seen as the centre of a large cluster of works in which treatment of the lawbreaker is presented in a particularly problematic light. *Lord Jim* offers an elaborately ambiguous example. Strikingly, Conrad commenced 'The Secret Sharer' amid his struggles to complete *Under Western Eyes*. In that novel of Russian political life, Haldin, an assassin, seeks sanctuary at

---

[30] Kirschner, *Typhoon and Other Stories*, 296.
[31] *Some Reminiscences* (London: Eveleigh Nash, 1912), 75–6.

the lodgings of Razumov; and Razumov, after tormented introspection, betrays the lawbreaker to the Tsarist authorities. It is typical of his dialectical imagination that Conrad should temporarily veer aside to compose a tale in which a lawbreaker is successfully concealed from the authorities. Joseph Conrad never forgot the time in his childhood when a Russian tribunal had sentenced his parents to exile for their patriotic conspiratorial activities, and when the 4-year-old boy accompanied his mother and father on that dreary journey from Poland to the penal settlement of Vologda. Not surprisingly, then, the eventual fiction-writer was deeply preoccupied by moral and political paradoxes. Loyalty to one cause might resemble treachery to another. A rebel may be a loyalist. The outsider may be a deluded egoist who causes havoc or an intense individual among mere conformists. The man who sells his soul has, at least, a soul to sell. As Conrad says:

It would take too long to explain the intimate alliance of contradictions in human nature which makes love itself wear at times the desperate shape of betrayal.[32]

The four tales in this volume provide an ample basis for exploring the distinctive, capacious, and paradoxical terrain of Joseph Conrad's imagination. As we explore it, we explore ourselves, and what we discover will be sometimes reassuring and sometimes troubling. Conrad declared:

The only legitimate basis of creative work lies in the courageous recognition of all the irreconcilable antagonisms that make our life so enigmatic, so burdensome, so fascinating, so dangerous—so full of hope.[33]

[32] *Some Reminiscences*, 76.   [33] *Letters*, ii. 348–9.

NOTE ON THE TEXT

The four tales in this volume are arranged in chronological order of composition. 'Typhoon' was written between September 1900 and January 1901. It was serialized in Britain in *Pall Mall Magazine* (January to March 1902) and in the United States in *Critic* (February to May 1902). On its own, it was published in book form by G. P. Putnam's Sons, New York, September 1902; in Britain, it was collected in *Typhoon and Other Stories* (London: Heinemann, April 1903). 'Falk: A Reminiscence' was written between January and May of 1901,[1] and was one of only two tales by Conrad not to be serialized. Conrad recalled: 'I think the copy was shown to the editor of some magazine, who rejected it indignantly on the sole ground that "the girl never says anything"' ('Author's Note', 1919, p. xi). It was initially published in 1903 in the *Typhoon* volume. 'Amy Foster' was written in late May and in June 1901, and first appeared in the *Illustrated London News* on 14, 21, and 28 December 1901. This tale, too, was included in *Typhoon and Other Stories*. In the USA, the volume *Falk, Amy Foster, To-morrow: Three Stories* was issued by McClure, Phillips in September 1903. 'The Secret Sharer' was composed in December 1909 and was originally published (as 'The Secret-Sharer') in *Harper's Monthly Magazine*, New York, in August and September 1910, before appearing in book form in the collection *'Twixt Land and Sea: Tales* (London: Dent, October 1912; New York: Doran, December 1912).

The manuscript and typescript of 'Typhoon' (bearing autograph corrections) were loaned to the Houghton Library, Harvard, Mass., from 1964 to 1974, before being returned to their private owner. The manuscript of 'Falk' is in the Yale University Library; that of 'Amy Foster' in the Beinecke Rare Book and Manuscript Library at Yale University; and that of 'The Secret Sharer' in the Berg Collection of New York Public Library. Relevant essays include Bruce Johnson's

---

[1] The *Oxford Reader's Companion to Conrad* (Oxford: Oxford University Press, 2000), 107, states that 'Falk' was written 'during the first three months of 1901'; but on 28 April 1901 Conrad remarked 'I am finishing the Falk story', and on 24 May 1901 he said that during the previous fortnight he had been 'finishing a story for Heinemann', namely 'Falk' (*Letters*, ii. 327–8).

'Conrad's "Falk": Manuscript and Meaning' (*Modern Language Quarterly*, 26 (1965), 267–84) and Gail Fraser's 'Conrad's Revisions to "Amy Foster"' (*Conradiana*, 20 (1988), 181–93).

Conrad repeatedly revised the text of 'Typhoon'. The American serial version (representing an earlier stage of the text) differs on numerous occasions from the British serial version. These differences have been scrupulously analysed by Dwight H. Purdy in 'Conrad at Work: The Two Serial Texts of "Typhoon"', *Conradiana*, 19: 2 (1987), 99–119. He finds that, among other alterations, the treatment of Jukes becomes somewhat less critical and that of MacWhirr somewhat less sympathetic; the narration becomes rather more objective in mode; and descriptive passages are given greater precision. Furthermore, there are various substantive variations between the British serial and the first British book edition; and Conrad made subsequent changes.

In the present volume, the base-texts of the fictional works are those of the first British publications in book form, which I have compared with the British serial versions (except for the never-serialized 'Falk'). I have preserved some spellings which, according to the *Oxford English Dictionary*, are not incorrect but are archaic or uncommon (e.g. 'decrepid' and 'blurr'). In compliance with the General Editor's prescriptions, various editorial emendations are made tacitly. Other emendations are listed below. In the following lists, the page and line numbers refer to the present volume, and the reading after the square bracket is that of the first British book edition. Emendations marked '*Per.*' derive from the serial version; all others are editorial.

Typhoon

8: 37	bosun] bo'ss'en
26: 18	that has] that had
30: 5	bridge, heads] bridge heads
36: 31	bosun] boss'n
36: 32	bosun] boss'n
37: 3	'tween-deck *Per.*] 'tween deck
41: 23	was as though *Per.*] was though
43: 17	Bosun] Boss'n
43: 18	bosun] boss'n
43: 24	bosun] boss'n

46: 12	striped] stripped
47: 30	stopped,] stopped
49: 39	below, the] below the
63: 7	bosun's] boss'en's
64: 38	plumet] plummet
72: 25	bosun] boss'en

Falk

77: 33	Plate] Platte
78: 11	forward were] were forward
80: 37	twice,] twice
82: 10	a-musing] a musing
83: 14	opened hopefully,] opened, hopefully
85: 2	trombone] trump *See explanatory note*
85: 7	my] any
85: 13	world-proof] world proof
86: 12	ironwork,] ironwork
89: 23	up-stream] up stream
91: 31	paddle-wheels,] paddle-wheels
94: 24	look-out] look out
96: 16	brought out the] brought the
97: 18	young can] young man can
100: 32	water-side] water side
101: 36	remarked that "it] remarked, "that it
102: 15	roads] Roads
102: 32	tam'] tam
103: 28	Gottverdamm!] Gottferdam!
103: 29	Schomberg,] Schomberg
105: 21	reiterated,] reiterated
105: 33	roads] Roads
106: 36	iron-grey] iron grey
108: 9	thoroughfare, ruinous] thoroughfare ruinous
116: 4	he didn't] "he didn't
116: 5	game.] game."
116: 6	this, Schomberg] this Schomberg
116: 7	said,] said
117: 30	"courting"] courting,
120: 29	Well] "Well
120: 30	ago.] ago."
124: 19	*Ach so!*] *Ach So!*
125: 26	called, vulgar] called vulgar
127: 9	roadstead] Roadstead

130: 28	quarter-deck] quarter deck
135: 12	Break-down] Break down
137: 11	chief engineer] chief-engineer
137: 38	ropes'] rope's
140: 11	on Falk,] on, Falk
140: 22	fresh-water pump] fresh water-pump
141: 2	brass-framed] brass framed
141: 4–5	unexpectedly and,] unexpectedly, and
141: 27	of *The*] of the
141: 29	wraith] wreath
142: 33	charms,] charms
144: 1	Yes!] "Yes!
144: 3	went . . .] went . . . "

Amy Foster

149: 13	Ship Inn *Per.*] "Ship Inn"
150: 15	brick] black *See explanatory note*
153: 27	startled—glance] startled, glance
157: 31	over-full] over full
158: 3	mirage of *Per.*] mirage or
160: 10	has admitted] had admitted
162: 10–11	Ship Inn, *Per.*] "Ship Inn,"
164: 21	here?] here.
168: 20	seeing] see
168: 32	would *Per.*] should
168: 39	Horses *Per.*] Horses,
170: 22	in all *Per.*] all in
172: 2	Coach and Horses,] 'Coach and Horses,'
174: 28	wicket gate] wicker-gate *See explanatory note*

The Secret Sharer

186: 24	*Conway*] Conway
186: 26	*Conway*] Conway
187: 26	forebitts] forebits
189: 6	L, the *Per.*] L the
190: 21	*Conway*] Conway
200: 1	"Sui—cide!] "Sui-cide!
201: 30	"*Sephora*s] "*Sephoras*
203: 30	bosun] bo's'n
205: 34	pâté *Per.*] paté
207: 21	eyes, I] eyes I

208: 33   Cambodian] Cambodje
211: 10   seeing] see
214: 31   on, sir?] on, sir,

The base-text of the extract from the 'Author's Note' (1919) is in *Typhoon and Other Tales* (London: Heinemann, 1921), pp. vii–xi. I omit material inappropriate to the present volume, which offers a different collection of material.

SELECT BIBLIOGRAPHY

Biographies and Letters

Baines, Jocelyn, *Joseph Conrad: A Critical Biography* (London: Weidenfeld & Nicolson, 1960).

Batchelor, John, *The Life of Joseph Conrad* (Oxford: Blackwell, 1994).

Ford, Ford Madox, *Joseph Conrad: A Personal Remembrance* (Boston: Little, Brown, 1924; New York: Ecco, 1989).

Jean-Aubry, G., *Joseph Conrad: Life and Letters*, 2 vols. (London: Heinemann, 1927).

Karl, Frederick R., *Joseph Conrad: The Three Lives* (London: Faber, 1979).

—— and Davies, Laurence (eds.), *The Collected Letters of Joseph Conrad* (Cambridge: Cambridge University Press, 1983–   ).

Knowles, Owen, *A Conrad Chronology* (Basingstoke: Macmillan, 1989).

Najder, Zdzisław, *Conrad's Polish Background* (Oxford: Oxford University Press, 1964).

—— *Joseph Conrad: A Chronicle* (Cambridge: Cambridge University Press, 1983).

Ray, Martin (ed.), *Joseph Conrad: Interviews and Recollections* (Basingstoke: Macmillan, 1990).

Sherry, Norman, *Conrad's Eastern World* (London: Cambridge University Press, 1966).

—— *Conrad's Western World* (London: Cambridge University Press, 1971).

—— *Conrad and His World* (London: Thames & Hudson, 1972).

Stape, J. H., and Knowles, Owen (eds.), *A Portrait in Letters: Correspondence to and about Conrad* (Amsterdam: Rodopi, 1996).

Watts, Cedric, *Joseph Conrad: A Literary Life* (Basingstoke: Macmillan, 1989).

Criticism

Berthoud, Jacques, *Joseph Conrad: The Major Phase* (Cambridge: Cambridge University Press, 1978).

Bradbrook, Muriel, *Joseph Conrad: Poland's English Genius* (Cambridge: Cambridge University Press, 1941).

Daleski, Hillel M., *Joseph Conrad: The Way of Dispossession* (London: Faber, 1977).

Erdinast-Vulcan, Daphna, *Joseph Conrad and the Modern Temper* (Oxford: Oxford University Press, 1991).

Fogel, Aaron, *Coercion to Speak: Conrad's Poetics of Dialogue* (Cambridge, Mass.: Harvard University Press, 1985).

Gordon, John Dozier, *Joseph Conrad: The Making of a Novelist* (Cambridge, Mass.: Harvard University Press, 1940).

Guerard, Albert J., *Conrad the Novelist* (Cambridge, Mass.: Harvard University Press, 1958).

Hampson, Robert, *Joseph Conrad: Betrayal and Identity* (Basingstoke: Macmillan, 1992).

Hawthorn, Jeremy, *Joseph Conrad: Language and Fictional Self-Consciousness* (London: Edward Arnold, 1979).

—— *Joseph Conrad: Narrative Technique and Ideological Commitment* (London: Edward Arnold, 1990).

Knowles, Owen, and Moore, Gene, *The Oxford Reader's Companion to Conrad* (Oxford: Oxford University Press, 2000).

Lothe, Jakob, *Conrad's Narrative Method* (Oxford: Oxford University Press, 1989).

Morf, Gustav, *The Polish Shades and Ghosts of Joseph Conrad* (New York: Astra, 1976).

Moser, Thomas, *Joseph Conrad: Achievement and Decline* (Cambridge, Mass.: Harvard University Press, 1957).

Murfin, Ross (ed.), *Conrad Revisited: Essays for the Eighties* (Tuscaloosa, Ala.: University of Alabama Press, 1985).

Said, Edward, *Joseph Conrad and the Fiction of Autobiography* (Cambridge, Mass.: Harvard University Press, 1966).

Sherry, Norman (ed.), *Conrad: The Critical Heritage* (London: Routledge & Kegan Paul, 1973).

Spittles, Brian, *Joseph Conrad* (Basingstoke: Macmillan, 1992).

Stape, J. H. (ed.), *The Cambridge Companion to Joseph Conrad* (Cambridge: Cambridge University Press, 1996).

Watt, Ian, *Conrad in the Nineteenth Century* (London: Chatto & Windus, 1980).

—— *Essays on Conrad* (Cambridge: Cambridge University Press, 2000).

Watts, Cedric, *A Preface to Conrad* (London: Longman, 1982, 1993).

—— *The Deceptive Text: An Introduction to Covert Plots* (Brighton: Harvester, 1984).

Chapters on Conrad in Critical Texts

Armstrong, Paul B., *The Challenge of Bewilderment: Understanding and Representation in James, Conrad and Ford* (Ithaca, NY: Cornell University Press, 1987).

Graham, Kenneth, *Indirections of the Novel: James, Conrad and Ford* (Cambridge: Cambridge University Press, 1988).

Leavis, F. R., *The Great Tradition: George Eliot, Henry James, Joseph Conrad* (London: Chatto & Windus, 1948).

Levenson, Michael, *A Genealogy of Modernism* (Cambridge: Cambridge University Press, 1984).

—— *Modernism and the Fate of Individuality* (Cambridge: Cambridge University Press, 1991).

White, Allon, *The Uses of Obscurity: The Fiction of Early Modernism* (London: Routledge & Kegan Paul, 1981).

Whiteley, Patrick J., *Knowledge and Experimental Realism in Conrad, Lawrence and Woolf* (Baton Rouge: Louisiana State University Press, 1987).

Periodicals and Bibliographies

There are two important journals devoted to Conrad—*The Conradian* and *Conradiana*—and several scholarly critical bibliographies, though to date there is no single comprehensive bibliography of Conrad's entire oeuvre. The most helpful selective guide for the student and general reader is Owen Knowles's *An Annotated Critical Bibliography of Joseph Conrad* (Hemel Hempstead: Harvester Wheatsheaf, 1992). Further details of recent scholarship can be found in the *MLA International Bibliography* which is also available on CD-Rom and on-line.

Useful Web Sites

http://lang.nagoya-u.ac.jp/~matsuoka/Conrad.html [offers a large number of hyperlinks to many other specialized Conrad web sites or relevant parts of other web sites]

http://www.library.utoronto.ca/utel/authors/conradj.html [a sound academic complement to the above]

http://members.tripod.com/~JTKNK/ [focuses mainly on the activities of the Joseph Conrad Foundation but also provides access to a number of e-texts]

On 'Typhoon', 'Falk', 'Amy Foster', and 'The Secret Sharer'

Andreach, Robert, 'The Two Narrators of "Amy Foster"', *Studies in Short Fiction*, 2 (1965), 262–9.

Busza, Andrzej, section on 'Amy Foster' in 'Conrad's Polish Literary Background and Some Illustrations of the Influence of Polish Literature on his Work', *Antemurale*, 10 (Rome: Institutum Historicum Polonicum, 1966), 224–30.

Carabine, Keith, 'Introduction' to Joseph Conrad, *Sea Stories: 'Typhoon', 'Falk' and 'The Shadow-Line'* (Ware: Wordsworth Editions, 1998).

Curreli, Mario, and Ciompi, Fausto, 'A Socio-Semiotic Reading of Conrad's "Falk"', *L'Epoque Conradienne*, 18 (1988), 35–46; repr. in Keith Carabine (ed.), *Joseph Conrad: Critical Assessments*, vol. ii (Robertsbridge: Helm Information, 1992).

Fraser, Gail, 'Conrad's Revisions to "Amy Foster"', *Conradiana*, 20 (1988), 181–92; repr. in Carabine (ed.), *Conrad: Critical Assessments*.

—— 'The Short Fiction', in J. H. Stape (ed.), *The Cambridge Companion to Joseph Conrad* (Cambridge: Cambridge University Press, 1996).

Harkness, Bruce (ed.), *Conrad's 'Secret Sharer' and the Critics* (Belmont: Wadsworth, 1962).

Herndon, Richard, 'The Genesis of Conrad's "Amy Foster"', *Studies in Philology*, 57 (1960), pp. 549–66.

Johnson, Bruce, 'Conrad's "Falk": Manuscript and Meaning', *Modern Language Quarterly*, 26 (1965), 267–84.

Purdy, Dwight H., 'Conrad at Work: The Two Serial Texts of "Typhoon"', *Conradiana*, 19 (1987), 99–119.

Schuster, Charles I., 'Comedy and the Limits of Language in Conrad's "Typhoon"', *Conradiana*, 16 (1984), 55–71.

Tanner, Tony, '"Gnawed Bones" and "Artless Tales"—Eating and Narrative in Conrad', in Norman Sherry (ed.), *Joseph Conrad: A Commemoration* (London: Macmillan, 1976); repr. in Carabine (ed.), *Conrad: Critical Assessments*.

Watt, Ian, 'Comedy and Humour in *Typhoon*', in Mario Curreli (ed.), *The Ugo Mursia Memorial Lectures* (Milan: Mursia International, 1988).

Watts, Cedric, 'The Mirror-Tale: An Ethico-Structural Analysis of "The Secret Sharer"', *Critical Quarterly*, 19 (1977), 25–37.

Further Reading in Oxford World's Classics

Conrad, Joseph, *Chance*, ed. Martin Ray.

—— *Heart of Darkness and Other Tales*, ed. Cedric Watts.

—— *The Lagoon and Other Stories*, ed. William Atkinson.

—— *Lord Jim*, ed. Jacques Berthoud.

—— *Nostromo*, ed. Keith Carabine.

—— *An Outcast of the Islands*, ed. J. H. Stape and Hans van Marle.

—— *The Secret Agent*, ed. Roger Tennant.

—— *The Shadow-Line*, ed. Jeremy Hawthorn.

—— *Under Western Eyes*, ed. Jeremy Hawthorn.

—— *Victory*, ed. John Batchelor.

A CHRONOLOGY OF JOSEPH CONRAD

<table>
<tr><td>Life</td><td>Historical and Cultural Background</td></tr>
</table>

The Polish Years: 1857–1873

Life	Historical and Cultural Background
1857 3 December: Józef Teodor Konrad Korzeniowski born to Apollo Korzeniowski and Ewa (née Bobrowska) Korzeniowska in Berdyczów (Berdichev), Polish Ukraine	Indian Mutiny; Flaubert, *Madame Bovary* 1859: Darwin, *On the Origin of Species* 1860: Turgenev, *On the Eve*
1861 October: Conrad's father arrested and imprisoned in Warsaw by the Russian authorities for anti-Russian conspiracy	American Civil War begins; emancipation of the serfs in Russia; Dickens, *Great Expectations*
1862 May: Conrad's parents convicted of 'political activities' and exiled to Vologda, Russia; Conrad goes with them	Rise of Bismarck in Prussia; Turgenev, *Fathers and Sons*; Victor Hugo, *Les Misérables*
1863 Exile continues in Chernikhov	Polish insurrection; death of Thackeray
1865 18 April: death of Ewa Korzeniowska	American Civil War ends; Tolstoy, *War and Peace* (1865–72) 1866: Dostoevsky, *Crime and Punishment* 1867: Karl Marx, *Das Kapital*
1868 Korzeniowski permitted to leave Russia; settles with his son in Lwów, Austrian Poland	Dostoevsky, *The Idiot*
1869 February: Conrad and his father move to Cracow; 23 May: death of Apollo Korzeniowski; Conrad's uncle Tadeusz Bobrowski becomes his unofficial guardian	Suez Canal opens; Flaubert, *L'Éducation sentimentale*; Matthew Arnold, *Culture and Anarchy*; J. S. Mill, *The Subjection of Women*
1870–3 Lives in Cracow with his maternal grandmother, Teofila Bobrowska; studies with his tutor, Adam Pulman	Franco-Prussian War; Education Act; death of Dickens 1871: Darwin, *The Descent of Man* 1872: George Eliot, *Middlemarch*
1873 Goes to school in Lwów; May–June: tours Switzerland and N. Italy with his tutor	Death of J. S. Mill; publication of his *Autobiography*

Life   *Historical and Cultural Background*

The Years at Sea: 1874–1893

1874 September: leaves for   First Impressionist Exhibition in Paris;
      Marseille and takes a position   Britain extends influence in Malaya
      with Delestang et Fils,
      bankers and shippers;
      December: Conrad's sea-life
      begins; sails as passenger in
      the *Mont-Blanc* to Martinique

1875 June–December: sails across   Tolstoy, *Anna Karenina* (1875–6)
      the Atlantic as apprentice in
      the *Mont-Blanc*

1876–7 July–February: steward in   Alexander Graham Bell demonstrates the
      the *Saint-Antoine* sailing from telephone; Wagner's 'The Ring Cycle'
      Marseille to South America   performed in Bayreuth; death of
                                       George Sand

1877 March–December: possibly   Russia declares war on Turkey; Britain
      involved in Carlist arms-   annexes Transvaal
      smuggling to Spain

1878 March: apparent suicide   The Congress of Berlin; James, *The
      attempt;   Europeans*
      April: sails in British steamer
      Mavis;
      June: lands in England for first
      time;
      July: joins British coastal ship
      Skimmer of the Sea as ordinary
      seaman;
      October: departs from
      London in the *Duke of
      Sutherland* bound for Australia

1879–80 October: arrives back in   British Zulu War; Ibsen, *A Doll's House*;
      London;   James, *Daisy Miller*; Meredith, *The Egoist*
      December–January: sails in
      the *Europa* bound for
      Australia

1880 Takes lodgings in London;   Edison develops electric lighting; deaths of
      May: passes second-mate's   George Eliot and Flaubert; Dostoevsky,
      examination;   *The Brothers Karamazov*
      August: joins the *Loch Etive*
      bound for Australia as third
      mate

1881 September: signs on as second   Tsar Alexander II assassinated; deaths of
      mate in the *Palestine* bound   Dostoevsky and Carlyle
      for Bangkok

Life	*Historical and Cultural Background*
1882–3 The *Palestine* repaired in Falmouth but sinks off Sumatra	Married Women's Property Act in Britain; deaths of Darwin and Garibaldi
1883 July: reunited with his uncle Tadeusz Bobrowski at Marienbad; September: signs on as second mate in the *Riversdale* bound for South Africa and Madras, India	Nietzsche, *Also Sprach Zarathustra*; deaths of Turgenev, Wagner, and Marx
1884 June: sails in the *Narcissus* from Bombay, India, to Dunkirk as second mate; December: passes examination as first mate	Berlin Conference (14 nations), 'The Scramble for Africa'; the Fabian Society founded; Mark Twain, *Huckleberry Finn*
1885 April: sails for Calcutta and Singapore aboard the *Tilkhurst* as second mate	Death of General Gordon at Khartoum; Zola, *Germinal*
1886 August: becomes a naturalized British subject; November: gains his Master's Certificate; briefly signs on as second mate in the *Falconhurst*	Stevenson, *Dr. Jekyll and Mr. Hyde*; Nietzsche, *Beyond Good and Evil*
1887–8 Makes four voyages to the Malay Archipelago as first mate; February (1887): sails for Java in the *Highland Forest* but is injured and hospitalized in Singapore; August: joins the *Vidar* in Singapore bound for Borneo; January (1888): appointed Master of the *Otago* at Bangkok and sails for Australia	Queen Victoria's Golden Jubilee; Verdi, *Otello*; 1888: Wilhelm II becomes Kaiser; British 'protectorate' over Matabeleland, Sarawak, North Borneo, and Brunei; death of Matthew Arnold
1889 Resigns from the *Otago*; March: released from his status as a Russian subject; June: settles briefly in London and in the autumn begins writing *Almayer's Folly*	London Dock Strike; Cecil Rhodes founds the British South Africa Co.; death of Robert Browning

	Life	Historical and Cultural Background
1890	February: returns to Polish Ukraine for the first time in 16 years and visits his uncle Tadeusz Bobrowski; April: in Brussels; appointed by the Société Anonyme Belge pour le Commerce du Haut-Congo; Mid-May: sails for the Congo; September–October: commands the *Roi des Belges* from Stanley Falls to Kinshasa but falls ill with dysentery and malaria; sails for Europe in November	The Partition of Africa; Ibsen, *Hedda Gabler*; William Morris, *News from Nowhere*; J. G. Frazer, *The Golden Bough* (1890–1914)
1891–3	January (1891): back in England; February–March: hospitalized in London; April–May: travels to Champel-les-Bains near Geneva for a cure and returns to London in June, to be temporarily employed by Barr, Moering & Co.; November: joins the *Torrens*, his last sailing ship, and makes four voyages as first mate; meets John Galsworthy and Edward (Ted) Sanderson on one return passage; July (1893): resigns from the *Torrens* but remains on the payroll till mid-October; August–September: visits his uncle in Ukraine; November: briefly joins the *Adowa* at Rouen, France	1891: Hardy, *Tess of the D'Urbervilles*; Wilde, *The Picture of Dorian Gray* 1892: Death of Tennyson 1893: Dvořák, 'New World' Symphony, Verdi, *Falstaff*

Life	*Historical and Cultural Background*

Conrad the Writer: 1894–1924

1894 January: leaves the *Adowa* and returns to London; 10 February: Tadeusz Bobrowski dies; April–May: finishes and revises *Almayer's Folly*; August: again at Champel-les-Bains for hydrotherapy; October: meets Edward Garnett; November: meets Jessie George, his future wife	Nicholas II becomes Tsar; 'Dreyfus case' in France; death of Robert Louis Stevenson
1895 April: *Almayer's Folly* published	Crane, *The Red Badge of Courage*; H. G. Wells, *The Time Machine*; death of Engels; Hardy, *Jude the Obscure*
1896 March: *An Outcast of the Islands*; marries Jessie George; they live in Stanford-le-Hope, Essex	Puccini, *La Bohème*; death of William Morris
1897 Meets R. B. Cunninghame Graham, Henry James, and Stephen Crane; March: moves to Ivy Walls, Essex; December: *The Nigger of the 'Narcissus'*	Queen Victoria's Diamond Jubilee; H. G. Wells, *The Invisible Man*
1898 Meets Ford Madox (Hueffer) Ford and H. G. Wells; 15 January: Alfred Borys Conrad born; April: *Tales of Unrest*; October: leases Pent Farm, Postling, Kent	Curies discover radium; Wilde, *The Ballad of Reading Gaol*; H. G. Wells, *The War of the Worlds*
1899 February: finishes 'Heart of Darkness'	Boer War begins
1900 September: J. B. Pinker becomes Conrad's literary agent; October: *Lord Jim*	Russia occupies Manchuria; Freud, *The Interpretation of Dreams*; deaths of Oscar Wilde, Ruskin, Nietzsche, Crane
1901 June: *The Inheritors* (with Ford)	Death of Queen Victoria; Marconi transmits first transatlantic Morse Code signal; Kipling, *Kim*

Life	*Historical and Cultural Background*
1902 November: *Youth: A Narrative and Two Other Stories* ('Heart of Darkness' and 'The End of the Tether')	Balfour's Education Act; death of Zola; Gorky, *The Lower Depths*
1903 April: *Typhoon and Other Stories* October: *Romance* (with Ford)	Wright brothers' first flight; Shaw, *Man and Superman*; James, *The Ambassadors*; Butler, *The Way of All Flesh*
1904 October: *Nostromo*	Russo-Japanese War; Anglo-French *Entente Cordiale*; Chekhov, *The Cherry Orchard*; James, *The Golden Bowl*; death of Chekhov
1905 January–May: resides in Capri, Italy; June: *One Day More* staged in London	Abortive revolution in Russia; beginning of the Women's Suffrage Movement; Freud, *Three Essays on the Theory of Sexuality*; Debussy, *La Mer*
1906 Meets Arthur Marwood, who becomes a close friend; 2 August: John Conrad born; October: *The Mirror of the Sea: Memories and Impressions*	Anglo-Russian Entente; death of Ibsen; Galsworthy, *The Man of Property*
1907 May–August: at Champel-les-Bains for the children's health; September: *The Secret Agent*; moves to Someries, Luton Hoo, Bedfordshire	Cubist Exhibition in Paris; Shaw, *Major Barbara*
1908 August: *A Set of Six*	Bennett, *The Old Wives' Tale*
1909 February: moves to rented rooms in Aldington, near Hythe, Kent; July: deteriorating relations with Ford culminate in a break	Peary reaches the North Pole; Blériot flies across the Channel; Marinetti launches the Futurist movement
1910 January: quarrels with Pinker; physical and mental breakdown for three months; June: moves to new home, Capel House, Orlestone, Kent	The Union of South Africa created; death of Tolstoy; Post-Impressionist Exhibition, London; E. M. Forster, *Howards End*; Yeats, *The Green Helmet*
1911 October: *Under Western Eyes*	Amundsen reaches the South Pole; the *Blaue Reiter* group formed, Munich
1912 January: *Some Reminiscences* (later retitled *A Personal Record*); October: *'Twixt Land and Sea*	*Titanic* sinks; Schoenberg, *Pierrot Lunaire*; Pound, *Ripostes*; Mann, *Death in Venice*

Life	Historical and Cultural Background
1913 March: meets F. N. Doubleday to discuss a collected edition of his work; September: first meets Bertrand Russell	D. H. Lawrence, *Sons and Lovers*; Proust, *A la recherche du temps perdu* (1913–27); Stravinsky, *The Rite of Spring*
1914 January: *Chance*; July–November: visits Poland with his family and is detained for several weeks by the outbreak of the war	Outbreak of First World War; Polish Legion fights Russians; Joyce, *Dubliners*
1915 February: *Within the Tides*; March: *Victory* (USA; September in UK)	Germans sink the *Lusitania*; Einstein, *General Theory of Relativity*; Pound, *Cathay*; D. H. Lawrence, *The Rainbow*; Ford, *The Good Soldier*
1916 March: sits for a bust by the sculptor Jo Davidson; August: visits Foreign Office and Admiralty to discuss propaganda articles	Battles of Verdun and Somme; Joyce, *A Portrait of the Artist as a Young Man*; death of Henry James
1917 March: *The Shadow-Line*; November: London for a three-month stay	The Russian Revolution; USA enters war; Jung, *The Psychology of the Unconscious*; T. S. Eliot, *Prufrock and Other Observations*; Shaw, *Heartbreak House*
1918 May: first meets G. Jean-Aubry; October: his son Borys hospitalized in Rouen, suffering from shell-shock	Spengler, *The Decline of the West*; death of Wilfred Owen; November, Armistice signed; Polish Republic restored
1919 March: stage version of *Victory* in London; April: *The Arrow of Gold*; May: sells film rights to four of his novels; October: moves to his last home—Oswalds, Bishopsbourne, near Canterbury, Kent	Treaty of Versailles; Keynes, *The Economic Consequences of the Peace*; Walter Gropius founds the *Bauhaus*
1920 May: *The Rescue* (USA; June in UK)	League of Nations founded; Poles rout Russian invaders; D. H. Lawrence, *Women in Love*
1921 February: *Notes on Life and Letters*; the Collected Edition begins publication in England (Heinemann) and the USA (Doubleday)	Irish Free State created; Rutherford and Chadwick work on splitting the atom

Life	*Historical and Cultural Background*
1922 November: stage version of *The Secret Agent*, London	Mussolini forms fascist government in Italy; BBC founded; T. S. Eliot, *The Waste Land*; Joyce, *Ulysses*; Woolf, *Jacob's Room*
1923 May–June: visits USA; December: *The Rover*	Yeats wins Nobel Prize for Literature
1924 11 January: birth of first grandson, Philip James; March: sits for sculptor Jacob Epstein; May: declines knighthood; 3 August: dies of a heart attack; buried in Canterbury Cemetery; September: *The Nature of a Crime* (with Ford); October: *Laughing Anne & One Day More: Two Plays*; November: Ford, *Joseph Conrad: A Personal Remembrance*	Death of Lenin; E. M. Forster, *A Passage to India*; Mann, *The Magic Mountain*; Shaw, *St. Joan*
1925 January: *Tales of Hearsay*; September: *Suspense* (unfinished)	Fall of Trotsky, rise of Stalin; Shaw wins the Nobel Prize for Literature; Hitler, *Mein Kampf*; Woolf, *Mrs. Dalloway*
1926 March: *Last Essays*	General Strike; Kafka, *The Castle*
1928 June: *The Sisters*	Death of Thomas Hardy; D. H. Lawrence, *Lady Chatterley's Lover*

TYPHOON

TYPHOON*

I

CAPTAIN MACWHIRR, of the steamer *Nan-Shan**, had a physiognomy that, in the order of material appearances, was the exact counterpart of his mind: it presented no marked characteristics of firmness or stupidity; it had no pronounced characteristics whatever; it was simply ordinary, irresponsive, and unruffled.

The only thing his aspect might have been said to suggest, at times, was bashfulness; because he would sit, in business offices ashore, sunburnt and smiling faintly, with downcast eyes. When he raised them, they were perceived to be direct in their glance and of blue colour. His hair was fair and extremely fine, clasping from temple to temple the bald dome of his skull in a clamp as of fluffy silk. The hair of his face, on the contrary, carroty and flaming, resembled a growth of copper wire clipped short to the line of the lip; while, no matter how close he shaved, fiery metallic gleams passed, when he moved his head, over the surface of his cheeks. He was rather below the medium height, a bit round-shouldered, and so sturdy of limb that his clothes always looked a shade too tight for his arms and legs. As if unable to grasp what is due to the difference of latitudes, he wore a brown bowler hat, a complete suit of a brownish hue, and clumsy black boots. These harbour togs gave to his thick figure an air of stiff and uncouth smartness. A thin silver watchchain looped his waistcoat, and he never left his ship for the shore without clutching in his powerful, hairy fist an elegant umbrella of the very best quality, but generally unrolled. Young Jukes, the chief mate, attending his commander to the gangway, would sometimes venture to say, with the greatest gentleness, "Allow me, sir,"—and possessing himself of the umbrella deferentially, would elevate the ferule, shake the folds, twirl a neat furl in a jiffy, and hand it back; going through the performance with a face of such portentous gravity, that Mr. Solomon Rout, the chief engineer, smoking his morning cigar over the skylight, would turn away his head in order to hide a smile. "Oh! aye! The blessed gamp. . . . Thank 'ee, Jukes, thank 'ee," would mutter Captain MacWhirr heartily, without looking up.

Having just enough imagination to carry him through each successive day, and no more, he was tranquilly sure of himself; and from the very same cause he was not in the least conceited. It is your imaginative superior who is touchy, overbearing, and difficult to please; but every ship Captain MacWhirr commanded was the floating abode of harmony and peace. It was, in truth, as impossible for him to take a flight of fancy as it would be for a watchmaker to put together a chronometer with nothing except a two-pound hammer and a whip-saw in the way of tools. Yet the uninteresting lives of men so entirely given to the actuality of the bare existence have their mysterious side. It was impossible in Captain MacWhirr's case, for instance, to understand what under heaven could have induced that perfectly satisfactory son of a petty grocer in Belfast to run away to sea. And yet he had done that very thing at the age of fifteen. It was enough, when you thought it over, to give you the idea of an immense, potent, and invisible hand thrust into the ant-heap of the earth, laying hold of shoulders, knocking heads together, and setting the unconscious faces of the multitude towards inconceivable goals and in undreamt-of directions.

His father never really forgave him for this undutiful stupidity. "We could have got on without him," he used to say later on, "but there's the business. And he an only son too!" His mother wept very much after his disappearance. As it had never occurred to him to leave word behind, he was mourned over for dead till, after eight months, his first letter arrived from Talcahuano. It was short, and contained the statement: "We had very fine weather on our passage out." But evidently, in the writer's mind, the only important intelligence was to the effect that his captain had, on the very day of writing, entered him regularly on the ship's articles as Ordinary Seaman. "Because I can do the work," he explained. The mother again wept copiously, while the remark, "Tom's an ass," expressed the emotions of the father. He was a corpulent man, with a gift for sly chaffing, which to the end of his life he exercised in his intercourse with his son, a little pityingly, as if upon a half-witted person.

MacWhirr's visits to his home were necessarily rare, and in the course of years he despatched other letters to his parents, informing them of his successive promotions and of his movements upon the vast earth. In these missives could be found sentences like this: "The heat here is very great." Or: "On Christmas day at 4 P.M. we fell in with some icebergs." The old people ultimately became acquainted with a good many names of ships, and with the names of the skippers who commanded them—with the names of Scots and English shipowners—with the names of seas, oceans, straits, promontories—with outlandish names of lumber-ports, of rice-ports, of cotton-ports—with the names of islands—with the name of their son's young woman. She was called Lucy. It did not suggest itself to him to mention whether he thought the name pretty. And then they died.

The great day of MacWhirr's marriage came in due course, following shortly upon the great day when he got his first command.

All these events had taken place many years before the morning when, in the chart-room of the steamer *Nan-Shan*, he stood confronted by the fall of a barometer he had no reason to distrust. The fall—taking into account the excellence of the instrument, the time of the year, and the ship's position on the terrestrial globe—was of a nature ominously prophetic; but the red face of the man betrayed no sort of inward disturbance. Omens were as nothing to him, and he was unable to discover the message of a prophecy till the fulfilment had brought it home to his very door. "That's a fall, and no mistake," he thought. "There must be some uncommonly dirty weather knocking about."

The *Nan-Shan* was on her way from the southward to the treaty port of Fu-chau, with some cargo in her lower holds, and two hundred Chinese coolies returning to their village homes in the province of Fo-kien, after a few years of work in various tropical colonies. The morning was fine, the oily sea heaved without a sparkle, and there was a queer white misty patch in the sky like a halo of the sun. The fore-deck, packed with Chinamen, was full of sombre clothing, yellow faces, and pigtails, sprinkled over with a good many naked shoulders, for there was no wind, and the heat was close. The coolies lounged, talked, smoked, or stared over the rail; some, drawing water over the side, sluiced each other; a few slept on hatches, while several small parties of six sat on their heels surrounding iron trays with plates of rice and tiny teacups; and every single Celestial of them was carrying with him all he had in the world—a wooden chest with a ringing lock and brass on the corners, containing the savings of his labours: some clothes of ceremony, sticks of incense, a little opium maybe, bits of nameless rubbish of conventional value, and a small hoard of silver dollars, toiled for in coal lighters, won in gambling-houses or in petty trading, grubbed out of earth, sweated out in mines, on railway lines, in deadly jungle, under heavy burdens—amassed patiently, guarded with care, cherished fiercely.

A cross swell had set in from the direction of Formosa Channel about ten o'clock, without disturbing these passengers much, because the *Nan-Shan*, with her flat bottom, rolling chocks on bilges, and great breadth of beam, had the reputation of an exceptionally steady ship in a sea-way. Mr. Jukes, in moments of expansion on shore, would proclaim loudly that the "old girl was as good as she was pretty." It would never have occurred to Captain MacWhirr to express his favourable opinion so loud or in terms so fanciful.

She was a good ship, undoubtedly, and not old either. She had been built in Dumbarton less than three years before, to the order of a firm of merchants in Siam—Messrs. Sigg and Son.* When she lay afloat, finished in every detail and ready to take up the work of her life, the builders contemplated her with pride.

"Sigg has asked us for a reliable skipper to take her out," remarked one of the partners; and the other, after reflecting for a while, said: "I think MacWhirr is ashore just at present." "Is he? Then wire him at once. He's the very man," declared the senior, without a moment's hesitation.

Next morning MacWhirr stood before them unperturbed, having travelled from London by the midnight express after a sudden but undemonstrative parting with his wife. She was the daughter of a superior couple who had seen better days.

"We had better be going together over the ship, Captain," said the senior partner; and the three men started to view the perfections of the *Nan-Shan* from stem to stern, and from her keelson to the trucks of her two stumpy pole-masts.

Captain MacWhirr had begun by taking off his coat, which he hung on the end of a steam windlass embodying all the latest improvements.

"My uncle wrote of you favourably by yesterday's mail to our good friends—Messrs. Sigg, you know—and doubtless they'll continue you out there in command," said the junior partner. "You'll be able to boast of being in charge of the handiest boat of her size on the coast of China, Captain," he added.

"Have you? Thank 'ee," mumbled vaguely MacWhirr, to whom

the view of a distant eventuality could appeal no more than the beauty of a wide landscape to a purblind tourist; and his eyes happening at the moment to be at rest upon the lock of the cabin door, he walked up to it, full of purpose, and began to rattle the handle vigorously, while he observed, in his low, earnest voice, "You can't trust the workmen nowadays. A brand-new lock, and it won't act at all. Stuck fast. See? See?"

As soon as they found themselves alone in their office across the yard: "You praised that fellow up to Sigg. What is it you see in him?" asked the nephew, with faint contempt.

"I admit he has nothing of your fancy skipper about him, if that's what you mean," said the elder man curtly. "Is the foreman of the joiners on the *Nan-Shan* outside? . . . Come in, Bates. How is it that you let Tait's people put us off with a defective lock on the cabin door? The Captain could see directly he set eye on it. Have it replaced at once. The little straws, Bates . . . the little straws. . . ."*

The lock was replaced accordingly, and a few days afterwards the *Nan-Shan* steamed out to the East, without MacWhirr having offered any further remark as to her fittings, or having been heard to utter a single word hinting at pride in his ship, gratitude for his appointment, or satisfaction at his prospects.

With a temperament neither loquacious nor taciturn, he found very little occasion to talk. There were matters of duty, of course—directions, orders, and so on; but the past being to his mind done with, and the future not there yet, the more general actualities of the day required no comment—because facts can speak for themselves with overwhelming precision.

Old Mr. Sigg liked a man of few words, and one that "you could be sure would not try to improve upon his instructions." MacWhirr satisfying these requirements, was continued in command of the *Nan-Shan*, and applied himself to the careful navigation of his ship in the China seas. She had come out on a British register, but after some time Messrs. Sigg judged it expedient to transfer her to the Siamese flag.

At the news of the contemplated transfer Jukes grew restless, as if under a sense of personal affront. He went about grumbling to himself, and uttering short scornful laughs. "Fancy having a ridiculous Noah's Ark elephant in the ensign of one's ship," he said once at the engine-room door. "Dash me if I can stand it: I'll throw up the billet.

Don't it make *you* sick, Mr. Rout?" The chief engineer only cleared his throat with the air of a man who knows the value of a good billet.

The first morning the new flag floated over the stern of the *Nan-Shan* Jukes stood looking at it bitterly from the bridge. He struggled with his feelings for a while, and then remarked, "Queer flag for a man to sail under, sir."

"What's the matter with the flag?" inquired Captain MacWhirr. "Seems all right to me." And he walked across to the end of the bridge to have a good look.

"Well, it looks queer to me," burst out Jukes, greatly exasperated, and flung off the bridge.

Captain MacWhirr was amazed at these manners. After a while he stepped quietly into the chart-room, and opened his International Signal Code-book at the plate where the flags of all the nations are correctly figured in gaudy rows. He ran his finger over them, and when he came to Siam he contemplated with great attention the red field and the white elephant. Nothing could be more simple; but to make sure he brought the book out on the bridge for the purpose of comparing the coloured drawing with the real thing at the flagstaff astern. When next Jukes, who was carrying on the duty that day with a sort of suppressed fierceness, happened on the bridge, his commander observed:

"There's nothing amiss with that flag."

"Isn't there?" mumbled Jukes, falling on his knees before a deck-locker and jerking therefrom viciously a spare lead-line.

"No. I looked up the book. Length twice the breadth and the elephant exactly in the middle. I thought the people ashore would know how to make the local flag. Stands to reason. You were wrong, Jukes. . . ."

"Well, sir," began Jukes, getting up excitedly, "all I can say——" He fumbled for the end of the coil of line with trembling hands.

"That's all right." Captain MacWhirr soothed him, sitting heavily on a little canvas folding-stool he greatly affected. "All you have to do is to take care they don't hoist the elephant upside-down before they get quite used to it."

Jukes flung the new lead-line over on the fore-deck with a loud "Here you are, bosun—don't forget to wet it thoroughly," and turned with immense resolution towards his commander; but Captain MacWhirr spread his elbows on the bridge-rail comfortably.

"Because it would be, I suppose, understood as a signal of distress," he went on. "What do you think? That elephant there, I take it, stands for something in the nature of the Union Jack in the flag. . . ."

"Does it!" yelled Jukes, so that every head on the *Nan-Shan's* decks looked towards the bridge. Then he sighed, and with sudden resignation: "It would certainly be a dam' distressful sight," he said meekly.

Later in the day he accosted the chief engineer with a confidential "Here, let me tell you the old man's latest."

Mr. Solomon Rout (frequently alluded to as Long Sol, Old Sol, or Father Rout), from finding himself almost invariably the tallest man on board every ship he joined, had acquired the habit of a stooping, leisurely condescension. His hair was scant and sandy, his flat cheeks were pale, his bony wrists and long scholarly hands were pale too, as though he had lived all his life in the shade.

He smiled from on high at Jukes, and went on smoking and glancing about quietly, in the manner of a kind uncle lending an ear to the tale of an excited schoolboy. Then, greatly amused but impassive, he asked:

"And did you throw up the billet?"

"No," cried Jukes, raising a weary, discouraged voice above the harsh buzz of the *Nan-Shan's* friction winches. All of them were hard at work, snatching slings of cargo, high up, to the end of long derricks, only, as it seemed, to let them rip down recklessly by the run. The cargo chains groaned in the gins, clinked on coamings, rattled over the side; and the whole ship quivered, with her long grey flanks smoking in wreaths of steam. "No," cried Jukes, "I didn't. What's the good? I might just as well fling my resignation at this bulkhead. I don't believe you can make a man like that understand anything. He simply knocks me over."

At that moment Captain MacWhirr, back from the shore, crossed the deck, umbrella in hand, escorted by a mournful, self-possessed Chinaman, walking behind in paper-soled silk shoes, and who also carried an umbrella.

The master of the *Nan-Shan*, speaking just audibly and gazing at his boots as his manner was, remarked that it would be necessary to call at Fu-chau this trip, and desired Mr. Rout to have steam up tomorrow afternoon at one o'clock sharp. He pushed back his hat to wipe his forehead, observing at the same time that he hated going ashore anyhow; while overtopping him Mr. Rout, without deigning a word, smoked austerely, nursing his right elbow in the palm of his left hand. Then Jukes was directed in the same subdued voice to keep the forward 'tween-deck clear of cargo. Two hundred coolies were going to be put down there. The Bun Hin Company were sending that lot home. Twenty-five bags of rice would be coming off in a sampan directly, for stores. All seven-years'-men they were, said Captain MacWhirr, with a camphor-wood chest to every man. The carpenter should be set to work nailing three-inch battens along the deck below, fore and aft, to keep these boxes from shifting in a sea-way. Jukes had better look to it at once. "D'ye hear, Jukes?" This Chinaman here was coming with the ship as far as Fu-chau,—a sort of interpreter he would be. Bun Hin's clerk he was, and wanted to have a look at the space. Jukes had better take him forward. "D'ye hear, Jukes?"

Jukes took care to punctuate these instructions in proper places with the obligatory "Yes, sir," ejaculated without enthusiasm. His brusque "Come along John; make look see" set the Chinaman in motion at his heels.

"Wanchee look see, all same look see can do," said Jukes, who having no talent for foreign languages mangled the very pidgin-English cruelly. He pointed at the open hatch. "Catchee number one piecie place to sleep in. Eh?"

He was gruff, as became his racial superiority, but not unfriendly. The Chinaman, gazing sad and speechless into the darkness of the hatchway, seemed to stand at the head of a yawning grave.

"No catchee rain down there—savee?" pointed out Jukes. "Suppose all 'ee same fine weather, one piecie coolie-man come top-side," he pursued, warming up imaginatively. "Make so—Phooooo!" He expanded his chest and blew out his cheeks. "Savee, John? Breathe—fresh air. Good. Eh? Washee him piecie pants, chow-chow top-side—see, John?"

With his mouth and hands he made exuberant motions of eating rice and washing clothes; and the Chinaman, who concealed his distrust of this pantomime under a collected demeanour tinged by a gentle and refined melancholy, glanced out of his almond eyes from Jukes to the hatch and back again. "Velly good," he murmured, in a disconsolate undertone, and hastened smoothly along the decks, dodging obstacles in his course. He disappeared, ducking low under a sling of ten dirty gunny-bags full of some costly merchandise and exhaling a repulsive smell.

Captain MacWhirr meantime had gone on the bridge, and into the chart-room, where a letter, commenced two days before, awaited termination. These long letters began with the words, "My darling wife," and the steward, between the scrubbing of the floors and the dusting of chronometer-boxes, snatched at every opportunity to read them. They interested him much more than they possibly could the woman for whose eye they were intended; and this for the reason that they related in minute detail each successive trip of the *Nan-Shan*.

Her master, faithful to facts, which alone his consciousness reflected, would set them down with painstaking care upon many pages. The house in a northern suburb to which these pages were addressed had a bit of garden before the bow-windows, a deep porch of good appearance, coloured glass with imitation lead frame in the front door. He paid five-and-forty pounds a year for it, and did not think the rent too high, because Mrs. MacWhirr (a pretentious person with a scraggy neck and a disdainful manner) was admittedly ladylike, and in the neighbourhood considered as "quite superior." The only secret of her life was her abject terror of the time when her husband would come home to stay for good. Under the same roof there dwelt also a daughter called Lydia and a son, Tom. These two were but slightly acquainted with their father. Mainly, they knew him as a rare but privileged visitor, who of an evening smoked his pipe in the dining-room and slept in the house. The lanky girl, upon the whole, was rather ashamed of him; the boy was frankly and utterly indifferent in a straightforward, delightful, unaffected way manly boys have.

And Captain MacWhirr wrote home from the coast of China twelve times every year, desiring queerly to be "remembered to the children," and subscribing himself "your loving husband," as calmly as if the words so long used by so many men were, apart from their shape, worn-out things, and of a faded meaning.

The China seas north and south are narrow seas. They are seas full of every-day, eloquent facts, such as islands, sand-banks, reefs, swift and changeable currents—tangled facts that nevertheless speak to a seaman in clear and definite language. Their speech appealed to

Captain MacWhirr's sense of realities so forcibly that he had given up his state-room below and practically lived all his days on the bridge of his ship, often having his meals sent up, and sleeping at night in the chart-room. And he indited there his home letters. Each of them, without exception, contained the phrase, "The weather has been very fine this trip," or some other form of a statement to that effect. And this statement, too, in its wonderful persistence, was of the same perfect accuracy as all the others they contained.

Mr. Rout likewise wrote letters; only no one on board knew how chatty he could be pen in hand, because the chief engineer had enough imagination to keep his desk locked. His wife relished his style greatly. They were a childless couple, and Mrs. Rout, a big, high-bosomed, jolly woman of forty, shared with Mr. Rout's tooth-less and venerable mother a little cottage near Teddington. She would run over her correspondence, at breakfast, with lively eyes, and scream out interesting passages in a joyous voice at the deaf old lady, prefacing each extract by the warning shout, "Solomon says!"* She had the trick of firing off Solomon's utterances also upon strangers, astonishing them easily by the unfamiliar text and the unexpectedly jocular vein of these quotations. On the day the new curate called for the first time at the cottage, she found occasion to remark, "As Solomon says: 'the engineers that go down to the sea in ships behold the wonders of sailor nature';" when a change in the visitor's countenance made her stop and stare.

"Solomon . . . Oh! . . . Mrs. Rout," stuttered the young man, very red in the face, "I must say . . . I don't . . ."

"He's my husband," she announced in a great shout, throwing herself back in the chair. Perceiving the joke, she laughed immoder-ately with a handkerchief to her eyes, while he sat wearing a forced smile, and, from his inexperience of jolly women, fully persuaded that she must be deplorably insane. They were excellent friends afterwards; for, absolving her from irreverent intention, he came to think she was a very worthy person indeed; and he learned in time to receive without flinching other scraps of Solomon's wisdom.

"For my part," Solomon was reported by his wife to have said once, "give me the dullest ass for a skipper before a rogue. There is a way to take a fool; but a rogue is smart and slippery." This was an airy generalisation drawn from the particular case of Captain MacWhirr's honesty, which, in itself, had the heavy obviousness of a lump of clay. On the other hand, Mr. Jukes, unable to generalise, unmarried, and unengaged, was in the habit of opening his heart after another fashion to an old chum and former shipmate, actually serving as second officer on board an Atlantic liner.

First of all he would insist upon the advantages of the Eastern trade, hinting at its superiority to the Western ocean service. He extolled the sky, the seas, the ships, and the easy life of the Far East. The *Nan-Shan*, he affirmed, was second to none as a sea-boat.

"We have no brass-bound uniforms, but then we are like brothers here," he wrote. "We all mess together and live like fighting-cocks. . . . All the chaps of the black-squad are as decent as they make that kind, and old Sol, the Chief, is a dry stick. We are good friends. As to our old man, you could not find a quieter skipper. Sometimes you would think he hadn't sense enough to see anything wrong. And yet it isn't that. Can't be. He has been in command for a good few years now. He doesn't do anything actually foolish, and gets his ship along all right without worrying anybody. I believe he hasn't brains enough to enjoy kicking up a row. I don't take advantage of him. I would scorn it. Outside the routine of duty he doesn't seem to understand more than half of what you tell him. We get a laugh out of this at times; but it is dull, too, to be with a man like this—in the long-run. Old Sol says he hasn't much conversation. Conversation! O Lord! He never talks. The other day I had been yarning under the bridge with one of the engineers, and he must have heard us. When I came up to take my watch, he steps out of the chart-room and has a good look all round, peeps over at the sidelights, glances at the compass, squints upwards at the stars. That's his regular perform-ance. By-and-by he says: 'Was that you talking just now in the port alleyway?' 'Yes, sir.' 'With the third engineer?' 'Yes, sir.' He walks off to starboard, and sits under the dodger on a little campstool of his, and for half an hour perhaps he makes no sound, except that I heard him sneeze once. Then after a while I hear him getting up over there, and he strolls across to port, where I was. 'I can't understand what you can find to talk about,' says he. 'Two solid hours. I am not blaming you. I see people ashore at it all day long, and then in the evening they sit down and keep at it over the drinks. Must be saying the same things over and over again. I can't understand.'

"Did you ever hear anything like that? And he was so patient about it. It made me quite sorry for him. But he is exasperating too sometimes. Of course one would not do anything to vex him even if it were worth while. But it isn't. He's so jolly innocent that if you were to put your thumb to your nose and wave your fingers at him he would only wonder gravely to himself what got into you. He told me once quite simply that he found it very difficult to make out what made people always act so queerly. He's too dense to trouble about, and that's the truth."

Thus wrote Mr. Jukes to his chum in the Western ocean trade, out of the fulness of his heart and the liveliness of his fancy.

He had expressed his honest opinion. It was not worth while trying to impress a man of that sort. If the world had been full of such men, life would have probably appeared to Jukes an unentertaining and unprofitable business. He was not alone in his opinion. The sea itself, as if sharing Mr. Jukes' good-natured forbearance, had never put itself out to startle the silent man, who seldom looked up, and wandered innocently over the waters with the only visible purpose of getting food, raiment, and house-room for three people ashore. Dirty weather he had known, of course. He had been made wet, uncomfortable, tired in the usual way, felt at the time and presently forgotten. So that upon the whole he had been justified in reporting fine weather at home. But he had never been given a glimpse of immeasurable strength and of immoderate wrath, the wrath that passes exhausted but never appeased—the wrath and fury of the passionate sea. He knew it existed, as we know that crime and abominations exist; he had heard of it as a peaceable citizen in a town hears of battles, famines, and floods, and yet knows nothing of what these things mean—though, indeed, he may have been mixed up in a street row, have gone without his dinner once, or been soaked to the skin in a shower. Captain MacWhirr had sailed over the surface of the oceans as some men go skimming over the years of existence to sink gently into a placid grave, ignorant of life to the last, without ever having been made to see all it may contain of perfidy, of violence, and of terror. There are on sea and land such men thus fortunate—or thus disdained by destiny or by the sea.

OBSERVING the steady fall of the barometer, Captain MacWhirr thought, "There's some dirty weather knocking about." This is precisely what he thought. He had had an experience of moderately dirty weather—the term dirty as applied to the weather implying only moderate discomfort to the seaman. Had he been informed by an indisputable authority that the end of the world was to be finally accomplished by a catastrophic disturbance of the atmosphere, he would have assimilated the information under the simple idea of dirty weather, and no other, because he had no experience of cataclysms, and belief does not necessarily imply comprehension. The wisdom of his country had pronounced by means of an Act of Parliament that before he could be considered as fit to take charge of a ship he should be able to answer certain simple questions on the subject of circular storms such as hurricanes, cyclones, typhoons; and apparently he had answered them, since he was now in command of the *Nan-Shan* in the China seas during the season of typhoons. But if he had answered he remembered nothing of it. He was, however, conscious of being made uncomfortable by the clammy heat. He came out on the bridge, and found no relief to this oppression. The air seemed thick. He gasped like a fish, and began to believe himself greatly out of sorts.

The *Nan-Shan* was ploughing a vanishing furrow upon the circle of the sea that had the surface and the shimmer of an undulating piece of grey silk. The sun, pale and without rays, poured down leaden heat in a strangely indecisive light, and the Chinamen were lying prostrate about the decks. Their bloodless, pinched, yellow faces were like the faces of bilious invalids. Captain MacWhirr noticed two of them especially, stretched out on their backs below the bridge. As soon as they had closed their eyes they seemed dead. Three others, however, were quarrelling barbarously away forward; and one big fellow, half naked, with herculean shoulders, was hanging limply over a winch; another, sitting on the deck, his knees up and his head drooping sideways in a girlish attitude, was plaiting his pigtail with infinite languor depicted in his whole person and in the very movement of his fingers. The smoke struggled with difficulty out of the funnel, and instead of streaming away spread itself out like an infernal sort of cloud, smelling of sulphur and raining soot all over the decks.

"What the devil are you doing there, Mr. Jukes?" asked Captain MacWhirr.

This unusual form of address, though mumbled rather than spoken, caused the body of Mr. Jukes to start as though it had been prodded under the fifth rib. He had had a low bench brought on the bridge, and sitting on it, with a length of rope curled about his feet and a piece of canvas stretched over his knees, was pushing a sail-needle vigorously. He looked up, and his surprise gave to his eyes an expression of innocence and candour.

"I am only roping some of that new set of bags we made last trip for whipping up coals," he remonstrated gently. "We shall want them for the next coaling, sir."

"What became of the others?"

"Why, worn out of course, sir."

Captain MacWhirr, after glaring down irresolutely at his chief mate, disclosed the gloomy and cynical conviction that more than half of them had been lost overboard, "if only the truth was known," and retired to the other end of the bridge. Jukes, exasperated by this unprovoked attack, broke the needle at the second stitch, and dropping his work got up and cursed the heat in a violent undertone.

The propeller thumped, the three Chinamen forward had given up squabbling very suddenly, and the one who had been plaiting his tail clasped his legs and stared dejectedly over his knees. The lurid sunshine cast faint and sickly shadows. The swell ran higher and swifter every moment, and the ship lurched heavily in the smooth, deep hollows of the sea.

"I wonder where that beastly swell comes from," said Jukes aloud, recovering himself after a stagger.

"North-east," grunted the literal MacWhirr, from his side of the bridge. "There's some dirty weather knocking about. Go and look at the glass."

When Jukes came out of the chart-room, the cast of his countenance had changed to thoughtfulness and concern. He caught hold of the bridge-rail and stared ahead.

The temperature in the engine-room had gone up to a hundred and seventeen degrees. Irritated voices were ascending through the skylight and through the fiddle of the stokehold in a harsh and resonant uproar, mingled with angry clangs and scrapes of metal, as if men with limbs of iron and throats of bronze had been quarrelling down there. The second engineer was falling foul of the stokers for letting the steam go down. He was a man with arms like a black-smith, and generally feared; but that afternoon the stokers were answering him back recklessly, and slammed the furnace doors with the fury of despair. Then the noise ceased suddenly, and the second engineer appeared, emerging out of the stokehold streaked with grime and soaking wet like a chimney-sweep coming out of a well. As soon as his head was clear of the fiddle he began to scold Jukes for not trimming properly the stokehold ventilators; and in answer Jukes made with his hands deprecatory soothing signs meaning: No wind—can't be helped—you can see for yourself. But the other wouldn't hear reason. His teeth flashed angrily in his dirty face. He didn't mind, he said, the trouble of punching their blanked heads down there, blank his soul, but did the condemned sailors think you could keep steam up in the God-forsaken boilers simply by knocking the blanked stokers about? No, by George! You had to get some draught too—may he be everlastingly blanked for a swab-headed deck-hand if you didn't! And the chief, too, rampaging before the steam-gauge and carrying on like a lunatic up and down the engine-room ever since noon. What did Jukes think he was stuck up there for, if he couldn't get one of his decayed, good-for-nothing deck-cripples to turn the ventilators to the wind?

The relations of the "engine-room" and the "deck" of the *Nan-Shan* were, as is known, of a brotherly nature; therefore Jukes leaned over and begged the other in a restrained tone not to make a disgust-ing ass of himself; the skipper was on the other side of the bridge. But the second declared mutinously that he didn't care a rap who was on the other side of the bridge, and Jukes, passing in a flash from lofty disapproval into a state of exaltation, invited him in unflattering terms to come up and twist the beastly things to please himself, and catch such wind as a donkey of his sort could find. The second rushed up to the fray. He flung himself at the port ventilator as though he meant to tear it out bodily and toss it overboard. All he did was to move the cowl round a few inches, with an enormous expend-iture of force, and seemed spent in the effort. He leaned against the back of the wheel-house, and Jukes walked up to him.

"Oh, Heavens!" ejaculated the engineer in a feeble voice. He lifted his eyes to the sky, and then let his glassy stare descend to meet the horizon that, tilting up to an angle of forty degrees, seemed to hang on a slant for a while and settled down slowly. "Heavens! Phew! What's up, anyhow?"

Jukes, straddling his long legs like a pair of compasses, put on an air of superiority. "We're going to catch it this time," he said. "The barometer is tumbling down like anything, Harry. And you trying to kick up that silly row . . ."

The word "barometer" seemed to revive the second engineer's mad animosity. Collecting afresh all his energies, he directed Jukes in a low and brutal tone to shove the unmentionable instrument down his gory throat. Who cared for his crimson* barometer? It was the steam—the steam—that was going down; and what between the firemen going faint and the chief going silly, it was worse than a dog's life for him; he didn't care a tinker's curse how soon the whole show was blown out of the water. He seemed on the point of having a cry, but after regaining his breath he muttered darkly, "I'll faint them," and dashed off. He stopped upon the fiddle long enough to shake his fist at the unnatural daylight, and dropped into the dark hole with a whoop.

When Jukes turned, his eyes fell upon the rounded back and the big red ears of Captain MacWhirr, who had come across. He did not look at his chief officer, but said at once, "That's a very violent man, that second engineer."

"Jolly good second, anyhow," grunted Jukes. "They can't keep up steam," he added rapidly, and made a grab at the rail against the coming lurch.

Captain MacWhirr, unprepared, took a run and brought himself up with a jerk by an awning stanchion.

"A profane man," he said obstinately. "If this goes on, I'll have to get rid of him the first chance."

"It's the heat," said Jukes. "The weather's awful. It would make a saint swear. Even up here I feel exactly as if I had my head tied up in a woollen blanket."

Captain MacWhirr looked up. "D'ye mean to say, Mr. Jukes, you ever had your head tied up in a blanket? What was that for?"

"It's a manner of speaking, sir," said Jukes stolidly.

"Some of you fellows do go on! What's that about saints swearing?

I wish you wouldn't talk so wild. What sort of saint would that be that would swear? No more saint than yourself, I expect. And what's a blanket got to do with it—or the weather either . . . The heat does not make me swear—does it? It's filthy bad temper. That's what it is. And what's the good of your talking like this?"

Thus Captain MacWhirr expostulated against the use of images in speech, and at the end electrified Jukes by a contemptous snort, followed by words of passion and resentment: "Damme! I'll fire him out of the ship if he don't look out."

And Jukes, incorrigible, thought: "Goodness me! Somebody's put a new inside to my old man. Here's temper, if you like. Of course it's the weather; what else? It would make an angel quarrelsome—let alone a saint."

All the Chinamen on deck appeared at their last gasp.

At its setting the sun had a diminished diameter and an expiring brown, rayless glow, as if millions of centuries elapsing since the morning had brought it near its end. A dense bank of cloud became visible to the northward; it had a sinister dark olive tint, and lay low and motionless upon the sea, resembling a solid obstacle in the path of the ship. She went floundering towards it like an exhausted creature driven to its death. The coppery twilight retired slowly, and the darkness brought out overhead a swarm of unsteady, big stars, that, as if blown upon, flickered exceedingly and seemed to hang very near the earth. At eight o'clock Jukes went into the chart-room to write up the ship's log.

He copied neatly out of the rough-book the number of miles, the course of the ship, and in the column for "wind" scrawled the word "calm" from top to bottom of the eight hours since noon. He was exasperated by the continuous, monotonous rolling of the ship. The heavy inkstand would slide away in a manner that suggested perverse intelligence in dodging the pen. Having written in the large space under the head of "Remarks" "Heat very oppressive," he stuck the end of the penholder in his teeth, pipe fashion, and mopped his face carefully.

"Ship rolling heavily in a high cross swell," he began again, and commented to himself, "Heavily is no word for it." Then he wrote: "Sunset threatening, with a low bank of clouds to N. and E. Sky clear overhead."

Sprawling over the table with arrested pen, he glanced out of the door, and in that frame of his vision he saw all the stars flying upwards between the teak-wood jambs on a black sky. The whole lot took flight together and disappeared, leaving only a blackness flecked with white flashes, for the sea was as black as the sky and speckled with foam afar. The stars that had flown to the roll came back on the return swing of the ship, rushing downwards in their glittering multitude, not of fiery points, but enlarged to tiny discs brilliant with a clear wet sheen.

Jukes watched the flying big stars for a moment, and then wrote: "8 P.M. Swell increasing. Ship labouring and taking water on her decks. Battened down the coolies for the night. Barometer still falling." He paused, and thought to himself, "Perhaps nothing whatever'll come of it." And then he closed resolutely his entries: "Every appearance of a typhoon coming on."

On going out he had to stand aside, and Captain MacWhirr strode over the doorstep without saying a word or making a sign.

"Shut the door, Mr. Jukes, will you?" he cried from within.

Jukes turned back to do so, muttering ironically: "Afraid to catch cold, I suppose." It was his watch below, but he yearned for communion with his kind; and he remarked cheerily to the second mate: "Doesn't look so bad, after all—does it?"

The second mate was marching to and fro on the bridge, tripping down with small steps one moment, and the next climbing with difficulty the shifting slope of the deck. At the sound of Jukes's voice he stood still, facing forward, but made no reply.

"Hallo! That's a heavy one," said Jukes, swaying to meet the long roll till his lowered hand touched the planks. This time the second mate made in his throat a noise of an unfriendly nature.

He was an oldish, shabby little fellow, with bad teeth and no hair on his face. He had been shipped in a hurry in Shanghai, that trip when the second officer brought from home had delayed the ship three hours in port by contriving (in some manner Captain MacWhirr could never understand) to fall overboard into an empty coal-lighter lying alongside, and had to be sent ashore to the hospital with concussion of the brain and a broken limb or two.

Jukes was not discouraged by the unsympathetic sound. "The Chinamen must be having a lovely time of it down there," he said. "It's lucky for them the old girl has the easiest roll of any ship I've ever been in. There now! This one wasn't so bad."

"You wait," snarled the second mate.

With his sharp nose, red at the tip, and his thin pinched lips, he always looked as though he were raging inwardly; and he was concise in his speech to the point of rudeness. All his time off duty he spent in his cabin with the door shut, keeping so still in there that he was supposed to fall asleep as soon as he had disappeared; but the man who came in to wake him for his watch on deck would invariably find him with his eyes wide open, flat on his back in the bunk, and glaring irritably from a soiled pillow. He never wrote any letters, did not seem to hope for news from anywhere; and though he had been heard once to mention West Hartlepool, it was with extreme bitterness, and only in connection with the extortionate charges of a boarding-house. He was one of those men who are picked up at need in the ports of the world. They are competent enough, appear hopelessly hard up, show no evidence of any sort of vice, and carry about them all the signs of manifest failure. They come aboard on an emergency, care for no ship afloat, live in their own atmosphere of casual connection amongst their shipmates who know nothing of them, and make up their minds to leave at inconvenient times. They clear out with no words of leave-taking in some God-forsaken port other men would fear to be stranded in, and go ashore in company of a shabby sea-chest, corded like a treasure-box, and with an air of shaking the ship's dust off their feet.

"You wait," he repeated, balanced in great swings with his back to Jukes, motionless and implacable.

"Do you mean to say we are going to catch it hot?" asked Jukes with boyish interest.

"Say? . . . I say nothing. You don't catch me," snapped the little second mate, with a mixture of pride, scorn, and cunning, as if Jukes' question had been a trap cleverly detected. "Oh no! None of you here shall make a fool of me if I know it," he mumbled to himself.

Jukes reflected rapidly that this second mate was a mean little beast, and in his heart he wished poor Jack Allen had never smashed himself up in the coal-lighter. The far-off blackness ahead of the ship was like another night seen through the starry night of the earth—the starless night of the immensities beyond the created universe, revealed in its appalling stillness through a low fissure in the glittering sphere of which the earth is the kernel.

"Whatever there might be about," said Jukes, "we are steaming straight into it."

"*You've* said it," caught up the second mate, always with his back to Jukes. "You've said it, mind—not I."

"Oh, go to Jericho!" said Jukes frankly; and the other emitted a triumphant little chuckle.

"You've said it," he repeated.

"And what of that?"

"I've known some real good men get into trouble with their skippers for saying a dam' sight less," answered the second mate feverishly. "Oh no! You don't catch me."

"You seem deucedly anxious not to give yourself away," said Jukes, completely soured by such absurdity. "I wouldn't be afraid to say what I think."

"Aye, to me! That's no great trick. I am nobody, and well I know it."

The ship, after a pause of comparative steadiness, started upon a series of rolls, one worse than the other, and for a time Jukes, preserving his equilibrium, was too busy to open his mouth. As soon as the violent swinging had quieted down somewhat, he said: "This is a bit too much of a good thing. Whether anything is coming or not I think she ought to be put head on to that swell. The old man is just gone in to lie down. Hang me if I don't speak to him."

But when he opened the door of the chart-room he saw his captain reading a book. Captain MacWhirr was not lying down: he was standing up with one hand grasping the edge of the bookshelf and the other holding open before his face a thick volume. The lamp wriggled in the gimbals, the loosened books toppled from side to side on the shelf, the long barometer swung in jerky circles, the table altered its slant every moment. In the midst of all this stir and movement Captain MacWhirr, holding on, showed his eyes above the upper edge, and asked, "What's the matter?"

"Swell getting worse, sir."

"Noticed that in here," muttered Captain MacWhirr. "Anything wrong?"

Jukes, inwardly disconcerted by the seriousness of the eyes looking at him over the top of the book, produced an embarrassed grin.

"Rolling like old boots," he said sheepishly.

"Aye! Very heavy—very heavy. What do you want?"

At this Jukes lost his footing and began to flounder.

"I was thinking of our passengers," he said, in the manner of a man clutching at a straw.

"Passengers?" wondered the Captain gravely. "What passengers?"

"Why, the Chinamen, sir," explained Jukes, very sick of this conversation.

"The Chinamen! Why don't you speak plainly? Couldn't tell what you meant. Never heard a lot of coolies spoken of as passengers before. Passengers, indeed! What's come to you?"

Captain MacWhirr, closing the book on his forefinger, lowered his arm and looked completely mystified. "Why are you thinking of the Chinamen, Mr. Jukes?" he inquired.

Jukes took a plunge, like a man driven to it. "She's rolling her decks full of water, sir. Thought you might put her head on perhaps—for a while. Till this goes down a bit—very soon, I dare say. Head to the eastward. I never knew a ship roll like this."

He held on in the doorway, and Captain MacWhirr, feeling his grip on the shelf inadequate, made up his mind to let go in a hurry, and fell heavily on the couch.

"Head to the eastward?" he said, struggling to sit up. "That's more than four points off her course."

"Yes, sir. Fifty degrees . . . Would just bring her head far enough round to meet this . . ."

Captain MacWhirr was now sitting up. He had not dropped the book, and he had not lost his place.

"To the eastward?" he repeated, with dawning astonishment. "To the . . . Where do you think we are bound to? You want me to haul a full-powered steamship four points off her course to make the Chinamen comfortable! Now, I've heard more than enough of mad things done in the world—but this . . . If I didn't know you, Jukes, I would think you were in liquor. Steer four points off . . . And what afterwards? Steer four points over the other way, I suppose, to make the course good. What put it into your head that I would start to tack a steamer as if she were a sailing-ship?"

"Jolly good thing she isn't," threw in Jukes, with bitter readiness. "She would have rolled every blessed stick out of her this afternoon."

"Aye! And you just would have had to stand and see them go," said Captain MacWhirr, showing a certain animation. "It's a dead calm, isn't it?"

"It is, sir. But there's something out of the common coming, for sure."

"Maybe. I suppose you have a notion I should be getting out of the way of that dirt," said Captain MacWhirr, speaking with the utmost simplicity of manner and tone, and fixing the oilcloth on the floor with a heavy stare. Thus he noticed neither Jukes' discomfiture nor the mixture of vexation and astonished respect on his face.

"Now, here's this book," he continued with deliberation, slapping his thigh with the closed volume. "I've been reading the chapter on the storms* there."

This was true. He had been reading the chapter on the storms. When he had entered the chart-room, it was with no intention of taking the book down. Some influence in the air—the same influence, probably, that caused the steward to bring without orders the Captain's sea-boots and oilskin coat up to the chart-room—had as it were guided his hand to the shelf; and without taking the time to sit down he had waded with a conscious effort into the terminology of the subject. He lost himself amongst advancing semi-circles, left- and right-hand quadrants, the curves of the tracks, the probable bearing of the centre, the shifts of wind and the readings of barometer. He tried to bring all these things into a definite relation to himself, and ended by becoming contemptuously angry with such a lot of words and with so much advice, all head-work and supposition, without a glimmer of certitude.

"It's the damnedest thing, Jukes," he said. "If a fellow was to believe all that's in there, he would be running most of his time all over the sea trying to get behind the weather."

Again he slapped his leg with the book; and Jukes opened his mouth, but said nothing.

"Running to get behind the weather! Do you understand that, Mr. Jukes? It's the maddest thing!" ejaculated Captain MacWhirr, with pauses, gazing at the floor profoundly. "You would think an old woman had been writing this. It passes me. If that thing means anything useful, then it means that I should at once alter the course away, away to the devil somewhere, and come booming down on Fuchau from the northward at the tail of this dirty weather that's supposed to be knocking about in our way. From the north! Do you understand, Mr. Jukes? Three hundred extra miles to the distance, and a pretty coal bill to show. I couldn't bring myself to do that if

every word in there was gospel truth, Mr. Jukes. Don't you expect
me . . ."

And Jukes, silent, marvelled at this display of feeling and
loquacity.

"But the truth is that you don't know if the fellow is right anyhow.
How can you tell what a gale is made of till you get it? He isn't
aboard here, is he? Very well. Here he says that the centre of them
things bears eight points off the wind; but we haven't got any wind,
for all the barometer falling. Where's his centre now?"

"We will get the wind presently," mumbled Jukes.

"Let it come, then," said Captain MacWhirr, with dignified
indignation. "It's only to let you see, Mr. Jukes, that you don't find
everything in books. All these rules for dodging breezes and circum-
venting the winds of heaven, Mr. Jukes, seem to me the maddest
thing, when you come to look at it sensibly."

He raised his eyes, saw Jukes gazing at him dubiously, and tried to
illustrate his meaning.

"About as queer as your extraordinary notion of dodging the ship
head to sea, for I don't know how long, to make the Chinamen
comfortable; whereas all we've got to do is to take them to Fu-chau,
being timed to get there before noon on Friday. If the weather delays
me—very well. There's your log-book to talk straight about the
weather. But suppose I went swinging off my course and came in two
days late, and they asked me: 'Where have you been all that time,
Captain?' What could I say to that? 'Went around to dodge the bad
weather,' I would say. 'It must've been dam' bad,' they would say.
'Don't know,' I would have to say; 'I've dodged clear of it.' See that,
Jukes? I have been thinking it all out this afternoon."

He looked up again in his unseeing, unimaginative way. No one
had ever heard him say so much at one time. Jukes, with his arms
open in the doorway, was like a man invited to behold a miracle.
Unbounded wonder was the intellectual meaning of his eye, while
incredulity was seated in his whole countenance.

"A gale is a gale, Mr. Jukes," resumed the Captain, "and a full-
powered steam-ship has got to face it. There's just so much dirty
weather knocking about the world, and the proper thing is to go
through it with none of what old Captain Wilson of the *Melita** calls
'storm strategy.' The other day ashore I heard him hold forth about
it to a lot of shipmasters who came in and sat at a table next to mine.

It seemed to me the greatest nonsense. He was telling them how he—out-manœuvred, I think he said, a terrific gale, so that it never came nearer than fifty miles to him. A neat piece of head-work he called it. How he knew there was a terrific gale fifty miles off beats me altogether. It was like listening to a crazy man. I would have thought Captain Wilson was old enough to know better."

Captain MacWhirr ceased for a moment, then said, "It's your watch below, Mr. Jukes?"

Jukes came to himself with a start. "Yes, sir."

"Leave orders to call me at the slightest change," said the Captain. He reached up to put the book away, and tucked his legs upon the couch. "Shut the door so that it don't fly open, will you? I can't stand a door banging. They've put a lot of rubbishy locks into this ship, I must say."

Captain MacWhirr closed his eyes.

He did so to rest himself. He was tired, and he experienced that state of mental vacuity which comes at the end of an exhaustive discussion that has liberated some belief matured in the course of meditative years. He had indeed been making his confession of faith, had he only known it; and its effect was to make Jukes, on the other side of the door, stand scratching his head for a good while.

Captain MacWhirr opened his eyes.

He thought he must have been asleep. What was that loud noise? Wind? Why had he not been called? The lamp wriggled in its gimbals, the barometer swung in circles, the table altered its slant every moment; a pair of limp seaboots with collapsed tops went sliding past the couch. He put out his hand instantly, and captured one.

Jukes' face appeared in a crack of the door: only his face, very red, with staring eyes. The flame of the lamp leaped, a piece of paper flew up, a rush of air enveloped Captain MacWhirr. Beginning to draw on the boot, he directed an expectant gaze at Jukes' swollen, excited features.

"Came on like this," shouted Jukes, "five minutes ago . . . all of a sudden."

The head disappeared with a bang, and a heavy splash and patter of drops swept past the closed door as if a pailful of melted lead had been flung against the house. A whistling could be heard now upon the deep vibrating noise outside. The stuffy chart-room seemed as full of draughts as a shed. Captain MacWhirr collared the other sea-boot on its violent passage along the floor. He was not flustered, but he could not find at once the opening for inserting his foot. The shoes he had flung off were scurrying from end to end of the cabin, gambolling playfully over each other like puppies. As soon as he stood up he kicked at them viciously, but without effect.

He threw himself into the attitude of a lunging fencer, to reach after his oilskin coat; and afterwards he staggered all over the confined space while he jerked himself into it. Very grave, straddling his legs far apart, and stretching his neck, he started to tie deliberately the strings of his sou'-wester under his chin, with thick fingers that trembled slightly. He went through all the movements of a woman putting on her bonnet before a glass, with a strained, listening attention, as though he had expected every moment to hear the shout of his name in the confused clamour that had suddenly beset his ship. Its increase filled his ears while he was getting ready to go out and confront whatever it might mean. It was tumultuous and very loud—made up of the rush of the wind, the crashes of the sea, with that prolonged deep vibration of the air, like the roll of an immense and remote drum beating the charge of the gale.

He stood for a moment in the light of the lamp, thick, clumsy, shapeless in his panoply of combat, vigilant and red-faced.

"There's a lot of weight in this," he muttered.

As soon as he attempted to open the door the wind caught it. Clinging to the handle, he was dragged out over the doorstep, and at once found himself engaged with the wind in a sort of personal scuffle whose object was the shutting of that door. At the last moment a tongue of air scurried in and licked out the flame of the lamp.

Ahead of the ship he perceived a great darkness lying upon a multitude of white flashes; on the starboard beam a few amazing stars drooped, dim and fitful, above an immense waste of broken seas, as if seen through a mad drift of smoke.

On the bridge a knot of men, indistinct and toiling, were making great efforts in the light of the wheelhouse windows that shone mistily on their heads and backs. Suddenly darkness closed upon one pane, then on another. The voices of the lost group reached him after the manner of men's voices in a gale, in shreds and fragments of forlorn shouting snatched past the ear. All at once Jukes appeared at his side, yelling, with his head down.

"Watch — put in — wheelhouse shutters — glass — afraid — blow in."

Jukes heard his commander upbraiding.

"This—come—anything—warning—call me."

He tried to explain, with the uproar pressing on his lips.

"Light air — remained — bridge — sudden — north-east — could turn — thought — you — sure — hear."

They had gained the shelter of the weather-cloth, and could converse with raised voices, as people quarrel.

"I got the hands along to cover up all the ventilators. Good job I had remained on deck. I didn't think you would be asleep, and so . . . What did you say, sir? What?"

"Nothing," cried Captain MacWhirr. "I said—all right."

"By all the powers! We've got it this time," observed Jukes in a howl.

"You haven't altered her course?" inquired Captain MacWhirr, straining his voice.

"No, sir. Certainly not. Wind came out right ahead. And here comes the head sea."

A plunge of the ship ended in a shock as if she had landed her forefoot upon something solid. After a moment of stillness a lofty flight of sprays drove hard with the wind upon their faces.

"Keep her at it as long as we can," shouted Captain MacWhirr.

Before Jukes had squeezed the salt water out of his eyes all the stars had disappeared.

III

JUKES was as ready a man as any half-dozen young mates that may be caught by casting a net upon the waters; and though he had been somewhat taken aback by the startling viciousness of the first squall, he had pulled himself together on the instant, had called out the hands and had rushed them along to secure such openings about the deck as had not been already battened down earlier in the evening. Shouting in his fresh, stentorian voice, "Jump, boys, and bear a hand!" he led in the work, telling himself the while that he had "just expected this."

But at the same time he was growing aware that this was rather more than he had expected. From the first stir of the air felt on his cheek the gale seemed to take upon itself the accumulated impetus of an avalanche. Heavy sprays enveloped the *Nan-Shan* from stem to stern, and instantly in the midst of her regular rolling she began to jerk and plunge as though she had gone mad with fright.

Jukes thought, "This is no joke." While he was exchanging explanatory yells with his captain, a sudden lowering of the darkness came upon the night, falling before their vision like something palpable. It was as if the masked lights of the world had been turned down. Jukes was uncritically glad to have his captain at hand. It relieved him as though that man had, by simply coming on deck, taken most of the gale's weight upon his shoulders. Such is the prestige, the privilege, and the burden of command.

Captain MacWhirr could expect no relief of that sort from any one on earth. Such is the loneliness of command. He was trying to see, with that watchful manner of a seaman who stares into the wind's eye as if into the eye of an adversary, to penetrate the hidden intention and guess the aim and force of the thrust. The strong wind swept at him out of a vast obscurity; he felt under his feet the uneasiness of his ship, and he could not even discern the shadow of her shape. He wished it were not so; and very still he waited, feeling stricken by a blind man's helplessness.

To be silent was natural to him, dark or shine. Jukes, at his elbow, made himself heard yelling cheerily in the gusts, "We must have got the worst of it at once, sir." A faint burst of lightning quivered all round, as if flashed into a cavern—into a black and secret chamber of the sea, with a floor of foaming crests.

It unveiled for a sinister, fluttering moment a ragged mass of clouds hanging low, the lurch of the long outlines of the ship, the black figures of men caught on the bridge, heads forward, as if petrified in the act of butting. The darkness palpitated down upon all this, and then the real thing came at last.

It was something formidable and swift, like the sudden smashing of a vial of wrath. It seemed to explode all round the ship with an overpowering concussion and a rush of great waters, as if an immense dam had been blown up to windward. In an instant the men lost touch of each other. This is the disintegrating power of a great wind: it isolates one from one's kind. An earthquake, a landslip, an avalanche, overtake a man incidentally, as it were—without passion. A furious gale attacks him like a personal enemy, tries to grasp his limbs, fastens upon his mind, seeks to rout his very spirit out of him.

Jukes was driven away from his commander. He fancied himself whirled a great distance through the air. Everything disappeared—even, for a moment, his power of thinking; but his hand had found one of the rail-stanchions. His distress was by no means alleviated by an inclination to disbelieve the reality of this experience. Though young, he had seen some bad weather, and had never doubted his ability to imagine the worst; but this was so much beyond his powers of fancy that it appeared incompatible with the existence of any ship whatever. He would have been incredulous about himself in the same way, perhaps, had he not been so harassed by the necessity of exerting a wrestling effort against a force trying to tear him away from his hold. Moreover, the conviction of not being utterly destroyed returned to him through the sensations of being half-drowned, bestially shaken, and partly choked.

It seemed to him he remained there precariously alone with the stanchion for a long, long time. The rain poured on him, flowed, drove in sheets. He breathed in gasps; and sometimes the water he swallowed was fresh and sometimes it was salt. For the most part he kept his eyes shut tight, as if suspecting his sight might be destroyed in the immense flurry of the elements. When he ventured to blink hastily, he derived some moral support from the green gleam of the starboard light shining feebly upon the flight of rain and sprays. He was actually looking at it when its ray fell upon the uprearing sea which put it out. He saw the head of the wave topple over, adding the mite of its crash to the tremendous uproar raging around him, and almost at the same instant the stanchion was wrenched away from his embracing arms. After a crushing thump on his back he found himself suddenly afloat and borne upwards. His first irresistible notion was that the whole China Sea had climbed on the bridge. Then, more sanely, he concluded himself gone overboard. All the time he was being tossed, flung, and rolled in great volumes of water, he kept on repeating mentally, with the utmost precipitation, the words: "My God! My God! My God! My God!"

All at once, in a revolt of misery and despair, he formed the crazy resolution to get out of that. And he began to thresh about with his arms and legs. But as soon as he commenced his wretched struggles he discovered that he had become somehow mixed up with a face, an oilskin coat, somebody's boots. He clawed ferociously all these things in turn, lost them, found them again, lost them once more, and finally was himself caught in the firm clasp of a pair of stout arms. He returned the embrace closely round a thick solid body. He had found his captain.

They tumbled over and over, tightening their hug. Suddenly the water let them down with a brutal bang; and, stranded against the side of the wheelhouse, out of breath and bruised, they were left to stagger up in the wind and hold on where they could.

Jukes came out of it rather horrified, as though he had escaped some unparalleled outrage directed at his feelings. It weakened his faith in himself. He started shouting aimlessly to the man he could feel near him in that fiendish blackness, "Is it you, sir? Is it you, sir?" till his temples seemed ready to burst. And he heard in answer a voice, as if crying far away, as if screaming to him fretfully from a very great distance, the one word "Yes!" Other seas swept again over the bridge. He received them defencelessly right over his bare head, with both his hands engaged in holding.

The motion of the ship was extravagant. Her lurches had an appalling helplessness: she pitched as if taking a header into a void, and seemed to find a wall to hit every time. When she rolled she fell on her side headlong, and she would be righted back by such a demolishing blow that Jukes felt her reeling as a clubbed man reels before he collapses. The gale howled and scuffled about gigantically in the darkness, as though the entire world were one black gully. At certain moments the air streamed against the ship as if sucked through a tunnel with a concentrated solid force of impact that seemed to lift her clean out of the water and keep her up for an instant with only a quiver running through her from end to end. And then she would begin her tumbling again as if dropped back into a boiling cauldren. Jukes tried hard to compose his mind and judge things coolly.

The sea, flattened down in the heavier gusts, would uprise and overwhelm both ends of the *Nan-Shan* in snowy rushes of foam, expanding wide, beyond both rails, into the night. And on this dazzling sheet, spread under the blackness of the clouds and emitting a bluish glow, Captain MacWhirr could catch a desolate glimpse of a few tiny specks black as ebony, the tops of the hatches, the battened companions, the heads of the covered winches, the foot of a mast. This was all he could see of his ship. Her middle structure, covered by the bridge which bore him, his mate, the closed wheelhouse where a man was steering shut up with the fear of being swept overboard together with the whole thing in one great crash—her middle structure was like a half-tide rock awash upon a coast. It was like an outlying rock with the water boiling up, streaming over, pouring off, beating round—like a rock in the surf to which shipwrecked people cling before they let go—only it rose, it sank, it rolled continuously, without respite and rest, like a rock that should have miraculously struck adrift from a coast and gone wallowing upon the sea.

The *Nan-Shan* was being looted by the storm with a senseless, destructive fury: trysails torn out of the extra gaskets, double-lashed awnings blown away, bridge swept clean, weather-cloths burst, rails twisted, light-screens smashed—and two of the boats had gone already. They had gone unheard and unseen, melting, as it were, in the shock and smother of the wave. It was only later, when upon the white flash of another high sea hurling itself amidships, Jukes had a vision of two pairs of davits leaping black and empty out of the solid blackness, with one overhauled fall flying and an iron-bound block capering in the air, that he became aware of what had happened within about three yards of his back.

He poked his head forward, groping for the ear of his commander. His lips touched it—big, fleshy, very wet. He cried in an agitated tone, "Our boats are going now, sir."

And again he heard that voice, forced and ringing feebly, but with a penetrating effect of quietness in the enormous discord of noises,* as if sent out from some remote spot of peace beyond the black wastes of the gale; again he heard a man's voice—the frail and indomitable sound that can be made to carry an infinity of thought, resolution and purpose, that shall be pronouncing confident words on the last day,* when heavens fall, and justice is done*—again he heard it, and it was crying to him, as if from very, very far—"All right."

He thought he had not managed to make himself understood. "Our boats—I say boats—the boats, sir! Two gone!"

The same voice, within a foot of him and yet so remote, yelled sensibly, "Can't be helped."

Captain MacWhirr had never turned his face, but Jukes caught some more words on the wind.

"What can — expect — when hammering through — such —— Bound to leave—something behind—stands to reason."

Watchfully Jukes listened for more. No more came. This was all Captain MacWhirr had to say; and Jukes could picture to himself rather than see the broad squat back before him. An impenetrable obscurity pressed down upon the ghostly glimmers of the sea. A dull conviction seized upon Jukes that there was nothing to be done.

If the steering-gear did not give way, if the immense volumes of water did not burst the deck in or smash one of the hatches, if the engines did not give up, if way could be kept on the ship against this terrific wind, and she did not bury herself in one of these awful seas, of whose white crests alone, topping high above her bows, he could now and then get a sickening glimpse—then there was a chance of her coming out of it. Something within him seemed to turn over, bringing uppermost the feeling that the *Nan-Shan* was lost.

"She's done for," he said to himself, with a surprising mental agitation, as though he had discovered an unexpected meaning in this thought. One of these things was bound to happen. Nothing could be prevented now, and nothing could be remedied. The men on board did not count, and the ship could not last. This weather was too impossible.

Jukes felt an arm thrown heavily over his shoulders; and to this overture he responded with great intelligence by catching hold of his captain round the waist.

They stood clasped thus in the blind night, bracing each other against the wind, cheek to cheek and lip to ear, in the manner of two hulks lashed stem to stern together.

And Jukes heard the voice of his commander hardly any louder than before, but nearer, as though, starting to march athwart the prodigious rush of the hurricane, it had approached him, bearing that strange effect of quietness like the serene glow of a halo.

"D'ye know where the hands got to?" it asked, vigorous and evanescent at the same time, overcoming the strength of the wind, and swept away from Jukes instantly.

Jukes didn't know. They were all on the bridge when the real force of the hurricane struck the ship. He had no idea where they had crawled to. Under the circumstances they were nowhere, for all the use that could be made of them. Somehow the Captain's wish to know distressed Jukes.

"Want the hands, sir?" he cried apprehensively.

"Ought to know," asserted Captain MacWhirr. "Hold hard."

They held hard. An outburst of unchained fury, a vicious rush of the wind absolutely steadied the ship; she rocked only, quick and light like a child's cradle, for a terrific moment of suspense, while the whole atmosphere, as it seemed, streamed furiously past her, roaring away from the tenebrous earth.

It suffocated them, and with eyes shut they tightened their grasp. What from the magnitude of the shock might have been a column of water running upright in the dark, butted against the ship, broke short, and fell on her bridge, crushingly, from on high, with a dead burying weight.

A flying fragment of that collapse, a mere splash, enveloped them in one swirl from their feet over their heads, filling violently their ears, mouths and nostrils with salt water. It knocked out their legs, wrenched in haste at their arms, seethed away swiftly under their chins; and opening their eyes, they saw the piled-up masses of foam dashing to and fro amongst what looked like the fragments of a ship. She had given way as if driven straight in. Their panting hearts yielded too before the tremendous blow; and all at once she sprang up again to her desperate plunging, as if trying to scramble out from under the ruins.

The seas in the dark seemed to rush from all sides to keep her back where she might perish. There was hate in the way she was handled, and a ferocity in the blows that fell. She was like a living creature thrown to the rage of a mob: hustled terribly, struck at, borne up, flung down, leaped upon. Captain MacWhirr and Jukes kept hold of each other, deafened by the noise, gagged by the wind; and the great physical tumult beating about their bodies, brought, like an unbridled display of passion, a profound trouble to their souls. One of these wild and appalling shrieks that are heard at times passing mysteriously overhead in the steady roar of a hurricane, swooped, as if borne on wings, upon the ship, and Jukes tried to outscream it.

"Will she live through this?"

The cry was wrenched out of his breast. It was as unintentional as the birth of a thought in the head, and he heard nothing of it himself. It all became extinct at once—thought, intention, effort—and of his cry the inaudible vibration added to the tempest waves of the air.

He expected nothing from it. Nothing at all. For indeed what answer could be made? But after a while he heard with amazement the frail and resisting voice in his ear, the dwarf sound, unconquered in the giant tumult.

"She may!"

It was a dull yell, more difficult to seize than a whisper. And presently the voice returned again, half submerged in the vast crashes, like a ship battling against the waves of an ocean.

"Let's hope so!" it cried—small, lonely and unmoved, a stranger to the visions of hope or fear; and it flickered into disconnected words: "Ship . . . This . . . Never—Anyhow . . . for the best." Jukes gave it up.

Then, as if it had come suddenly upon the one thing fit to withstand the power of a storm, it seemed to gain force and firmness for the last broken shouts:

"Keep on hammering . . . builders . . . good men . . . And chance it . . . engines . . . Rout . . . good man."

Captain MacWhirr removed his arm from Jukes' shoulders, and thereby ceased to exist for his mate, so dark it was; Jukes, after a tense stiffening of every muscle, would let himself go limp all over. The gnawing of profound discomfort existed side by side with an incredible disposition to somnolence, as though he had been buffeted and worried into drowsiness. The wind would get hold of his head and try to shake it off his shoulders; his clothes, full of water, were as heavy as lead, cold and dripping like an armour of melting ice: he shivered—it lasted a long time; and with his hands closed hard on his hold, he was letting himself sink slowly into the depths of bodily misery. His mind became concentrated upon himself in an aimless, idle way, and when something pushed lightly at the back of his knees he nearly, as the saying is, jumped out of his skin.

In the start forward he bumped the back of Captain MacWhirr, who didn't move; and then a hand gripped his thigh. A lull had come, a menacing lull of the wind, the holding of a stormy breath—and he felt himself pawed all over. It was the boatswain. Jukes recognised these hands, so thick and enormous that they seemed to belong to some new species of man.

The boatswain had arrived on the bridge, crawling on all fours against the wind, and had found the chief mate's legs with the top of his head. Immediately he crouched and began to explore Jukes' person upwards, with prudent, apologetic touches, as became an inferior.

He was an ill-favoured, undersized, gruff sailor of fifty, coarsely hairy, short-legged, long-armed, resembling an elderly ape. His strength was immense; and in his great lumpy paws, bulging like brown boxing-gloves on the end of furry forearms, the heaviest objects were handled like playthings. Apart from the grizzled pelt on his chest, the menacing demeanour and the hoarse voice, he had none of the classical attributes of his rating. His good nature almost amounted to imbecility: the men did what they liked with him, and he had not an ounce of initiative in his character, which was easy-going and talkative. For these reasons Jukes disliked him; but Captain MacWhirr, to Jukes' scornful disgust, seemed to regard him as a first-rate petty officer.

He pulled himself up by Jukes' coat, taking that liberty with the greatest moderation, and only so far as it was forced upon him by the hurricane.

"What is it, bosun, what is it?" yelled Jukes, impatiently. What could that fraud of a bosun want on the bridge? The typhoon had got on Jukes' nerves. The husky bellowings of the other, though unintelligible, seemed to suggest a state of lively satisfaction. There could be no mistake. The old fool was pleased with something.

The boatswain's other hand had found some other body, for in a changed tone he began to inquire: "Is it you, sir? Is it you, sir?" The wind strangled his howls.

"Yes!" cried Captain MacWhirr.

IV

ALL that the boatswain, out of a superabundance of yells, could make clear to Captain MacWhirr was the bizarre intelligence that "All them Chinamen in the fore 'tween-deck have fetched away, sir."

Jukes to leeward could hear these two shouting within six inches of his face, as you may hear on a still night half a mile away two men conversing across a field. He heard Captain MacWhirr's exasperated "What? What?" and the strained pitch of the other's hoarseness. "In a lump . . . seen them myself. . . . Awful sight, sir . . . thought . . . tell you."

Jukes remained indifferent, as if rendered irresponsible by the force of the hurricane, which made the very thought of action utterly vain. Besides, being very young, he had found the occupation of keeping his heart completely steeled against the worst so engrossing that he had come to feel an overpowering dislike towards any other form of activity whatever. He was not scared; he knew this because, firmly believing he would never see another sunrise, he remained calm in that belief.

These are the moments of do-nothing heroics to which even good men surrender at times. Many officers of ships can no doubt recall a case in their experience when just such a trance of confounded stoicism would come all at once over a whole ship's company. Jukes, however, had no wide experience of men or storms. He conceived himself to be calm—inexorably clam; but as a matter of fact he was daunted; not abjectly, but only so far as a decent man may, without becoming loathsome to himself.

It was rather like a forced-on numbness of spirit. The long, long stress of a gale does it; the suspense of the interminably culminating catastrophe; and there is a bodily fatigue in the mere holding on to existence within the excessive tumult; a searching and insidious fatigue that penetrates deep into a man's breast to cast down and sadden his heart, which is incorrigible, and of all the gifts of the earth—even before life itself—aspires to peace.

Jukes was benumbed much more than he supposed. He held on—very wet, very cold, stiff in every limb; and in a momentary hallucination of swift visions (it is said that a drowning man thus reviews all his life) he beheld all sorts of memories altogether unconnected with his present situation. He remembered his father, for instance: a worthy business man, who at an unfortunate crisis in his affairs went quietly to bed and died forthwith in a state of resignation. Jukes did not recall these circumstances, of course, but remaining otherwise unconcerned he seemed to see distinctly the poor man's face; a certain game of nap played when quite a boy in Table Bay on board a ship, since lost with all hands; the thick eyebrows of his first skipper; and without any emotion, as he might years ago have walked listlessly into her room and found her sitting there with a book, he remembered his mother—dead, too, now—the resolute woman, left badly off, who had been very firm in his bringing up.

It could not have lasted more than a second, perhaps not so much. A heavy arm had fallen about his shoulders; Captain MacWhirr's voice was speaking his name into his ear.

"Jukes! Jukes!"

He detected the tone of deep concern. The wind had thrown its weight on the ship, trying to pin her down amongst the seas. They made a clean breach over her, as over a deep-swimming log; and the gathered weight of crashes menaced monstrously from afar. The breakers flung out of the night with a ghostly light on their crests— the light of sea-foam that in a ferocious, boiling-up pale flash showed upon the slender body of the ship the toppling rush, the downfall, and the seething mad scurry of each wave. Never for a moment could she shake herself clear of the water; Jukes, rigid, perceived in her motion the ominous sign of haphazard floundering. She was no longer struggling intelligently. It was the beginning of the end; and the note of busy concern in Captain MacWhirr's voice sickened him like an exhibition of blind and pernicious folly.

The spell of the storm had fallen upon Jukes. He was penetrated by it, absorbed by it; he was rooted in it with a rigour of dumb attention. Captain MacWhirr persisted in his cries, but the wind got between them like a solid wedge. He hung round Jukes' neck as heavy as a millstone, and suddenly the sides of their heads knocked together.

"Jukes! Mr. Jukes, I say!"

He had to answer that voice that would not be silenced. He answered in the customary manner: ". . . Yes, sir."

And directly, his heart, corrupted by the storm that breeds a craving for peace, rebelled against the tyranny of training and command.

Captain MacWhirr had his mate's head fixed firm in the crook of his elbow, and pressed it to his yelling lips mysteriously. Sometimes Jukes would break in, admonishing hastily: "Look out, sir!" or Captain MacWhirr would bawl an earnest exhortation to "Hold hard, there!" and the whole black universe seemed to reel together with the ship. They paused. She floated yet. And Captain MacWhirr would resume his shouts. ". . . Says . . . whole lot . . . fetched away . . . Ought to see . . . what's the matter."

Directly the full force of the hurricane had struck the ship, every part of her deck became untenable; and the sailors, dazed and dismayed, took shelter in the port alleyway under the bridge. It had a door aft, which they shut; it was very black, cold, and dismal. At each heavy fling of the ship they would groan all together in the dark, and tons of water could be heard scuttling about as if trying to get at them from above. The boatswain had been keeping up a gruff talk, but a more unreasonable lot of men, he said afterwards, he had never been with. They were snug enough there, out of harm's way, and not wanted to do anything, either; and yet they did nothing but grumble and complain peevishly like so many sick kids. Finally, one of them said that if there had been at least some light to see each other's noses by, it wouldn't be so bad. It was making him crazy, he declared, to lie there in the dark waiting for the blamed hooker to sink.

"Why don't you step outside, then, and be done with it at once?" the boatswain turned on him.

This called up a shout of execration. The boatswain found himself overwhelmed with reproaches of all sorts. They seemed to take it ill that a lamp was not instantly created for them out of nothing. They would whine after a light to get drowned by—anyhow! And though the unreason of their revilings was patent—since no one could hope to reach the lamp-room, which was forward—he became greatly distressed. He did not think it was decent of them to be nagging at him like this. He told them so, and was met by general contumely. He sought refuge, therefore, in an embittered silence. At the same time their grumbling and sighing and muttering worried him greatly, but by-and-by it occurred to him that there were six globe lamps hung in the 'tween-deck, and that there could be no harm in depriving the coolies of one of them.

The *Nan-Shan* had an athwartship coal-bunker, which, being at times used as cargo space, communicated by an iron door with the fore 'tween-deck. It was empty then, and its manhole was the foremost one in the alleyway. The boatswain could get in, therefore, without coming out on deck at all; but to his great surprise he found he could induce no one to help him in taking off the manhole cover. He groped for it all the same, but one of the crew lying in his way refused to budge.

"Why, I only want to get you that blamed light you are crying for," he expostulated, almost pitifully.

Somebody told him to go and put his head in a bag. He regretted he could not recognise the voice, and that it was too dark to see, otherwise, as he said, he would have put a head on *that* son of a sea-cook, anyway, sink or swim. Nevertheless, he had made up his mind to show them he could get a light, if he were to die for it.

Through the violence of the ship's rolling, every movement was dangerous. To be lying down seemed labour enough. He nearly broke his neck dropping into the bunker. He fell on his back, and was sent shooting helplessly from side to side in the dangerous company of a heavy iron bar—a coal-trimmer's slice probably— left down there by somebody. This thing made him as nervous as though it had been a wild beast. He could not see it, the inside of the bunker coated with coal-dust being perfectly and impenetrably black; but he heard it sliding and clattering, and striking here and there, always in the neighbourhood of his head. It seemed to make an extraordinary noise, too—to give heavy thumps as though it had been as big as a bridge girder. This was remarkable enough for him to notice while he was flung from port to starboard and back again, and clawing desperately the smooth sides of the bunker in the endeavour to stop himself. The door into the 'tween-deck not fitting quite true, he saw a thread of dim light at the bottom.

Being a sailor, and a still active man, he did not want much of a chance to regain his feet; and as luck would have it, in scrambling up he put his hand on the iron slice, picking it up as he rose. Otherwise he would have been afraid of the thing breaking his legs, or at least knocking him down again. At first he stood still. He felt unsafe in this darkness that seemed to make the ship's motion unfamiliar, unforeseen, and difficult to counteract. He felt so much shaken for a moment that he dared not move for fear of "taking charge again." He had no mind to get battered to pieces in that bunker.

He had struck his head twice; he was dazed a little. He seemed to hear yet so plainly the clatter and bangs of the iron slice flying about his ears that he tightened his grip to prove to himself he had it there safely in his hand. He was vaguely amazed at the plainness with which down there he could hear the gale raging. Its howls and shrieks seemed to take on, in the emptiness of the bunker, something of the human character, of human rage and pain—being not vast but infinitely poignant. And there were, with every roll, thumps too—profound, ponderous thumps, as if a bulky object of five-ton weight or so had got play in the hold. But there was no such thing in the cargo. Something on deck? Impossible. Or alongside? Couldn't be.

He thought all this quickly, clearly, competently, like a seaman, and in the end remained puzzled. This noise, though, came deadened from outside, together with the washing and pouring of water on deck above his head. Was it the wind? Must be. It made down there a row like the shouting of a big lot of crazed men. And he discovered in himself a desire for a light too—if only to get drowned by—and a nervous anxiety to get out of that bunker as quickly as possible.

He pulled back the bolt: the heavy iron plate turned on its hinges; and it was as though he had opened the door to the sounds of the tempest. A gust of hoarse yelling met him: the air was still; and the rushing of water overhead was covered by a tumult of strangled, throaty shrieks that produced an effect of desperate confusion. He straddled his legs the whole width of the doorway and stretched his neck. And at first he perceived only what he had come to seek: six small yellow flames swinging violently on the great body of the dusk.

It was stayed like the gallery of a mine, with a row of stanchions in the middle, and cross-beams overhead, penetrating into the gloom ahead—indefinitely. And to port there loomed, like the caving in of one of the sides, a bulky mass with a slanting outline. The whole place, with the shadows and the shapes, moved all the time. The boatswain glared: the ship lurched to starboard, and a great howl came from that mass that had the slant of fallen earth.

Pieces of wood whizzed past. Planks, he thought, inexpressibly startled, and flinging back his head. At his feet a man went sliding over, open-eyed, on his back, straining with uplifted arms for nothing: and another came bounding like a detached stone with his head between his legs and his hands clenched. His pigtail whipped in the air; he made a grab at the boatswain's legs, and from his opened hand a bright white disc rolled against the boatswain's foot. He recognised a silver dollar, and yelled at it with astonishment. With a precipitated sound of trampling and shuffling of bare feet, and with guttural cries, the mound of writhing bodies piled up to port detached itself from the ship's side and shifted to starboard, sliding, inert and struggling, to a dull, brutal thump. The cries ceased. The boatswain heard a long moan through the roar and whistling of the wind; he saw an inextricable confusion of heads and shoulders, naked soles kicking upwards, fists raised, tumbling backs, legs, pigtails, faces.

"Good Lord!" he cried, horrified, and banged-to the iron door upon this vision.

This was what he had come on the bridge to tell. He could not keep it to himself; and on board ship there is only one man to whom it is worth while to unburden yourself. On his passage back the hands in the alleyway swore at him for a fool. Why didn't he bring that lamp? What the devil did the coolies matter to anybody? And when he came out, the extremity of the ship made what went on inside of her appear of little moment.

At first he thought he had left the alleyway in the very moment of her sinking. The bridge ladders had been washed away, but an enormous sea filling the after-deck floated him up. After that he had to lie on his stomach for some time, holding to a ring-bolt, getting his breath now and then, and swallowing salt water. He struggled farther on his hands and knees, too frightened and distracted to turn back. In this way he reached the after-part of the wheelhouse. In that comparatively sheltered spot he found the second mate. The boatswain was pleasantly surprised—his impression being that everybody on deck must have been washed away a long time ago. He asked eagerly where the captain was.

The second mate was lying low, like a malignant little animal under a hedge.

"Captain? Gone overboard, after getting us into this mess." The mate, too, for all he knew or cared. Another fool. Didn't matter. Everybody was going by-and-by.

The boatswain crawled out again into the strength of the wind;

not because he much expected to find anybody, he said, but just to get away from "that man." He crawled out as outcasts go to face an inclement world. Hence his great joy at finding Jukes and the Captain. But what was going on in the 'tween-deck was to him a minor matter by that time. Besides, it was difficult to make yourself heard. But he managed to convey the idea that the Chinamen had broken adrift together with their boxes, and that he had come up on purpose to report this. As to the hands, they were all right. Then, appeased, he subsided on the deck in a sitting posture, hugging with his arms and legs the stand of the engine-room telegraph—an iron casting as thick as a post. When that went, why, he expected he would go too. He gave no more thought to the coolies.

Captain MacWhirr had made Jukes understand that he wanted him to go down below—to see.

"What am I to do then, sir?" And the trembling of his whole wet body caused Jukes' voice to sound like bleating.

"See first . . . Bosun . . . says . . . adrift."

"That bosun is a confounded fool," howled Jukes shakily.

The absurdity of the demand made upon him revolted Jukes. He was as unwilling to go as if the moment he had left the deck the ship were sure to sink.

"I must know . . . can't leave . . . ."

"They'll settle, sir."

"Fight . . . bosun says they fight. . . . Why? Can't have . . . fighting . . . board ship. . . . Much rather keep you here . . . case . . . I should . . . washed overboard myself. . . . Stop it . . . some way. You see and tell me . . . through engine-room tube. Don't want you . . . come up here . . . too often. Dangerous . . . moving about . . . deck."

Jukes, held with his head in chancery, had to listen to what seemed horrible suggestions.

"Don't want . . . you get lost . . . so long . . . ship isn't. . . . Rout . . . Good man . . . Ship . . . may . . . through this . . . all right yet."

All at once Jukes understood he would have to go.

"Do you think she may?" he screamed.

But the wind devoured the reply, out of which Jukes heard only the one word, pronounced with great energy ". . . Always . . ."

Captain MacWhirr released Jukes, and bending over the

boatswain, yelled "Get back with the mate." Jukes only knew that the arm was gone off his shoulders. He was dismissed with his orders—to do what? He was exasperated into letting go his hold carelessly, and on the instant was blown away. It seemed to him that nothing could stop him from being blown right over the stern. He flung himself down hastily, and the boatswain, who was following, fell on him.

"Don't you get up yet, sir," cried the boatswain. "No hurry!"

A sea swept over. Jukes understood the boatswain to splutter that the bridge ladders were gone. "I'll lower you down, sir, by your hands," he screamed. He shouted also something about the smoke-stack being as likely to go overboard as not. Jukes thought it very possible, and imagined the fires out, the ship helpless. . . . The boat-swain by his side kept on yelling. "What? What is it?" Jukes cried distressfully; and the other repeated, "What would my old woman say if she saw me now?"

In the alleyway, where a lot of water had got in and splashed in the dark, the men were still as death, till Jukes stumbled against one of them and cursed him savagely for being in the way. Two or three voices then asked, eager and weak, "Any chance for us, sir?"

"What's the matter with you fools?" he said brutally. He felt as though he could throw himself down amongst them and never move any more. But they seemed cheered; and in the midst of obsequious warnings, "Look out! Mind that manhole lid, sir," they lowered him into the bunker. The boatswain tumbled down after him, and as soon as he had picked himself up he remarked, "She would say, 'Serve you right, you old fool, for going to sea.'"

The boatswain had some means, and made a point of alluding to them frequently. His wife—a fat woman—and two grown-up daughters kept a greengrocer's shop in the East-end of London.

In the dark, Jukes, unsteady on his legs, listened to a faint thunderous patter. A deadened screaming went on steadily at his elbow, as it were; and from above the louder tumult of the storm descended upon these near sounds. His head swam. To him, too, in that bunker, the motion of the ship seemed novel and menacing, sapping his resolution as though he had never been afloat before.

He had half a mind to scramble out again; but the remembrance of Captain MacWhirr's voice made this impossible. His orders were to go and see. What was the good of it, he wanted to know. Enraged, he told himself he would see—of course. But the boatswain, staggering clumsily, warned him to be careful how he opened that door; there was a blamed fight going on. And Jukes, as if in great bodily pain, desired irritably to know what the devil they were fighting for.

"Dollars! Dollars, sir. All their rotten chests got burst open. Blamed money skipping all over the place, and they are tumbling after it head over heels—tearing and biting like anything. A regular little hell in there."

Jukes convulsively opened the door. The short boatswain peered under his arm.

One of the lamps had gone out, broken perhaps. Rancorous, guttural cries burst out loudly on their ears, and a strange panting sound, the working of all these straining breasts. A hard blow hit the side of the ship: water fell above with a stunning shock, and in the forefront of the gloom, where the air was reddish and thick, Jukes saw a head bang the deck violently, two thick calves waving on high, muscular arms twined round a naked body, a yellow-face, open-mouthed and with a set wild stare, look up and slide away. An empty chest clattered turning over; a man fell head first with a jump, as if lifted by a kick; and farther off, indistinct, others streamed like a mass of rolling stones down a bank, thumping the deck with their feet and flourishing their arms wildly. The hatchway ladder was loaded with coolies swarming on it like bees on a branch. They hung on the steps in a crawling, stirring cluster, beating madly with their fists the underside of the battened hatch, and the headlong rush of the water above was heard in the intervals of their yelling. The ship heeled over more, and they began to drop off: first one, then two, then all the rest went away together, falling straight off with a great cry.

Jukes was confounded. The boatswain, with gruff anxiety, begged him, "Don't you go in there, sir."

The whole place seemed to twist upon itself, jumping incessantly the while; and when the ship rose to a sea Jukes fancied that all these men would be shot upon him in a body. He backed out, swung the door to, and with trembling hands pushed at the bolt. . . .

As soon as his mate had gone Captain MacWhirr, left alone on the bridge, sidled and staggered as far as the wheelhouse. Its door being hinged forward, he had to fight the gale for admittance, and when at last he managed to enter, it was with an instantaneous clatter and a bang, as though he had been fired through the wood. He stood within, holding on to the handle.

The steering-gear leaked steam, and in the confined space the glass of the binnacle made a shiny oval of light in a thin white fog. The wind howled, hummed, whistled, with sudden booming gusts that rattled the doors and shutters in the vicious patter of sprays. Two coils of lead-line and a small canvas bag hung on a long lanyard, swung wide off, and came back clinging to the bulkheads. The gratings underfoot were nearly afloat; with every sweeping blow of a sea, water squirted violently through the cracks all round the door, and the man at the helm had flung down his cap, his coat, and stood propped against the gear-casing in a striped cotton shirt open on his breast. The little brass wheel in his hands had the appearance of a bright and fragile toy. The cords of his neck stood hard and lean, a dark patch lay in the hollow of his throat, and his face was still and sunken as in death.

Captain MacWhirr wiped his eyes. The sea that had nearly taken him overboard had, to his great annoyance, washed his sou'-wester hat off his bald head. The fluffy, fair hair, soaked and darkened, resembled a mean skein of cotton threads festooned round his bare skull. His face, glistening with sea-water, had been made crimson with the wind, with the sting of sprays. He looked as though he had come off sweating from before a furnace.

"You here?" he muttered heavily.

The second mate had found his way into the wheelhouse some time before. He had fixed himself in a corner with his knees up, a fist pressed against each temple; and this attitude suggested rage, sorrow, resignation, surrender, with a sort of concentrated unforgiveness. He said mournfully and defiantly, "Well, it's my watch below now: ain't it?"

The steam gear clattered, stopped, clattered again; and the helmsman's eyeballs seemed to project out of a hungry face as if the compass card behind the binnacle glass had been meat. God knows how long he had been left there to steer, as if forgotten by all his shipmates. The bells had not been struck; there had been no reliefs; the ship's routine had gone down wind; but he was trying to keep her head north-north-east. The rudder might have been gone for all he knew, the fires out, the engines broken down, the ship ready to roll over like a corpse. He was anxious not to get muddled and lose control of her head, because the compass-card swung far both ways, wriggling on the pivot, and sometimes seemed to whirl right round. He suffered from mental stress. He was horribly afraid, also, of the wheelhouse going. Mountains of water kept on tumbling against it. When the ship took one of her desperate dives the corners of his lips twitched.

Captain MacWhirr looked up at the wheelhouse clock. Screwed to the bulk-head, it had a white face on which the black hands appeared to stand quite still. It was half-past one in the morning.

"Another day," he muttered to himself.

The second mate heard him, and lifting his head as one grieving amongst ruins, "You won't see it break," he exclaimed. His wrists and his knees could be seen to shake violently. "No, by God! You won't . . ."

He took his face again between his fists.

The body of the helmsman had moved slightly, but his head didn't budge on his neck,—like a stone head fixed to look one way from a column. During a roll that all but took his booted legs from under him, and in the very stagger to save himself, Captain MacWhirr said austerely, "Don't you pay any attention to what that man says." And then, with an indefinable change of tone, very grave, he added, "He isn't on duty."

The sailor said nothing.

The hurricane boomed, shaking the little place, which seemed air-tight; and the light of the binnacle flickered all the time.

"You haven't been relieved," Captain MacWhirr went on, looking down. "I want you to stick to the helm, though, as long as you can. You've got the hang of her. Another man coming here might make a mess of it. Wouldn't do. No child's play. And the hands are probably busy with a job down below. . . . Think you can?"

The steering gear leaped into an abrupt short clatter, stopped, smouldering like an ember; and the still man, with a motionless gaze, burst out, as if all the passion in him had gone into his lips: "By Heavens, sir! I can steer for ever if nobody talks to me."*

"Oh! aye! All right, . . ." The Captain lifted his eyes for the first time to the man, ". . . Hackett."

And he seemed to dismiss this matter from his mind. He stooped to the engine-room speaking-tube, blew in, and bent his head. Mr. Rout below answered, and at once Captain MacWhirr put his lips to the mouthpiece.

With the uproar of the gale around him he applied alternately his lips and his ear, and the engineer's voice mounted to him, harsh and as if out of the heat of an engagement. One of the stokers was disabled, the others had given in, the second engineer and the donkey-man were firing-up. The third engineer was standing by the steam-valve. The engines were being tended by hand. How was it above?

"Bad enough. It mostly rests with you," said Captain MacWhirr. Was the mate down there yet? No? Well, he would be presently. Would Mr. Rout let him talk through the speaking-tube?—through the deck speaking-tube, because he—the Captain—was going out again on the bridge directly. There was some trouble amongst the Chinamen. They were fighting, it seemed. Couldn't allow fighting anyhow. . . .

Mr. Rout had gone away, and Captain MacWhirr could feel against his ear the pulsation of the engines, like the beat of the ship's heart. Mr. Rout's voice down there shouted something distantly. The ship pitched headlong, the pulsation leaped with a hissing tumult, and stopped dead. Captain MacWhirr's face was impassive, and his eyes were fixed aimlessly on the crouching shape of the second mate. Again Mr. Rout's voice cried out in the depths, and the pulsating beats recommenced, with slow strokes—growing swifter.

Mr. Rout had returned to the tube. "It don't matter much what they do," he said hastily; and then, with irritation, "She takes these dives as if she never meant to come up again."

"Awful sea," said the Captain's voice from above.

"Don't let me drive her under," barked Solomon Rout up the pipe.

"Dark and rain. Can't see what's coming," uttered the voice. "Must—keep—her—moving—enough to steer—and chance it," it went on to state distinctly.

"I am doing as much as I dare."

"We are—getting—smashed up—a good deal up here," proceeded the voice mildly. "Doing—fairly well—though. Of course, if the wheelhouse should go . . ."

Mr. Rout, bending an attentive ear, muttered peevishly something under his breath.

But the deliberate voice up there became animated to ask: "Jukes turned up yet?" Then, after a short wait, "I wish he would bear a hand. I want him to be done and come up here in case of anything. To look after the ship. I am all alone. The second mate's lost. . . ."

"What?" shouted Mr. Rout into the engine-room, taking his head away. Then up the tube he cried, "Gone overboard?" and clapped his ear to.

"Lost his nerve," the voice from above continued in a matter-of-fact tone. "Damned awkward circumstance."

Mr. Rout, listening with bowed neck, opened his eyes wide at this. However, he heard something like the sounds of a scuffle and broken exclamations coming down to him. He strained his hearing; and all the time Beale, the third engineer, with his arms uplifted, held between the palms of his hands the rim of a little black wheel projecting at the side of a big copper pipe. He seemed to be poising it above his head, as though it were a correct attitude in some sort of game.

To steady himself, he pressed his shoulder against the white bulkhead, one knee bent, and a sweat-rag tucked in his belt hanging on his hip. His smooth cheek was begrimed and flushed, and the coal dust on his eyelids, like the black pencilling of a make-up, enhanced the liquid brilliance of the whites, giving to his youthful face something of a feminine, exotic and fascinating aspect. When the ship pitched he would with hasty movements of his hands screw hard at the little wheel.

"Gone crazy," began the Captain's voice suddenly in the tube. "Rushed at me. . . . Just now. Had to knock him down. . . . This minute. You heard, Mr. Rout?"

"The devil!" muttered Mr. Rout. "Look out, Beale!"

His shout rang out like the blast of a warning trumpet, between the iron walls of the engine-room. Painted white, they rose high into the dusk of the skylight, sloping like a roof; and the whole lofty space resembled the interior of a monument, divided by floors of iron grating, with lights flickering at different levels, and a mass of gloom lingering in the middle, within the columnar stir of machinery under the motionless swelling of the cylinders. A loud and wild resonance, made up of all the noises of the hurricane, dwelt in the still warmth of the air. There was in it the smell of hot metal, of oil, and a slight mist of steam. The blows of the sea seemed to traverse it in an unringing, stunning shock, from side to side.

Gleams, like pale long flames, trembled upon the polish of metal; from the flooring below, the enormous crank-heads emerged in their turns with a flash of brass and steel—going over; while the connecting-rods, big-jointed, like skeleton limbs, seemed to thrust them down and pull them up again with an irresistible precision. And deep in the half-light other rods dodged deliberately to and fro, crossheads nodded, discs of metal rubbed smoothly against each other, slow and gentle, in a commingling of shadows and gleams.

Sometimes all those powerful and unerring movements would slow down simultaneously, as if they had been the functions of a living organism, stricken suddenly by the blight of languor; and Mr. Rout's eyes would blaze darker in his long sallow face. He was fighting this fight in a pair of carpet slippers. A short shiny jacket barely covered his loins, and his white wrists protruded far out of the tight sleeves, as though the emergency had added to his stature, had lengthened his limbs, augmented his pallor, hollowed his eyes.

He moved, climbing high up, disappearing low down, with a restless, purposeful industry, and when he stood still, holding the guard-rail in front of the starting-gear, he would keep glancing to the right at the steam-gauge, at the water-gauge, fixed upon the white wall in the light of a swaying lamp. The mouths of two speaking-tubes gaped stupidly at his elbow, and the dial of the engine-room telegraph resembled a clock of large diameter, bearing on its face curt words instead of figures. The grouped letters stood out heavily black, around the pivot-head of the indicator, emphatically symbolic of loud exclamations: AHEAD, ASTERN, SLOW, HALF, STAND BY; and the fat black hand pointed downwards to the word FULL, which, thus singled out, captured the eye as a sharp cry secures attention.

The wood-encased bulk of the low-pressure cylinder, frowning portly from above, emitted a faint wheeze at every thrust, and except for that low hiss the engines worked their steel limbs headlong or slow with a silent, determined smoothness. And all this, the white walls, the moving steel, the floor plates under Solomon Rout's feet, the floors of iron grating above his head, the dusk and the gleams, uprose and sank continuously, with one accord, upon the harsh wash of the waves against the ship's side. The whole loftiness of the place, booming hollow to the great voice of the wind, swayed at the top like a tree, would go over bodily, as if borne down this way and that by the tremendous blasts.

"You've got to hurry up," shouted Mr. Rout, as soon as he saw Jukes appear in the stokehold doorway.

Jukes' glance was wandering and tipsy; his red face was puffy, as though he had overslept himself. He had had an arduous road, and had travelled over it with immense vivacity, the agitation of his mind corresponding to the exertions of his body. He had rushed up out of the bunker, stumbling in the dark alleyway amongst a lot of bewildered men who, trod upon, asked "What's up, sir?" in awed mutters all round him;—down the stokehold ladder, missing many iron rungs in his hurry, down into a place deep as a well, black as Tophet, tipping over back and forth like a see-saw. The water in the bilges thundered at each roll, and lumps of coal skipped to and fro, from end to end, rattling like an avalanche of pebbles on a slope of iron.

Somebody in there moaned with pain, and somebody else could be seen crouching over what seemed the prone body of a dead man; a lusty voice blasphemed; and the glow under each fire-door was like a pool of flaming blood radiating quietly in a velvety blackness.

A gust of wind struck upon the nape of Jukes' neck, and next moment he felt it streaming about his wet ankles. The stokehold ventilators hummed: in front of the six fire-doors two wild figures, stripped to the waist, staggered and stooped, wrestling with two shovels.

"Hallo! Plenty of draught now," yelled the second engineer at once, as though he had been all the time looking out for Jukes. The donkeyman, a dapper little chap with a dazzling fair skin and a tiny, gingery moustache, worked in a sort of mute transport. They were keeping a full head of steam, and a profound rumbling, as of an empty furniture van trotting over a bridge, made a sustained bass to all the other noises of the place.

"Blowing off all the time," went on yelling the second.* With a sound as of a hundred scoured saucepans, the orifice of a ventilator spat upon his shoulder a sudden gush of salt water, and he volleyed a stream of curses upon all things on earth including his own soul, ripping and raving, and all the time attending to his business. With a sharp clash of metal the ardent pale glare of the fire opened upon his bullet head, showing his spluttering lips, his insolent face, and with another clang closed like the white-hot wink of an iron eye.

"Where's the blooming ship? Can you tell me? blast my eyes! Under water—or what? It's coming down here in tons. Are the condemned cowls gone to Hades? Hey? Don't you know anything— you jolly sailor-man you . . . ?"

Jukes, after a bewildered moment, had been helped by a roll to dart through; and as soon as his eyes took in the comparative vastness, peace and brilliance of the engine-room, the ship, setting her stern heavily in the water, sent him charging head down upon Mr. Rout.

The chief's arm, long like a tentacle, and straightening as if worked by a spring, went out to meet him, and deflected his rush into a spin towards the speaking-tubes. At the same time Mr. Rout repeated earnestly: "You've got to hurry up, whatever it is."

Jukes yelled "Are you there, sir?" and listened. Nothing. Suddenly the roar of the wind fell straight into his ear, but presently a small voice shoved aside the shouting hurricane quietly.

"You, Jukes?—Well?"

Jukes was ready to talk: it was only time that seemed to be wanting. It was easy enough to account for everything. He could perfectly imagine the coolies battened down in the reeking 'tween-deck, lying sick and scared between the rows of chests. Then one of these chests—or perhaps several at once—breaking loose in a roll, knocking out others, sides splitting, lids flying open, and all these clumsy Chinamen rising up in a body to save their property. Afterwards every fling of the ship would hurl that tramping, yelling mob here and there, from side to side, in a whirl of smashed wood, torn clothing, rolling dollars. A struggle once started, they would be unable to stop themselves. Nothing could stop them now except main force. It was a disaster. He had seen it, and that was all he could say. Some of them must be dead, he believed. The rest would go on fighting. . . .

He sent up his words, tripping over each other, crowding the narrow tube. They mounted as if into a silence of an enlightened comprehension dwelling alone up there with a storm. And Jukes wanted to be dismissed from the face of that odious trouble intruding on the great need of the ship.

V

HE waited. Before his eyes the engines turned with slow labour, that in the moment of going off into a mad fling would stop dead at Mr. Rout's shout, "Look out, Beale!" They paused in an intelligent immobility, stilled in mid-stroke, a heavy crank arrested on the cant, as if conscious of danger and the passage of time. Then, with a "Now, then!" from the chief, and the sound of a breath expelled through clenched teeth, they would accomplish the interrupted revolution and begin another.

There was the prudent sagacity of wisdom and the deliberation of enormous strength in their movements. This was their work—this patient coaxing of a distracted ship over the fury of the waves and into the very eye of the wind. At times Mr. Rout's chin would sink on his breast, and he watched them with knitted eyebrows as if lost in thought.

The voice that kept the hurricane out of Jukes' ear began: "Take the hands with you . . . ;" and left off unexpectedly.

"What could I do with them, sir?"

A harsh, abrupt, imperious clang exploded suddenly. The three pairs of eyes flew up to the telegraph dial to see the hand jump from FULL to STOP, as if snatched by a devil. And then these three men in the engine-room had the intimate sensation of a check upon the ship, of a strange shrinking, as if she had gathered herself for a desperate leap.

"Stop her!" bellowed Mr. Rout.

Nobody—not even Captain MacWhirr, who alone on deck had caught sight of a white line of foam coming on at such a height that he couldn't believe his eyes—nobody was to know the steepness of that sea and the awful depth of the hollow the hurricane had scooped out behind the running wall of water.

It raced to meet the ship, and, with a pause, as of girding the loins,* the Nan-Shan lifted her bows and leaped. The flames in all the lamps sank, darkening the engine-room. One went out. With a tearing crash and a swirling, raving tumult, tons of water fell upon the deck, as though the ship had darted under the foot of a cataract.

Down there they looked at each other, stunned.

"Swept from end to end, by God!" bawled Jukes.

She dipped into the hollow straight down, as if going over the edge of the world. The engine-room toppled forward menacingly, like the inside of a tower nodding in an earthquake. An awful racket, of iron things falling, came from the stokehold. She hung on this appalling slant long enough for Beale to drop on his hands and knees and begin to crawl as if he meant to fly on all fours out of the engine-room, and for Mr. Rout to turn his head slowly, rigid, cavernous, with the lower jaw dropping. Jukes had shut his eyes, and his face in a moment became hopelessly blank and gentle, like the face of a blind man.

At last she rose slowly, staggering, as if she had to lift a mountain with her bows.

Mr. Rout shut his mouth; Jukes blinked; and little Beale stood up hastily.

"Another one like this, and that's the last of her," cried the chief.

He and Jukes looked at each other, and the same thought came into their heads. The Captain! Everything must have been swept away. Steering gear gone—ship like a log. All over directly.

"Rush!" ejaculated Mr. Rout thickly, glaring with enlarged, doubtful eyes at Jukes, who answered him by an irresolute glance.

The clang of the telegraph gong soothed them instantly. The black hand dropped in a flash from STOP to FULL.

"Now then, Beale!" cried Mr. Rout.

The steam hissed low. The piston-rods slid in and out. Jukes put his ear to the tube. The voice was ready for him. It said: "Pick up all the money. Bear a hand now. I'll want you up here." And that was all.

"Sir?" called up Jukes. There was no answer.

He staggered away like a defeated man from the field of battle. He had got, in some way or other, a cut above his left eyebrow—a cut to the bone. He was not aware of it in the least: quantities of the China Sea, large enough to break his neck for him, had gone over his head, had cleaned, washed, and salted that wound. It did not bleed, but only gaped red; and this gash over the eye, his dishevelled hair, the disorder of his clothes, gave him the aspect of a man worsted in a fight with fists.

"Got to pick up the dollars." He appealed to Mr. Rout, smiling pitifully at random.

"What's that?" asked Mr. Rout wildly. "Pick up . . . ? I don't care. . . ." Then, quivering in every muscle, but with an exaggeration of paternal tone, "Go away now, for God's sake. You deck people'll drive me silly. There's that second mate been going for the old man. Don't you know? You fellows are going wrong for want of something to do. . . ."

At these words Jukes discovered in himself the beginnings of anger. Want of something to do—indeed. . . . Full of hot scorn against the chief, he turned to go the way he had come. In the stokehold the plump donkeyman toiled with his shovel mutely, as if his tongue had been cut out; but the second was carrying on like a noisy, undaunted maniac, who had preserved his skill in the art of stoking under a marine boiler.

"Hallo, you wandering officer! Hey! Can't you get some of your slush-slingers to wind up a few of them ashes? I am getting choked with them here. Curse it! Hallo! Hey! Remember the articles: *Sailors and firemen to assist each other*. Hey! D'ye hear?"

Jukes was climbing out frantically, and the other, lifting up his face after him, howled, "Can't you speak? What are you poking about here for? What's your game, anyhow?"

A frenzy possessed Jukes. By the time he was back amongst the men in the darkness of the alleyway, he felt ready to wring all their necks at the slightest sign of hanging back. The very thought of it exasperated him. *He* couldn't hang back. They shouldn't.

The impetuosity with which he came amongst them carried them along. They had already been excited and startled at all his comings and goings—by the fierceness and rapidity of his movements; and more felt than seen in his rushes, he appeared formidable—busied with matters of life and death that brooked no delay. At his first word he heard them drop into the bunker one after another obediently, with heavy thumps.

They were not clear as to what would have to be done. "What is it? What is it?" they were asking each other. The boatswain tried to explain; the sounds of a great scuffle surprised them: and the mighty shocks, reverberating awfully in the black bunker, kept them in mind of their danger. When the boatswain threw open the door it seemed that an eddy of the hurricane, stealing through the iron sides of the ship, had set all these bodies whirling like dust: there came to them a confused uproar, a tempestuous tumult, a fierce mutter, gusts of screams dying away, and the tramping of feet mingling with the blows of the sea.

For a moment they glared amazed, blocking the doorway. Jukes pushed through them brutally. He said nothing, and simply darted in. Another lot of coolies on the ladder, struggling suicidally to break through the battened hatch to a swamped deck, fell off as before, and he disappeared under them like a man overtaken by a landslide.

The boatswain yelled excitedly: "Come along. Get the mate out. He'll be trampled to death. Come on."

They charged in, stamping on breasts, on fingers, on faces, catching their feet in heaps of clothing, kicking broken wood; but before they could get hold of him Jukes emerged waist deep in a multitude of clawing hands. In the instant he had been lost to view, all the buttons of his jacket had gone, its back had got split up to the collar, his waistcoat had been torn open. The central struggling mass of Chinamen went over to the roll, dark, indistinct, helpless, with a wild gleam of many eyes in the dim light of the lamps.

"Leave me alone—damn you. I am all right," screeched Jukes. "Drive them forward. Watch your chance when she pitches. Forward with 'em. Drive them against the bulkhead. Jam 'em up."

The rush of the sailors into the seething 'tween-deck was like a splash of cold water into a boiling cauldron. The commotion sank for a moment.

The bulk of Chinamen were locked in such a compact scrimmage that, linking their arms and aided by an appalling dive of the ship, the seamen sent it forward in one great shove, like a solid block. Behind their backs small clusters and loose bodies tumbled from side to side.

The boatswain performed prodigious feats of strength. With his long arms open, and each great paw clutching at a stanchion, he stopped the rush of seven entwined Chinamen rolling like a boulder. His joints cracked; he said, "Ha!" and they flew apart. But the carpenter showed the greater intelligence. Without saying a word to anybody he went back into the alleyway, to fetch several coils of cargo gear he had seen there—chain and rope. With these life-lines were rigged.

There was really no resistance. The struggle, however it began, had turned into a scramble of blind panic. If the coolies had started up after their scattered dollars they were by that time fighting only for their footing. They took each other by the throat merely to save themselves from being hurled about. Whoever got a hold anywhere would kick at the others who caught at his legs and hung on, till a roll sent them flying together across the deck.

The coming of the white devils was a terror. Had they come to kill? The individuals torn out of the ruck became very limp in the seamen's hands: some, dragged aside by the heels, were passive, like dead bodies, with open, fixed eyes. Here and there a coolie would fall on his knees as if begging for mercy; several, whom the excess of fear made unruly, were hit with hard fists between the eyes, and cowered; while those who were hurt submitted to rough handling, blinking rapidly without a plaint. Faces streamed with blood; there were raw places on the shaven heads, scratches, bruises, torn wounds, gashes. The broken porcelain out of the chests was mostly responsible for the latter. Here and there a Chinaman, wild-eyed, with his tail unplaited, nursed a bleeding sole.

They had been ranged closely, after having been shaken into submission, cuffed a little to allay excitement, addressed in gruff words of encouragement that sounded like promises of evil. They sat on the deck in ghastly, drooping rows, and at the end the carpenter, with two hands to help him, moved busily from place to place, setting taut and hitching the life-lines. The boatswain, with one leg and one arm embracing a stanchion, struggled with a lamp pressed to his breast, trying to get a light, and growling all the time like an industrious gorilla. The figures of seamen stooped repeatedly, with the movements of gleaners, and everything was being flung into the bunker: clothing, smashed wood, broken china, and the dollars too, gathered up in men's jackets. Now and then a sailor would stagger towards the doorway with his arms full of rubbish; and dolorous, slanting eyes followed his movements.

With every roll of the ship the long rows of sitting Celestials would sway forward brokenly, and her headlong dives knocked together the line of shaven polls from end to end. When the wash of water rolling on the deck died away for a moment, it seemed to Jukes, yet quivering from his exertions, that in his mad struggle down there he had overcome the wind somehow: that a silence had fallen upon the ship, a silence in which the sea struck thunderously at her sides.

Everything had been cleared out of the 'tween-deck—all the wreckage, as the men said. They stood erect and tottering above the level of heads and drooping shoulders. Here and there a coolie sobbed for his breath. Where the high light fell, Jukes could see the salient ribs of one, the yellow, wistful face of another; bowed necks; or would meet a dull stare directed at his face. He was amazed that there had been no corpses; but the lot of them seemed at their last gasp, and they appeared to him more pitiful than if they had been all dead.

Suddenly one of the coolies began to speak. The light came and went on his lean, straining face; he threw his head up like a baying hound. From the bunker came the sounds of knocking and the tinkle of some dollars rolling loose; he stretched out his arm, his mouth yawned black, and the incomprehensible guttural hooting sounds, that did not seem to belong to a human language, penetrated Jukes with a strange emotion as if a brute had tried to be eloquent.

Two more started mouthing what seemed to Jukes fierce denunciations; the others stirred with grunts and growls. Jukes ordered the hands out of the 'tween-decks hurriedly. He left last himself, backing through the door, while the grunts rose to a loud murmur and hands were extended after him as after a malefactor. The boatswain shot the bolt, and remarked uneasily, "Seems as if the wind had dropped, sir."

The seamen were glad to get back into the alleyway. Secretly each of them thought that at the last moment he could rush out on deck—and that was a comfort. There is something horribly repugnant in the idea of being drowned under a deck. Now they had done with the Chinamen, they again became conscious of the ship's position.

Jukes on coming out of the alleyway found himself up to the neck in the noisy water. He gained the bridge, and discovered he could detect obscure shapes as if his sight had become preternaturally acute. He saw faint outlines. They recalled not the familiar aspect of the *Nan-Shan*, but something remembered—an old dismantled steamer he had seen years ago rotting on a mudbank. She recalled that wreck.

There was no wind, not a breath, except the faint currents created by the lurches of the ship. The smoke tossed out of the funnel was settling down upon her deck. He breathed it as he passed forward. He felt the deliberate throb of the engines, and heard small sounds that seemed to have survived the great uproar: the knocking of broken fittings, the rapid tumbling of some piece of wreckage on the bridge. He perceived dimly the squat shape of his captain holding on to a twisted bridge-rail, motionless and swaying as if rooted to the planks. The unexpected stillness of the air oppressed Jukes.

"We have done it, sir," he gasped.

"Thought you would," said Captain MacWhirr.

"Did you?" murmured Jukes to himself.

"Wind fell all at once," went on the Captain.

Jukes burst out: "If you think it was an easy job——"

But his captain, clinging to the rail, paid no attention. "According to the books the worst is not over yet."

"If most of them hadn't been half dead with sea-sickness and fright, not one of us would have come out of that 'tween-deck alive," said Jukes.

"Had to do what's fair by them," mumbled MacWhirr stolidly. "You don't find everything in books."

"Why, I believe they would have risen on us if I hadn't ordered the hands out of that pretty quick," continued Jukes with warmth.

After the whisper of their shouts, their ordinary tones, so distinct, rang out very loud to their ears in the amazing stillness of the air. It seemed to them they were talking in a dark and echoing vault.

Through a jagged aperture in the dome of clouds the light of a few stars fell upon the black sea, rising and falling confusedly. Sometimes the head of a watery cone would topple on board and mingle with the rolling flurry of foam on the swamped deck; and the *Nan-Shan* wallowed heavily at the bottom of a circular cistern of clouds. This ring of dense vapours, gyrating madly round the calm of the centre, encompassed the ship like a motionless and unbroken wall of an aspect inconceivably sinister. Within, the sea, as if agitated by an internal commotion, leaped in peaked mounds that jostled each other, slapping heavily against her sides; and a low moaning sound, the infinite plaint of the storm's fury, came from beyond the limits of the menacing calm. Captain MacWhirr remained silent, and Jukes' ready ear caught suddenly the faint, long-drawn roar of some immense wave rushing unseen under that thick blackness, which made the appalling boundary of his vision.

"Of course," he started resentfully, "they thought we had caught at the chance to plunder them. Of course! You said—pick up the money. Easier said than done. They couldn't tell what was in our heads. We came in, smash—right into the middle of them. Had to do it by a rush."

"As long as it's done...," mumbled the Captain, without attempting to look at Jukes. "Had to do what's fair."

"We shall find yet there's the devil to pay when this is over," said Jukes, feeling very sore. "Let them only recover a bit, and you'll see. They will fly at our throats, sir. Don't forget, sir, she isn't a British ship now. These brutes know it well, too. The damn'd Siamese flag."

"We are on board, all the same," remarked Captain MacWhirr.

"The trouble's not over yet," insisted Jukes prophetically, reeling and catching on. "She's a wreck," he added faintly.

"The trouble's not over yet," assented Captain MacWhirr, half aloud. . . . "Look out for her a minute."

"Are you going off the deck, sir?" asked Jukes hurriedly, as if the storm were sure to pounce upon him as soon as he had been left alone with the ship.

He watched her, battered and solitary, labouring heavily in a wild scene of mountainous black waters lit by the gleams of distant worlds. She moved slowly, breathing into the still core of the hurricane the excess of her strength in a white cloud of steam—and the deep-toned vibration of the escape was like the defiant trumpeting of a living creature of the sea impatient for the renewal of the contest. It ceased suddenly. The still air moaned. Above Jukes' head a few stars shone into the pit of black vapours. The inky edge of the cloud-disc frowned upon the ship under the patch of glittering sky. The stars too seemed to look at her intently, as if for the last time, and the cluster of their splendour sat like a diadem on a lowering brow.

Captain MacWhirr had gone into the chart-room. There was no light there; but he could feel the disorder of that place where he used to live tidily. His armchair was upset. The books had tumbled out on the floor: he scrunched a piece of glass under his boot. He groped for the matches, and found a box on a shelf with a deep ledge. He struck one, and puckering the corners of his eyes, held out the little flame towards the barometer whose glittering top of glass and metals nodded at him continuously.

It stood very low—incredibly low, so low that Captain MacWhirr grunted. The match went out, and hurriedly he extracted another, with thick, stiff fingers.

Again a little flame flared up before the nodding glass and metal of the top. His eyes looked at it, narrowed with attention, as if expecting an imperceptible sign. With his grave face he resembled a booted and misshapen pagan burning incense before the oracle of a Joss. There was no mistake. It was the lowest reading he had ever seen in his life.

Captain MacWhirr emitted a low whistle. He forgot himself till the flame diminished to a blue spark, burnt his fingers and vanished. Perhaps something had gone wrong with the thing!

There was an aneroid glass screwed above the couch. He turned that way, struck another match, and discovered the white face of the other instrument looking at him from the bulkhead, meaningly, not to be gainsaid, as though the wisdom of men were made unerring by the indifference of matter. There was no room for doubt now. Captain MacWhirr pshawed at it, and threw the match down.

The worst was to come, then—and if the books were right this worst would be very bad. The experience of the last six hours had enlarged his conception of what heavy weather could be like. "It'll be terrific," he pronounced mentally. He had not consciously looked at anything by the light of the matches except at the barometer; and yet somehow he had seen that his water-bottle and the two tumblers had been flung out of their stand. It seemed to give him a more intimate knowledge of the tossing the ship had gone through. "I wouldn't have believed it," he thought. And his table had been cleared too; his rulers, his pencils, the inkstand—all the things that had their safe appointed places—they were gone, as if a mischievous hand had plucked them out one by one and flung them on the wet floor. The hurricane had broken in upon the orderly arrangements of his privacy. This had never happened before, and the feeling of dismay reached the very seat of his composure. And the worst was to come yet! He was glad the trouble in the 'tween-deck had been discovered in time. If the ship had to go after all, then, at least, she wouldn't be going to the bottom with a lot of people in her fighting teeth and claw. That would have been odious. And in that feeling there was a humane intention and a vague sense of the fitness of things.

These instantaneous thoughts were yet in their essence heavy and slow, partaking of the nature of the man. He extended his hand to put back the matchbox in its corner of the shelf. There were always matches there—by his order. The steward had his instructions impressed upon him long before. "A box . . . just there, see? Not so very full . . . where I can put my hand on it, steward. Might want a light in a hurry. Can't tell on board ship *what* you might want in a hurry. Mind, now."

And of course on his side he would be careful to put it back in its place scrupulously. He did so now, but before he removed his hand it occurred to him that perhaps he would never have occasion to use that box any more. The vividness of the thought checked him, and for an infinitesimal fraction of a second his fingers closed again on the small object as though it had been the symbol of all these little habits that chain us to the weary round of life. He released it at last, and letting himself fall on the settee, listened for the first sounds of returning wind.

Not yet. He heard only the wash of water, the heavy splashes, the dull shocks of the confused seas boarding his ship from all sides. She would never have a chance to clear her decks.

But the quietude of the air was startlingly tense and unsafe, like a slender hair holding a sword suspended over his head.* By this awful pause the storm penetrated the defences of the man and unsealed his lips. He spoke out in the solitude and the pitch darkness of the cabin, as if addressing another being awakened within his breast.

"I shouldn't like to lose her," he said half aloud.

He sat unseen, apart from the sea, from his ship, isolated, as if withdrawn from the very current of his own existence, where such freaks as talking to himself surely had no place. His palms reposed on his knees, he bowed his short neck and puffed heavily, surrendering to a strange sensation of weariness he was not enlightened enough to recognise for the fatigue of mental stress.

From where he sat he could reach the door of a washstand locker. There should have been a towel there. There was. Good. . . . He took it out, wiped his face, and afterwards went on rubbing his wet head. He towelled himself with energy in the dark, and then remained motionless with the towel on his knees. A moment passed, of a stillness so profound that no one could have guessed there was a man sitting in that cabin. Then a murmur arose.

"She may come out of it yet."

When Captain MacWhirr came out on deck, which he did brusquely, as though he had suddenly become conscious of having stayed away too long, the calm had lasted already more than fifteen minutes—long enough to make itself intolerable even to his imagination. Jukes, motionless on the forepart of the bridge, began to speak at once. His voice, blank and forced as though he were talking through hard-set teeth, seemed to flow away on all sides into the darkness, deepening again upon the sea.

"I had the wheel relieved. Hackett began to sing out that he was done. He's lying in there alongside the steering gear with a face like death. At first I couldn't get anybody to crawl out and relieve the poor devil. That bosun's worse than no good, I always said. Thought I would have had to go myself and haul out one of them by the neck."

"Ah, well," muttered the Captain. He stood watchful by Jukes' side.

"The second mate's in there too, holding his head. Is he hurt, sir?"

"No—crazy," said Captain MacWhirr, curtly.

"Looks as if he had a tumble, though."

"I had to give him a push," explained the Captain.

Jukes gave an impatient sigh.

"It will come very sudden," said Captain MacWhirr, "and from over there, I fancy. God only knows, though. These books are only good to muddle your head and make you jumpy. It will be bad, and there's an end. If we only can steam her round in time to meet it . . ."

A minute passed. Some of the stars winked rapidly and vanished.

"You left them pretty safe?" began the Captain abruptly, as though the silence were unbearable.

"Are you thinking of the coolies, sir? I rigged life-lines all ways across that 'tween-deck."

"Did you? Good idea, Mr. Jukes."

"I didn't . . . think you cared to . . . know," said Jukes—the lurching of the ship cut his speech as though somebody had been jerking him around while he talked—"how I got on with . . . that infernal job. We did it. And it may not matter in the end."

"Had to do what's fair, for all—they are only Chinamen. Give them the same chance with ourselves—hang it all. She isn't lost yet. Bad enough to be shut up below in a gale——"

"That's what I thought when you gave me the job, sir," interjected Jukes moodily.

"——without being battered to pieces," pursued Captain MacWhirr with rising vehemence. "Couldn't let that go on in my ship, if I knew she hadn't five minutes to live. Couldn't bear it, Mr. Jukes."

A hollow echoing noise, like that of a shout rolling in a rocky chasm, approached the ship and went away again. The last star, blurred, enlarged, as if returning to the fiery mist of its beginning, struggled with the colossal depth of blackness hanging over the ship—and went out.

"Now for it!" muttered Captain MacWhirr. "Mr. Jukes."

"Here, sir."

The two men were growing indistinct to each other.

"We must trust her to go through it and come out on the other side. That's plain and straight. There's no room for Captain Wilson's storm-strategy here."

"No, sir."

"She will be smothered and swept again for hours," mumbled the Captain. "There's not much left by this time above deck for the sea to take away—unless you or me."

"Both, sir," whispered Jukes breathlessly.

"You are always meeting trouble half way, Jukes," Captain MacWhirr remonstrated quaintly. "Though it's a fact that the second mate is no good. D'ye hear, Mr. Jukes? You would be left alone if . . ."

Captain MacWhirr interrupted himself, and Jukes, glancing on all sides, remained silent.

"Don't you be put out by anything," the Captain continued, mumbling rather fast. "Keep her facing it. They may say what they like, but the heaviest seas run with the wind. Facing it—always facing it—that's the way to get through. You are a young sailor. Face it. That's enough for any man. Keep a cool head."

"Yes, sir," said Jukes, with a flutter of the heart.

In the next few seconds the Captain spoke to the engine-room and got an answer.

For some reason Jukes experienced an access of confidence, a sensation that came from outside like a warm breath, and made him feel equal to every demand. The distant muttering of the darkness stole into his ears. He noted it unmoved, out of that sudden belief in himself, as a man safe in a shirt of mail would watch a point.

The ship laboured without intermission amongst the black hills of water, paying with this hard tumbling the price of her life. She rumbled in her depths, shaking a white plumet of steam into the night, and Jukes' thought skimmed like a bird through the engine-room, where Mr. Rout—good man—was ready. When the rumbling ceased it seemed to him that there was a pause of every sound, a dead pause in which Captain MacWhirr's voice rang out startlingly.

"What's that? A puff of wind?"—it spoke much louder than Jukes had ever heard it before—"On the bow. That's right. She may come out of it yet."

The mutter of the winds drew near apace. In the forefront could be distinguished a drowsy waking plaint passing on, and far off the growth of a multiple clamour, marching and expanding. There was the throb as of many drums in it, a vicious rushing note, and like the chant of a tramping multitude.

Jukes could no longer see his captain distinctly. The darkness was absolutely piling itself upon the ship. At most he made out movements, a hint of elbows spread out, of a head thrown up.

Captain MacWhirr was trying to do up the top button of his oilskin coat with unwonted haste. The hurricane, with its power to madden the seas, to sink ships, to uproot trees, to overturn strong walls and dash the very birds of the air to the ground, had found this taciturn man in its path, and, doing its utmost, had managed to wring out a few words. Before the renewed wrath of winds swooped on his ship, Captain MacWhirr was moved to declare, in a tone of vexation, as it were: "I wouldn't like to lose her."

He was spared that annoyance.

VI

ON a bright sunshiny day, with the breeze chasing her smoke far ahead, the *Nan-Shan* came into Fu-chau. Her arrival was at once noticed on shore, and the seamen in harbour said: "Look! Look at that steamer. What's that? Siamese—isn't she? Just look at her!"

She seemed, indeed, to have been used as a running target for the secondary batteries of a cruiser. A hail of minor shells could not have given her upper works a more broken, torn, and devastated aspect: and she had about her the worn, weary air of ships coming from the far ends of the world—and indeed with truth, for in her short passage she had been very far; sighting, verily, even the coast of the Great Beyond, whence no ship ever returns to give up her crew to the dust of the earth. She was incrusted and grey with salt to the trucks of her masts and to the top of her funnel; as though (as some facetious seaman said) "the crowd on board had fished her out somewhere from the bottom of the sea and brought her in here for salvage." And further, excited by the felicity of his own wit, he offered to give five pounds for her—"as she stands."

Before she had been quite an hour at rest, a meagre little man, with a red-tipped nose and a face cast in an angry mould, landed from a sampan on the quay of the Foreign Concession, and incontinently turned to shake his fist at her.

A tall individual, with legs much too thin for a rotund stomach, and with watery eyes, strolled up and remarked, "Just left her—eh? Quick work."

He wore a soiled suit of blue flannel with a pair of dirty cricketing shoes; a dingy grey moustache dropped from his lip, and daylight could be seen in two places between the rim and the crown of his hat.

"Hallo! what are you doing here?" asked the ex-second-mate of the *Nan-Shan*, shaking hands hurriedly.

"Standing by for a job—chance worth taking—got a quiet hint," explained the man with the broken hat, in jerky, apathetic wheezes.

The second shook his fist again at the *Nan-Shan*, "There's a fellow there that ain't fit to have the command of a scow," he declared, quivering with passion, while the other looked about listlessly.

"Is there?"

But he caught sight on the quay of a heavy seaman's chest, painted brown under a fringed sailcloth cover, and lashed with new manila line. He eyed it with awakened interest.

"I would talk and raise trouble if it wasn't for that damned Siamese flag. Nobody to go to—or I would make it hot for him. The fraud! Told his chief engineer—that's another fraud for you—I had lost my nerve. The greatest lot of ignorant fools that ever sailed the seas. No! You can't think . . ."

"Got your money all right?" inquired his seedy acquaintance suddenly.

"Yes. Paid me off on board," raged the second mate. " 'Get your breakfast on shore,' says he."

"Mean skunk!" commented the tall man vaguely, and passed his tongue on his lips. "What about having a drink of some sort?"

"He struck me," hissed the second mate.

"No! Struck! You don't say?" The man in blue began to bustle about sympathetically. "Can't possibly talk here. I want to know all about it. Struck—eh? Let's get a fellow to carry your chest. I know a quiet place where they have some bottled beer. . . ."

Mr. Jukes, who had been scanning the shore through a pair of glasses, informed the chief engineer afterwards that "our late second mate hasn't been long in finding a friend. A chap looking uncommonly like a bummer. I saw them walk away together from the quay."

The hammering and banging of the needful repairs did not disturb Captain MacWhirr. The steward found in the letter he wrote, in a tidy chart-room, passages of such absorbing interest that twice he was nearly caught in the act. But Mrs. MacWhirr, in the drawing-room of the forty-pound house, stifled a yawn—perhaps out of self-respect—for she was alone.

She reclined in a plush-bottomed and gilt hammock-chair near a tiled fireplace, with Japanese fans on the mantel and a glow of coals in the grate. Lifting her hands, she glanced wearily here and there into the many pages. It was not her fault they were so prosy, so completely uninteresting—from "My darling wife" at the beginning, to "Your loving husband" at the end. She couldn't be really expected to understand all these ship affairs. She was glad, of course, to hear from him, but she had never asked herself why, precisely.

". . . They are called typhoons . . . The mate did not seem to like it . . . Not in books . . . Couldn't think of letting it go on. . . ."

The paper rustled sharply. ". . . . A calm that lasted over twenty minutes," she read perfunctorily; and the next words her thoughtless eyes caught, on the top of another page, were: "see you and the children again. . . ." She had a movement of impatience. He was always thinking of coming home. He had never had such a good salary before. What was the matter now?

It did not occur to her to turn back overleaf to look. She would have found it recorded there that between 4 and 6 A.M. on December 25th, Captain MacWhirr did actually think that his ship could not possibly live another hour in such a sea, and that he would never see his wife and children again. Nobody was to know this (his letters got mislaid so quickly)—nobody whatever but the steward, who had been greatly impressed by that disclosure. So much so, that he tried to give the cook some idea of the "narrow squeak we all had" by saying solemnly, "The old man himself had a dam' poor opinion of our chance."

"How do you know?" asked contemptuously the cook, an old soldier, "He hasn't told you, maybe?"

"Well, he did give me a hint to that effect," the steward brazened it out.

"Get along with you! He will be coming to tell *me* next," jeered the old cook over his shoulder.

Mrs. MacWhirr glanced farther, on the alert. ". . . Do what's fair. . . . Miserable objects. . . . Only three, with a broken leg each, and one . . . Thought had better keep the matter quiet . . . hope to have done the fair thing. . . ."

She let fall her hands. No: there was nothing more about coming home. Must have been merely expressing a pious wish. Mrs. MacWhirr's mind was set at ease, and a black marble clock, priced by the local jeweller at £3 18s. 6d., had a discreet stealthy tick.

The door flew open, and a girl in the long-legged, short-frocked period of existence, flung into the room. A lot of colourless, rather lanky hair was scattered over her shoulders. Seeing her mother, she stood still, and directed her pale prying eyes upon the letter.

"From father," murmured Mrs. MacWhirr. "What have you done with your ribbon?"

The girl put her hands up to her head and pouted.

"He's well," continued Mrs. MacWhirr languidly. "At least I think so. He never says." She had a little laugh. The girl's face expressed a wandering indifference, and Mrs. MacWhirr surveyed her with fond pride.

"Go and get your hat," she said after a while. "I am going out to do some shopping. There is a sale at Linom's."

"Oh, how jolly!" uttered the child impressively, in unexpectedly grave vibrating tones, and bounded out of the room.

It was a fine afternoon, with a grey sky and dry sidewalks. Outside the draper's Mrs. MacWhirr smiled upon a woman in a black mantle of generous proportions, armoured in jet and crowned with flowers blooming falsely above a bilious matronly countenance. They broke into a swift little babble of greetings and exclamations both together, very hurried, as if the street were ready to yawn open and swallow all that pleasure before it could be expressed.

Behind them the high glass doors were kept on the swing. People couldn't pass, men stood aside waiting patiently, and Lydia was absorbed in poking the end of her parasol between the stone flags. Mrs. MacWhirr talked rapidly.

"Thank you very much. He's not coming home yet. Of course it's very sad to have him away, but it's such a comfort to know he keeps so well." Mrs. MacWhirr drew breath. "The climate there agrees with him," she added beamingly, as if poor MacWhirr had been away touring in China for the sake of his health.

Neither was the chief engineer coming home yet. Mr. Rout knew too well the value of a good billet.

"Solomon says wonders will never cease," cried Mrs. Rout joyously at the old lady in her armchair by the fire. Mr. Rout's mother moved slightly, her withered hands lying in black half-mittens on her lap.

The eyes of the engineer's wife fairly danced on the paper. "That captain of the ship he is in—a rather simple man, you remember, mother?—has done something rather clever, Solomon says."

"Yes, my dear," said the old woman meekly, sitting with bowed silvery head, and that air of inward stillness characteristic of very old people who seem lost in watching the last flickers of life. "I think I remember."

Solomon Rout, Old Sol, Father Sol, The Chief, "Rout, good man"—Mr. Rout, the condescending and paternal friend of youth, had been the baby of her many children—all dead by this time. And she remembered him best as a boy of ten—long before he went away to serve his apprenticeship in some great engineering works in the North. She had seen so little of him since, she had gone through so many years, that she had now to retrace her steps very far back to recognise him plainly in the mist of time. Sometimes it seemed that her daughter-in-law was talking of some strange man.

Mrs. Rout junior was disappointed. "H'm. H'm." She turned the page. "How provoking! He doesn't say what it is. Says I couldn't understand how much there was in it. Fancy! What could it be so very clever? What a wretched man not to tell us!"

She read on without further remark soberly, and at last sat looking into the fire. The chief wrote just a word or two of the typhoon; but something had moved him to express an increased longing for the companionship of the jolly woman. "If it hadn't been that mother must be looked after, I would send you your passage-money today. You could set up a small house out here. I would have a chance to see you sometimes then. We are not growing younger. . . ."

"He's well, mother," sighed Mrs. Rout, rousing herself.

"He always was a strong healthy boy," said the old woman placidly.

But Mr. Jukes' account was really animated and very full. His friend in the Western Ocean trade imparted it freely to the other officers of his liner. "A chap I know writes to me about an extraordinary affair that happened on board his ship in that typhoon—you know—that we read of in the papers two months ago. It's the funniest thing! Just see for yourself what he says. I'll show you his letter."

There were phrases in it calculated to give the impression of light-hearted, indomitable resolution. Jukes had written them in good faith, for he felt thus when he wrote. He described with lurid effect the scenes in the 'tween-deck. ". . . It struck me in a flash that those confounded Chinamen couldn't tell we weren't a desperate kind of robbers. 'Tisn't good to part the Chinaman from his money if he is the stronger party. We need have been desperate indeed to go thieving in such weather, but what could these beggars know of us? So, without thinking of it twice, I got the hands away in a jiffy. Our work was done—that the old man had set his heart on. We cleared out without staying to inquire how they felt. I am convinced that if they had not been so unmercifully shaken, and afraid—each individual one of them—to stand up, we would have been torn to pieces.

Oh! It was pretty complete, I can tell you; and you may run to and fro across the Pond to the end of time before you find yourself with such a job on your hands."

After this he alluded professionally to the damage done to the ship, and went on thus:

"It was when the weather quieted down that the situation became confoundedly delicate. It wasn't made any better by us having been lately transferred to the Siamese flag; though the skipper can't see that it makes any difference—'as long as *we* are on board'—he says. There are feelings that this man simply hasn't got—and there's an end of it. You might just as well try to make a bedpost understand. But apart from this it is an infernally lonely state for a ship to be going about the China seas with no proper consuls, not even a gunboat of her own anywhere, nor a body to go to in case of some trouble.

"My notion was to keep these Johnnies under hatches for another fifteen hours or so; as we weren't much farther than that from Fu-chau. We would find there, most likely, some sort of a man-of-war, and once under her guns we were safe enough; for surely any skipper of a man-of-war—English, French or Dutch—would see white men through as far as row on board goes. We could get rid of them and their money afterwards by delivering them to their Mandarin or Taotai, or whatever they call these chaps in goggles you see being carried about in sedan-chairs through their stinking streets.

"The old man wouldn't see it somehow. He wanted to keep the matter quiet. He got that notion into his head, and a steam windlass couldn't drag it out of him. He wanted as little fuss made as possible, for the sake of the ship's name and for the sake of the owners—'for the sake of all concerned,' says he, looking at me very hard. It made me angry hot. Of course you couldn't keep a thing like that quiet; but the chests had been secured in the usual manner and were safe enough for any earthly gale, while this had been an altogether fiendish business I couldn't give you even an idea of.

"Meantime, I could hardly keep on my feet. None of us had a spell of any sort for nearly thirty hours, and there the old man sat rubbing his chin, rubbing the top of his head, and so bothered he didn't even think of pulling his long boots off.

"'I hope, sir,' says I, 'you won't be letting them out on deck before we make ready for them in some shape or other.' Not, mind you, that I felt very sanguine about controlling these beggars if they meant to take charge. A trouble with a cargo of Chinamen is no child's play. I was dam' tired too. 'I wish,' said I, 'you would let us throw the whole lot of these dollars down to them and leave them to fight it out amongst themselves, while we get a rest.'

"'Now you talk wild, Jukes,' says he, looking up in his slow way that makes you ache all over, somehow. 'We must plan out something that would be fair to all parties.'

"I had no end of work on hand, as you may imagine, so I set the hands going, and then I thought I would turn in a bit. I hadn't been asleep in my bunk ten minutes when in rushes the steward and begins to pull at my leg.

"'For God's sake, Mr. Jukes, come out! Come on deck quick, sir. Oh, do come out!'

"The fellow scared all the sense out of me. I didn't know what had happened: another hurricane—or what. Could hear no wind.

"'The Captain's letting them out. Oh, he is letting them out! Jump on deck, sir, and save us. The chief engineer has just run below for his revolver.'

"That's what I understood the fool to say. However, Father Rout swears he went in there only to get a clean pocket-handkerchief. Anyhow, I made one jump into my trousers and flew on deck aft. There was certainly a good deal of noise going on forward of the bridge. Four of the hands with the bosun were at work abaft. I passed up to them some of the rifles all the ships on the China coast carry in the cabin, and led them on the bridge. On the way I ran against Old Sol, looking startled and sucking at an unlighted cigar.

"'Come along,' I shouted to him.

"We charged, the seven of us, up to the chart-room. All was over. There stood the old man with his sea-boots still drawn up to the hips and in shirt-sleeves—got warm thinking it out, I suppose. Bun-hin's dandy clerk at his elbow, as dirty as a sweep, was still green in the face. I could see directly I was in for something.

"'What the devil are these monkey tricks, Mr. Jukes?' asks the old man, as angry as ever he could be. I tell you frankly it made me lose my tongue. 'For God's sake, Mr. Jukes,' says he, 'do take away these rifles from the men. Somebody's sure to get hurt before long if you don't. Damme, if this ship isn't worse than Bedlam! Look sharp now.

I want you up here to help me and Bun-hin's Chinaman to count that money. You wouldn't mind lending a hand too, Mr. Rout, now you are here. The more of us the better.'

"He had settled it all in his mind while I was having a snooze. Had we been an English ship, or only going to land our cargo of coolies in an English port, like Hong-Kong, for instance, there would have been no end of inquiries and bother, claims for damages and so on. But these Chinamen know their officials better than we do.

"The hatches had been taken off already, and they were all on deck after a night and a day down below. It made you feel queer to see so many gaunt, wild faces together. The beggars stared about at the sky, at the sea, at the ship, as though they had expected the whole thing to have been blown to pieces. And no wonder! They had had a doing that would have shaken the soul out of a white man. But then they say a Chinaman has no soul. He has, though, something about him that is deuced tough. There was a fellow (amongst others of the badly hurt) who had had his eye all but knocked out. It stood out of his head the size of half a hen's egg. This would have laid out a white man on his back for a month: and yet there was that chap elbowing here and there in the crowd and talking to the others as if nothing had been the matter. They made a great hubbub amongst themselves, and whenever the old man showed his bald head on the fore-side of the bridge, they would all leave off jawing and look at him from below.

"It seems that after he had done his thinking he made that Bun-hin's fellow go down and explain to them the only way they could get their money back. He told me afterwards that, all the coolies having worked in the same place and for the same length of time, he reckoned he would be doing the fair thing by them as near as possible if he shared all the cash we had picked up equally among the lot. You couldn't tell one man's dollars from another's, he said, and if you asked each man how much money he brought on board he was afraid they would lie, and he would find himself a long way short. I think he was right there. As to giving up the money to any Chinese official he could scare up in Fu-chau, he said he might just as well put the lot in his own pocket at once for all the good it would be to them. I suppose they thought so too.

"We finished the distribution before dark. It was rather a sight: the sea running high, the ship a wreck to look at, these Chinamen staggering up on the bridge one by one for their share, and the old man still booted, and in his shirt-sleeves, busy paying out at the chartroom door, perspiring like anything, and now and then coming down sharp on myself or Father Rout about one thing or another not quite to his mind. He took the share of those who were disabled himself to them on the No. 2 hatch. There were three dollars left over, and these went to the three most damaged coolies, one to each. We turned-to afterwards, and shovelled out on deck heaps of wet rags, all sorts of fragments of things without shape, and that you couldn't give a name to, and let them settle the ownership themselves.

"This certainly is coming as near as can be to keeping the thing quiet for the benefit of all concerned. What's your opinion, you pampered mail-boat swell? The old chief says that this was plainly the only thing that could be done. The skipper remarked to me the other day, 'There are things you find nothing about in books.' I think that he got out of it very well for such a stupid man."

FALK:
A REMINISCENCE

FALK: A REMINISCENCE

SEVERAL of us, all more or less connected with the sea,* were dining in a small river-hostelry not more than thirty miles from London, and less than twenty from that shallow and dangerous puddle to which our coasting men give the grandiose name of "German Ocean." And through the wide windows we had a view of the Thames; an enfilading view down the Lower Hope Reach. But the dinner was execrable, and all the feast was for the eyes.

That flavour of salt-water which for so many of us had been the very water of life permeated our talk. He who hath known the bitterness of the Ocean shall have its taste for ever in his mouth. But one or two of us, pampered by the life of the land, complained of hunger.* It was impossible to swallow any of that stuff. And indeed there was a strange mustiness in everything. The wooden dining-room stuck out over the mud of the shore like a lacustrine dwelling; the planks of the floor seemed rotten; a decrepid old waiter tottered pathetically to and fro before an antediluvian and worm-eaten sideboard; the chipped plates might have been disinterred from some kitchen midden near an inhabited lake; and the chops recalled times more ancient still. They brought forcibly to one's mind the night of ages when the primeval man, evolving the first rudiments of cookery from his dim consciousness, scorched lumps of flesh at a fire of sticks in the company of other good fellows; then, gorged and happy, sat him back among the gnawed bones to tell his artless tales of experience—the tales of hunger and hunt—and of women, perhaps!

But luckily the wine happened to be as old as the waiter. So, comparatively empty, but upon the whole fairly happy, we sat back and told our artless tales. We talked of the sea and all its works. The sea never changes, and its works for all the talk of men are wrapped in mystery. But we agreed that the times were changed. And we talked of old ships, of sea-accidents, of break-downs, dismastings; and of a man who brought his ship safe to Liverpool all the way from the River Plate under a jury rudder. We talked of wrecks, of short rations and of heroism—or at least of what the newspapers would have called heroism at sea—a manifestation of virtues quite different from the heroism of primitive times. And now and then falling silent all together we gazed at the sights of the river.

A P. & O. boat passed bound down. "One gets jolly good dinners on board these ships," remarked one of our band. A man with sharp eyes read out the name on her bows: *Arcadia*. "What a beautiful model of a ship!" murmured some of us. She was followed by a small cargo-steamer, and the flag they hauled down aboard while we were looking showed her to be a Norwegian. She made an awful lot of smoke; and before it had quite blown away, a high-sided, short, wooden barque, in ballast and towed by a paddle-tug, appeared in front of the windows. All her hands forward were busy setting up the headgear; and aft a woman in a red hood, quite alone with the man at the wheel, paced the length of the poop back and forth, with the grey wool of some knitting work in her hands.

"German I should think," muttered one. "The skipper has his wife on board," remarked another; and the light of the crimson sunset all ablaze behind the London smoke, throwing a glow of Bengal light upon the barque's spars, faded away from the Hope Reach.

Then one of us, who had not spoken before, a man of over fifty,* that had commanded ships for a quarter of a century, looking after the barque now gliding far away, all black on the lustre of the river, said:

This reminds me of an absurd episode in my life, now many years ago, when I got first the command of an iron barque, loading then in a certain Eastern seaport. It was also the capital of an Eastern kingdom,* lying up a river as might be London lies up this old Thames of ours. No more need be said of the place; for this sort of thing might have happened anywhere where there are ships, skippers, tugboats, and orphan nieces of indescribable splendour. And the absurdity of the episode concerns only me, my enemy Falk, and my friend Hermann.*

There seemed to be something like peculiar emphasis on the words "My friend Hermann," which caused one of us (for we had just been speaking of heroism at sea) to say idly and nonchalantly:

"And was this Hermann a hero?"

Not at all, said our grizzled friend. No hero at all. He was a Schiff-führer: Ship-conductor. That's how they call a Master Mariner in Germany. I prefer our way. The alliteration is good, and there is something in the nomenclature that gives to us as a body the sense of corporate existence: Apprentice, Mate, Master, in the ancient and honourable craft of the sea. As to my friend Hermann, he might have been a consummate master of the honourable craft, but he was called officially Schiff-führer, and had the simple, heavy appearance of a well-to-do farmer, combined with the good-natured shrewdness of a small shopkeeper. With his shaven chin, round limbs, and heavy eyelids he did not look like a toiler, and even less like an adventurer of the sea. Still, he toiled upon the seas, in his own way, much as a shopkeeper works behind his counter. And his ship was the means by which he maintained his growing family.

She was a heavy, strong, blunt-bowed affair, awakening the ideas of primitive solidity, like the wooden plough of our forefathers. And there were, about her, other suggestions of a rustic and homely nature. The extraordinary timber projections which I have seen in no other vessel made her square stern resemble the tail end of a miller's waggon. But the four stern ports of her cabin, glazed with six little greenish panes each, and framed in wooden sashes painted brown, might have been the windows of a cottage in the country. The tiny white curtains and the greenery of flower-pots behind the glass completed the resemblance. On one or two occasions when passing under her stern I had detected from my boat a round arm in the act of tilting a watering-pot, and the bowed sleek head of a maiden whom I shall always call Hermann's niece, because as a matter of fact I've never heard her name, for all my intimacy with the family.

This, however, sprang up later on. Meantime in common with the rest of the shipping in that Eastern port, I was left in no doubt as to Hermann's notions of hygienic clothing. Evidently he believed in wearing good stout flannel next his skin. On most days little frocks and pinafores could be seen drying in the mizzen rigging of his ship, or a tiny row of socks fluttering on the signal halyards; but once a fortnight the family washing was exhibited in force. It covered the poop entirely. The afternoon breeze would incite to a weird and flabby activity all that crowded mass of clothing, with its vague suggestions of drowned, mutilated and flattened humanity. Trunks without heads waved at you arms without hands; legs without feet kicked fantastically with collapsible flourishes; and there were long white garments, that taking the wind fairly through their neck openings edged with lace, became for a moment violently distended as by the passage of obese and invisible bodies. On these days you could make out that ship at a great distance by the multi-coloured grotesque riot going on abaft her mizzen-mast.

She had her berth just ahead of me, and her name was *Diana*,—Diana not of Ephesus* but of Bremen. This was proclaimed in white letters a foot long spaced widely across the stern (somewhat like the lettering of a shop-sign) under the cottage windows. This ridiculously unsuitable name struck one as an impertinence towards the memory of the most charming of goddesses; for, apart from the fact that the old craft was physically incapable of engaging in any sort of chase, there was a gang of four children belonging to her. They peeped over the rail at passing boats and occasionally dropped various objects into them. Thus, sometime before I knew Hermann to speak to, I received on my hat a horrid rag-doll belonging to Hermann's eldest daughter. However, these youngsters were upon the whole well behaved. They had fair heads, round eyes, round little knobby noses, and they resembled their father a good deal.

This *Diana* of Bremen was a most innocent old ship, and seemed to know nothing of the wicked sea, as there are on shore households that know nothing of the corrupt world. And the sentiments she suggested were unexceptionable and mainly of a domestic order. She was a home. All these dear children had learned to walk on her roomy quarter-deck. In such thoughts there is something pretty, even touching. Their teeth, I should judge, they had cut on the ends of her running gear. I have many times observed the baby Hermann (Nicholas) engaged in gnawing the whipping of the fore-royal brace. Nicholas' favourite place of residence was under the main fife-rail. Directly he was let loose he would crawl off there, and the first seaman who came along would bring him, carefully held aloft in tarry hands, back to the cabin door. I fancy there must have been a standing order to that effect. In the course of these transportations the baby, who was the only peppery person in the ship, tried to smite these stalwart young German sailors on the face.

Mrs. Hermann, an engaging, stout housewife, wore on board baggy blue dresses with white dots. When, as happened once or twice, I caught her at an elegant little wash-tub rubbing hard on white collars, baby's socks, and Hermann's summer neck-ties, she would blush in girlish confusion, and raising her wet hands greet me from afar with many friendly nods. Her sleeves would be rolled up to the elbows, and the gold hoop of her wedding ring glittered among the soap-suds. Her voice was pleasant, she had a serene brow, smooth bands of very fair hair, and a good-humoured expression of the eyes. She was motherly and moderately talkative. When this simple matron smiled, youthful dimples broke out on her fresh broad cheeks. Hermann's niece on the other hand, an orphan and very silent, I never saw attempt a smile. This, however, was not gloom on her part but the restraint of youthful gravity.

They had carried her about with them for the last three years, to help with the children and be company for Mrs. Hermann, as Hermann mentioned once to me. It had been very necessary while they were all little, he had added in a vexed manner. It was her arm and her sleek head that I had glimpsed one morning, through the stern-windows of the cabin, hovering over the pots of fuchsias and mignonette; but the first time I beheld her full length I surrendered to her proportions. They fix her in my mind, as great beauty, great intelligence, quickness of wit or kindness of heart might have made some other woman equally memorable.

With her it was form and size. It was her physical personality that had this imposing charm. She might have been witty, intelligent, and kind to an exceptional degree. I don't know, and this is not to the point. All I know is that she was built on a magnificent scale. Built is the only word. She was constructed, she was erected, as it were, with a regal lavishness. It staggered you to see this reckless expenditure of material upon a chit of a girl. She was youthful and also perfectly mature, as though she had been some fortunate immortal. She was heavy too, perhaps, but that's nothing. It only added to that notion of permanence. She was barely nineteen. But such shoulders! Such round arms! Such a shadowing forth of mighty limbs when with three long strides she pounced across the deck upon the overturned Nicholas—it's perfectly indescribable! She seemed a good, quiet girl, vigilant as to Lena's needs, Gustav's tumbles, the state of Carl's dear little nose—conscientious, hardworking, and all that. But what magnificent hair she had! Abundant, long, thick, of a tawny colour. It had the sheen of precious metals. She wore it plaited tightly into one single tress hanging girlishly down her back; and its end reached down to her waist. The massiveness of it surprised you. On my word it reminded one of a club. Her face was big, comely, of an unruffled expression. She had a good complexion, and her blue eyes were so pale that she appeared to look at the world with the empty white candour of a statue. You could not call her good-looking. It was something much more impressive. The simplicity of her apparel, the opulence of her form, her imposing stature, and the extraordinary sense of vigorous life that seemed to emanate from her like a perfume exhaled by a flower, made her beautiful with a beauty of a rustic and olympian order. To watch her reaching up to the clothes-line with both arms raised high above her head, caused you to fall a-musing in a strain of pagan piety. Excellent Mrs. Hermann's baggy cotton gowns had some sort of rudimentary frills at neck and bottom, but this girl's print frocks hadn't even a wrinkle; nothing but a few straight folds in the skirt falling to her feet, and these, when she stood still, had a severe and statuesque quality. She was inclined naturally to be still whether sitting or standing. However, I don't mean to say she was statuesque. She was too generously alive; but she could have stood for an allegoric statue of the Earth. I don't mean the worn-out earth of our possession, but a young Earth, a virginal planet undisturbed by the vision of a future teeming with the monstrous forms of life and death, clamorous with the cruel battles of hunger and thought.

The worthy Hermann himself was not very entertaining, though his English was fairly comprehensible. Mrs. Hermann, who always let off one speech at least at me in an hospitable, cordial tone (and in Platt-Deutsch I suppose) I could not understand. As to their niece, however satisfactory to look upon (and she inspired you somehow with a hopeful view as to the prospects of mankind) she was a modest and silent presence, mostly engaged in sewing, only now and then, as I observed, falling over that work into a stare of maidenly meditation. Her aunt sat opposite her, sewing also, with her feet propped on a wooden footstool. On the other side of the deck Hermann and I would get a couple of chairs out of the cabin and settle down to a smoking match, accompanied at long intervals by the pacific exchange of a few words. I came nearly every evening. Hermann I would find in his shirt sleeves. As soon as he returned from the shore on board his ship he commenced operations by taking off his coat; then he put on his head an embroidered round cap with a tassel, and changed his boots for a pair of cloth slippers. Afterwards he smoked at the cabin-door, looking at his children with an air of civic virtue, till they got caught one after another and put to bed in various staterooms. Lastly, we would drink some beer in the cabin, which was furnished with a wooden table on cross legs, and with black straight-backed chairs—more like a farm kitchen than a ship's cuddy. The sea and all nautical affairs seemed very far removed from the hospitality of this exemplary family.

And I liked this because I had a rather worrying time on board my own ship. I had been appointed ex-officio by the British Consul to take charge of her after a man who had died suddenly,* leaving for the guidance of his successor some suspiciously unreceipted bills, a few dry-dock estimates hinting at bribery, and a quantity of vouchers for three years' extravagant expenditure; all these mixed up together in a dusty old violin-case lined with ruby velvet. I found besides a large account-book, which, when opened hopefully, turned out to my infinite consternation to be filled with verses—page after page of rhymed doggerel of a jovial and improper character, written in the neatest minute hand I ever did see. In the same fiddle-case a photograph of my predecessor, taken lately in Saigon, represented in front of a garden view, and in company of a female in strange draperies, an elderly, squat, rugged man of stern aspect in a clumsy suit of black broadcloth, and with the hair brushed forward above the temples in a manner reminding one of a boar's tusks. Of a fiddle, however, the only trace on board was the case, its empty husk as it were; but of the two last freights the ship had indubitably earned of late, there were not even the husks left. It was impossible to say where all that money had gone to. It wasn't on board. It had not been remitted home; for a letter from the owners, preserved in a desk evidently, by the merest accident, complained mildly enough that they had not been favoured by a scratch of the pen for the last eighteen months.* There were next to no stores on board, not an inch of spare rope or a yard of canvas. The ship had been run bare, and I foresaw no end of difficulties before I could get her ready for sea.

As I was young then—not thirty yet—I took myself and my troubles very seriously. The old mate, who had acted as chief mourner at the captain's funeral, was not particularly pleased at my coming.* But the fact is the fellow was not legally qualified for command, and the Consul was bound, if at all possible, to put a properly certificated man on board. As to the second mate, all I can say is his name was Tottersen, or something like that.* His practice was to wear on his head, in that tropical climate, a mangy fur cap. He was, without exception, the stupidest man I had ever seen on board ship. And he looked it too. He looked so confoundedly stupid that it was a matter of surprise for me when he answered to his name.

I drew no great comfort from their company, to say the least of it; while the prospect of making a long sea passage with those two fellows was depressing. And my other thoughts in solitude could not be of a gay complexion. The crew was sickly,* the cargo was coming very slow; I foresaw I would have lots of trouble with the charterers, and doubted whether they would advance me enough money for the ship's expenses. Their attitude towards me was unfriendly. Altogether I was not getting on. I would discover at odd times (generally about midnight) that I was totally inexperienced, greatly ignorant of business, and hopelessly unfit for any sort of command; and when the steward had to be taken to the hospital ill with choleraic symptoms I felt bereaved of the only decent person at the after end of the ship. He was fully expected to recover, but in the meantime had to be replaced by some sort of servant. And on the recommendation of a certain Schomberg,* the proprietor of the smaller of the two hotels in the place, I engaged a Chinaman. Schomberg, a brawny, hairy Alsatian, and an awful gossip, assured me that it was all right. "First-class boy that. Came in the *suite* of his Excellency Tseng the Commissioner—you know. His Excellency Tseng lodged with me here for three weeks."

He mouthed the Chinese Excellency at me with great unction, though the specimen of the "*suite*" did not seem very promising. At the time, however, I did not know what an untrustworthy humbug Schomberg was. The "boy" might have been forty or a hundred and forty for all you could tell—one of those Chinamen of the death's-head type of face and completely inscrutable. Before the end of the third day he had revealed himself as a confirmed opium-smoker, a gambler, a most audacious thief, and a first-class sprinter.* When he departed at the top of his speed with thirty-two golden sovereigns of my own hard-earned savings it was the last straw. I had reserved that money in case my difficulties came to the worst. Now it was gone I felt as poor and naked as a fakir. I clung to my ship, for all the bother she caused me, but what I could not bear were the long lonely evenings in her cuddy, where the atmosphere, made smelly by a leaky lamp, was agitated by the snoring of the mate. That fellow shut himself up in his stuffy cabin punctually at eight, and made gross and revolting noises like a water-logged trombone.* It was odious not to be able to worry oneself in comfort on board one's own ship. Everything in this world, I reflected, even the command of a nice little barque, may be made a delusion and a snare for the unwary spirit of pride in man.

From such reflections I was glad to make my escape on board that Bremen *Diana*. There apparently no whisper of the world's iniquities had ever penetrated. And yet she lived upon the wide sea: and the sea tragic and comic, the sea with its horrors and its peculiar scandals, the sea peopled by men and ruled by iron necessity is indubitably a part of the world. But that patriarchal old tub, like some saintly retreat, echoed nothing of it. She was world-proof. Her venerable innocence apparently had put a restraint on the roaring lusts of the sea. And yet I have known the sea too long to believe in its respect for decency. An elemental force is ruthlessly frank. It may, of course, have been Hermann's skilful seamanship, but to me it looked as if the allied oceans had refrained from smashing these high bulwarks, unshipping the lumpy rudder, frightening the children, and generally opening this family's eyes out of sheer reticence. It looked like reticence. The ruthless disclosure was, in the end, left for a man to make; a man strong and elemental enough and driven to unveil some secrets of the sea by the power of a simple and elemental desire.

This, however, occurred much later, and meantime I took sanctuary in that serene old ship early every evening. The only person on board that seemed to be in trouble was little Lena, and in due course I perceived that the health of the rag-doll was more than delicate. This object led a sort of "in extremis" existence in a wooden box placed against the starboard mooring-bitts, tended and nursed with the greatest sympathy and care by all the children, who greatly enjoyed pulling long faces and moving with hushed footsteps. Only the baby—Nicholas—looked on with a cold, ruffianly leer, as if he had belonged to another tribe altogether. Lena perpetually sorrowed over the box, and all of them were in deadly earnest. It was wonderful the way these children would work up their compassion for that bedraggled thing I wouldn't have touched with a pair of tongs. I suppose they were exercising and developing their racial sentimentalism by the means of that dummy. I was only surprised that Mrs. Hermann let Lena cherish and hug that bundle of rags to that extent, it was so disreputably and completely unclean. But Mrs. Hermann would raise her fine womanly eyes from her needlework to look on with amused sympathy, and did not seem to see it, somehow, that this object of affection was a disgrace to the ship's purity. Purity, not cleanliness, is the word. It was pushed so far that I seemed to detect in this too a sentimental excess, as if dirt had been removed in very love. It is impossible to give you an idea of such a meticulous neatness. It was as if every morning that ship had been arduously explored with—with toothbrushes. Her very bowsprit three times a week had its toilette made with a cake of soap and a piece of soft flannel. Arrayed—I *must* say arrayed—arrayed artlessly in dazzling white paint as to wood and dark green as to ironwork, the simple-minded distribution of these colours evoked the images of simple-minded peace, of arcadian felicity; and the childish comedy of disease and sorrow struck me sometimes as an abominably real blot upon that ideal state.

I enjoyed it greatly, and on my part I brought a little mild excitement into it. Our intimacy arose from the pursuit of that thief. It was in the evening, and Hermann, who, contrary to his habits, had stayed on shore late that day, was extricating himself backwards out of a little gharry on the river bank, opposite his ship, when the hunt passed. Realising the situation as though he had eyes in his shoulder-blades, he joined us with a leap and took the lead. The Chinaman fled silent like a rapid shadow on the dust of an extremely oriental road. I followed. A long way in the rear my mate whooped like a savage. A young moon threw a bashful light on a plain like a monstrous waste ground: the architectural mass of a Buddhist temple far away projected itself in dead black on the sky. We lost the thief of course; but in my disappointment I had to admire Hermann's presence of mind. The velocity that stodgy man developed in the interests of a complete stranger earned my warm gratitude—there was something truly cordial in his exertions.

He seemed as vexed as myself at our failure, and would hardly listen to my thanks. He said it was "nothings," and invited me on the spot to come on board his ship and drink a glass of beer with him. We poked sceptically for a while amongst the bushes, peered without conviction into a ditch or two. There was not a sound: patches of slime glimmered feebly amongst the reeds. Slowly we trudged back, drooping under the thin sickle of the moon, and I heard him mutter to himself, "Himmel! Zwei und dreissig Pfund!" He was impressed by the figure of my loss. For a long time we had ceased to hear the mate's whoops and yells.

Then he said to me, "Everybody has his troubles," and as we went on remarked that he would never have known anything of mine hadn't he by an extraordinary chance been detained on shore by Captain Falk. He didn't like to stay late ashore—he added with a sigh. The something doleful in his tone I put to his sympathy with my misfortune, of course.

On board the *Diana* Mrs. Hermann's fine eyes expressed much interest and commiseration. We had found the two women sewing face to face under the open skylight in the strong glare of the lamp. Hermann walked in first, starting in the very doorway to pull off his coat, and encouraging me with loud, hospitable ejaculations: "Come in! This way! Come in, captain!" At once, coat in hand, he began to tell his wife all about it. Mrs. Hermann put the palms of her plump hands together; I smiled and bowed with a heavy heart: the niece got up from her sewing to bring Hermann's slippers and his embroidered calotte, which he assumed pontifically, talking (about me) all the time. Billows of white stuff lay between the chairs on the cabin floor; I caught the words "Zwei und dreissig Pfund" repeated several times, and presently came the beer, which seemed delicious to my throat, parched with running and the emotions of the chase.

I didn't get away till well past midnight, long after the women had retired. Hermann had been trading in the East for three years or more, carrying freights of rice and timber mostly. His ship was well known in all the ports from Vladivostok to Singapore. She was his own property. The profits had been moderate, but the trade answered well enough while the children were small yet. In another year or so he hoped he would be able to sell the old *Diana* to a firm in Japan for a fair price. He intended to return home, to Bremen, by mail boat, second class, with Mrs. Hermann and the children. He told me all this stolidly, with slow puffs at his pipe. I was sorry when knocking the ashes out he began to rub his eyes. I would have sat with him till morning. What had I to hurry on board my own ship for? To face the broken rifled drawer in my state-room. Ugh! The very thought made me feel unwell.

I became their daily guest, as you know. I think that Mrs. Hermann from the first looked upon me as a romantic person. I did

not, of course, tear my hair *coram populo* over my loss, and she took it
for lordly indifference. Afterwards, I daresay, I did tell them some of
my adventures—such as they were—and they marvelled greatly at
the extent of my experience. Hermann would translate what he
thought the most striking passages. Getting upon his legs, and as if
delivering a lecture on a phenomenon, he addressed himself, with
gestures, to the two women, who would let their sewing sink slowly
on their laps. Meantime I sat before a glass of Hermann's beer,
trying to look modest. Mrs. Hermann would glance at me quickly,
emit slight "Ach's!" The girl never made a sound. Never. But she too
would sometimes raise her pale eyes to look at me in her unseeing
gentle way. Her glance was by no means stupid; it beamed out soft
and diffuse as the moon beams upon a landscape—quite differently
from the scrutinising inspection of the stars. You were drowned in it,
and imagined yourself to appear blurred. And yet this same glance
when turned upon Christian Falk must have been as efficient as the
searchlight of a battle-ship.

Falk was the other assiduous visitor on board, but from his
behaviour he might have been coming to see the quarter-deck capstan. He certainly used to stare at it a good deal when keeping us
company outside the cabin door, with one muscular arm thrown over
the back of the chair, and his big shapely legs, in very tight white
trousers, extended far out and ending in a pair of black shoes as
roomy as punts. On arrival he would shake Hermann's hand with a
mutter, bow to the women, and take up his careless and misanthropic
attitude by our side. He departed abruptly, with a jump, going
through the performance of grunts, hand-shakes, bow, as if in a
panic. Sometimes, with a sort of discreet and convulsive effort, he
approached the women and exchanged a few low words with them,
half a dozen at most. On these occasions Hermann's usual stare
became positively glassy and Mrs. Hermann's kind countenance
would colour up. The girl herself never turned a hair.

Falk was a Dane or perhaps a Norwegian, I can't tell now. At all
events he was a Scandinavian of some sort, and a bloated monopolist
to boot. It is possible he was unacquainted with the word, but he had
a clear perception of the thing itself. His tariff of charges for towing
ships in and out was the most brutally inconsiderate document of the
sort I had ever seen. He was the commander and owner of the only
tug-boat on the river, a very trim white craft of 150 tons or more, as

elegantly neat as a yacht, with a round wheelhouse rising like a glazed turret high above her sharp bows, and with one slender varnished pole mast forward. I daresay there are yet a few shipmasters afloat who remember Falk and his tug very well. He extracted his pound and a half of flesh* from each of us merchant-skippers with an inflexible sort of indifference which made him detested and even feared. Schomberg used to remark: "I won't talk about the fellow. I don't think he has six drinks from year's end to year's end in my place. But my advice is, gentleman, don't you have anything to do with him, if you can help it."

This advice, apart from unavoidable business relations, was easy to follow because Falk intruded upon no one. It seems absurd to compare a tug-boat skipper to a centaur: but he reminded me somehow of an engraving in a little book I had as a boy, which represented centaurs at a stream, and there was one, especially in the foreground, prancing bow and arrows in hand, with regular severe features and an immense curled wavy beard, flowing down his breast. Falk's face reminded me of that centaur. Besides, he was a composite creature. Not a man-horse, it is true, but a man-boat. He lived on board his tug, which was always dashing up and down the river from early morn till dewy eve. In the last rays of the setting sun,* you could pick out far away down the reach his beard borne high up on the white structure, foaming up-stream to anchor for the night. There was the white-clad man's body, and the rich brown patch of the hair, and nothing below the waist but the 'thwart-ship white lines of the bridge-screens, that led the eye to the sharp white lines of the bows cleaving the muddy water of the river.

Separated from his boat, to me at least he seemed incomplete. The tug herself without his head and torso on the bridge looked mutilated as it were. But he left her very seldom. All the time I remained in harbour I saw him only twice on shore. On the first occasion it was at my charterers, where he came in misanthropically to get paid for towing out a French barque the day before. The second time I could hardly believe my eyes, for I beheld him reclining under his beard in a cane-bottomed chair in the billiard-room of Schomberg's hotel.

It was very funny to see Schomberg ignoring him pointedly. The artificiality of it contrasted strongly with Falk's natural unconcern. The big Alsatian talked loudly with his other customers, going from one little table to the other, and passing Falk's place of repose with his eyes fixed straight ahead. Falk sat there with an untouched glass at his elbow. He must have known by sight and name every white man in the room, but he never addressed a word to anybody. He acknowledged my presence by a drop of his eyelids, and that was all. Sprawling there in the chair, he would, now and again, draw the palms of both his hands down his face, giving at the same time a slight, almost imperceptible, shudder.

It was a habit he had, and of course I was perfectly familiar with it, since you could not remain an hour in his company without being made to wonder at such a movement breaking some long period of stillness. It was a passionate and inexplicable gesture. He used to make it at all sorts of times; as likely as not after he had been listening to little Lena's chatter about the suffering doll, for instance. The Hermann children always besieged him about his legs closely, though, in a gentle way, he shrank from them a little. He seemed, however, to feel a great affection for the whole family. For Hermann himself especially. He sought his company. In this case, for instance, he must have been waiting for him, because as soon as he appeared Falk rose hastily, and they went out together. Then Schomberg expounded in my hearing to three or four people his theory that Falk was after Captain Hermann's niece, and asserted confidently that nothing would come of it. It was the same last year when Captain Hermann was loading here, he said.

Naturally, I did not believe Schomberg, but I own that for a time I observed closely what went on. All I discovered was some impatience on Hermann's part. At the sight of Falk, stepping over the gangway, the excellent man would begin to mumble and chew between his teeth something that sounded like German swear-words. However, as I've said, I'm not familiar with the language, and Hermann's soft, round-eyed countenance remained unchanged. Staring stolidly ahead he greeted him with, "Wie geht's," or in English, "How are you?" with a throaty enunciation. The girl would look up for an instant and move her lips slightly: Mrs. Hermann let her hands rest on her lap to talk volubly to him for a minute or so in her pleasant voice before she went on with her sewing again. Falk would throw himself into a chair, stretch his big legs, as like as not draw his hands down his face passionately. As to myself, he was not pointedly impertinent: it was rather as though he could not be bothered with such trifles as my existence; and the truth is that being a monopolist he was under no necessity to be amiable. He was sure to get his own extortionate terms out of me for towage whether he frowned or smiled. As a matter of fact, he did neither: but before many days elapsed he managed to astonish me not a little and to set Schomberg's tongue clacking more than ever.

It came about in this way. There was a shallow bar at the mouth of the river which ought to have been kept down, but the authorities of the State were piously busy gilding afresh the great Buddhist Pagoda* just then, and I suppose had no money to spare for dredging operations. I don't know how it may be now, but at the time I speak of that sandbank was a great nuisance to the shipping. One of its consequences was that vessels of a certain draught of water, like Hermann's or mine, could not complete their loading in the river. After taking in as much as possible of their cargo, they had to go outside to fill up. The whole procedure was an unmitigated bore. When you thought you had as much on board as your ship could carry safely over the bar, you went and gave notice to your agents. They, in their turn, notified Falk that so-and-so was ready to go out. Then Falk (ostensibly when it fitted in with his other work, but, if the truth were known, simply when his arbitrary spirit moved him), after ascertaining carefully in the office that there was enough money to meet his bill, would come along unsympathetically, glaring at you with his yellow eyes from the bridge, and would drag you out dishevelled as to rigging, lumbered as to the decks, with unfeeling haste, as if to execution. And he would force you too to take the end of his own wire hawser, for the use of which there was of course an extra charge. To your shouted remonstrances against this extortion this towering trunk with one hand on the engine-room telegraph only shook its bearded head above the splash, the racket and the clouds of smoke, in which the tug, backing and filling in the smother of churning paddle-wheels, behaved like a ferocious and impatient creature. He had her manned by the cheekiest gang of lascars I ever did see, whom he allowed to bawl at you insolently, and, once fast, he plucked you out of your berth as if he did not care what he smashed. Eighteen miles down the river you had to go behind him, and then three more along the coast to where a group of uninhabited rocky islets enclosed a sheltered anchorage. There you would have to lie at single anchor with your naked spars showing to seaward over these barren fragments of land scattered upon a very intensely blue sea. There was nothing to look at besides but a bare coast, the muddy edge of the brown plain with the sinuosities of the river you had left, traced in dull green, and the Great Pagoda uprising lonely and massive with shining curves and pinnacles like the gorgeous and stony efflorescence of tropical rocks. You had nothing to do but to wait fretfully for the balance of your cargo, which was sent out of the river with the greatest irregularity. And it was open to you to console yourself with the thought that, after all, this stage of bother meant that your departure from these shores was indeed approaching at last.

We both had to go through that stage, Hermann and I, and there was a sort of tacit emulation between the ships as to which should be ready first. We kept on neck and neck almost to the finish, when I won the race by going personally to give notice in the forenoon; whereas Hermann, who was very slow in making up his mind to go ashore, did not get to the agents' office till late in the day. They told him there that my ship was first on turn for next morning, and I believe he told them he was in no hurry. It suited him better to go the day after.

That evening, on board the *Diana*, he sat with his plump knees well apart, staring and puffing at the curved mouthpiece of his pipe. Presently he spoke with some impatience to his niece about putting the children to bed. Mrs. Hermann, who was talking to Falk, stopped short and looked at her husband uneasily, but the girl got up at once and drove the children before her into the cabin. In a little while Mrs. Hermann had to leave us to quell what, from the sounds inside, must have been a dangerous mutiny. At this Hermann grumbled to himself. For half an hour longer Falk left alone with us fidgeted on his chair, sighed lightly, then at last, after drawing his hands down his face, got up, and as if renouncing the hope of making himself understood (he hadn't opened his mouth once) he said in English: "Well . . . Good night, Captain Hermann." He stopped for a moment before my chair and looked down fixedly; I may even say he glared: and he went so far as to make a deep noise in his throat. There was in all this something so marked that for the first time in our limited intercourse of nods and grunts he excited in me something like interest. But next moment he disappointed me—for he strode away hastily without a nod even.

His manner was usually odd it is true, and I certainly did not pay much attention to it; but that sort of obscure intention, which seemed to lurk in his nonchalance like a wary old carp in a pond, had never before come so near the surface. He had distinctly aroused my expectations. I would have been unable to say what it was I expected, but at all events I did not expect the absurd developments he sprung upon me no later than the break of the very next day.

I remember only that there was, on that evening, enough point in his behaviour to make me, after he had fled, wonder audibly what he might mean.* To this Hermann, crossing his legs with a swing and settling himself viciously away from me in his chair, said: "That fellow don't know himself what he means."

There might have been some insight in such a remark. I said nothing, and, still averted, he added: "When I was here last year he was just the same." An eruption of tobacco smoke enveloped his head as if his temper had exploded like gunpowder.

I had half a mind to ask him point blank whether he, at least, didn't know why Falk, a notoriously unsociable man, had taken to visiting his ship with such assiduity. After all, I reflected suddenly, it was a most remarkable thing. I wonder now what Hermann would have said. As it turned out he didn't let me ask. Forgetting all about Falk apparently, he started a monologue on his plans for the future: the selling of the ship, the going home; and falling into a reflective and calculating mood he mumbled between regular jets of smoke about the expense. The necessity of disbursing passage-money for all his tribe seemed to disturb him in a manner that was the more striking because otherwise he gave no signs of a miserly disposition. And yet he fussed over the prospect of that voyage home in a mail-boat like a sedentary grocer who has made up his mind to see the world. He was racially thrifty I suppose, and for him there must have been a great novelty in finding himself obliged to pay for travelling — for sea travelling which was the normal state of life for the family — from the very cradle for most of them. I could see he grudged prospectively every single shilling which must be spent so absurdly. It was rather funny. He would become doleful over it, and then again, with a fretful sigh, he would suppose there was nothing for it now but to take three second-class tickets — and there were the four children to pay for besides. A lot of money that to spend at once. A big lot of money.

I sat with him listening (not for the first time) to these heart-searchings till I grew thoroughly sleepy, and then I left him and turned in on board my ship. At daylight I was awakened by a yelping of shrill voices, accompanied by a great commotion in the water, and the short, bullying blasts of a steam-whistle. Falk with his tug had come for me.

I began to dress. It was remarkable that the answering noise on board my ship together with the patter of feet above my head ceased suddenly. But I heard more remote guttural cries which seemed to express surprise and annoyance. Then the voice of my mate reached me howling expostulations to somebody at a distance. Other voices joined, apparently indignant; a chorus of something that sounded like abuse replied. Now and then the steam-whistle screeched.

Altogether that unnecessary uproar was distracting, but down there in my cabin I took it calmly. In another moment, I thought, I should be going down that wretched river, and in another week at the most I should be totally quit of the odious place and all the odious people in it.

Greatly cheered by the idea, I seized the hair-brushes and looking at myself in the glass began to use them. Suddenly a hush fell upon the noise outside, and I heard (the ports of my cabin were thrown open)—I heard a deep calm voice, not on board my ship, however, hailing resolutely in English, but with a strong foreign twang, "Go ahead!"

There may be tides in the affairs of men which taken at the flood . . . and so on.* Personally I am still on the look-out for that important turn. I am, however, afraid that most of us are fated to flounder for ever in the dead water of a pool whose shores are arid indeed. But I know that there are often in men's affairs unexpectedly—even irrationally—illuminating moments when an otherwise insignificant sound, perhaps only some perfectly commonplace gesture, suffices to reveal to us all the unreason, all the fatuous unreason, of our complacency. "Go ahead" are not particularly striking words even when pronounced with a foreign accent; yet they petrified me in the very act of smiling at myself in the glass. And then, refusing to believe my ears, but already boiling with indignation, I ran out of the cabin and up on deck.

It was incredibly true. It was perfectly true. I had no eyes for anything but the *Diana*. It was she that was being taken away. She was already out of her berth and shooting athwart the river. "The way this loonatic plucked that ship out is a caution," said the awed voice of my mate close to my ear. "Hey! Hallo! Falk! Hermann! What's this infernal trick?" I yelled in a fury.

Nobody heard me. Falk certainly could not hear me. His tug was turning at full speed away under the other bank. The wire hawser between her and the *Diana*, stretched as taut as a harpstring, vibrated alarmingly.

The high black craft careened over to the awful strain. A loud crack came out of her, followed by the tearing and splintering of wood. "There!" said the awed voice in my ear. "He's carried away their towing chock." And then, with enthusiasm, "Oh! Look! Look, sir! Look at them Dutchmen skipping out of the way on the forecastle. I hope to goodness he'll break a few of their shins before he's done with 'em."

I yelled my vain protests. The rays of the rising sun coursing level along the plain warmed my back, but I was hot enough with rage. I could not have believed that a simple towing operation could suggest so plainly the idea of abduction, of rape. Falk was simply running off with the *Diana*.

The white tug careered out into the middle of the river. The red floats of her paddle-wheels revolving with mad rapidity tore up the whole reach into foam. The *Diana* in mid-stream waltzed round with as much grace as an old barn, and flew after her ravisher. Through the ragged fog of smoke driving headlong upon the water I had a glimpse of Falk's square motionless shoulders under a white hat as big as a cart-wheel, of his red face, his yellow staring eyes, his great beard. Instead of keeping a look-out ahead, he was deliberately turning his back on the river to glare at his tow. The tall heavy craft, never so used before in her life, seemed to have lost her senses; she took a wild sheer against her helm, and for a moment came straight at us, menacing and clumsy, like a runaway mountain. She piled up a streaming, hissing, boiling wave half-way up her blunt stem, my crew let out one great howl,—and then we held our breaths. It was a near thing. But Falk had her! He had her in his clutch. I fancied I could hear the steel hawser ping as it surged across the *Diana*'s forecastle, with the hands on board of her bolting away from it in all directions. It was a near thing. Hermann, with his hair rumpled, in a snuffy flannel shirt and a pair of mustard-coloured trousers, had rushed to help with the wheel. I saw his terrified round face; I saw his very teeth uncovered by a sort of ghastly fixed grin; and in a great leaping tumult of water between the two ships the *Diana* whisked past so close that I could have flung a hair-brush at his head, for, it seems, I had kept them in my hands all the time. Meanwhile Mrs. Hermann sat placidly on the skylight, with a woollen shawl on her shoulders. The excellent woman in response to my indignant gesticulations fluttered a handkerchief, nodding and smiling in the kindest way imaginable. The boys, only half-dressed, were jumping about the poop in great glee, displaying their gaudy braces; and Lena in a short scarlet petticoat, with peaked elbows and thin bare arms, nursed the rag-doll with devotion. The whole family passed before my sight as if dragged across a scene of unparalleled violence. The last I saw was Hermann's niece with the baby Hermann in her arms standing apart from the others. Magnificent in her close-fitting print frock, she displayed something so commanding in the manifest perfection of her figure that the sun seemed to be rising for her alone. The flood of light brought out the opulence of her form and the vigour of her youth in a glorifying way. She went by perfectly motionless and as if lost in meditation; only the hem of her skirt stirred in the draught; the sun rays broke on her sleek tawny hair; that bald-headed ruffian, Nicholas, was whacking her on the shoulder. I saw his tiny fat arm rise and fall in a workmanlike manner. And then the four cottage windows of the *Diana* came into view retreating swiftly down the river. The sashes were up, and one of the white calico curtains fluttered straight out like a streamer above the agitated water of the wake.

To be thus tricked out of one's turn was an unheard-of occurrence. In my agent's office, where I went to complain at once, they protested with apologies they couldn't understand how the mistake arose: but Schomberg, when I dropped in later to get some tiffin, though surprised to see me, was perfectly ready with an explanation. I found him seated at the end of a long narrow table, facing his wife—a scraggy little woman, with long ringlets and a blue tooth, who smiled abroad stupidly and looked frightened when you spoke to her.* Between them a waggling punkah fanned twenty vacant canebottomed chairs and two rows of shiny plates. Three Chinamen in white jackets loafed with napkins in their hands around that desolation. Schomberg's pet *table-d'hôte* was not much of a success that day. He was feeding himself furiously and seemed to overflow with bitterness.

He began by ordering in a brutal voice the chops to be brought back for me, and turning in his chair: "Mistake they told you? Not a bit of it! Don't you believe it for a moment, captain! Falk isn't a man to make mistakes unless on purpose." His firm conviction was that Falk had been trying all along to curry favour on the cheap with Hermann. "On the cheap—mind you! It doesn't cost him a cent to put that insult upon you, and Captain Hermann gets in a day ahead of your ship. Time's money! Eh? You are very friendly with Captain Hermann I believe, but a man is bound to be pleased at any little advantage he may get. Captain Hermann is a good business man, and there's no such thing as a friend in business. Is there?" He leaned forward and began to cast stealthy glances as usual. "But Falk is, and always was, a miserable fellow. I would despise him."

I muttered, grumpily, that I had no particular respect for Falk.

"I would despise him," he insisted, with an appearance of anxiety which would have amused me if I had not been fathoms deep in discontent. To a young man fairly conscientious and as well-meaning as only the young can be, the current ill-usage of life comes with a peculiar cruelty. Youth that is fresh enough to believe in guilt, in innocence, and in itself, will always doubt whether it have not perchance deserved its fate. Sombre of mind and without appetite, I struggled with the chop while Mrs. Schomberg sat with her everlasting stupid grin and Schomberg's talk gathered way like a slide of rubbish.

"Let me tell you. It's all about that girl. I don't know what Captain Hermann expects, but if he asked me I could tell him something about Falk. He's a miserable fellow. That man is a perfect slave. That's what I call him. A slave. Last year I started this *table d'hôte*, and sent cards out—you know. You think he had one meal in the house? Give the thing a trial? Not once. He has got hold now of a Madras cook—a blamed fraud that I hunted out of my cookhouse with a rattan. He was not fit to cook for white men. No, not for the white men's dogs either; but, see, any damned native that can boil a pot of rice is good enough for Mr. Falk. Rice and a little fish he buys for a few cents from the fishing-boats outside is what he lives on. You would hardly credit it—eh? A white man, too. . . ."

He wiped his lips, using the napkin with indignation, and looking at me. It flashed through my mind in the midst of my depression that if all the meat in the town was like these *table-d'hôte* chops,

Falk wasn't so far wrong. I was on the point of saying this, but Schomberg's stare was intimidating. "He's a vegetarian, perhaps," I murmured instead.

"He's a miser. A miserable miser," affirmed the hotel-keeper with great force. "The meat here is not so good as at home—of course. And dear too. But look at me. I only charge a dollar for the tiffin, and one dollar and fifty cents for the dinner. Show me anything cheaper. Why am I doing it? There's little profit in this game. Falk wouldn't look at it. I do it for the sake of a lot of young white fellows here that hadn't a place where they could get a decent meal and eat it decently in good company. There's first-rate company always at my table."

The convinced way he surveyed the empty chairs made me feel as if I had intruded upon a tiffin of ghostly Presences.

"A white man should eat like a white man, dash it all," he burst out impetuously. "Ought to eat meat, must eat meat. I manage to get meat for my patrons all the year round. Don't I? I am not catering for a dam' lot of coolies: Have another chop, captain. . . . No? You, boy—take away!"

He threw himself back and waited grimly for the curry. The half-closed jalousies darkened the room pervaded by the smell of fresh whitewash: a swarm of flies buzzed and settled in turns, and poor Mrs. Schomberg's smile seemed to express the quintessence of all the imbecility that had ever spoken, had ever breathed, had ever been fed on infamous buffalo meat within these bare walls. Schomberg did not open his lips till he was ready to thrust therein a spoonful of greasy rice. He rolled his eyes ridiculously before he swallowed the hot stuff, and only then broke out afresh.

"It is the most degrading thing. They take the dish up to the wheelhouse for him with a cover on it, and he shuts both the doors before he begins to eat. Fact! Must be ashamed of himself. Ask the engineer. He can't do without an engineer—don't you see—and as no respectable man can be expected to put up with such a table, he allows them fifteen dollars a month extra mess money. I assure you it is so! You just ask Mr. Ferdinand da Costa. That's the engineer he has now. You may have seen him about my place, a delicate dark young man, with very fine eyes and a little moustache. He arrived here a year ago from Calcutta. Between you and me, I guess the money-lenders there must have been after him. He rushes here for a meal every chance he can get, for just please tell me what satisfaction is that for a well-educated young fellow to feed all alone in his cabin—like a wild beast? That's what Falk expects his engineers to put up with for fifteen dollars extra. And the rows on board every time a little smell of cooking gets about the deck! You wouldn't believe! The other day da Costa got the cook to fry a steak for him—a turtle steak it was too, not beef at all—and the fat caught or something. Young da Costa himself was telling me of it here in this room. 'Mr. Schomberg'—says he—'if I had let a cylinder cover blow off through the skylight by my negligence Captain Falk couldn't have been more savage. He frightened the cook so that he won't put anything on the fire for me now.' Poor da Costa had tears in his eyes. Only try to put yourself in his place, captain: a sensitive, gentlemanly young fellow. Is he expected to eat his food raw? But that's your Falk all over. Ask any one you like. I suppose the fifteen dollars extra he has to give keep on rankling—in there."

And Schomberg tapped his manly breast. I sat half stunned by his irrelevant babble. Suddenly he gripped my forearm in an impressive and cautious manner, as if to lead me into a very cavern of confidence.

"It's nothing but enviousness," he said in a lowered tone, which had a stimulating effect upon my wearied hearing. "I don't suppose there is one person in this town that he isn't envious of. I tell you he's dangerous. Even I myself am not safe from him. I know for certain he tried to poison . . . ."

"Oh, come now," I cried, revolted.

"But I know for certain. The people themselves came and told me of it. He went about saying everywhere I was a worse pest to this town than the cholera. He had been talking against me ever since I opened this hotel. And he poisoned Captain Hermann's mind too. Last time the *Diana* was loading here Captain Hermann used to come in every day for a drink or a cigar. This time he hasn't been here twice in a week. How do you account for that?"

He squeezed my arm till he extorted from me some sort of mumble.

"He makes ten times the money I do. I've another hotel to fight against, and there is no other tug on the river. I am not in his way, am I? He wouldn't be fit to run an hotel if he tried. But that's just his nature. He can't bear to think I am making a living. I only hope it makes him properly wretched. He's like that in everything. He would like to keep a decent table well enough. But no—for the sake of a few cents. Can't do it. It's too much for him. That's what I call being a slave to it. But he's mean enough to kick up a row when his nose gets tickled a bit. See that? That just paints him. Miserly and envious. You can't account for it any other way. Can you? I have been studying him these three years."

He was anxious I should assent to his theory. And indeed on thinking it over it would have been plausible enough if there hadn't been always the essential falseness of irresponsibility in Schomberg's chatter. However, I was not disposed to investigate the psychology of Falk. I was engaged just then in eating despondently a piece of stale Dutch cheese, being too much crushed to care what I swallowed myself, let alone bothering my head about Falk's ideas of gastronomy. I could expect from their study no clue to his conduct in matters of business, which seemed to me totally unrestrained by morality or even by the commonest sort of decency. How insignificant and contemptible I must appear, for the fellow to dare treat me like this—I reflected suddenly, writhing in silent agony. And I consigned Falk and all his peculiarities to the devil with so much mental fervour as to forget Schomberg's existence, till he grabbed my arm urgently. "Well, you may think and think till every hair of your head falls off, captain; but you can't explain it in any other way."

For the sake of peace and quietness I admitted hurriedly that I couldn't; persuaded that now he would leave off. But the only result was to make his moist face shine with the pride of cunning. He removed his hand for a moment to scare a black mass of flies off the sugar-basin, and caught hold of my arm again.

"To be sure. And in the same way everybody is aware he would like to get married. Only he can't. Let me quote you an instance. Well, two years ago a Miss Vanlo, a very ladylike girl, came from home to keep house for her brother, Fred, who had an engineering shop for small repairs by the water-side. Suddenly Falk takes to going up to their bungalow after dinner and sitting for hours in the verandah saying nothing. The poor girl couldn't tell for the life of her what to do with such a man, so she would keep on playing the piano and singing to him evening after evening till she was ready to drop. And it wasn't as if she had been a strong young woman either. She was thirty, and the climate had been playing the deuce with her. Then—don't you know—Fred had to sit up with them for propriety, and during whole weeks on end never got a single chance to get to bed before midnight. That was not pleasant for a tired man—was it? And besides Fred had worries then because his shop didn't pay and he was dropping money fast. He just longed to get away from here and try his luck somewhere else, but for the sake of his sister he hung on and on till he ran himself into debt over his ears—I can tell you. I, myself, could show a handful of his chits for meals and drinks in my drawer. I could never find out tho' where he found all the money at last. Can't be but he must have got something out of that brother of his, a coal merchant in Port Said. Anyhow he paid everybody before he left, but the girl nearly broke her heart. Disappointment, of course, and at her age, don't you know. . . . Mrs. Schomberg here was very friendly with her, and she could tell you. Awful despair. Fainting fits. It was a scandal. A notorious scandal. To that extent that old Mr. Siegers—not your present charterer, but Mr. Siegers the father, the old gentleman who retired from business on a fortune and got buried at sea going home, *he* had to interview Falk in his private office. He was a man who could speak like a Dutch Uncle, and besides, Messrs. Siegers had been helping Falk with a good bit of money from the start. In fact you may say they made him as far as that goes. It so happened that just at the time he turned up here, their firm was chartering a lot of sailing-ships every year, and it suited their business that there should be good towing facilities on the river. See? . . . Well—there's always an ear at the keyhole—isn't there? In fact," he lowered his tone confidentially, "in this case it was a good friend of mine; a man you can see here any evening; only they conversed rather low. Anyhow my friend's certain that Falk was trying to make all sorts of excuses, and old Mr. Siegers was coughing a lot. And yet Falk wanted all the time to be married too. Why! It's notorious the man has been longing for years to make a home for himself. Only he can't face the expense. When it comes to putting his hand in his pocket—it chokes him off. That's the truth and no other. I've always said so, and everybody agrees with me by this time. What do you think of that—eh?"

He appealed confidently to my indignation, but having a mind to annoy him I remarked that "it seemed to me very pitiful—if true."

He bounced in his chair as if I had run a pin into him. I don't know what he might have said, only at that moment we heard through the half open door of the billiard-room the footsteps of two men entering from the verandah, a murmur of two voices; at the sharp tapping of a coin on a table Mrs. Schomberg half rose irresolutely. "Sit still," he hissed at her, and then, in an hospitable, jovial tone, contrasting amazingly with the angry glance that had made his wife sink in her chair, he cried very loud: "Tiffin still going on in here, gentlemen."

There was no answer, but the voices dropped suddenly. The head Chinaman went out. We heard the clink of ice in the glasses, pouring sounds, the shuffling of feet, the scraping of chairs. Schomberg, after wondering in a low mutter who the devil could be there at this time of the day, got up napkin in hand to peep through the doorway cautiously. He retreated rapidly on tip-toe, and whispering behind his hand informed me that it was Falk, Falk himself who was in there, and, what's more, he had Captain Hermann with him.

The return of the tug from the outer roads was unexpected but possible, for Falk had taken away the *Diana* at half-past five, and it was now two o'clock. Schomberg wished me to observe that neither of these men would spend a dollar on a tiffin, which they must have wanted. But by the time I was ready to leave the dining-room Falk had gone. I heard the last of his big boots on the planks of the verandah. Hermann was sitting quite alone in the large, wooden room with the two lifeless billiard tables shrouded in striped covers, mopping his face diligently. He wore his best go-ashore clothes, a stiff collar, black coat, large white waistcoat, grey trousers. A white cotton sunshade with a cane handle reposed between his legs, his side whiskers were neatly brushed, his chin had been freshly shaved; and he only distantly resembled the dishevelled and terrified man in a snuffy night shirt and ignoble old trousers I had seen in the morning hanging on to the wheel of the *Diana*.

He gave a start at my entrance, and addressed me at once in some confusion, but with genuine eagerness. He was anxious to make it clear he had nothing to do with what he called the "tam' pizness" of the morning. It was most inconvenient. He had reckoned upon another day up in town to settle his bills and sign certain papers. There were also some few stores to come, and sundry pieces of "my ironwork," as he called it quaintly, landed for repairs, had been left behind. Now he would have to hire a native boat to take all this out to the ship. It would cost five or six dollars perhaps. He had had no warning from Falk. Nothing. . . . . He hit the table with his dumpy fist. . . . Der verfluchte Kerl came in the morning like a "tam' ropper," making a great noise, and took him away. His mate was not prepared, his ship was moored fast—he protested it was shameful to come upon a man in that way. Shameful! Yet such was the power Falk had on the river that when I suggested in a chilling tone that he might have simply refused to have his ship moved, Hermann was quite startled at the idea. I never realised so well before that this is an age of steam. The exclusive possession of a marine boiler had given Falk the whip hand of us all. Hermann recovering, put it to me appealingly that I knew very well how unsafe it was to contradict that fellow. At this I only smiled distantly.

"Der Kerl!" he cried. He was sorry he had not refused. He was indeed. The damage! The damage! What for all that damage! There was no occasion for damage. Did I know how much damage he had done? It gave me a certain satisfaction to tell him that I had heard his old waggon of a ship crack fore and aft as she went by. "You passed close enough to me," I added significantly.

He threw both his hands up to heaven at the recollection. One of them grasped by the middle the white parasol, and he resembled curiously a caricature of a shopkeeping citizen in one of his own German comic papers. "Ach! That was dangerous," he cried. I was amused. But directly he added with an appearance of simplicity, "The side of your iron ship would have been crushed in like—like this matchbox."

"Would it?" I growled, much less amused now; but by the time I had decided that this remark was not meant for a dig at me he had worked himself into a high state of resentfulness against Falk. The inconvenience, the damage, the expense! Gottverdamm! Devil take the fellow. Behind the bar Schomberg, with a cigar in his teeth, pretended to be writing with a pencil on a large sheet of paper; and as Hermann's excitement increased it made me comfortingly aware of my own calmness and superiority. But it occurred to me while I listened to his revilings, that after all the good man had come up in the tug. There perhaps—since he must come to town—he had no option. But evidently he had had a drink with Falk, either accepted or offered. How was that? So I checked him by saying loftily that I hoped he would make Falk pay for every penny of the damage.

"That's it! That's it! Go for him," called out Schomberg from the bar, flinging his pencil down and rubbing his hands.

We ignored his noise. But Hermann's excitement suddenly went off the boil as when you remove a saucepan from the fire. I urged on his consideration that he had done now with Falk and Falk's confounded tug. He, Hermann, would not, perhaps, turn up again in this part of the world for years to come, since he was going to sell the *Diana* at the end of this very trip ("Go home passenger in a mail boat," he murmured mechanically). He was therefore safe from Falk's malice. All he had to do was to race off to his consignees and stop payment of the towage bill before Falk had the time to get in and lift the money.

Nothing could have been less in the spirit of my advice than the thoughtful way in which he set about to make his parasol stay propped against the edge of the table.

While I watched his concentrated efforts with astonishment he threw at me one or two perplexed, half-shy glances. Then he sat down. "That's all very well," he said reflectively.

It cannot be doubted that the man had been thrown off his balance by being hauled out of the harbour against his wish. His stolidity had been profoundly stirred, else he would never have made up his mind to ask me unexpectedly whether I had not remarked that Falk had been casting eyes upon his niece. "No more than myself," I answered with literal truth. The girl was of the sort one necessarily casts eyes at in a sense. She made no noise, but she filled most satisfactorily a good bit of space.

"But you, captain, are not the same kind of man," observed Hermann.

I was not, I am happy to say, in a position to deny this. "What about the lady?" I could not help asking. At this he gazed for a time into my face, earnestly, and made as if to change the subject. I heard him beginning to mutter something unexpected, about his children growing old enough to require schooling. He would have to leave them ashore with their grandmother when he took up that new command he expected to get in Germany.

This constant harping on his domestic arrangements was funny. I suppose it must have been like the prospect of a complete alteration in his life. An epoch. He was going, too, to part with the *Diana*! He had served in her for years. He had inherited her. From an uncle, if I remember rightly. And the future loomed big before him, occupying his thought exclusively with all its aspects as on the eve of a venturesome enterprise. He sat there frowning and biting his lip, and suddenly he began to fume and fret.

I discovered to my momentary amusement that he seemed to imagine I could, should or ought, have caused Falk in some way to pronounce himself. Such a hope was incomprehensible, but funny. Then the contact with all this foolishness irritated me. I said crossly that I had seen no symptoms, but if there were any—since he, Hermann, was so sure—then it was still worse. What pleasure Falk found in humbugging people in just that way I couldn't say. It was, however, my solemn duty to warn him. It had lately, I said, come to my knowledge that there was a man (not a very long time ago either) who had been taken in just like this.

All this passed in undertones, and at this point Schomberg, exasperated at our secrecy, went out of the room slamming the door with a crash that positively lifted us in our chairs. This, or else what I had said, huffed my Hermann. He supposed, with a contemptuous toss of his head towards the door which trembled yet, that I had got hold of some of that man's silly tales. It looked, indeed, as though his mind had been thoroughly poisoned against Schomberg. "His tales were—they were," he repeated, seeking for the word— "trash." They were trash, he reiterated, and moreover I was young yet . . .

This horrid aspersion (I regret I am no longer exposed to that sort of insult) made me huffy too. I felt ready in my own mind to back up every assertion of Schomberg's and on any subject. In a moment, devil only knows why, Hermann and I were looking at each other most inimically. He caught up his hat without more ado and I gave myself the pleasure of calling after him:

"Take my advice and make Falk pay for breaking up your ship. You aren't likely to get anything else out of him."

When I got on board my ship later on, the old mate, who was very full of the events of the morning, remarked:

"I saw the tug coming back from the outer roads just before two P.M." (He never by any chance used the words morning or afternoon. Always P.M. or A.M., log-book style.) "Smart work that. Man's always in a state of hurry. He's a regular chucker-out, ain't he, sir? There's a few pubs I know of in the East-end of London that would be all the better for one of his sort around the bar." He chuckled at his joke. "A regular chucker-out. Now he has fired out that Dutchman head over heels, I suppose our turn's coming tomorrow morning."

We were all on deck at break of day (even the sick—poor devils—had crawled out) ready to cast off in the twinkling of an eye. Nothing came. Falk did not come. At last, when I began to think that probably something had gone wrong in his engine-room, we perceived the tug going by, full pelt, down the river, as if we hadn't existed. For a moment I entertained the wild notion that he was going to turn round in the next reach. Afterwards I watched his smoke appear above the plain, now here, now there, according to the windings of the river. It disappeared. Then without a word I went down to breakfast. I just simply went down to breakfast.

Not one of us uttered a sound till the mate, after imbibing—by means of suction out of a saucer—his second cup of tea, exclaimed: "Where the devil is the man gone to?"

"Courting!" I shouted, with such a fiendish laugh that the old chap didn't venture to open his lips any more.

I started to the office perfectly calm. Calm with excessive rage. Evidently they knew all about it already, and they treated me to a show of consternation. The manager, a soft-footed, immensely obese man, breathing short, got up to meet me, while all round the room the young clerks, bending over the papers on their desks, cast upward glances in my direction. The fat man, without waiting for my complaint, wheezing heavily and in a tone as if he himself were incredulous, conveyed to me the news that Falk—Captain Falk—had declined—had absolutely declined—to tow my ship—to have anything to do with my ship—this day or any other day. Never!

I did my best to preserve a cool appearance, but, all the same, I must have shown how much taken aback I was. We were talking in the middle of the room. Suddenly behind my back some ass blew his nose with great force, and at the same time another quill-driver jumped up and went out on the landing hastily. It occurred to me I was cutting a foolish figure there. I demanded angrily to see the principal in his private room.

The skin of Mr. Siegers' head showed dead white between the iron-grey streaks of hair lying plastered cross-wise from ear to ear over the top of his skull in the manner of a bandage. His narrow sunken face was of an uniform and permanent terra-cotta colour, like a piece of pottery. He was sickly, thin, and short, with wrists like a boy of ten. But from that debile body there issued a bullying voice, tremendously loud, harsh and resonant, as if produced by some powerful mechanical contrivance in the nature of a fog-horn. I do not know what he did with it in the private life of his home, but in the larger sphere of business it presented the advantage of over-coming arguments without the slightest mental effort, by the mere volume of sound. We had had several passages of arms. It took me all I knew to guard the interests of my owners—whom, *nota bene*, I had never seen—while Siegers (who had made their acquaintance some years before, during a business tour in Australia) pretended to the knowledge of their innermost minds, and, in the character of "our very good friends," threw them perpetually at my head.

He looked at me with a jaundiced eye (there was no love lost between us), and declared at once that it was strange, very strange. His pronunciation of English was so extravagant that I can't even attempt to reproduce it. For instance, he said "Fferie strantch." Combined with the bellowing intonation it made the language of one's childhood sound weirdly startling, and even if considered purely as a kind of unmeaning noise it filled you with astonishment at first. "They had," he continued, "been acquainted with Captain Falk for very many years, and never had any reason. . . ."

"That's why I come to you, of course," I interrupted. "I've the right to know the meaning of this infernal nonsense." In the half-light of the room, which was greenish, because of the tree-tops screening the window, I saw him writhe his meagre shoulders. It came into my head, as disconnected ideas will come at all sorts of times into one's head, that this, most likely, was the very room where, if the tale were true, Falk had been lectured by Mr. Siegers, the father. Mr. Siegers' (the son's) overwhelming voice, in brassy blasts, as though he had been trying to articulate his words through a trombone, was expressing his great regret at conduct characterised by a very marked want of discretion . . . As I lived I was being lectured too! His deafening gibberish was difficult to follow, but it was *my* conduct—mine!—that . . . Damn! I wasn't going to stand this.

"What on earth are you driving at?" I asked in a passion. I put my hat on my head (he never offered a seat to anybody), and as he seemed for the moment struck dumb by my irreverence, I turned my back on him and marched out. His vocal arrangements blared after me a few threats of coming down on the ship for the demurrage of the lighters, and all the other expenses consequent upon the delays arising from my frivolity.

Once outside in the sunshine my head swam. It was no longer a question of mere delay. I perceived myself involved in hopeless and humiliating absurdities that were leading me to something very like a disaster. "Let us be calm," I muttered to myself, and ran into the shade of a leprous wall. From that short side-street I could see the broad main thoroughfare, ruinous and gay, running away, away between stretches of decaying masonry, bamboo fences, ranges of arcades of brick and plaster, hovels of lath and mud, lofty temple gates of carved timber, huts of rotten mats—an immensely wide thoroughfare, loosely packed as far as the eye could reach with a barefooted and brown multitude paddling ankle deep in the dust. For a moment I felt myself about to go out of my mind with worry and desperation.

Some allowance must be made for the feelings of a young man new to responsibility. I thought of my crew. Half of them were ill, and I really began to think that some of them would end by dying on board if I couldn't get them out to sea soon. Obviously I should have to take my ship down the river, either working under canvas or dredging with the anchor down; operations which, in common with many modern sailors, I only knew theoretically. And I almost shrank from undertaking them shorthanded and without local knowledge of the river bed, which is so necessary for the confident handling of the ship. There were no pilots, no beacons, no buoys of any sort; but there was a very devil of a current for anybody to see, no end of shoal places, and at least two obviously awkward turns of the channel between me and the sea. But how dangerous these turns were I could not tell. I didn't even know what my ship was capable of! I had never handled her in my life. A misunderstanding between a man and his ship, in a difficult river with no room to make it up, is bound to end in trouble for the man. On the other hand, it must be owned I had not much reason to count upon a general run of good luck. And suppose I had the misfortune to pile her up high and dry on some beastly shoal? That would have been the final undoing of that voyage. It was plain that if Falk refused to tow me out he would also refuse to pull me off. This meant—what? A day lost at the very best; but more likely a whole fortnight of frizzling on some pestilential mudflat, of desperate work, of discharging cargo; more than likely it meant borrowing money at an exorbitant rate of interest—from the Siegers' gang too at that. They were a power in the port. And that elderly seaman of mine, Gambril,* had looked pretty ghastly when I went forward to dose him with quinine that morning. *He* would certainly die—not to speak of two or three others that seemed nearly as bad, and of the rest of them just ready to catch any tropical disease going. Horror, ruin and everlasting remorse. And no help. None. I had fallen amongst a lot of unfriendly lunatics!

At any rate, if I must take my ship down myself it was my duty to procure if possible some local knowledge. But that was not easy. The only person I could think of for that service was a certain Johnson, formerly captain of a country ship, but now spliced to a country wife and gone utterly to the bad. I had only heard of him in the vaguest way, as living concealed in the thick of two hundred thousand natives, and only emerging into the light of day for the purpose of hunting up some brandy. I had a notion that if I could lay my hands on him I would sober him on board my ship and use him for a pilot. Better than nothing. Once a sailor always a sailor—and he had known the river for years. But in our Consulate (where I arrived dripping after a sharp walk) they could tell me nothing. The excellent young men on the staff, though willing to help me, belonged to a sphere of the white colony for which that sort of Johnson does not exist. Their suggestion was that I should hunt the man up myself with the help of the Consulate's constable—an ex-sergeant-major of a regiment of Hussars.

This man, whose usual duty apparently consisted in sitting behind a little table in an outer room of Consular offices, when ordered to assist me in my search for Johnson displayed lots of energy and a marvellous amount of local knowledge of a sort. But he did not conceal an immense and sceptical contempt for the whole business. We explored together on that afternoon an infinity of infamous grog shops, gambling dens, opium dens. We walked up narrow lanes where our gharry—a tiny box of a thing on wheels, attached to a jibbing Burmah pony—could by no means have passed. The constable seemed to be on terms of scornful intimacy with Maltese, with Eurasians, with Chinamen, with Klings, and with the sweepers attached to a temple, with whom he talked at the gate. We interviewed also through a grating in a mud wall closing a blind alley an immensely corpulent Italian, who, the ex-sergeant-major remarked to me perfunctorily, had "killed another man last year." Thereupon he addressed him as "Antonio" and "Old Buck," though that bloated carcase, apparently more than half filling the sort of cell wherein it sat, recalled rather a fat pig in a stye. Familiar and never unbending, the sergeant chucked—absolutely chucked—under the chin a horribly wrinkled and shrivelled old hag propped on a stick, who had volunteered some sort of information: and with the same stolid face he kept up an animated conversation with the groups of swathed brown women, who sat smoking cheroots on the doorsteps of a long range of clay hovels. We got out of the gharry and clambered into dwellings airy like packing crates, or descended into places sinister like cellars. We got in, we drove on, we got out again for the sole purpose, as it seemed, of looking behind a heap of rubble. The sun declined; my companion was curt and sardonic in his answers, but it appears we were just missing Johnson all along. At last our conveyance stopped once more with a jerk, and the driver jumping down opened the door.

A black mudhole blocked the lane. A mound of garbage crowned with the dead body of a dog arrested us not. An empty Australian beef tin bounded cheerily before the toe of my boot. Suddenly we clambered through a gap in a prickly fence. . . .

It was a very clean native compound: and the big native woman, with bare brown legs as thick as bedposts, pursuing on all fours a silver dollar that came rolling out from somewhere, was Mrs. Johnson herself. "Your man's at home," said the ex-sergeant, and stepped aside in complete and marked indifference to anything that might follow. Johnson—at home—stood with his back to a native house built on posts and with its walls made of mats. In his left hand he held a banana. Out of the right he dealt another dollar into space. The woman captured this one on the wing, and there and then plumped down on the ground to look at us with greater comfort.

"My man" was sallow of face, grizzled, unshaven, muddy on elbows and back; where the seams of his serge coat yawned you could see his white nakedness. The vestiges of a paper collar encircled his neck. He looked at us with a grave, swaying surprise. "Where do you come from?" he asked. My heart sank. How could I have been stupid enough to waste energy and time for this?

But having already gone so far I approached a little nearer and declared the purpose of my visit. He would have to come at once with me, sleep on board my ship, and tomorrow, with the first of the ebb, he would give me his assistance in getting my ship down to the sea, without steam. A six-hundred-ton barque, drawing nine feet aft. I proposed to give him eighteen dollars for his local knowledge; and all the time I was speaking he kept on considering attentively the various aspects of the banana, holding first one side up to his eye, then the other.

"You've forgotten to apologise," he said at last with extreme precision. "Not being a gentleman yourself, you don't know apparently when you intrude upon a gentleman. I am one. I wish you to understand that when I am in funds I don't work, and now . . ."

I would have pronounced him perfectly sober had he not paused in great concern to try and brush a hole off the knee of his trousers.

"I have money—and friends. Every gentleman has. Perhaps you would like to know my friend? His name is Falk. You could borrow some money. Try to remember. F-A-L-K. Falk." Abruptly his tone changed. "A noble heart," he said muzzily.

"Has Falk been giving you some money?" I asked, appalled by the detailed finish of the dark plot.

"Lent me, my good man, not given me," he corrected suavely. "Met me taking the air last evening, and being as usual anxious to oblige—— Hadn't you better go to the devil out of my compound?"

And upon this, without other warning, he let fly with the banana, which missed my head and took the constable just under the left eye. He rushed at the miserable Johnson, stammering with fury. They fell. . . . But why dwell on the wretchedness, the breathlessness, the degradation, the senselessness, the weariness, the ridicule and humiliation and—and—the perspiration, of these moments? I dragged the ex-hussar off. He was like a wild beast. It seems he had been greatly annoyed at losing his free afternoon on my account. The garden of his bungalow required his personal attention, and at the slight blow of the banana the brute in him had broken loose. We left Johnson on his back still black in the face, but beginning to kick feebly. Meantime, the big woman had remained sitting on the ground, apparently paralysed with extreme terror.

For half an hour we jolted inside our rolling box, side by side, in profound silence. The ex-sergeant was busy staunching the blood of a long scratch on his cheek. "I hope you're satisfied," he said suddenly. "That's what comes of all that tomfool business. If you hadn't quarrelled with that tugboat skipper over some girl or other, all this wouldn't have happened."

"You heard *that* story?" I said.

"Of course I heard. And I shouldn't wonder if the Consul-General himself doesn't come to hear of it. How am I to go before him tomorrow with that thing on my cheek—I want to know. It's *you* who ought to have got this!"

After that, till the gharry stopped and he jumped out without leave-taking, he swore to himself steadily, horribly; muttering great, purposeful, trooper oaths, to which the worst a sailor can do is like the prattle of a child. For my part I had just the strength to crawl into Schomberg's coffee-room, where I wrote at a little table a note to the mate instructing him to get everything ready for dropping down the river next day. I couldn't face my ship. Well! she had a clever sort of skipper and no mistake—poor thing! What a horrid mess! I took my head between my hands. At times the obviousness of my innocence would reduce me to despair. What had I done? If I had done something to bring about the situation I should at least have learned not to do it again. But I felt guiltless to the point of imbecility. The room was empty yet; only Schomberg prowled round me goggle-eyed and with a sort of awed respectful curiosity. No doubt he had set the story going himself; but he was a good-hearted chap, and I am really persuaded he participated in all my troubles. He did what he could for me. He ranged aside the heavy matchstand, set a chair straight, pushed a spittoon slightly with his foot—as you show small attentions to a friend under a great sorrow—sighed, and at last, unable to hold his tongue:

"Well! I warned you, captain. That's what comes of running your head against Mr. Falk. Man'll stick at nothing."

I sat without stirring, and after surveying me with a sort of commiseration in his eyes, he burst out in a hoarse whisper: "But for a fine lump of a girl, she's a fine lump of a girl." He made a loud smacking noise with his thick lips. "The finest lump of a girl that I ever . . ." he was going on with great unction, but for some reason or other broke off. I fancied myself throwing something at his head. "I don't blame you, captain. Hang me if I do," he said with a patronising air.

"Thank you," I said resignedly. It was no use fighting against this false fate. I don't know even if I was sure myself where the truth of the matter began. The conviction that it would end disastrously had been driven into me by all the successive shocks my sense of security had received. I began to ascribe an extraordinary potency to agents in themselves powerless. It was as if Schomberg's baseless gossip had the power to bring about the thing itself or the abstract enmity of Falk could put my ship ashore.

I have already explained how fatal this last would have been. For my further action, my youth, my inexperience, my very real concern for the health of my crew must be my excuse. The action itself, when it came, was purely impulsive. It was set in movement quite undiplomatically and simply by Falk's appearance in the doorway of the coffee-room.

The room was full by then and buzzing with voices. I had been looked at with curiosity by every one, but how am I to describe the sensation produced by the appearance of Falk himself blocking the doorway? The tension of expectation could be measured by the profundity of the silence that fell upon the very click of the billiard balls. As to Schomberg, he looked extremely frightened; he hated mortally any sort of row (*fracas* he called it) in his establishment. *Fracas* was bad for business, he affirmed; but, in truth, this specimen of portly, middle-aged manhood was of a timid disposition. I don't know what, considering my presence in the place, they all hoped would come of it. A sort of stag fight, perhaps. Or they may have supposed Falk had come in only to annihilate me completely. As a matter of fact, Falk had come in because Hermann had asked him to inquire after the precious white cotton parasol which, in the worry and excitement of the previous day, he had forgotten at the table where we had held our little discussion.

It was this that gave me my opportunity. I don't think I would have gone to seek Falk out. No. I don't think so. There are limits. But there was an opportunity and I seized it—I have already tried to explain why. Now I will merely state that, in my opinion, to get his sickly crew into the sea air and secure a quick despatch for his ship a skipper would be justified in going to any length, short of absolute crime. He should put his pride in his pocket; he may accept confidences; he must explain his innocence as if it were a sin; he may take advantage of misconceptions, of desires and of weaknesses; he ought to conceal his horror and other emotions, and, if the fate of a human being, and that human being a magnificent young girl, is strangely involved—why, he should contemplate that fate (whatever it might seem to be) without turning a hair. And all these things I have done; the explaining, the listening, the pretending—even to the discretion—and nobody, not even Hermann's niece, I believe, need throw stones at me now. Schomberg at all events needn't, since from first to last, I am happy to say, there was not the slightest "*fracas*."

Overcoming a nervous contraction of the windpipe, I had managed to exclaim "Captain Falk!" His start of surprise was perfectly genuine, but afterwards he neither smiled nor scowled. He simply waited. Then, when I had said, "I must have a talk with you," and had pointed to a chair at my table, he moved up to me, though he didn't sit down. Schomberg, however, with a long tumbler in his hand, was making towards us prudently, and I discovered then the only sign of weakness in Falk. He had for Schomberg a repulsion resembling that sort of physical fear some people experience at the sight of a toad. Perhaps to a man so essentially and silently concentrated upon himself (though he could talk well enough, as I was to find out presently) the other's irrepressible loquacity, embracing every human being within range of the tongue, might have appeared unnatural, disgusting, and monstrous. He suddenly gave signs of restiveness—positively like a horse about to rear, and, muttering hurriedly as if in great pain, "No. I can't stand that fellow," seemed ready to bolt. This weakness of his gave me the advantage at the very start. "Verandah," I suggested, as if rendering him a service, and walked him out by the arm. We stumbled over a few chairs; we had the feeling of open space before us, and felt the fresh breath of the river—fresh, but tainted. The Chinese theatres across the water made, in the sparsely twinkling masses of gloom an Eastern town presents at night, blazing centres of light, and of a distant and howling uproar. I felt him become suddenly tractable again like an animal, like a good-tempered horse when the object that scares him is removed. Yes. I felt in the darkness there how tractable he was, without my conviction of his inflexibility—tenacity, rather, perhaps—being in the least weakened. His very arm abandoning itself to my grasp was as hard as marble—like a limb of iron. But I heard a tumultuous scuffling of boot-soles within. The unspeakable idiots inside were crowding to the windows, climbing over each other's backs behind the blinds, billiard cues and all. Somebody broke a window-pane, and with the sound of falling glass, so suggestive of riot and devastation, Schomberg reeled out after us in a state of funk which had prevented his parting with his brandy and soda. He must have trembled like an aspen leaf. The piece of ice in the long tumbler he held in his hand tinkled with an effect of chattering teeth. "I beg you, gentlemen," he expostulated thickly. "Come! Really, now, I must insist . . ."

How proud I am of my presence of mind! "Hallo," I said instantly in a loud and naïve tone, "somebody's breaking your windows, Schomberg. Would you please tell one of your boys to bring out here a pack of cards and a couple of lights? And two long drinks. Will you?"

To receive an order soothed him at once. It was business. "Certainly," he said in an immensely relieved tone. The night was rainy, with wandering gusts of wind, and while we waited for the candles Falk said, as if to justify his panic, "I don't interfere in anybody's business. I don't give any occasion for talk. I am a respectable man. But this fellow is always making out something wrong, and can never rest till he gets somebody to believe him."

This was the first of my knowledge of Falk. This desire of respectability, of being like everybody else, was the only recognition he vouchsafed to the organisation of mankind. For the rest he might have been the member of a herd, not of a society. Self-preservation was his only concern. Not selfishness, but mere self-preservation. Selfishness presupposes consciousness, choice, the presence of other men; but his instinct acted as though he were the last of mankind nursing that law like the only spark of a sacred fire. I don't mean to say that living naked in a cavern would have satisfied him. Obviously he was the creature of the conditions to which he was born. No doubt self-preservation meant also the preservation of these conditions. But essentially it meant something much more simple, natural, and powerful. How shall I express it? It meant the preservation of the five senses of his body—let us say—taking it in its narrowest as well as in its widest meaning. I think you will admit before long the justice of this judgment. However, as we stood there together in the dark verandah I had judged nothing as yet—and I had no desire to judge—which is an idle practice anyhow. The light was long in coming.

"Of course," I said in a tone of mutual understanding, "it isn't exactly a game of cards I want with you."

I saw him draw his hands down his face—the vague stir of the passionate and meaningless gesture; but he waited in silent patience. It was only when the lights had been brought out that he opened his lips. I understood his mumble to mean that he didn't know any game.*

"Like this, Schomberg and all the other fools will have to keep off," I said, tearing open the pack. "Have you heard that we are universally supposed to be quarrelling about a girl? You know who— of course. I am really ashamed to ask, but is it possible that you do me the honour to think me dangerous?"

As I said these words I felt how absurd it was and also I felt flattered—for, really, what else could it be? His answer, spoken in his usual dispassionate undertone, made it clear that it was so, but not precisely as flattering as I supposed. He thought me dangerous with Hermann, more than with the girl herself; but, as to quarrelling, I saw at once how inappropriate the word was. We had no quarrel. Natural forces are not quarrelsome. You can't quarrel with the wind that inconveniences and humiliates you by blowing off your hat in a street full of people. He had no quarrel with me. Neither would a boulder, falling on my head, have had. He fell upon me in accordance with the law by which he was moved—not of gravitation, like a detached stone, but of self-preservation. Of course this is giving it a rather wide interpretation. Strictly speaking, he had existed and could have existed without being married. Yet he told me that he had found it more and more difficult to live alone. Yes. He told me this in his low, careless voice, to such a pitch of confidence had we arrived at the end of half an hour.

It took me just about that time to convince him that I had never dreamed of marrying Hermann's niece. Could any necessity have been more extravagant? And the difficulty was the greater because he was so hard hit that he couldn't imagine anybody being able to remain in a state of indifference. Any man with eyes in his head, he seemed to think, could not help coveting so much bodily magnificence. This profound belief was conveyed by the manner he listened sitting sideways to the table and playing absently with a few cards I had dealt to him at random. And the more I saw into him the more I saw of him. The wind swayed the lights so that his sunburnt face, whiskered to the eyes, seemed to successively flicker crimson at me and to go out. I saw the extraordinary breadth of the high cheek-bones, the perpendicular style of the features, the massive forehead, steep like a cliff, denuded at the top, largely uncovered at the temples. The fact is I had never before seen him without his hat; but now, as if my fervour had made him hot, he had taken it off and laid it gently on the floor. Something peculiar in the shape and setting of his yellow eyes gave them the provoking silent intensity which characterised his glance. But the face was thin, furrowed, worn; I discovered that through the bush of his hair, as you may detect the gnarled shape of a tree trunk lost in a dense undergrowth. These overgrown cheeks were sunken. It was an anchorite's bony head fitted with a Capuchin's beard and adjusted to a herculean body. I don't mean athletic. Hercules, I take it, was not an athlete. He was a strong man, susceptible to female charms, and not afraid of dirt. And thus with Falk, who was a strong man. He was extremely strong, just as the girl (since I must think of them together) was magnificently attractive by the masterful power of flesh and blood, expressed in shape, in size, in attitude—that is by a straight appeal to the senses. His mind meantime, preoccupied with respectability, quailed before Schomberg's tongue and seemed absolutely impervious to my protestations; and I went so far as to protest that I would just as soon think of marrying my mother's (dear old lady!) faithful female cook as Hermann's niece. Sooner, I protested, in my desperation, much sooner; but it did not appear that he saw anything outrageous in the proposition, and in his sceptical immobility he seemed to nurse the argument that at all events the cook was very, very far away. It must be said that, just before, I had gone wrong by appealing to the evidence of my manner whenever I called on board the *Diana*. I had never attempted to approach the girl, or to speak to her, or even to look at her in any marked way. Nothing could be clearer. But, as his own idea of—let us say—"courting" seemed to consist* precisely in sitting silently for hours in the vicinity of the beloved object, that line of argument inspired him with distrust. Staring down his extended legs he let out a grunt—as much as to say, "That's all very fine, but you can't throw dust in *my* eyes."

At last I was exasperated into saying, "Why don't you put the matter at rest by talking to Hermann?" and I added sneeringly: "You don't expect me perhaps to speak for you?"

To this he said, very loud for him, "Would you?"

And for the first time he lifted his head to look at me with wonder

and incredulity. He lifted his head so sharply that there could be no
mistake. I had touched a spring. I saw the whole extent of my
opportunity, and could hardly believe in it.

"Why. Speak to . . . Well, of course," I proceeded very slowly,
watching him with great attention, for, on my word, I feared a joke.
"Not, perhaps, to the young lady herself. I can't speak German, you
know. But . . ."

He interrupted me with the earnest assurance that Hermann
had the highest opinion of me; and at once I felt the need for the
greatest possible diplomacy at this juncture. So I demurred just
enough to draw him on. Falk sat up, but except for a very noticeable
enlargement of the pupils, till the irises of his eyes were reduced
to two narrow yellow rings, his face, I should judge, was incapable
of expressing excitement. "Oh, yes! Hermann did have the
greatest . . ."

"Take up your cards. Here's Schomberg peeping at us through
the blind!" I said.

We went through the motions of what might have been a game of
écarté. Presently the intolerable scandalmonger withdrew, probably
to inform the people in the billiard-room that we two were gambling
on the verandah like mad.

We were not gambling, but it was a game; a game in which I felt I
held the winning cards. The stake, roughly speaking, was the success
of the voyage—for me; and he, I apprehended, had nothing to lose.
Our intimacy matured rapidly, and before many words had been
exchanged I perceived that the excellent Hermann had been making
use of me. That simple and astute Teuton had been, it seems, holding me up to Falk in the light of a rival. I was young enough to be
shocked at so much duplicity. "Did he tell you that in so many
words?" I asked with indignation.

Hermann had not. He had given hints only; and of course it had
not taken very much to alarm Falk; but, instead of declaring himself,
he had taken steps to remove the family from under my influence.
He was perfectly straightforward about it—as straightforward as a
tile falling on your head. There was no duplicity in that man; and
when I congratulated him on the perfection of his arrangements—
even to the bribing of the wretched Johnson against me—he had a
genuine movement of protest. Never bribed. He knew the man
wouldn't work as long as he had a few cents in his pocket to get

drunk on, and, naturally (he said—"*naturally*") he let him have a dollar or two. He was himself a sailor, he said, and anticipated the view another sailor, like myself, was bound to take. On the other hand, he was sure that I should have to come to grief. He hadn't been knocking about for the last seven years up and down that river for nothing. It would have been no disgrace to me—but he asserted confidently I would have had my ship very awkwardly ashore at a spot two miles below the Great Pagoda. . . .

And with all that he had no ill-will. That was evident. This was a crisis in which his only object had been to gain time—I fancy. And presently he mentioned that he had written for some jewellery, real good jewellery—had written to Hong-Kong for it. It would arrive in a day or two.

"Well, then," I said cheerily, "everything is all right. All you've got to do is to present it to the lady together with your heart, and live happy ever after."

Upon the whole he seemed to accept that view as far as the girl was concerned, but his eyelids drooped. There was still something in the way. For one thing Hermann disliked him so much. As to me, on the contrary, it seemed as though he could not praise me enough. Mrs. Hermann too. He didn't know why they disliked him so. It made everything most difficult.

I listened impassive, feeling more and more diplomatic. His speech was not transparently clear. He was one of those men who seem to live, feel, suffer in a sort of mental twilight. But as to being fascinated by the girl and possessed by the desire of home life with her—it was as clear as daylight. So much being at stake, he was afraid of putting it to the hazard of the declaration. Besides, there was something else. And with Hermann being so set against him . . .

"I see," I said thoughtfully, while my heart beat fast with the excitement of my diplomacy. "I don't mind sounding Hermann. In fact, to show you how mistaken you were, I am ready to do all I can for you in that way."

A light sigh escaped him. He drew his hands down his face, and it emerged, bony, unchanged of expression, as if all the tissues had been ossified. All the passion was in those big brown hands. He was satisfied. Then there was that other matter. If there were anybody on earth it was I who could persuade Hermann to take a reasonable view! I had a knowledge of the world and lots of experience.

Hermann admitted this himself. And then I was a sailor too. Falk thought that a sailor would be able to understand certain things best. . . .

He talked as if the Hermanns had been living all their life in a rural hamlet, and I alone had been capable, with my practice in life, of a large and indulgent view of certain occurrences. That was what my diplomacy was leading me to. I began suddenly to dislike it.

"I say, Falk," I asked quite brusquely, "you haven't already a wife put away somewhere?"

The pain and disgust of his denial were very striking. Couldn't I understand that he was as respectable as any white man hereabouts; earning his living honestly. He was suffering from my suspicion, and the low undertone of his voice made his protestations sound very pathetic. For a moment he shamed me, but, my diplomacy notwithstanding, I seemed to develop a conscience, as if in very truth it were in my power to decide the success of this matrimonial enterprise. By pretending hard enough we come to believe anything—anything to our advantage. And I had been pretending very hard, because I meant yet to be towed safely down the river. But, through conscience or stupidity, I couldn't help alluding to the Vanlo affair. "You acted rather badly there. Didn't you?" was what I ventured actually to say—for the logic of our conduct is always at the mercy of obscure and unforeseen impulses.

His dilated pupils swerved from my face, glancing at the window with a sort of scared fury. We heard behind the blinds the continuous and sudden clicking of ivory, a jovial murmur of many voices, and Schomberg's deep manly laugh.

"That confounded old woman of a hotel-keeper then would never, never let it rest!" Falk exclaimed. Well, yes! It had happened two years ago. When it came to the point he owned he couldn't make up his mind to trust Fred Vanlo—no sailor, a bit of a fool too. He could not trust him, but, to stop his row, he had lent him enough money to pay all his debts before he left. I was greatly surprised to hear this. Then Falk could not be such a miser after all. So much the better for the girl. For a time he sat silent; then he picked up a card, and while looking at it he said:

"You need not think of anything bad. It was an accident. I've been unfortunate once."

"Then in heaven's name say nothing about it."

As soon as these words were out of my mouth I fancied I had said something immoral. He shook his head negatively. It had to be told. He considered it proper that the relations of the lady should know. No doubt—I thought to myself—had Miss Vanlo not been thirty and damaged by the climate he would have found it possible to entrust Fred Vanlo with this confidence. And then the figure of Hermann's niece appeared before my mind's eye, with the wealth of her opulent form, her rich youth, her lavish strength. With that powerful and immaculate vitality, her girlish form must have shouted aloud of life to that man, whereas poor Miss Vanlo could only sing sentimental songs to the strumming of a piano.

"And that Hermann hates me, I know it!" he cried in his undertone, with a sudden recrudescence of anxiety. "I must tell them. It is proper that they should know. You would say so yourself."

He then murmured an utterly mysterious allusion to the necessity for peculiar domestic arrangements.* Though my curiosity was excited I did not want to hear any of his confidences. I feared he might give me a piece of information that would make my assumed *rôle* of match-maker odious—however unreal it was. I was aware that he could have the girl for the asking; and keeping down a desire to laugh in his face, I expressed a confident belief in my ability to argue away Hermann's dislike for him. "I am sure I can make it all right," I said. He looked very pleased.

And when we rose not a word had been said about towage! Not a word! The game was won and the honour was safe. Oh! blessed white cotton umbrella! We shook hands, and I was holding myself with difficulty from breaking into a step dance of joy when he came back, striding all the length of the verandah, and said doubtfully:

"I say, captain, I have your word? You—you—won't turn round?"

Heavens! The fright he gave me. Behind his tone of doubt there was something desperate and menacing. The infatuated ass. But I was equal to the situation.

"My dear Falk," I said, beginning to lie with a glibness and effrontery that amazed me even at the time—"confidence for confidence." (He had made no confidences.) "I will tell you that I am already engaged to an extremely charming girl at home, and so you understand . . ."

He caught my hand and wrung it in a crushing grip.

"Pardon me. I feel it every day more difficult to live alone . . ."

"On rice and fish," I interrupted smartly, giggling with the sheer nervousness of a danger escaped.

He dropped my hand as if it had become suddenly red hot. A moment of profound silence ensued, as though something extraordinary had happened.

"I promise you to obtain Hermann's consent," I faltered out at last, and it seemed to me that he could not help seeing through that humbugging promise. "If there's anything else to get over I shall endeavour to stand by you," I conceded further, feeling somehow defeated and overborne; "but you must do your best yourself."

"I have been unfortunate once," he muttered unemotionally, and turning his back on me he went away, thumping slowly the plank floor as if his feet had been shod with iron.

Next morning, however, he was lively enough as man-boat, a combination of splashing and shouting; of the insolent commotion below with the steady overbearing glare of the silent head-piece above. He turned us out most unnecessarily at an ungodly hour, but it was nearly eleven in the morning before he brought me up a cable's length from Hermann's ship. And he did it very badly too, in a hurry, and nearly contriving to miss altogether the patch of good holding ground, because, forsooth, he had caught sight of Hermann's niece on the poop. And so did I; and probably as soon as he had seen her himself. I saw the modest, sleek glory of the tawny head, and the full, grey shape of the girlish print frock she filled so perfectly, so satisfactorily, with the seduction of unfaltering curves—a very nymph of Diana the Huntress. And *Diana* the ship sat, high-walled and as solid as an institution, on the smooth level of the water, the most uninspiring and respectable craft upon the seas, useful and ugly, devoted to the support of domestic virtues like any grocer's shop on shore. At once Falk steamed away; for there was some work for him to do. He would return in the evening.

He ranged close by us, passing out dead slow, without a hail. The beat of the paddle-wheels reverberating amongst the stony islets, as if from the ruined walls of a vast arena, filled the anchorage confusedly with the clapping sounds of a mighty and leisurely applause. Abreast of Hermann's ship he stopped the engines; and a profound silence reigned over the rocks, the shore and the sea, for the time it took him to raise his hat aloft before the nymph of the grey print frock. I had snatched up my binoculars, and I can answer for it she didn't stir a limb, standing by the rail shapely and erect, with one of her hands grasping a rope at the height of her head, while the way of the tug carried slowly past her the lingering and profound homage of the man. There was for me an enormous significance in the scene, the sense of having witnessed a solemn declaration. The die was cast. After such a manifestation he couldn't back out. And I reflected that it was nothing whatever to me now. With a rush of black smoke belching suddenly out of the funnel, and a mad swirl of paddle-wheels provoking a burst of weird and precipitated clapping, the tug shot out of the desolate arena. The rocky islets lay on the sea like the heaps of a cyclopean ruin on a plain; the centipedes and scorpions lurked under the stones; there was not a single blade of grass in sight anywhere, not a single lizard sunning himself on a boulder by the shore. When I looked again at Hermann's ship the girl had disappeared. I could not detect the smallest dot of a bird on the immense sky, and the flatness of the land continued the flatness of the sea to the naked line of the horizon.

This is the setting now inseparably connected with my knowledge of Falk's misfortune. My diplomacy had brought me there, and now I had only to wait the time for taking up the *rôle* of an ambassador. My diplomacy was a success; my ship was safe; old Gambril would probably live; a feeble sound of a tapping hammer came intermittently from the *Diana*. During the afternoon I looked at times at the old homely ship, the faithful nurse of Hermann's progeny, or yawned towards the distant temple of Buddha, like a lonely hillock on the plain, where shaven priests cherish the thoughts of that Annihilation which is the worthy reward of us all.* Unfortunate! He had been unfortunate once. Well, that was not so bad as life goes. And what the devil could be the nature of that misfortune? I remembered that I had known a man before who had declared himself to have fallen, years ago, a victim to misfortune; but this misfortune, whose effects appeared permanent (he looked desperately hard up) when considered dispassionately, seemed indistinguishable from a breach of trust. Could it be something of that nature? Apart, however, from the utter improbability that he would offer to talk of it even to his future uncle-in-law I had a strange feeling that Falk's physique unfitted him for that sort of delinquency. As the person of Hermann's niece exhaled the profound physical charm of feminine form, so her adorer's big frame embodied to my senses the hard, straight masculinity that would conceivably kill but would not condescend to cheat. The thing was obvious. I might just as well have suspected the girl of a curvature of the spine. And I perceived that the sun was about to set.

The smoke of Falk's tug hove in sight, far away at the mouth of the river. It was time for me to assume the character of an ambassador, and the negotiation would not be difficult except in the matter of keeping my countenance. It was all too extravagantly nonsensical, and I conceived that it would be best to compose for myself a grave demeanour. I practised this in my boat as I went along, but the bashfulness that came secretly upon me the moment I stepped on the deck of the *Diana* is inexplicable. As soon as we had exchanged greetings Hermann asked me eagerly if I knew whether Falk had found his white parasol.

"He's going to bring it to you himself directly," I said with great solemnity. "Meantime I am charged with an important message for which he begs your favourable consideration. He is in love with your niece. . . ."

"*Ach so!*" he hissed with an animosity that made my assumed gravity change into the most genuine concern. What meant this tone? And I hurried on.

"He wishes, with your consent of course, to ask her to marry him at once—before you leave here, that is. He would speak to the Consul."

Hermann sat down and smoked violently. Five minutes passed in that furious meditation, and then, taking the long pipe out of his mouth, he burst into a hot diatribe against Falk—against his cupidity, his stupidity (a fellow that can hardly be got to say "yes" or "no" to the simplest question)—against his outrageous treatment of the shipping in port (because he saw they were at his mercy)—and against his manner of walking, which to his (Hermann's) mind showed a conceit positively unbearable. The damage to the old *Diana* was not forgotten, of course, and there was nothing of any nature said or done by Falk (even to the last offer of refreshment in the hotel) that did not seem to have been a cause of offence. "Had the cheek" to drag him (Hermann) into that coffee room; as though a drink from him could make up for forty-seven dollars and fifty cents of damage in the cost of wood alone—not counting two days' work for the carpenter. Of course he would not stand in the girl's way.

He was going home to Germany. There were plenty of poor girls walking about in Germany.

"He's very much in love," was all I found to say.

"Yes," he cried. "And it is time too after making himself and me talked about ashore the last voyage I was here, and then now again; coming on board every evening unsettling the girl's mind, and saying nothing. What sort of conduct is that?"

The seven thousand dollars the fellow was always talking about did not, in his opinion, justify such behaviour. Moreover, nobody had seen them. He (Hermann) seriously doubted if there were seven thousand cents, and the tug, no doubt, was mortgaged up to the top of the funnel to the firm of Siegers. But let that pass. He wouldn't stand in the girl's way. Her head was so turned that she had become no good to them of late. Quite unable even to put the children to bed without her aunt. It was bad for the children; they got unruly; and yesterday he actually had to give Gustav a thrashing.

For that, too, Falk was made responsible apparently. And looking at my Hermann's heavy, puffy, good-natured face, I knew he would not exert himself till greatly exasperated, and, therefore, would thrash very hard, and being fat would resent the necessity. How Falk had managed to turn the girl's head was more difficult to understand. I supposed Hermann would know. And then hadn't there been Miss Vanlo? It could not be his silvery tongue, or the subtle seduction of his manner; he had no more of what is called "manner" than an animal—which, however, on the other hand, is never, and can never be called, vulgar. Therefore it must have been his bodily appearance, exhibiting a virility of nature as exaggerated as his beard, and resembling a sort of constant ruthlessness. It was seen in the very manner he lolled in the chair. He meant no offence, but his intercourse was characterised by that sort of frank disregard of susceptibilities a man of seven foot six, living in a world of dwarfs, would naturally assume, without in the least wishing to be unkind. But amongst men of his own stature, or nearly, this frank use of his advantages, in such matters as the awful towage bills for instance, caused much impotent gnashing of teeth. When attentively considered it seemed appalling at times. He was a strange beast. But maybe women liked it. Seen in that light he was well worth taming, and I suppose every woman at the bottom of her heart considers herself as a tamer of strange beasts. But Hermann arose with precipitation to carry the news to his wife. I had barely the time, as he made for the cabin door, to grab him by the seat of his inexpressibles. I begged him to wait till Falk in person had spoken with him. There remained some small matter to talk over, as I understood.

He sat down again at once, full of suspicion.

"What matter?" he said surlily. "I have had enough of his nonsense. There's no matter at all, as he knows very well; the girl has nothing in the world. She came to us in one thin dress when my brother died, and I have a growing family."

"It can't be anything of that kind," I opined. "He's desperately enamoured of your niece. I don't know why he did not say so before. Upon my word, I believe it is because he was afraid to lose, perhaps, the felicity of sitting near her on your quarter deck."

I intimated my conviction that his love was so great as to be in a sense cowardly. The effects of a great passion are unaccountable. It has been known to make a man timid. But Hermann looked at me as if I had foolishly raved; and the twilight was dying out rapidly.

"You don't believe in passion, do you, Hermann?" I said cheerily. "The passion of fear will make a cornered rat courageous. Falk's in a corner. He will take her off your hands in one thin frock just as she came to you. And after ten years' service it isn't a bad bargain," I added.

Far from taking offence, he resumed his air of civic virtue. The sudden night came upon him while he stared placidly along the deck, bringing in contact with his thick lips, and taking away again after a jet of smoke, the curved mouthpiece fitted to the stem of his pipe. The night came upon him and buried in haste his whiskers, his globular eyes, his puffy pale face, his fat knees and the vast flat slippers on his fatherly feet. Only his short arms in respectable white shirt-sleeves remained very visible, propped up like the flippers of a seal reposing on the strand.

"Falk wouldn't settle anything about repairs. Told me to find out first how much wood I should require and he would see," he remarked; and after he had spat peacefully in the dusk we heard over the water the beat of the tug's floats. There is, on a calm night, nothing more suggestive of fierce and headlong haste than the rapid sound made by the paddle-wheels of a boat threshing her way through a quiet sea; and the approach of Falk towards his fate seemed to be urged by an impatient and passionate desire. The engines must have been driven to the very utmost of their revolutions. We heard them slow down at last, and, vaguely, the white hull of the tug appeared moving against the black islets, whilst a slow and rhythmical clapping as of thousands of hands rose on all sides. It ceased all at once, just before Falk brought her up. A single brusque splash was followed by the long drawn rumbling of iron links running through the hawse pipe. Then a solemn silence fell upon the roadstead.

"He will soon be here," I murmured, and after that we waited for him without a word. Meantime, raising my eyes, I beheld the glitter of a lofty sky above the *Diana*'s mastheads. The multitude of stars gathered into clusters, in rows, in lines, in masses, in groups, shone all together, unanimously—and the few isolated ones, blazing by themselves in the midst of dark patches, seemed to be of a superior kind and of an inextinguishable nature. But long striding footsteps were heard hastening along the deck; the high bulwarks of the *Diana* made a deeper darkness. We rose from our chairs quickly, and Falk, appearing before us, all in white, stood still.

Nobody spoke at first, as though we had been covered with confusion. His arrival was fiery, but his white bulk, of indefinite shape and without features, made him loom up like a man of snow.

"The captain here has been telling me . . ." Hermann began in a homely and amicable voice; and Falk had a low, nervous laugh. His cool, negligent undertone had no inflexions, but the strength of a powerful emotion made him ramble in his speech. He had always desired a home. It was difficult to live alone, though he was not answerable. He was domestic; there had been difficulties; but since he had seen Hermann's niece he found that it had become at last impossible to live by himself. "I mean—impossible," he repeated with no sort of emphasis and only with the slightest of pauses, but the word fell into my mind with the force of a new idea.

"I have not said anything to her yet," Hermann observed quietly. And Falk dismissed this by a "That's all right. Certainly. Very proper." There was a necessity for perfect frankness—in marrying, especially. Hermann seemed attentive, but he seized the first opportunity to ask us into the cabin. "And by-the-by, Falk," he said innocently, as we passed in, "the timber came to no less than forty-seven dollars and fifty cents."

Falk, uncovering his head, lingered in the passage. "Some other time," he said; and Hermann nudged me angrily—I don't know why. The girl alone in the cabin sat sewing at some distance from the table. Falk stopped short in the doorway. Without a word, without a sign, without the slightest inclination of his bony head, by the silent intensity of his look alone, he seemed to lay his herculean frame at her feet. Her hands sank slowly on her lap, and raising her clear eyes, she let her soft, beaming glance enfold him from head to foot like a slow and pale caress. He was very hot when he sat down; she, with bowed head, went on with her sewing; her neck was very white under the light of the lamp; but Falk, hiding his face in the palms of his hands, shuddered faintly. He drew them down, even to his beard, and his uncovered eyes astonished me by their tense and irrational expression—as though he had just swallowed a heavy gulp of alcohol. It passed away while he was binding us to secrecy. Not that he cared, but he did not like to be spoken about; and I looked at the girl's marvellous, at her wonderful, at her regal hair, plaited tight into that one astonishing and maidenly tress. Whenever she moved her well-shaped head it would stir stiffly to and fro on her back. The thin cotton sleeve fitted the irreproachable roundness of her arm like a skin; and her very dress, stretched on her bust, seemed to palpitate like a living tissue with the strength of vitality animating her body. How good her complexion was, the outline of her soft cheek and the small convoluted conch of her rosy ear! To pull her needle she kept the little finger apart from the others; it seemed a waste of power to see her sewing—eternally sewing—with that industrious and precise movement of her arm, going on eternally upon all the oceans, under all the skies, in innumerable harbours. And suddenly I heard Falk's voice declare that he could not marry a woman unless she knew of something in his life that had happened ten years ago. It was an accident. An unfortunate accident. It would affect the domestic arrangements of their home, but, once told, it need not be alluded to again for the rest of their lives. "I should want my wife to feel for me," he said. "It has made me unhappy." And how could he keep the knowledge of it to himself—he asked us—perhaps through years and years of companionship? What sort of companionship would that be? He had thought it over. A wife must know. Then why not at once? He counted on Hermann's kindness for presenting the affair in the best possible light. And Hermann's countenance, mystified before, became very sour. He stole an inquisitive glance at me. I shook my head blankly. Some people thought, Falk went on, that such an experience changed a man for the rest of his life. He couldn't say. It was hard, awful, and not to be forgotten, but he did not think himself a worse man than before. Only he talked in his sleep now, he believed. . . . At last I began to think he had accidentally killed some one; perhaps a friend—his own father maybe; when he went on to say that probably we were aware he never touched meat. Throughout he spoke English, of course on my account.

He swayed forward heavily.

The girl, with her hands raised before her pale eyes, was threading her needle. He glanced at her, and his mighty trunk overshadowed the table, bringing nearer to us the breadth of his shoulders, the thickness of his neck, and that incongruous, anchorite head, burnt in the desert, hollowed and lean as if by excesses of vigils and fasting. His beard flowed imposingly downwards, out of sight, between the two brown hands gripping the edge of the table, and his persistent glance made sombre by the wide dilations of the pupils, fascinated.

"Imagine to yourselves," he said in his ordinary voice, "that I have eaten man."*

I could only ejaculate a faint "Ah!" of complete enlightenment. But Hermann, dazed by the excessive shock, actually murmured, "Himmel! What for?"

"It was my terrible misfortune to do so," said Falk in a measured undertone. The girl, unconscious, sewed on. Mrs. Hermann was absent in one of the state-rooms, sitting up with Lena, who was feverish; but Hermann suddenly put both his hands up with a jerk. The embroidered calotte fell, and, in the twinkling of an eye, he had rumpled his hair all ends up in a most extravagent manner. In this state he strove to speak; with every effort his eyes seemed to start further out of their sockets; his head looked like a mop. He choked, gasped, swallowed, and managed to shriek out the one word, "Beast!"

From that moment till Falk went out of the cabin the girl, with her hands folded on the work lying in her lap, never took her eyes off him. His own, in the blindness of his heart, darted all over the cabin, only seeking to avoid the sight of Hermann's raving. It was ridiculous, and was made almost terrible by the stillness of every other person present. It was contemptible, and was made appalling by the man's overmastering horror of this awful sincerity, coming to him suddenly, with the confession of such a fact. He walked with great strides; he gasped. He wanted to know from Falk how dared he to come and tell him this? Did he think himself a proper person to be sitting in this cabin where his wife and children lived? Tell his niece! Expected him to tell his niece! His own brother's daughter! Shameless! Did I ever hear tell of such impudence?—he appealed to me. "This man here ought to have gone and hidden himself out of sight instead of . . ."

"But it's a great misfortune for me. But it's a great misfortune for me," Falk would ejaculate from time to time.

However, Hermann kept on running frequently against the corners of the table. At last he lost a slipper, and crossing his arms on his breast, walked up with one stocking foot very close to Falk, in order to ask him whether he did think there was anywhere on earth a woman abandoned enough to mate with such a monster. "Did he? Did he? Did he?" I tried to restrain him. He tore himself out of my hands; he found his slipper, and, endeavouring to put it on, stormed standing on one leg—and Falk, with a face unmoved and averted eyes, grasped all his mighty beard in one vast palm.

"Was it right then for me to die myself?" he asked thoughtfully. I laid my hand on his shoulder.

"Go away," I whispered imperiously, without any clear reason for this advice, except that I wished to put an end to Hermann's odious noise. "Go away."

He looked searchingly for a moment at Hermann before he made a move. I left the cabin too to see him out of the ship. But he hung about the quarter-deck.

"It is my misfortune," he said in a steady voice.

"You were stupid to blurt it out in such a manner. After all, we don't hear such confidences every day."

"What does the man mean?" he mused in deep undertones. "Somebody had to die—but why me?"

He remained still for a time in the dark—silent; almost invisible. All at once he pinned my elbows to my sides. I felt utterly powerless in his grip, and his voice, whispering in my ear, vibrated.

"It's worse than hunger. Captain, do you know what that means? And I could kill then—or be killed. I wish the crowbar had smashed my skull ten years ago. And I've got to live now. Without her. Do you understand? Perhaps many years. But how? What can be done? If I had allowed myself to look at her once I would have carried her off before that man in my hands—like this."

I felt myself snatched off the deck, then suddenly dropped—and I staggered backwards, feeling bewildered and bruised. What a man! All was still; he was gone. I heard Hermann's voice declaiming in the cabin, and I went in.

I could not at first make out a single word, but Mrs. Hermann, who, attracted by the noise, had come in some time before, with an expression of surprise and mild disapproval depicted broadly on her face, was giving now all the signs of profound, helpless agitation. Her husband shot a string of guttural words at her, and instantly putting out one hand to the bulkhead as if to save herself from falling, she clutched the loose bosom of her dress with the other. He harangued the two women extraordinarily; with much of his shirt hanging out of his waistbelt, stamping his foot, turning from one to the other, sometimes throwing both his arms together, straight up above his rumpled hair, and keeping them in that position while he uttered a passage of loud denunciation; at others folding them tight across his breast—and then he hissed with indignation, elevating his shoulders and protruding his head. The girl was crying.

She had not changed her attitude. From her steady eyes that, following Falk in his retreat, had remained fixed wistfully on the cabin door, the tears fell rapid, thick, on her hands, on the work in her lap, warm and gentle like a shower in spring. She wept without grimacing, without noise—very touching, very quiet, with something more of pity than of pain in her face, as one weeps in compassion rather than in grief—and Hermann, before her, declaimed. I caught several times the word "Mensch," man; and also "Fressen," which last I looked up afterwards in my dictionary. It means "Devour." Hermann seemed to be requesting an answer of some sort from her; his whole body swayed. She remained mute and perfectly still; at last his agitation gained her; she put the palms of her hands together, her full lips parted, no sound came. His voice scolded shrilly, his arms went like a windmill—suddenly he shook a thick fist at her. She burst out into loud sobs. He seemed stupefied.

Mrs. Hermann rushed forward babbling rapidly. The two women fell on each other's necks, and, with an arm round her niece's waist, she led her away. Her own eyes were simply streaming, her face was flooded. She shook her head back at me negatively, I wonder why to this day. The girl's head dropped heavily on her shoulder. They disappeared together.

Then Hermann sat down and stared at the cabin floor.

"We don't know all the circumstances," I ventured to break the silence. He retorted tartly that he didn't want to know of any. According to his ideas no circumstances could excuse a crime—and certainly not such a crime. This was the opinion generally received. The duty of a human being was to starve. Falk therefore was a beast, an animal; base, low, vile, despicable, shameless, and deceitful. He had been deceiving him since last year. He was, however, inclined to think that Falk must have gone mad quite recently; for no sane person, without necessity, uselessly, for no earthly reason, and regardless of another's self-respect and peace of mind, would own to having devoured human flesh. "Why tell?" he cried. "Who was asking him?" It showed Falk's brutality because after all he had selfishly caused him (Hermann) much pain. He would have preferred not to know that such an unclean creature had been in the habit of caressing his children. He hoped I would say nothing of all this ashore, though. He wouldn't like it to get about that he had been intimate with an eater of men—a common cannibal. As to the scene he had made (which I judged quite unnecessary) he was not going to inconvenience and restrain himself for a fellow that went about courting and upsetting girls' heads, while he knew all the time that no decent housewifely girl could think of marrying him. At least he (Hermann) could not conceive how any girl could. "Fancy Lena! . . . No, it was impossible. The thoughts that would come into their heads every time they sat down to a meal. Horrible! Horrible!"

"You are too squeamish, Hermann," I said.

He seemed to think it was eminently proper to be squeamish if the word meant disgust at Falk's conduct; and turning up his eyes sentimentally he drew my attention to the horrible fate of the victims—the victims of that Falk. I said that I knew nothing about them. He seemed surprised. Could not anybody imagine without knowing? He—for instance—felt he would like to avenge them. But what if—said I—there had not been any? They might have died as it were, naturally—of starvation. He shuddered. But to be eaten—after death! To be devoured! He gave another deep shudder, and asked suddenly, "Do you think it is true?"

His indignation and his personality together would have been enough to spoil the reality of the most authentic thing. When I looked at him I doubted the story—but the remembrance of Falk's words, looks, gestures, invested it not only with an air of reality but with the absolute truth of primitive passion.

"It is true just as much as you are able to make it; and exactly in the way you like to make it. For my part, when I hear you clamouring about it, I don't believe it is true at all."

And I left him pondering. The men in my boat, lying at the foot of *Diana*'s side-ladder, told me that the captain of the tug had gone away in his gig some time ago.

I let my fellows pull an easy stroke; because of the heavy dew the clear sparkle of the stars seemed to fall on me cold and wetting. There was a sense of lurking gruesome horror somewhere in my mind, and it was mingled with clear and grotesque images. Schomberg's gastronomic tittle-tattle was responsible for these; and I half hoped I should never see Falk again. But the first thing my anchor-watchman told me was that the captain of the tug was on board. He had sent his boat away and was now waiting for me in the cuddy.

He was lying full length on the stern settee, his face buried in the cushions. I had expected to see it discomposed, contorted, despairing. It was nothing of the kind; it was just as I had seen it twenty times, steady and glaring from the bridge of the tug. It was immovably set and hungry, dominated like the whole man by the singleness of one instinct.

He wanted to live. He had always wanted to live. So we all do—but in us the instinct serves a complex conception, and in him this instinct existed alone. There is in such simple development a gigantic force, and like the pathos of a child's naïve and uncontrolled desire. He wanted that girl, and the utmost that can be said for him was that he wanted that particular girl alone. I think I saw then the obscure beginning, the seed germinating in the soil of an unconscious need, the first shoot of that tree bearing now for a mature mankind the flower and the fruit, the infinite gradation in shades and in flavour of our discriminating love. He was a child. He was as frank as a child too. He was hungry for the girl, terribly hungry, as he had been terribly hungry for food.

Don't be shocked if I declare that in my belief it was the same

Falk

need, the same pain, the same torture. We are in his case allowed to contemplate the foundation of all the emotions—that one joy which is to live, and the one sadness at the root of the innumerable torments. It was made plain by the way he talked. He had never suffered so. It was gnawing, it was fire; it was there, like this! And after pointing below his breastbone, he made a hard wringing motion with his hands. And I assure you that, seen as I saw it with my bodily eyes, it was anything but laughable. And again, as he was presently to tell me (alluding to an early incident of the disastrous voyage when some damaged meat had been flung overboard), he said that a time soon came when his heart ached (that was the expression he used), and he was ready to tear his hair out at the thought of all that rotten beef thrown away.

I had heard all this; I witnessed his physical struggles, seeing the working of the rack and hearing the true voice of pain. I witnessed it all patiently, because the moment I came into the cuddy he had called upon me to stand by him—and this, it seems, I had diplomatically promised.

His agitation was impressive and alarming in the little cabin, like the floundering of a great whale driven into a shallow cove in a coast. He stood up; he flung himself down headlong; he tried to tear the cushion with his teeth; and again hugging it fiercely to his face he let himself fall on the couch. The whole ship seemed to feel the shock of his despair; and I contemplated with wonder the lofty forehead, the noble touch of time on the uncovered temples, the unchanged hungry character of the face—so strangely ascetic and so incapable of portraying emotion.

What should he do? He had lived by being near her. He had sat—in the evening—I knew?—all his life! She sewed. Her head was bent—so. Her head—like this—and her arms. Ah! Had I seen? Like this.

He dropped on a stool, bowed his powerful neck whose nape was red, and with his hands stitched the air, ludicrous, sublimely imbecile and comprehensible.

And now he couldn't have her? No! That was too much. After thinking too that . . . . What had he done? What was my advice? Take her by force? No? Mustn't he? Who was there then to kill him? For the first time I saw one of his features move; a fighting teeth-baring curl of the lip. . . . "Not Hermann, perhaps." He lost himself in thought as though he had fallen out of the world.

I may note that the idea of suicide apparently did not enter his head for a single moment. It occurred to me to ask:

"Where was it that this shipwreck of yours took place?"

"Down south," he said vaguely with a start.

"You are not down south now," I said. "Violence won't do. They would take her away from you in no time. And what was the name of the ship?"

"*Borgmester Dahl*," he said. "It was no shipwreck."

He seemed to be waking up by degrees from that trance, and waking up calmed.

"Not a shipwreck? What was it?"

"Break-down," he answered, looking more like himself every moment. By this only I learned that it was a steamer. I had till then supposed they had been starving in boats or on a raft—or perhaps on a barren rock.

"She did not sink then?" I asked in surprise. He nodded. "We sighted the southern ice," he pronounced dreamily.

"And you alone survived?"

He sat down. "Yes. It was a terrible misfortune for me. Everything went wrong. All the men went wrong. I survived."

Remembering the things one reads of it was difficult to realise the true meaning of his answers. I ought to have seen at once—but I did not; so difficult is it for our minds, remembering so much, instructed so much, informed of so much, to get in touch with the real actuality at our elbow. And with my head full of preconceived notions as to how a case of "cannibalism and suffering at sea" should be managed I said—"You were then so lucky in the drawing of lots?"

"Drawing of lots?" he said. "What lots? Do you think I would have allowed my life to go for the drawing of lots?"

Not if he could help it, I perceived, no matter what other life went.

"It was a great misfortune. Terrible. Awful," he said. "Many heads went wrong, but the best men would live."

"The toughest, you mean," I said. He considered the word. Perhaps it was strange to him, though his English was so good.

"Yes," he asserted at last. "The best. It was everybody for himself at last and the ship open to all."

Thus from question to question I got the whole story. I fancy it was the only way I could that night have stood by him. Outwardly at least he was himself again; the first sign of it was the return of that incongruous trick he had of drawing both his hands down his face— and it had its meaning now, with that slight shudder of the frame and the passionate anguish of these hands uncovering a hungry immovable face, the wide pupils of the intent, silent, fascinating eyes.

It was an iron steamer of a most respectable origin. The burgomaster of Falk's native town had built her. She was the first steamer ever launched there. The burgomaster's daughter had christened her. Country people drove in carts from miles around to see her. He told me all this. He got the berth as, what we should call, a chief mate. He seemed to think it had been a feather in his cap; and, in his own corner of the world, this lover of life was of good parentage.

The burgomaster had advanced ideas in the shipowning line. At that time not every one would have known enough to think of despatching a cargo steamer to the Pacific. But he loaded her with pitch-pine deals and sent her off to hunt for her luck. Wellington was to be the first port, I fancy. It doesn't matter, because in latitude 44° south and somewhere halfway between Good Hope and New Zealand the tail-shaft broke and the propeller dropped off.

They were steaming then with a fresh gale on the quarter and all their canvas set, to help the engines. But by itself the sail power was not enough to keep way on her. When the propeller went the ship broached-to at once, and the masts got whipped overboard.

The disadvantage of being dismasted consisted in this, that they had nothing to hoist flags on to make themselves visible at a distance. In the course of the first few days several ships failed to sight them; and the gale was drifting them out of the usual track. The voyage had been, from the first, neither very successful nor very harmonious. There had been quarrels on board. The captain was a clever, melancholic man, who had no unusual grip on his crew. The ship had been amply provisioned for the passage, but, somehow or other, several barrels of meat were found spoiled on opening, and had been thrown overboard soon after leaving home, as a sanitary measure. Afterwards the crew of the *Borgmester Dahl* thought of that rotten carrion with tears of regret, covetousness and despair.

She drove south. To begin with, there had been an appearance of organisation, but soon the bonds of discipline became relaxed. A sombre idleness succeeded. They looked with sullen eyes at the horizon. The gales increased: she lay in the trough, the seas made a clean breach over her. On one frightful night, when they expected their hulk to turn over with them every moment, a heavy sea broke on board, deluged the store-rooms and spoiled the best part of the remaining provisions. It seems the hatch had not been properly secured. This instance of neglect is characteristic of utter discouragement. Falk tried to inspire some energy into his captain, but failed. From that time he retired more into himself, always trying to do his utmost in the situation. It grew worse. Gale succeeded gale, with black mountains of water hurling themselves on the *Borgmester Dahl*. Some of the men never left their bunks; many became quarrelsome. The chief engineer, an old man, refused to speak at all to anybody. Others shut themselves up in their berths to cry. On calm days the inert steamer rolled on a leaden sea under a murky sky, or showed, in sunshine, the squalor of sea waifs, the dried white salt, the rust, the jagged broken places. Then the gales came again. They kept body and soul together on short rations. Once, an English ship, scudding in a storm, tried to stand by them, heaving-to pluckily under their lee. The seas swept her decks; the men in oilskins clinging to her rigging looked at them, and they made desperate signs over their shattered bulwarks. Suddenly her main-topsail went, yard and all, in a terrific squall; she had to bear up under bare poles and disappeared.

Other ships had spoken them before, but at first they had refused to be taken off, expecting the assistance of some steamer. There were very few steamers in those latitudes then; and when they desired to leave this dead and drifting carcase, no ship came in sight. They had drifted south out of men's knowledge. They failed to attract the attention of a lonely whaler: and very soon the edge of the polar ice-cap rose from the sea and closed the southern horizon like a wall. One morning they were alarmed by finding themselves floating amongst detached pieces of ice. But the fear of sinking passed away like their vigour, like their hopes; the shocks of the floes knocking against the ship's side could not rouse them from their apathy: and the *Borgmester Dahl* drifted out again, unharmed, into open water. They hardly noticed the change.

The funnel had gone overboard in one of the heavy rolls; two of their three boats had disappeared, washed away in bad weather, and the davits swung to and fro, unsecured, with chafed ropes' ends waggling to the roll. Nothing was done on board, and Falk told me

how he had often listened to the water washing about the dark
engine-room where the engines, stilled for ever, were decaying
slowly into a mass of rust, as the stilled heart decays within the
lifeless body. At first, after the loss of the motive power, the tiller had
been thoroughly secured by lashings. But in course of time these had
rotted, chafed, rusted, parting one by one: and the rudder, freed,
banged heavily to and fro night and day, sending dull shocks through
the whole frame of the vessel. This was dangerous. Nobody cared
enough to lift a little finger. He told me that even now sometimes
waking up at night, he fancied he could hear the dull vibrating thuds.
The pintles carried away, and it dropped off at last.

The final catastrophe came with the sending off of their one
remaining boat. It was Falk who had managed to preserve her intact,
and now it was agreed that some of the hands should sail away into
the track of the shipping to procure assistance. She was provisioned
with all the food they could spare for the six who were to go. They
waited for a fine day. It was long in coming. At last one morning they
lowered her into the water.

Directly, in that demoralised crowd, trouble broke out. Two men
who had no business there had jumped into the boat under the
pretence of unhooking the tackles, while some sort of squabble arose
on the deck amongst these weak, tottering spectres of a ship's company. The captain, who had been for days living secluded and
unapproachable in the chart-room, came to the rail. He ordered the
two men to come up on board and menaced them with his revolver.
They pretended to obey, but suddenly cutting the boat's painter,
gave a shove against the ship's side and made ready to hoist the sail.

"Shoot, sir! Shoot them down!" cried Falk—"and I will jump
overboard to regain the boat." But the captain, after taking aim with
an irresolute arm, turned suddenly away.

A howl of rage arose. Falk dashed into his cabin for his own pistol.
When he returned it was too late. Two more men had leaped into the
water, but the fellows in the boat beat them off with the oars, hoisted
the boat's lug and sailed away. They were never heard of again.

Consternation and despair possessed the remaining ship's
company, till the apathy of utter hopelessness re-asserted its sway.
That day a fireman committed suicide, running up on deck with his
throat cut from ear to ear, to the horror of all hands. He was thrown
overboard. The captain had locked himself in the chart-room, and

Falk, knocking vainly for admittance, heard him reciting over and over again the names of his wife and children, not as if calling upon them or commending them to God, but in a mechanical voice like an exercise of memory. Next day the doors of the chart-room were swinging open to the roll of the ship, and the captain had disappeared. He must during the night have jumped into the sea. Falk locked both the doors and kept the keys.

The organised life of the ship had come to an end. The solidarity of the men had gone. They became indifferent to each other. It was Falk who took in hand the distribution of such food as remained. They boiled their boots for soup to eke out the rations, which only made their hunger more intolerable. Sometimes whispers of hate were heard passing between the languid skeletons that drifted endlessly to and fro, north and south, east and west, upon that carcase of a ship.

And in this lies the grotesque horror of this sombre story. The last extremity of sailors, overtaking a small boat or a frail craft, seems easier to bear, because of the direct danger of the seas. The confined space, the close contact, the imminent menace of the waves, seem to draw men together, in spite of madness, suffering and despair. But there was a ship—safe, convenient, roomy: a ship with beds, bedding, knives, forks, comfortable cabins, glass and china, and a complete cook's galley, pervaded, ruled and possessed by the pitiless spectre of starvation. The lamp oil had been drunk, the wicks cut up for food, the candles eaten. At night she floated dark in all her recesses, and full of fears. One day Falk came upon a man gnawing a splinter of pine wood. Suddenly he threw the piece of wood away, tottered to the rail, and fell over. Falk, too late to prevent the act, saw him claw the ship's side desperately before he went down. Next day another man did the same thing, after uttering horrible imprecations. But this one somehow managed to get hold of the broken rudder chains and hung on there, silently. Falk set about trying to save him, and all the time the man, holding with both hands, looked at him anxiously with his sunken eyes. Then, just as Falk was ready to put his hand on him, the man let go his hold and sank like a stone. Falk reflected on these sights. His heart revolted against the horror of death, and he said to himself that he would struggle for every precious minute of his life.

One afternoon—as the survivors lay about on the after deck—the carpenter, a tall man with a black beard, spoke of the last sacrifice. There was nothing eatable left on board. Nobody said a word to this; but that company separated quickly, these listless feeble spectres slunk off one by one to hide in fear of each other. Falk and the carpenter remained on deck together. Falk liked the big carpenter. He had been the best man of the lot, helpful and ready as long as there was anything to do, the longest hopeful, and had preserved to the last some vigour and decision of mind.

They did not speak to each other. Henceforth no voices were to be heard conversing sadly on board that ship. After a time the carpenter tottered away forward; but later on Falk, going to drink at the fresh-water pump, had the inspiration to turn his head. The carpenter had stolen upon him from behind, and, summoning all his strength, was aiming with a crowbar a blow at the back of his skull.

Dodging just in time, Falk made his escape and ran into his cabin. While he was loading his revolver there, he heard the sound of heavy blows struck upon the bridge. The locks of the chart-room doors were slight, they flew open, and the carpenter, possessing himself of the captain's revolver, fired a shot of defiance.

Falk was about to go on deck and have it out at once, when he remarked that one of the ports of his cabin commanded the approaches to the fresh-water pump. Instead of going out he remained in and secured the door. "The best man shall survive," he said to himself—and the other, he reasoned, must at some time or other come there to drink. These starving men would drink often to cheat the pangs of their hunger. But the carpenter too must have noticed the position of the port. They were the two best men in the ship, and the game was with them. All the rest of the day Falk saw no one and heard no sound. At night he strained his eyes. It was dark— he heard a rustling noise once, but he was certain that no one could have come near the pump. It was to the left of his deck port, and he could not have failed to see a man, for the night was clear and starry. He saw nothing; towards morning another faint noise made him suspicious. Deliberately and quietly he unlocked his door. He had not slept, and had not given way to the horror of the situation. He wanted to live.

But during the night the carpenter, without at all trying to approach the pump, had managed to creep quietly along the starboard bulwark, and, unseen, had crouched down right under Falk's deck port. When daylight came he rose up suddenly, looked in, and putting his arm through the round brass-framed opening, fired at Falk within a foot. He missed—and Falk, instead of attempting to seize the arm holding the weapon, opened his door unexpectedly and, with the muzzle of his long revolver nearly touching the other's side, shot him dead.

The best man had survived. Both of them had at the beginning just strength enough to stand on their feet, and both had displayed pitiless resolution, endurance, cunning and courage—all the qualities of classic heroism. At once Falk threw overboard the captain's revolver. He was a born monopolist. Then after the report of the two shots, followed by a profound silence, there crept out into the cold, cruel dawn of Antarctic regions, from various hiding-places, over the deck of that dismantled corpse of a ship floating on a grey sea ruled by iron necessity and with a heart of ice—there crept into view one by one, cautious, slow, eager, glaring, and unclean, a band of hungry and livid skeletons. Falk faced them, the possessor of the only firearm on board, and the second best man—the carpenter—was lying dead between him and them.

"He was eaten, of course," I said.

He bent his head slowly, shuddered a little, drawing his hands over his face, and said, "I had never any quarrel with that man. But there were our lives between him and me."

Why continue the story of that ship, that story before which, with its fresh-water pump like a spring of death, its man with the weapon, the sea ruled by iron necessity, its spectral band swayed by terror and hope, its mute and unhearing heaven?—the fable of *The Flying Dutchman** with its convention of crime and its sentimental retribution fades like a graceful wraith, like a wisp of white mist. What is there to say that every one of us cannot guess for himself? I believe Falk began by going through the ship, revolver in hand, to annex all the matches. Those starving wretches had plenty of matches! He had no mind to have the ship set on fire under his feet, either from hate or from despair. He lived in the open, camping on the bridge, commanding all the after deck and the only approach to the pump. He lived! Some of the others lived too—concealed, anxious, coming out one by one from their hiding-places at the seductive sound of a shot. And he was not selfish. They shared, but only three of them all were alive when a whaler, returning from her cruising-ground, nearly ran over the water-logged hull of the *Borgmester Dahl*, which, it seems, in the end had in some way sprung a leak in both her holds, but being loaded with deals could not sink.

"They all died," Falk said. "These three too, afterwards. But I would not die. All died, all! under this terrible misfortune. But was I too to throw away my life? Could I? Tell me, captain? I was alone there, quite alone, just like the others. Each man was alone. Was I to give up my revolver? Who to? Or was I to throw it into the sea? What would have been the good? Only the best man would survive. It was a great, terrible, and cruel misfortune."

He had survived! I saw him before me as though preserved for a witness to the mighty truth of an unerring and eternal principle.* Great beads of perspiration stood on his forehead. And suddenly it struck the table with a heavy blow, as he fell forward throwing his hands out.

"And this is worse," he cried. "This is a worse pain! This is more terrible."

He made my heart thump with the profound conviction of his cry. And after he had left me alone I called up before my mental eye the image of the girl weeping silently, abundantly, patiently, and as if irresistibly. I thought of her tawny hair. I thought how, if unplaited, it would have covered her all round as low as the hips, like the hair of a siren. And she had bewitched him. Fancy a man who would guard his own life with the inflexibility of a pitiless and immovable fate, being brought to lament that once a crowbar had missed his skull! The sirens sing and lure to death, but this one had been weeping silently as if for the pity of his life. She was the tender and voiceless siren of this appalling navigator. He evidently wanted to live his whole conception of life. Nothing else would do. And she too was a servant of that life that, in the midst of death, cries aloud to our senses. She was eminently fitted to interpret for him its feminine side. And in her own way, and with her own profusion of sensuous charms, she also seemed to illustrate the eternal truth of an unerring principle. I don't know though what sort of principle Hermann illustrated when he turned up early on board my ship with a most perplexed air. It struck me, however, that he too would do his best to survive. He seemed greatly calmed on the subject of Falk, but still very full of it.

"What is it you said I was last night? You know"—he asked after some preliminary talk. "Too—too—I don't know. A very funny word."

"Squeamish?" I suggested.

"Yes. What does it mean?"

"That you exaggerate things—to yourself. Without inquiry, and so on."

He seemed to turn it over in his mind. We went on talking. This Falk was the plague of his life. Upsetting everybody like this! Mrs. Hermann was unwell rather this morning. His niece was crying still. There was nobody to look after the children. He struck his umbrella on the deck. She would be like that for months. Fancy carrying all the way home, second class, a perfectly useless girl who is crying all the time. It was bad for Lena too, he observed; but on what grounds I could not guess. Perhaps of the bad example. That child was already sorrowing and crying enough over the rag doll. Nicholas was really the least sentimental person of the family.

"Why does she weep?" I asked.

"From pity," cried Hermann.

It was impossible to make out women. Mrs. Hermann was the only one he pretended to understand. She was very, very upset and doubtful.

"Doubtful about what?" I asked.

He averted his eyes and did not answer this. It was impossible to make them out. For instance, his niece was weeping for Falk. Now he (Hermann) would like to wring his neck—but then . . . He supposed he had too tender a heart. "Frankly," he asked at last, "what do you think of what we heard last night, captain?"

"In all these tales," I observed, "there is always a good deal of exaggeration."

And not letting him recover from his surprise I assured him that I knew all the details. He begged me not to repeat them. His heart was too tender. They made him feel unwell. Then, looking at his feet and speaking very slowly, he supposed that he need not see much of them after they were married. For, indeed, he could not bear the sight of Falk. On the other hand it was ridiculous to take home a girl with her head turned. A girl that weeps all the time and is of no help to her aunt.

"Now you will be able to do with one cabin only on your passage home," I said.

"Yes, I had thought of that," he said brightly, almost. Yes! Himself, his wife, four children—one cabin might do. Whereas if his niece went . . . *

"And what does Mrs. Hermann say to it?" I inquired.

Mrs. Hermann did not know whether a man of that sort could make a girl happy—she had been greatly deceived in Captain Falk. She had been very upset last night.

Those good people did not seem to be able to retain an impression for a whole twelve hours. I assured him on my own personal knowledge that Falk possessed in himself all the qualities to make his niece's future prosperous. He said he was glad to hear this, and that he would tell his wife. Then the object of the visit came out. He wished me to help him to resume relations with Falk. His niece, he said, had expressed the hope I would do so in my kindness. He was evidently anxious that I should, for though he seemed to have forgotten nine-tenths of his last night's opinions and the whole of his indignation, yet he evidently feared to be sent to the right-about. "You told me he was very much in love," he concluded slyly, and leered in a sort of bucolic way.

As soon as he had left my ship I called Falk on board by signal— the tug still lying at the anchorage. He took the news with calm gravity, as though he had all along expected the stars to fight for him in their courses.

I saw them once more together, and only once—on the quarter-deck of the *Diana*. Hermann sat smoking with a shirt-sleeved elbow hooked over the back of his chair. Mrs. Hermann was sewing alone. As Falk stepped over the gangway, Hermann's niece, with a slight swish of the skirt and a swift friendly nod to me, glided past my chair.

They met in sunshine abreast of the mainmast. He held her hands and looked down at them, and she looked up at him with her candid and unseeing glance. It seemed to me they had come together as if attracted, drawn and guided to each other by a mysterious influence. They were a complete couple. In her grey frock, palpitating with life, generous of form, olympian and simple, she was indeed the siren to fascinate that dark navigator, this ruthless lover of the five senses. From afar I seemed to feel the masculine strength with which he grasped those hands she had extended to him with a womanly swiftness. Lena, a little pale, nursing her beloved lump of dirty rags, ran towards her big friend; and then in the drowsy silence of the good old ship Mrs. Hermann's voice rang out so changed that it made me spin round in my chair to see what was the matter.

"Lena, come here!" she screamed. And this good-natured matron gave me a wavering glance, dark and full of fearsome distrust. The child ran back, surprised, to her knee. But the two, standing before each other in sunlight with clasped hands, had heard nothing, had seen nothing and no one. Three feet away from them in the shade a seaman sat on a spar, very busy splicing a strop, and dipping his fingers into a tar-pot, as if utterly unaware of their existence.

When I returned in command of another ship, some five years afterwards, Mr. and Mrs. Falk had left the place. I should not wonder if Schomberg's tongue had succeeded at last in scaring Falk away for good; and, indubitably, there was a tale still going about the town of a certain Falk, owner of a tug, who had won his wife at cards from the captain of an English ship.

AMY FOSTER

AMY FOSTER*

KENNEDY is a country doctor, and lives in Colebrook, on the shores of Eastbay. The high ground rising abruptly behind the red roofs of the little town crowds the quaint High Street against the wall which defends it from the sea. Beyond the sea-wall there curves for miles in a vast and regular sweep the barren beach of shingle, with the village of Brenzett standing out darkly across the water, a spire in a clump of trees; and still further out the perpendicular column of a light-house, looking in the distance no bigger than a lead-pencil, marks the vanishing-point of the land. The country at the back of Brenzett is low and flat; but the bay is fairly well sheltered from the seas, and occasionally a big ship, windbound or through stress of weather, makes use of the anchoring ground a mile and a half due north from you as you stand at the back door of the Ship Inn in Brenzett.* A dilapidated windmill near by lifting its shattered arms from a mound no loftier than a rubbish-heap, and a Martello tower squatting at the water's edge half a mile to the south of the Coastguard cottages, are familiar to the skippers of small craft. These are the official seamarks for the patch of trustworthy bottom represented on the Admiralty charts by an irregular oval of dots enclosing several figures six, with a tiny anchor engraved among them, and the legend "mud and shells" over all.

The brow of the upland overtops the square tower of the Colebrook Church. The slope is green and looped by a white road. Ascending along this road, you open a valley broad and shallow, a wide green trough of pastures and hedges merging inland into a vista of purple tints and flowing lines closing the view.

In this valley down to Brenzett and Colebrook and up to Darnford, the market town fourteen miles away, lies the practice of my friend Kennedy. He had begun life as surgeon in the Navy, and afterwards had been the companion of a famous traveller, in the days when there were continents with unexplored interiors. His papers on the fauna and flora made him known to scientific societies. And now he had come to a country practice—from choice. The penetrating power of his mind, acting like a corrosive fluid, had destroyed his ambition, I fancy. His intelligence is of a scientific order, of an investigating habit, and of that unappeasable curiosity which believes that there is a particle of a general truth in every mystery.

A good many years ago now, on my return from abroad, he invited me to stay with him. I came readily enough, and as he could not neglect his patients to keep me company, he took me on his rounds— thirty miles or so of an afternoon, sometimes. I waited for him on the roads; the horse reached after the leafy twigs, and, sitting high in the dogcart, I could hear Kennedy's laugh through the half-open door of some cottage. He had a big, hearty laugh that would have fitted a man twice his size, a brisk manner, a bronzed face, and a pair of grey, profoundly attentive eyes. He had the talent of making people talk to him freely, and an inexhaustible patience in listening to their tales.

One day, as we trotted out of a large village into a shady bit of road, I saw on our left hand a low, brick cottage,* with diamond panes in the windows, a creeper on the end wall, a roof of shingle, and some roses climbing on the rickety trellis-work of the tiny porch. Kennedy pulled up to a walk. A woman, in full sunlight, was throwing a dripping blanket over a line stretched between two old apple-trees. And as the bobtailed, long-necked chestnut, trying to get his head, jerked the left hand, covered by a thick dogskin glove, the doctor raised his voice over the hedge: "How's your child, Amy?"

I had the time to see her dull face, red, not with a mantling blush, but as if her flat cheeks had been vigorously slapped, and to take in the squat figure, the scanty, dusty brown hair drawn into a tight knot at the back of the head. She looked quite young. With a distinct catch in her breath, her voice sounded low and timid.

"He's well, thank you."

We trotted again. "A young patient of yours," I said; and the doctor, flicking the chestnut absently, muttered, "Her husband used to be."

"She seems a dull creature," I remarked listlessly.

"Precisely," said Kennedy. "She is very passive. It's enough to look at the red hands hanging at the end of those short arms, at those slow, prominent brown eyes, to know the inertness of her mind—an inertness that one would think made it everlastingly safe from all the surprises of imagination. And yet which of us is safe? At any rate, such as you see her, she had enough imagination to fall in love. She's the daughter of one Isaac Foster, who from a small farmer has sunk into a shepherd; the beginning of his misfortunes dating from his runaway marriage with the cook of his widowed father—a well-to-do, apoplectic grazier, who passionately struck his name off his will, and had been heard to utter threats against his life. But this old affair, scandalous enough to serve as a motive for a Greek tragedy, arose from the similarity of their characters. There are other tragedies, less scandalous and of a subtler poignancy, arising from irreconcilable differences and from that fear of the Incomprehensible that hangs over all our heads—over all our heads. . . ."

The tired chestnut dropped into a walk; and the rim of the sun, all red in a speckless sky, touched familiarly the smooth top of a ploughed rise near the road as I had seen it times innumerable touch the distant horizon of the sea. The uniform brownness of the harrowed field glowed with a rosy tinge, as though the powdered clods had sweated out in minute pearls of blood the toil of uncounted ploughmen. From the edge of a copse a waggon with two horses was rolling gently along the ridge. Raised above our heads upon the skyline, it loomed up against the red sun, triumphantly big, enormous, like a chariot of giants drawn by two slow-stepping steeds of legendary proportions. And the clumsy figure of the man plodding at the head of the leading horse projected itself on the background of the Infinite with a heroic uncouthness. The end of his carter's whip quivered high up in the blue. Kennedy discoursed.

"She's the eldest of a large family. At the age of fifteen they put her out to service at the New Barns Farm. I attended Mrs. Smith, the tenant's wife, and saw that girl there for the first time. Mrs. Smith, a genteel person with a sharp nose, made her put on a black dress every afternoon. I don't know what induced me to notice her at all. There are faces that call your attention by a curious want of definiteness in their whole aspect, as, walking in a mist, you peer attentively at a vague shape which, after all, may be nothing more curious or strange than a signpost. The only peculiarity I perceived in her was a slight hesitation in her utterance, a sort of preliminary stammer which passes away with the first word. When sharply spoken to, she was apt to lose her head at once; but her heart was of the kindest. She had never been heard to express a dislike for a single human being, and she was tender to every living creature. She was devoted to Mrs. Smith, to Mr. Smith, to their dogs, cats, canaries;

and as to Mrs. Smith's grey parrot, its peculiarities exercised upon her a positive fascination. Nevertheless, when that outlandish bird, attacked by the cat, shrieked for help in human accents, she ran out into the yard stopping her ears,* and did not prevent the crime. For Mrs. Smith this was another evidence of her stupidity; on the other hand, her want of charm, in view of Smith's well-known frivolousness, was a great recommendation. Her short-sighted eyes would swim with pity for a poor mouse in a trap, and she had been seen once by some boys on her knees in the wet grass helping a toad in difficulties. If it's true, as some German fellow has said, that without phosphorus there is no thought,* it is still more true that there is no kindness of heart without a certain amount of imagination. She had some. She had even more than is necessary to understand suffering and to be moved by pity. She fell in love under circumstances that leave no room for doubt in the matter; for you need imagination to form a notion of beauty at all, and still more to discover your ideal in an unfamiliar shape.

"How this aptitude came to her, what it did feed upon, is an inscrutable mystery. She was born in the village, and had never been further away from it than Colebrook or perhaps Darnford. She lived for four years with the Smiths. New Barns is an isolated farmhouse a mile away from the road, and she was content to look day after day at the same fields, hollows, rises; at the trees and the hedgerows; at the faces of the four men about the farm, always the same—day after day, month after month, year after year. She never showed a desire for conversation, and, as it seemed to me, she did not know how to smile. Sometimes of a fine Sunday afternoon she would put on her best dress, a pair of stout boots, a large grey hat trimmed with a black feather (I've seen her in that finery), seize an absurdly slender parasol, climb over two stiles, tramp over three fields and along two hundred yards of road—never further. There stood Foster's cottage. She would help her mother to give their tea to the younger children, wash up the crockery, kiss the little ones, and go back to the farm. That was all. All the rest, all the change, all the relaxation. She never seemed to wish for anything more. And then she fell in love. She fell in love silently, obstinately—perhaps helplessly. It came slowly, but when it came it worked like a powerful spell; it was love as the Ancients understood it: an irresistible and fateful impulse—a possession! Yes, it was in her to become haunted and possessed by a face, by a presence, fatally, as though she had been a pagan worship-per of form under a joyous sky—and to be awakened at last from that mysterious forgetfulness of self, from that enchantment, from that transport, by a fear resembling the unaccountable terror of a brute. . . ."

With the sun hanging low on its western limit, the expanse of the grass-lands framed in the counter-scarps of the rising ground took on a gorgeous and sombre aspect. A sense of penetrating sadness, like that inspired by a grave strain of music, disengaged itself from the silence of the fields. The men we met walked past, slow, unsmil-ing, with downcast eyes, as if the melancholy of an over-burdened earth had weighted their feet, bowed their shoulders, borne down their glances.

"Yes," said the doctor to my remark, "one would think the earth is under a curse, since of all her children these that cling to her the closest are uncouth in body and as leaden of gait as if their very hearts were loaded with chains. But here on this same road you might have seen amongst these heavy men a being lithe, supple and long-limbed, straight like a pine, with something striving upwards in his appearance as though the heart within him had been buoyant. Perhaps it was only the force of the contrast, but when he was passing one of these villagers here, the soles of his feet did not seem to me to touch the dust of the road. He vaulted over the stiles, paced these slopes with a long elastic stride that made him noticeable at a great distance, and had lustrous black eyes. He was so different from the mankind around that, with his freedom of movement, his soft—a little startled—glance, his olive complexion and graceful bearing, his humanity suggested to me the nature of a woodland creature. He came from there."

The doctor pointed with his whip, and from the summit of the descent over the rolling tops of the trees in a park by the side of the road, appeared the level sea far below us, like the floor of an immense edifice inlaid with bands of dark ripple, with still trails of glitter, ending in a belt of glassy water at the foot of the sky. The light blurr of smoke, from an invisible steamer, faded on the great clearness of the horizon like the mist of a breath on a mirror; and, inshore, the white sails of a coaster, with the appearance of disentan-gling themselves slowly from under the branches, floated clear of the foliage of the trees.

"Shipwrecked in the bay?" I said.

"Yes; he was a castaway.* A poor emigrant from Central Europe bound to America and washed ashore here in a storm. And for him, who knew nothing of the earth, England was an undiscovered country. It was some time before he learned its name; and for all I know he might have expected to find wild beasts or wild men here, when, crawling in the dark over the sea-wall, he rolled down the other side into a dyke, where it was another miracle he didn't get drowned. But he struggled instinctively like an animal under a net,* and this blind struggle threw him out into a field. He must have been, indeed, of a tougher fibre than he looked to withstand without expiring such buffetings, the violence of his exertions, and so much fear. Later on, in his broken English that resembled curiously the speech of a young child, he told me himself that he put his trust in God, believing he was no longer in this world. And truly—he would add—how was he to know? He fought his way against the rain and the gale on all fours, and crawled at last among some sheep huddled close under the lee of a hedge. They ran off in all directions, bleating in the darkness, and he welcomed the first familiar sound he heard on these shores. It must have been two in the morning then. And this is all we know of the manner of his landing, though he did not arrive unattended by any means. Only his grisly company did not begin to come ashore till much later in the day. . . ."

The doctor gathered the reins, clicked his tongue; we trotted down the hill. Then turning, almost directly, a sharp corner into the High Street, we rattled over the stones and were home.

Late in the evening Kennedy, breaking a spell of moodiness that had come over him, returned to the story. Smoking his pipe, he paced the long room from end to end. A reading-lamp concentrated all its light upon the papers on his desk; and, sitting by the open window, I saw, after the windless, scorching day, the frigid splendour of a hazy sea lying motionless under the moon. Not a whisper, not a splash, not a stir of the shingle, not a footstep, not a sigh came up from the earth below—never a sign of life but the scent of climbing jasmine: and Kennedy's voice, speaking behind me, passed through the wide casement, to vanish outside in a chill and sumptuous stillness.

". . . . The relations of shipwrecks in the olden time tell us of much suffering. Often the castaways were only saved from drowning to die miserably from starvation on a barren coast; others suffered violent death or else slavery, passing through years of precarious existence with people to whom their strangeness was an object of suspicion, dislike or fear. We read about these things, and they are very pitiful. It is indeed hard upon a man to find himself a lost stranger, helpless, incomprehensible, and of a mysterious origin, in some obscure corner of the earth. Yet amongst all the adventurers shipwrecked in all the wild parts of the world, there is not one, it seems to me, that ever had to suffer a fate so simply tragic as the man I am speaking of, the most innocent of adventurers cast out by the sea in the bight of this bay, almost within sight from this very window.

"He did not know the name of his ship. Indeed, in the course of time we discovered he did not even know that ships had names—'like Christian people'; and when, one day, from the top of the Talfourd Hill, he beheld the sea lying open to his view, his eyes roamed afar, lost in an air of wild surprise, as though he had never seen such a sight before. And probably he had not. As far as I could make out, he had been hustled together with many others on board an emigrant-ship lying at the mouth of the Elbe,* too bewildered to take note of his surroundings, too weary to see anything, too anxious to care. They were driven below into the 'tween-deck and battened down from the very start. It was a low timber dwelling—he would say—with wooden beams overhead, like the houses in his country, but you went into it down a ladder. It was very large, very cold, damp and sombre, with places in the manner of wooden boxes where people had to sleep one above another, and it kept on rocking all ways at once all the time. He crept into one of these boxes and lay down there in the clothes in which he had left his home many days before, keeping his bundle and his stick by his side. People groaned, children cried, water dripped, the lights went out, the walls of the place creaked, and everything was being shaken so that in one's little box one dared not lift one's head. He had lost touch with his only companion (a young man from the same valley, he said), and all the time a great noise of wind went on outside and heavy blows fell—boom! boom! An awful sickness overcame him, even to the point of making him neglect his prayers. Besides, one could not tell whether it was morning or evening. It seemed always to be night in that place.

"Before that he had been travelling a long, long time on the iron track. He looked out of the window, which had a wonderfully clear glass in it, and the trees, the houses, the fields, and the long roads seemed to fly round and round about him till his head swam. He gave me to understand that he had on his passage beheld uncounted multitudes of people—whole nations—all dressed in such clothes as the rich wear. Once he was made to get out of the carriage, and slept through a night on a bench in a house of bricks with his bundle under his head; and once for many hours he had to sit on a floor of flat stones dozing, with his knees up and with his bundle between his feet. There was a roof over him, which seemed made of glass, and was so high that the tallest mountain-pine he had ever seen would have had room to grow under it. Steam-machines rolled in at one end and out at the other. People swarmed more than you can see on a feast-day round the miraculous Holy Image in the yard of the Carmelite Convent down in the plains where, before he left his home, he drove his mother in a wooden cart:—a pious old woman who wanted to offer prayers and make a vow for his safety. He could not give me an idea of how large and lofty and full of noise and smoke and gloom, and clang of iron, the place was, but some one had told him it was called Berlin. Then they rang a bell, and another steam-machine came in, and again he was taken on and on through a land that wearied his eyes by its flatness without a single bit of a hill to be seen anywhere. One more night he spent shut up in a building like a good stable with a litter of straw on the floor, guarding his bundle amongst a lot of men, of whom not one could understand a single word he said. In the morning they were all led down to the stony shores of an extremely broad muddy river, flowing not between hills but between houses that seemed immense. There was a steam-machine that went on the water, and they all stood upon it packed tight, only now there were with them many women and children who made much noise. A cold rain fell, the wind blew in his face; he was wet through, and his teeth chattered. He and the young man from the same valley took each other by the hand.

"They thought they were being taken to America straight away, but suddenly the steam-machine bumped against the side of a thing like a great house on the water. The walls were smooth and black, and there uprose, growing from the roof as it were, bare trees in the shape of crosses, extremely high. That's how it appeared to him then, for he had never seen a ship before. This was the ship that was going to swim all the way to America. Voices shouted, everything swayed; there was a ladder dipping up and down. He went up on his hands and knees in mortal fear of falling into the water below, which made a great splashing. He got separated from his companion, and when he descended into the bottom of that ship his heart seemed to melt suddenly within him.

"It was then also, as he told me, that he lost contact for good and all with one of those three men who the summer before had been going about through all the little towns in the foothills of his country. They would arrive on market-days driving in a peasant's cart, and would set up an office in an inn or some other Jew's house. There were three of them, of whom one with a long beard looked venerable; and they had red cloth collars round their necks and gold lace on their sleeves like Government officials. They sat proudly behind a long table; and in the next room, so that the common people shouldn't hear, they kept a cunning telegraph machine, through which they could talk to the Emperor of America. The fathers hung about the door, but the young men of the mountains would crowd up to the table asking many questions, for there was work to be got all the year round at three dollars a day in America, and no military service to do.

"But the American Kaiser would not take everybody. Oh no! He himself had a great difficulty in getting accepted, and the venerable man in uniform had to go out of the room several times to work the telegraph on his behalf. The American Kaiser engaged him at last at three dollars, he being young and strong. However, many able young men backed out, afraid of the great distance; besides, those only who had some money could be taken. There were some who sold their huts and their land because it cost a lot of money to get to America; but then, once there, you had three dollars a day, and if you were clever you could find places where true gold could be picked up on the ground. His father's house was getting over-full. Two of his brothers were married and had children. He promised to send money home from America by post twice a year. His father sold an old cow, a pair of piebald mountain ponies of his own raising, and a cleared plot of fair pasture land on the sunny slope of a pine-clad pass to a Jew inn-keeper, in order to pay the people of the ship that took men to America to get rich in a short time.

"He must have been a real adventurer at heart, for how many of the greatest enterprises in the conquest of the earth had for their beginning just such a bargaining away of the paternal cow for the mirage of true gold far away! I have been telling you more or less in my own words what I learned fragmentarily in the course of two or three years, during which I seldom missed an opportunity of a friendly chat with him. He told me this story of his adventure with many flashes of white teeth and lively glances of black eyes, at first in a sort of anxious baby-talk, then, as he acquired the language, with great fluency, but always with that singing, soft, and at the same time vibrating intonation that instilled a strangely penetrating power into the sound of the most familiar English words, as if they had been the words of an unearthly language. And he always would come to an end, with many emphatic shakes of his head, upon that awful sensation of his heart melting within him directly he set foot on board that ship. Afterwards there seemed to come for him a period of blank ignorance, at any rate as to facts. No doubt he must have been abominably seasick and abominably unhappy—this soft and passionate adventurer, taken thus out of his knowledge, and feeling bitterly as he lay in his emigrant bunk his utter loneliness; for his was a highly sensitive nature. The next thing we know of him for certain is that he had been hiding in Hammond's pig-pound by the side of the road to Norton, six miles, as the crow flies, from the sea. Of these experiences he was unwilling to speak: they seemed to have seared into his soul a sombre sort of wonder and indignation. Through the rumours of the country-side, which lasted for a good many days after his arrival, we know that the fishermen of West Colebrook had been disturbed and startled by heavy knocks against the walls of weatherboard cottages, and by a voice crying piercingly strange words in the night. Several of them turned out even, but, no doubt, he had fled in sudden alarm at their rough angry tones hailing each other in the darkness. A sort of frenzy must have helped him up the steep Norton hill. It was he, no doubt, who early the following morning had been seen lying (in a swoon, I should say) on the roadside grass by the Brenzett carrier, who actually got down to have a nearer look, but drew back, intimidated by the perfect immobility, and by something queer in the aspect of that tramp, sleeping so still under the showers. As the day advanced, some children came dashing into school at Norton in such a fright that the schoolmistress went out and spoke indignantly to a 'horrid-looking man' on the road. He edged away, hanging his head, for a few steps, and then suddenly ran off with extraordinary fleetness. The driver of Mr. Bradley's milk-cart made no secret of it that he had lashed with his whip at a hairy sort of gipsy fellow who, jumping up at a turn of the road by the Vents, made a snatch at the pony's bridle. And he caught him a good one too, right over the face, he said, that made him drop down in the mud a jolly sight quicker than he had jumped up; but it was a good half a mile before he could stop the pony. Maybe that in his desperate endeavours to get help, and in his need to get in touch with some one, the poor devil had tried to stop the cart. Also three boys confessed afterwards to throwing stones at a funny tramp, knocking about all wet and muddy, and, it seemed, very drunk, in the narrow deep lane by the limekilns. All this was the talk of three villages for days; but we have Mrs. Finn's (the wife of Smith's waggoner) unimpeachable testimony that she saw him get over the low wall of Hammond's pig-pound and lurch straight at her, babbling aloud in a voice that was enough to make one die of fright. Having the baby with her in a perambulator, Mrs. Finn called out to him to go away, and as he persisted in coming nearer, she hit him courageously with her umbrella over the head, and, without once looking back, ran like the wind with the perambulator as far as the first house in the village. She stopped then, out of breath, and spoke to old Lewis, hammering there at a heap of stones; and the old chap, taking off his immense black wire goggles, got up on his shaky legs to look where she pointed. Together they followed with their eyes the figure of the man running over a field; they saw him fall down, pick himself up, and run on again, staggering and waving his long arms above his head, in the direction of the New Barns Farm. From that moment he is plainly in the toils of his obscure and touching destiny. There is no doubt after this of what happened to him. All is certain now: Mrs. Smith's intense terror; Amy Foster's stolid conviction held against the other's nervous attack, that the man 'meant no harm'; Smith's exasperation (on his return from Darnford Market) at finding the dog barking himself into a fit, the back-door locked, his wife in hysterics; and all for an unfortunate dirty tramp, supposed to be even then lurking in his stackyard. Was he? He would teach him to frighten women.

"Smith is notoriously hot-tempered, but the sight of some non-descript and miry creature sitting cross-legged amongst a lot of loose straw, and swinging itself to and fro like a bear in a cage, made him pause. Then this tramp stood up silently before him, one mass of mud and filth from head to foot. Smith, alone amongst his stacks with this apparition, in the stormy twilight ringing with the infuriated barking of the dog, felt the dread of an inexplicable strangeness. But when that being, parting with his black hands the long matted locks that hung before his face, as you part the two halves of a curtain, looked out at him with glistening, wild, black-and-white eyes, the weirdness of this silent encounter fairly staggered him. He has admitted since (for the story has been a legitimate subject of conversation about here for years) that he made more than one step backwards. Then a sudden burst of rapid, senseless speech persuaded him at once that he had to do with an escaped lunatic. In fact, that impression never wore off completely. Smith has not in his heart given up his secret conviction of the man's essential insanity to this very day.

"As the creature approached him, jabbering in a most discomposing manner, Smith (unaware that he was being addressed as 'gracious lord,' and adjured in God's name to afford food and shelter) kept on speaking firmly but gently to it, and retreating all the time into the other yard. At last, watching his chance, by a sudden charge he bundled him headlong into the wood-lodge, and instantly shot the bolt. Thereupon he wiped his brow, though the day was cold. He had done his duty to the community by shutting up a wandering and probably dangerous maniac. Smith isn't a hard man at all, but he had room in his brain only for that one idea of lunacy. He was not imaginative enough to ask himself whether the man might not be perishing with cold and hunger. Meantime, at first, the maniac made a great deal of noise in the lodge. Mrs. Smith was screaming upstairs, where she had locked herself in her bedroom; but Amy Foster sobbed piteously at the kitchen-door, wringing her hands and muttering, 'Don't! don't!' I daresay Smith had a rough time of it that evening with one noise and another, and this insane, disturbing voice crying obstinately through the door only added to his irritation. He couldn't possibly have connected this troublesome lunatic with the sinking of a ship in Eastbay, of which there had been a rumour in the Darnford market-place. And I daresay the man inside had been very near to insanity on that night. Before his excitement collapsed and he became unconscious he was throwing himself violently about in the dark, rolling on some dirty sacks, and biting his fists with rage, cold, hunger, amazement, and despair.

"He was a mountaineer of the eastern range of the Carpathians, and the vessel sunk the night before in Eastbay was the Hamburg emigrant-ship *Herzogin Sophia-Dorothea*, of appalling memory.

"A few months later we could read in the papers the accounts of the bogus 'Emigration Agencies' among the Sclavonian peasantry in the more remote provinces of Austria. The object of these scoundrels was to get hold of the poor ignorant people's homesteads, and they were in league with the local usurers. They exported their victims through Hamburg mostly. As to the ship, I had watched her out of this very window, reaching close-hauled under short canvas into the bay on a dark, threatening afternoon. She came to an anchor, correctly by the chart, off the Brenzett Coastguard station. I remember before the night fell looking out again at the outlines of her spars and rigging that stood out dark and pointed on a background of ragged, slaty clouds like another and a slighter spire to the left of the Brenzett church-tower. In the evening the wind rose. At midnight I could hear in my bed the terrific gusts and the sounds of a driving deluge.

"About that time the Coastguardmen thought they saw the lights of a steamer over the anchoring-ground. In a moment they vanished; but it is clear that another vessel of some sort had tried for shelter in the bay on that awful, blind night, had rammed the German ship amidships (a breach—as one of the divers told me afterwards—'that you could sail a Thames barge through'), and then had gone out either scathless or damaged, who shall say; but had gone out, unknown, unseen, and fatal, to perish mysteriously at sea. Of her nothing ever came to light, and yet the hue and cry that was raised all over the world would have found her out if she had been in existence anywhere on the face of the waters.

"A completeness without a clue, and a stealthy silence as of a neatly executed crime, characterise this murderous disaster, which, as you may remember, had its gruesome celebrity. The wind would have prevented the loudest outcries from reaching the shore; there had been evidently no time for signals of distress. It was death without any sort of fuss. The Hamburg ship, filling all at once, capsized as she sank, and at daylight there was not even the end of a spar to be seen above water. She was missed, of course, and at first the

Coastguardmen surmised that she had either dragged her anchor or parted her cable some time during the night, and had been blown out to sea. Then, after the tide turned, the wreck must have shifted a little and released some of the bodies, because a child—a little fair-haired child in a red frock—came ashore abreast of the Martello tower. By the afternoon you could see along three miles of beach dark figures with bare legs dashing in and out of the tumbling foam, and rough-looking men, women with hard faces, children, mostly fair-haired, were being carried, stiff and dripping, on stretchers, on wattles, on ladders, in a long procession past the door of the Ship Inn, to be laid out in a row under the north wall of the Brenzett Church.

"Officially, the body of the little girl in the red frock is the first thing that came ashore from that ship. But I have patients amongst the seafaring population of West Colebrook, and, unofficially, I am informed that very early that morning two brothers, who went down to look after their cobble hauled up on the beach, found, a good way from Brenzett, an ordinary ship's hencoop lying high and dry on the shore, with eleven drowned ducks inside. Their families ate the birds, and the hencoop was split into firewood with a hatchet. It is possible that a man (supposing he happened to be on deck at the time of the accident) might have floated ashore on that hencoop. He might. I admit it is improbable, but there was the man—and for days, nay, for weeks—it didn't enter our heads that we had amongst us the only living soul that had escaped from that disaster. The man himself, even when he learned to speak intelligibly, could tell us very little. He remembered he had felt better (after the ship had anchored, I suppose), and that the darkness, the wind, and the rain took his breath away. This looks as if he had been on deck some time during that night. But we mustn't forget he had been taken out of his knowledge, that he had been sea-sick and battened down below for four days, that he had no general notion of a ship or of the sea, and therefore could have no definite idea of what was happening to him. The rain, the wind, the darkness he knew; he understood the bleating of the sheep, and he remembered the pain of his wretchedness and misery, his heartbroken astonishment that it was neither seen nor understood, his dismay at finding all the men angry and all the women fierce. He had approached them as a beggar, it is true, he said; but in his country, even if they gave nothing, they spoke gently to beggars. The children in his country were not taught to throw stones at those who asked for compassion. Smith's strategy overcame him completely. The wood-lodge presented the horrible aspect of a dungeon. What would be done to him next? . . . No wonder that Amy Foster appeared to his eyes with the aureole of an angel of light. The girl had not been able to sleep for thinking of the poor man, and in the morning, before the Smiths were up, she slipped out across the back yard. Holding the door of the wood-lodge ajar, she looked in and extended to him half a loaf of white bread—'such bread as the rich eat in my country,' he used to say.

"At this he got up slowly from amongst all sorts of rubbish, stiff, hungry, trembling, miserable, and doubtful. 'Can you eat this?' she asked in her soft and timid voice. He must have taken her for a 'gracious lady.' He devoured ferociously, and tears were falling on the crust. Suddenly he dropped the bread, seized her wrist, and imprinted a kiss on her hand. She was not frightened. Through his forlorn condition she had observed that he was good-looking. She shut the door and walked back slowly to the kitchen. Much later on, she told Mrs. Smith, who shuddered at the bare idea of being touched by that creature.

"Through this act of impulsive pity he was brought back again within the pale of human relations with his new surroundings. He never forgot it—never.

"That very same morning old Mr. Swaffer (Smith's nearest neighbour) came over to give his advice, and ended by carrying him off. He stood, unsteady on his legs, meek, and caked over in half-dried mud, while the two men talked around him in an incomprehensible tongue. Mrs. Smith had refused to come downstairs till the madman was off the premises; Amy Foster, far from within the dark kitchen, watched through the open back door; and he obeyed the signs that were made to him to the best of his ability. But Smith was full of mistrust. 'Mind, sir! It may be all his cunning,' he cried repeatedly in a tone of warning. When Mr. Swaffer started the mare, the deplorable being sitting humbly by his side, through weakness, nearly fell out over the back of the high two-wheeled cart. Swaffer took him straight home. And it is then that I come upon the scene.

"I was called in by the simple process of the old man beckoning to me with his forefinger over the gate of his house as I happened to be driving past. I got down, of course.

"'I've got something here,' he mumbled, leading the way to an outhouse at a little distance from his other farm-buildings.

"It was there that I saw him first, in a long low room taken upon the space of that sort of coach-house. It was bare and whitewashed, with a small square aperture glazed with one cracked, dusty pane at its further end. He was lying on his back upon a straw pallet; they had given him a couple of horse-blankets, and he seemed to have spent the remainder of his strength in the exertion of cleaning himself. He was almost speechless; his quick breathing under the blankets pulled up to his chin, his glittering, restless black eyes reminded me of a wild bird caught in a snare. While I was examining him, old Swaffer stood silently by the door, passing the tips of his fingers along his shaven upper lip. I gave some directions, promised to send a bottle of medicine, and naturally made some inquiries.

"'Smith caught him in the stackyard at New Barns,' said the old chap in his deliberate, unmoved manner, and as if the other had been indeed a sort of wild animal, 'That's how I came by him. Quite a curiosity, isn't he? Now tell me, doctor—you've been all over the world—don't you think that's a bit of a Hindoo we've got hold of here?'

"I was greatly surprised. His long black hair scattered over the straw bolster contrasted with the olive pallor of his face. It occurred to me he might be a Basque. It didn't necessarily follow that he should understand Spanish; but I tried him with the few words I know, and also with some French. The whispered sounds I caught by bending my ear to his lips puzzled me utterly. That afternoon the young ladies from the Rectory (one of them read Goethe with a dictionary, and the other had struggled with Dante for years), coming to see Miss Swaffer, tried their German and Italian on him from the doorway. They retreated, just the least bit scared by the flood of passionate speech which, turning on his pallet, he let out at them. They admitted that the sound was pleasant, soft, musical—but, in conjunction with his looks perhaps, it was startling—so excitable, so utterly unlike anything one had ever heard. The village boys climbed up the bank to have a peep through the little square aperture. Everybody was wondering what Mr. Swaffer would do with him.

"He simply kept him.

"Swaffer would be called eccentric were he not so much respected. They will tell you that Mr. Swaffer sits up as late as ten o'clock at night to read books, and they will tell you also that he can write a cheque for two hundred pounds without thinking twice about it. He himself would tell you that the Swaffers had owned land between this and Darnford for these three hundred years. He must be eighty-five today, but he does not look a bit older than when I first came here. He is a great breeder of sheep, and deals extensively in cattle. He attends market days for miles around in every sort of weather, and drives sitting bowed low over the reins, his lank grey hair curling over the collar of his warm coat, and with a green plaid rug round his legs. The calmness of advanced age gives a solemnity to his manner. He is clean-shaved; his lips are thin and sensitive; something rigid and monachal in the set of his features lends a certain elevation to the character of his face. He has been known to drive miles in the rain to see a new kind of rose in somebody's garden, or a monstrous cabbage grown by a cottager. He loves to hear tell of or to be shown something what he calls 'outlandish.' Perhaps it was just that outlandishness of the man which influenced old Swaffer. Perhaps it was only an inexplicable caprice. All I know is that at the end of three weeks I caught sight of Smith's lunatic digging in Swaffer's kitchen garden. They had found out he could use a spade. He dug barefooted.

"His black hair flowed over his shoulders. I suppose it was Swaffer who had given him the striped old cotton shirt; but he wore still the national brown cloth trousers (in which he had been washed ashore) fitting to the leg almost like tights; was belted with a broad leathern belt studded with little brass discs; and had never yet ventured into the village. The land he looked upon seemed to him kept neatly, like the grounds round a landowner's house; the size of the cart-horses struck him with astonishment; the roads resembled garden walks, and the aspect of the people, especially on Sundays, spoke of opulence. He wondered what made them so hardhearted and their children so bold. He got his food at the back door, carried it in both hands, carefully, to his outhouse, and, sitting alone on his pallet, would make the sign of the cross before he began. Beside the same pallet, kneeling in the early darkness of the short days, he recited aloud the Lord's Prayer before he slept. Whenever he saw old Swaffer he would bow with veneration from the waist, and stand erect while the old man, with his fingers over his upper lip, surveyed him silently. He bowed also to Miss Swaffer, who kept house frugally for her father—a broad-shouldered, big-boned woman of forty-five, with the pocket of her dress full of keys, and a grey, steady eye. She was Church—as people said (while her father was one of the trustees of the Baptist Chapel)—and wore a little steel cross at her waist. She dressed severely in black, in memory of one of the innumerable Bradleys of the neighbourhood, to whom she had been engaged some twenty-five years ago—a young farmer who broke his neck out hunting on the eve of the wedding-day. She had the unmoved countenance of the deaf, spoke very seldom, and her lips, thin like her father's, astonished one sometimes by a mysteriously ironic curl.

"These were the people to whom he owed allegiance, and an overwhelming loneliness seemed to fall from the leaden sky of that winter without sunshine. All the faces were sad. He could talk to no one, and had no hope of ever understanding anybody. It was as if these had been the faces of people from the other world—dead people—he used to tell me years afterwards. Upon my word, I wonder he did not go mad. He didn't know where he was. Somewhere very far from his mountains—somewhere over the water. Was this America, he wondered?

"If it hadn't been for the steel cross at Miss Swaffer's belt he would not, he confessed, have known whether he was in a Christian country at all. He used to cast stealthy glances at it, and feel comforted. There was nothing here the same as in his country! The earth and the water were different; there were no images of the Redeemer by the roadside. The very grass was different, and the trees. All the trees but the three old Norway pines on the bit of lawn before Swaffer's house, and these reminded him of his country. He had been detected once, after dusk, with his forehead against the trunk of one of them, sobbing, and talking to himself. They had been like brothers to him at that time, he affirmed. Everything else was strange. Conceive you* the kind of an existence over-shadowed, oppressed, by the everyday material appearances, as if by the visions of a nightmare. At night, when he could not sleep, he kept on thinking of the girl who gave him the first piece of bread he had eaten in this foreign land. She had been neither fierce nor angry, nor frightened. Her face he remembered as the only comprehensible face amongst all these faces that were as closed, as mysterious, and as mute as the faces of the dead who are possessed of a knowledge beyond the comprehension of the living. I wonder whether the memory of her compassion prevented him from cutting his throat. But there! I suppose I am an old sentimentalist, and forget the instinctive love of life which it takes all the strength of an uncommon despair to overcome.

"He did the work which was given him with an intelligence which surprised old Swaffer. By-and-by it was discovered that he could help at the ploughing, could milk the cows, feed the bullocks in the cattle-yard, and was of some use with the sheep. He began to pick up words, too, very fast; and suddenly, one fine morning in spring, he rescued from an untimely death a grand-child of old Swaffer.

"Swaffer's younger daughter is married to Willcox, a solicitor and the Town Clerk of Colebrook. Regularly twice a year they come to stay with the old man for a few days. Their only child, a little girl not three years old at the time, ran out of the house alone in her little white pinafore, and, toddling across the grass of a terraced garden, pitched herself over a low wall head first into the horsepond in the yard below.

"Our man was out with the waggoner and the plough in the field nearest to the house, and as he was leading the team round to begin a fresh furrow, he saw, through the gap of a gate, what for anybody else would have been a mere flutter of something white. But he had straight-glancing, quick, far-reaching eyes, that only seemed to flinch and lose their amazing power before the immensity of the sea. He was barefooted, and looking as outlandish as the heart of Swaffer could desire. Leaving the horses on the turn, to the inexpressible disgust of the waggoner he bounded off, going over the ploughed ground in long leaps, and suddenly appeared before the mother, thrust the child into her arms, and strode away.

"The pond was not very deep; but still, if he had not had such good eyes, the child would have perished—miserably suffocated in the foot or so of sticky mud at the bottom. Old Swaffer walked out slowly into the field, waited till the plough came over to his side, had a good look at him, and without saying a word went back to the house. But from that time they laid out his meals on the kitchen table; and at first, Miss Swaffer, all in black and with an inscrutable face, would come and stand in the doorway of the living-room to see him make a big sign of the cross before he fell to. I believe that from that day, too, Swaffer began to pay him regular wages.

"I can't follow step by step his development. He cut his hair short, was seen in the village and along the road going to and fro to his work like any other man. Children ceased to shout after him. He became aware of social differences, but remained for a long time surprised at the bare poverty of the churches among so much wealth. He couldn't understand either why they were kept shut up on week-days. There was nothing to steal in them. Was it to keep people from praying too often? The rectory took much notice of him about that time, and I believe the young ladies attempted to prepare the ground for his conversion. They could not, however, break him of his habit of crossing himself, but he went so far as to take off the string with a couple of brass medals the size of a sixpence, a tiny metal cross, and a square sort of scapulary which he wore round his neck. He hung them on the wall by the side of his bed, and he was still to be heard every evening reciting the Lord's Prayer, in incomprehensible words and in a slow, fervent tone, as he had heard his old father do at the head of all the kneeling family, big and little, on every evening of his life. And though he wore corduroys at work, and a slop-made pepper-and-salt suit on Sundays, strangers would turn round to look after him on the road. His foreignness had a peculiar and indelible stamp. At last people became used to seeing him. But they never became used to him. His rapid, skimming walk; his swarthy complexion; his hat cocked on the left ear; his habit, on warm evenings, of wearing his coat over one shoulder, like a hussar's dolman; his manner of leaping over the stiles, not as a feat of agility, but in the ordinary course of progression—all these peculiarities were, as one may say, so many causes of scorn and offence to the inhabitants of the village. *They* wouldn't in their dinner hour lie flat on their backs on the grass to stare at the sky. Neither did they go about the fields screaming dismal tunes. Many times have I heard his high-pitched voice from behind the ridge of some sloping sheep-walk, a voice light and soaring, like a lark's, but with a melancholy human note, over our fields that hear only the song of birds. And I would be startled myself. Ah! He was different: innocent of heart, and full of good will, which nobody wanted, this castaway, that, like a man transplanted into another planet, was separated by an immense space from his past and by an immense ignorance from his future. His quick, fervent utterance positively shocked everybody. "An excitable devil," they called him. One evening, in the tap-room of the Coach and Horses (having drunk some whisky), he upset them all by singing a love-song of his country. They hooted him down, and he was pained; but Preble, the lame wheelwright, and Vincent, the fat blacksmith, and the other notables too, wanted to drink their evening beer in peace. On another occasion he tried to show them how to dance. The dust rose in clouds from the sanded floor; he leaped straight up amongst the deal tables, struck his heels together, squatted on one heel in front of old Preble, shooting out the other leg, uttered wild and exulting cries, jumped up to whirl on one foot, snapping his fingers above his head—and a strange carter who was having a drink in there began to swear, and cleared out with his half-pint in his hand into the bar. But when suddenly he sprang upon a table and continued to dance among the glasses, the landlord interfered. He didn't want any 'acrobat tricks in the tap-room.' They laid their hands on him. Having had a glass or two, Mr. Swaffer's foreigner tried to expostulate: was ejected forcibly: got a black eye.

"I believe he felt the hostility of his human surroundings. But he was tough—tough in spirit, too, as well as in body. Only the memory of the sea frightened him, with that vague terror that is left by a bad dream. His home was far away; and he did not want now to go to America. I had often explained to him that there is no place on earth where true gold can be found lying ready and to be got for the trouble of the picking up. How then, he asked, could he ever return home with empty hands when there had been sold a cow, two ponies, and a bit of land to pay for his going? His eyes would fill with tears, and, averting them from the immense shimmer of the sea, he would throw himself face down on the grass. But sometimes, cocking his hat with a little conquering air, he would defy my wisdom. He had found his bit of true gold. That was Amy Foster's heart; which was 'a golden heart, and soft to people's misery,' he would say in the accents of overwhelming conviction.

"He was called Yanko. He had explained that this meant Little John; but as he would also repeat very often that he was a mountaineer (some word sounding in the dialect of his country like Goorall) he got it for his surname.* And this is the only trace of him that the succeeding ages may find in the marriage register of the parish. There it stands—Yanko Goorall—in the rector's handwriting. The crooked cross made by the castaway, a cross whose tracing no doubt seemed to him the most solemn part of the whole ceremony, is all that remains now to perpetuate the memory of his name.

"His courtship had lasted some time—ever since he got his precarious footing in the community. It began by his buying for Amy Foster a green satin ribbon in Darnford. This was what you did in his country. You bought a ribbon at a Jew's stall on a fair-day. I don't suppose the girl knew what to do with it, but he seemed to think that his honourable intentions could not be mistaken.

"It was only when he declared his purpose to get married that I fully understood how, for a hundred futile and inappreciable reasons, how—shall I say odious?—he was to all the countryside. Every old woman in the village was up in arms. Smith, coming upon him near the farm, promised to break his head for him if he found him about again. But he twisted his little black moustache with such a bellicose air and rolled such big, black fierce eyes at Smith that this promise came to nothing. Smith, however, told the girl that she must be mad to take up with a man who was surely wrong in his head. All the same, when she heard him in the gloaming whistle from beyond the orchard a couple of bars of a weird and mournful tune, she would drop whatever she had in her hand—she would leave Mrs. Smith in the middle of a sentence—and she would run out to his call. Mrs. Smith called her a shameless hussy. She answered nothing. She said nothing at all to anybody, and went on her way as if she had been deaf. She and I alone in all the land, I fancy, could see his very real beauty. He was very good-looking, and most graceful in his bearing, with that something wild as of a woodland creature in his aspect. Her mother moaned over her dismally whenever the girl came to see her on her day out. The father was surly, but pretended not to know; and Mrs. Finn once told her plainly that 'this man, my dear, will do you some harm some day yet.' And so it went on. They could be seen on the roads, she tramping stolidly in her finery—grey dress, black feather, stout boots, prominent white cotton gloves that caught your eye a hundred yards away; and he, his coat slung picturesquely over one shoulder, pacing by her side, gallant of bearing and casting tender glances upon the girl with the golden heart. I wonder whether he saw how plain she was. Perhaps among types so different from what he had ever seen, he had not the power to judge; or perhaps he was seduced by the divine quality of her pity.

"Yanko was in great trouble meantime. In his country you get an old man for an ambassador in marriage affairs. He did not know how to proceed. However, one day in the midst of sheep in a field (he was now Swaffer's under-shepherd with Foster) he took off his hat to the father and declared himself humbly. 'I daresay she's fool enough to marry you,' was all Foster said. 'And then,' he used to relate, 'he puts his hat on his head, looks black at me as if he wanted to cut my throat, whistles the dog, and off he goes, leaving me to do the work.' The Fosters, of course, didn't like to lose the wages the girl earned: Amy used to give all her money to her mother. But there was in Foster a very genuine aversion to that match. He contended that the fellow was very good with sheep, but was not fit for any girl to marry. For one thing, he used to go along the hedges muttering to himself like a dam' fool; and then, these foreigners behave very queerly to women sometimes. And perhaps he would want to carry her off somewhere—or run off himself. It was not safe. He preached it to his daughter that the fellow might ill-use her in some way. She made no answer. It was, they said in the village, as if the man had done something to her. People discussed the matter. It was quite an excitement, and the two went on 'walking out' together in the face of opposition. Then something unexpected happened.

"I don't know whether old Swaffer ever understood how much he was regarded in the light of a father by his foreign retainer. Anyway the relation was curiously feudal. So when Yanko asked formally for an interview—'and the Miss too' (he called the severe, deaf Miss Swaffer simply *Miss*)—it was to obtain their permission to marry. Swaffer heard him unmoved, dismissed him by a nod, and then shouted the intelligence into Miss Swaffer's best ear. She showed no surprise, and only remarked grimly, in a veiled blank voice, 'He certainly won't get any other girl to marry him.'

"It is Miss Swaffer who has all the credit of the munificence: but in a very few days it came out that Mr. Swaffer had presented Yanko with a cottage (the cottage you've seen this morning) and something like an acre of ground—had made it over to him in absolute property. Willcox expedited the deed, and I remember him telling me he had a great pleasure in making it ready. It recited: 'In consideration of saving the life of my beloved grandchild, Bertha Willcox.'

"Of course, after that no power on earth could prevent them from getting married.

"Her infatuation endured. People saw her going out to meet him in the evening. She stared with unblinking, fascinated eyes up the road where he was expected to appear, walking freely, with a swing from the hip, and humming one of the love-tunes of his country. When the boy was born, he got elevated at the Coach and Horses, essayed again a song and a dance, and was again ejected. People expressed their commiseration for a woman married to that Jack-in-the-box. He didn't care. There was a man now (he told me boastfully) to whom he could sing and talk in the language of his country, and show how to dance by-and-by.

"But I don't know. To me he appeared to have grown less springy of step, heavier in body, less keen of eye. Imagination, no doubt; but it seems to me now as if the net of fate had been drawn closer round him already.

"One day I met him on the footpath over the Talfourd Hill. He told me that 'women were funny.' I had heard already of domestic differences. People were saying that Amy Foster was beginning to find out what sort of man she had married. He looked upon the sea with indifferent, unseeing eyes. His wife had snatched the child out of his arms one day as he sat on the doorstep crooning to it a song such as the mothers sing to babies in his mountains. She seemed to think he was doing it some harm. Women are funny. And she had objected to him praying aloud in the evening. Why? He expected the boy to repeat the prayer aloud after him by-and-by, as he used to do after his old father when he was a child—in his own country. And I discovered he longed for their boy to grow up so that he could have a man to talk with in that language that to our ears sounded so disturbing, so passionate, and so bizarre. Why his wife should dislike the idea he couldn't tell. But that would pass, he said. And tilting his head knowingly, he tapped his breastbone to indicate that she had a good heart: not hard, not fierce, open to compassion, charitable to the poor!

"I walked away thoughtfully; I wondered whether his difference, his strangeness, were not penetrating with repulsion that dull nature they had begun by irresistibly attracting. I wondered. . . ."

The Doctor came to the window and looked out at the frigid splendour of the sea, immense in the haze, as if enclosing all the earth with all the hearts lost among the passions of love and fear.

"Physiologically, now," he said, turning away abruptly, "it was possible. It was possible."

He remained silent. Then went on—

"At all events, the next time I saw him he was ill—lung trouble.

He was tough, but I daresay he was not acclimatised as well as I had supposed. It was a bad winter; and, of course, these mountaineers do get fits of home sickness; and a state of depression would make him vulnerable. He was lying half dressed on a couch downstairs.

"A table covered with a dark oilcloth took up all the middle of the little room. There was a wicker cradle on the floor, a kettle spouting steam on the hob, and some child's linen lay drying on the fender. The room was warm, but the door opens right into the garden, as you noticed perhaps.

"He was very feverish, and kept on muttering to himself. She sat on a chair and looked at him fixedly across the table with her brown, blurred eyes. 'Why don't you have him upstairs?' I asked. With a start and a confused stammer she said, 'Oh! ah! I couldn't sit with him upstairs, sir.'

"I gave her certain directions; and going outside, I said again that he ought to be in bed upstairs. She wrung her hands. 'I couldn't. I couldn't. He keeps on saying something—I don't know what.' With the memory of all the talk against the man that had been dinned into her ears, I looked at her narrowly. I looked into her short-sighted eyes, at her dumb eyes that once in her life had seen an enticing shape, but seemed, staring at me, to see nothing at all now. But I saw she was uneasy.

"'What's the matter with him?' she asked in a sort of vacant trepidation. 'He doesn't look very ill. I never did see anybody look like this before. . . .'

"'Do you think,' I asked indignantly, 'he is shamming?'

"'I can't help it, sir,' she said stolidly. And suddenly she clapped her hands and looked right and left. 'And there's the baby. I am so frightened. He wanted me just now to give him the baby. I can't understand what he says to it.'

"'Can't you ask a neighbour to come in tonight?' I asked.

"'Please, sir, nobody seems to care to come,' she muttered, dully resigned all at once.

"I impressed upon her the necessity of the greatest care, and then had to go. There was a good deal of sickness that winter. 'Oh, I hope he won't talk!' she exclaimed softly just as I was going away.

"I don't know how it is I did not see—but I didn't. And yet, turning in my trap, I saw her lingering before the door, very still, and as if meditating a flight up the miry road.

"Towards the night his fever increased.

"He tossed, moaned, and now and then muttered a complaint. And she sat with the table between her and the couch, watching every movement and every sound, with the terror, the unreasonable terror, of that man she could not understand creeping over her. She had drawn the wicker cradle close to her feet. There was nothing in her now but the maternal instinct and that unaccountable fear.

"Suddenly coming to himself, parched, he demanded a drink of water. She did not move. She had not understood, though he may have thought he was speaking in English. He waited, looking at her, burning with fever, amazed at her silence and immobility, and then he shouted impatiently, 'Water! Give me water!'

"She jumped to her feet, snatched up the child, and stood still. He spoke to her, and his passionate remonstrances only increased her fear of that strange man. I believe he spoke to her for a long time, entreating, wondering, pleading, ordering, I suppose. She says she bore it as long as she could. And then a gust of rage came over him.

"He sat up and called out terribly one word—some word. Then he got up as though he hadn't been ill at all, she says. And as in fevered dismay, indignation, and wonder he tried to get to her round the table, she simply opened the door and ran out with the child in her arms. She heard him call twice after her down the road in a terrible voice—and fled. . . . Ah! but you should have seen stirring behind the dull, blurred glance of these eyes the spectre of the fear which had hunted her on that night three miles and a half to the door of Foster's cottage! I did the next day.

"And it was I who found him lying face down and his body in a puddle, just outside the little wicket gate.*

"I had been called out that night to an urgent case in the village, and on my way home at daybreak passed by the cottage. The door stood open. My man helped me to carry him in. We laid him on the couch. The lamp smoked, the fire was out, the chill of the stormy night oozed from the cheerless yellow paper on the wall. 'Amy!' I called aloud, and my voice seemed to lose itself in the emptiness of this tiny house as if I had cried in a desert. He opened his eyes. 'Gone!' he said distinctly. 'I had only asked for water—only for a little water. . . .'

"He was muddy. I covered him up and stood waiting in silence, catching a painfully gasped word now and then. They were no longer in his own language. The fever had left him, taking with it the heat of life. And with his panting breast and lustrous eyes he reminded me again of a wild creature under the net; of a bird caught in a snare. She had left him. She had left him—sick—helpless—thirsty. The spear of the hunter had entered his very soul. 'Why?' he cried in the penetrating and indignant voice of a man calling to a responsible Maker. A gust of wind and a swish of rain answered.

"And as I turned away to shut the door he pronounced the word 'Merciful!' and expired.

"Eventually I certified heart-failure as the immediate cause of death. His heart must have indeed failed him, or else he might have stood this night of storm and exposure, too. I closed his eyes and drove away. Not very far from the cottage I met Foster walking sturdily between the dripping hedges with his collie at his heels.

"'Do you know where your daughter is?' I asked.

"'Don't I!' he cried. 'I am going to talk to him a bit. Frightening a poor woman like this.'

"'He won't frighten her any more,' I said. 'He is dead.'

"He struck with his stick at the mud.

"'And there's the child.'

"Then, after thinking deeply for a while—

"'I don't know that it isn't for the best.'

"That's what he said. And she says nothing at all now. Not a word of him. Never. Is his image as utterly gone from her mind as his lithe and striding figure, his carolling voice are gone from our fields? He is no longer before her eyes to excite her imagination into a passion of love or fear; and his memory seems to have vanished from her dull brain as a shadow passes away upon a white screen. She lives in the cottage and works for Miss Swaffer. She is Amy Foster for everybody, and the child is 'Amy Foster's boy.' She calls him Johnny—which means Little John.

"It is impossible to say whether this name recalls anything to her. Does she ever think of the past? I have seen her hanging over the boy's cot in a very passion of maternal tenderness. The little fellow was lying on his back, a little frightened at me, but very still, with his big black eyes, with his fluttered air of a bird in a snare. And looking at him I seemed to see again the other one—the father, cast out mysteriously by the sea to perish in the supreme disaster of loneliness and despair."

THE SECRET SHARER:
AN EPISODE FROM THE COAST

THE SECRET SHARER*

I

ON my right hand there were lines of fishing-stakes resembling a mysterious system of half-submerged bamboo fences, incomprehensible in its division of the domain of tropical fishes, and crazy of aspect as if abandoned forever by some nomad tribe of fishermen now gone to the other end of the ocean; for there was no sign of human habitation as far as the eye could reach.* To the left a group of barren islets, suggesting ruins of stone walls, towers, and blockhouses,* had its foundations set in a blue sea that itself looked solid, so still and stable did it lie below my feet; even the track of light from the westering sun shone smoothly, without that animated glitter which tells of an imperceptible ripple. And when I turned my head to take a parting glance at the tug which had just left us anchored outside the bar, I saw the straight line of the flat shore joined to the stable sea, edge to edge, with a perfect and unmarked closeness, in one levelled floor half brown, half blue under the enormous dome of the sky. Corresponding in their insignificance to the islets of the sea, two small clumps of trees, one on each side of the only fault in the impeccable joint, marked the mouth of the river Meinam we had just left on the first preparatory stage of our homeward journey; and, far back on the inland level, a larger and loftier mass, the grove surrounding the great Paknam pagoda, was the only thing on which the eye could rest from the vain task of exploring the monotonous sweep of the horizon. Here and there gleams as of a few scattered pieces of silver marked the windings of the great river; and on the nearest of them, just within the bar, the tug steaming right into the land became lost to my sight, hull and funnel and masts, as though the impassive earth had swallowed her up without an effort, without a tremor. My eye followed the light cloud of her smoke, now here, now there, above the plain, according to the devious curves of the stream, but always fainter and farther away, till I lost it at last behind the mitre-shaped hill of the great pagoda. And then I was left alone with my ship, anchored at the head of the Gulf of Siam.

She floated at the starting-point of a long journey, very still in an immense stillness, the shadows of her spars flung far to the eastward by the setting sun. At that moment I was alone on her decks. There was not a sound in her—and around us nothing moved, nothing lived, not a canoe on the water, not a bird in the air, not a cloud in the sky. In this breathless pause at the threshold of a long passage we seemed to be measuring our fitness for a long and arduous enterprise, the appointed task of both our existences to be carried out, far from all human eyes, with only sky and sea for spectators and for judges.

There must have been some glare in the air to interfere with one's sight, because it was only just before the sun left us that my roaming eyes made out beyond the highest ridge of the principal islet of the group something which did away with the solemnity of perfect solitude. The tide of darkness flowed on swiftly; and with tropical suddenness a swarm of stars came out above the shadowy earth, while I lingered yet, my hand resting lightly on my ship's rail as if on the shoulder of a trusted friend. But, with all that multitude of celestial bodies staring down at one, the comfort of quiet communion with her was gone for good. And there were also disturbing sounds by this time—voices, footsteps forward; the steward flitted along the main-deck, a busily ministering spirit; a hand-bell tinkled urgently under the poop-deck. . . .

I found my two officers waiting for me near the supper table, in the lighted cuddy. We sat down at once, and as I helped the chief mate, I said:

"Are you aware that there is a ship anchored inside the islands? I saw her mastheads above the ridge as the sun went down."

He raised sharply his simple face, overcharged by a terrible growth of whisker, and emitted his usual ejaculations: "Bless my soul, sir! You don't say so!"

My second mate was a round-cheeked, silent young man, grave beyond his years, I thought; but as our eyes happened to meet I detected a slight quiver on his lips. I looked down at once. It was not my part to encourage sneering on board my ship. It must be said, too, that I knew very little of my officers. In consequence of certain events of no particular significance, except to myself, I had been appointed to the command only a fortnight before. Neither did I know much of the hands forward. All these people had been together for eighteen months or so, and my position was that of the only stranger on board. I mention this because it has some bearing on what is to follow. But what I felt most was my being a stranger to the ship; and if all the truth must be told, I was somewhat of a stranger to myself. The youngest man on board (barring the second mate), and untried as yet by a position of the fullest responsibility, I was willing to take the adequacy of the others for granted. They had simply to be equal to their tasks; but I wondered how far I should turn out faithful to that ideal conception of one's own personality every man sets up for himself secretly.*

Meantime the chief mate, with an almost visible effect of collaboration on the part of his round eyes and frightful whiskers, was trying to evolve a theory of the anchored ship. His dominant trait was to take all things into earnest consideration. He was of a painstaking turn of mind. As he used to say, he "liked to account to himself" for practically everything that came in his way, down to a miserable scorpion he had found in his cabin a week before. The why and the wherefore of that scorpion—how it got on board and came to select his room rather than the pantry (which was a dark place and more what a scorpion would be partial to), and how on earth it managed to drown itself in the inkwell of his writing-desk—had exercised him infinitely. The ship within the islands was much more easily accounted for; and just as we were about to rise from table he made his pronouncement. She was, he doubted not, a ship from home lately arrived. Probably she drew too much water to cross the bar except at the top of spring tides. Therefore she went into that natural harbour to wait for a few days in preference to remaining in an open roadstead.

"That's so," confirmed the second mate, suddenly, in his slightly hoarse voice. "She draws over twenty feet. She's the Liverpool ship *Sephora** with a cargo of coal. Hundred and twenty-three days from Cardiff."

We looked at him in surprise.

"The tugboat skipper told me when he came on board for your letters, sir," explained the young man. "He expects to take her up the river the day after tomorrow."

After thus overwhelming us with the extent of his information he slipped out of the cabin. The mate observed regretfully that he "could not account for that young fellow's whims." What prevented him telling us all about it at once, he wanted to know.

I detained him as he was making a move. For the last two days the crew had had plenty of hard work, and the night before they had very little sleep. I felt painfully that I—a stranger—was doing something unusual when I directed him to let all hands turn in without setting an anchor-watch. I proposed to keep on deck myself till one o'clock or thereabouts. I would get the second mate to relieve me at that hour.

"He will turn out the cook and the steward at four," I concluded, "and then give you a call. Of course at the slightest sign of any sort of wind we'll have the hands up and make a start at once."

He concealed his astonishment. "Very well, sir." Outside the cuddy he put his head in the second mate's door to inform him of my unheard-of caprice to take a five hours' anchor-watch on myself. I heard the other raise his voice incredulously—"What? The captain himself?" Then a few more murmurs, a door closed, then another. A few moments later I went on deck.

My strangeness, which had made me sleepless, had prompted that unconventional arrangement, as if I had expected in those solitary hours of the night to get on terms with the ship of which I knew nothing, manned by men of whom I knew very little more. Fast alongside a wharf, littered like any ship in port with a tangle of unrelated things, invaded by unrelated shore people, I had hardly seen her yet properly. Now, as she lay cleared for sea, the stretch of her main-deck seemed to me very fine under the stars. Very fine, very roomy for her size, and very inviting. I descended the poop and paced the waist, my mind picturing to myself the coming passage through the Malay Archipelago, down the Indian Ocean, and up the Atlantic. All its phases were familiar enough to me, every characteristic, all the alternatives which were likely to face me on the high seas—everything! . . . except the novel responsibility of command. But I took heart from the reasonable thought that the ship was like other ships, the men like other men, and that the sea was not likely to keep any special surprises expressly for my discomfiture.

Arrived at that comforting conclusion, I bethought myself of a cigar and went below to get it. All was still down there. Everybody at the after end of the ship was sleeping profoundly. I came out again on the quarter-deck, agreeably at ease in my sleeping-suit on that warm breathless night, barefooted, a glowing cigar in my teeth, and, going forward, I was met by the profound silence of the fore end of the ship. Only as I passed the door of the forecastle I heard a deep, quiet, trustful sigh of some sleeper inside. And suddenly I rejoiced in the great security of the sea as compared with the unrest of the land, in my choice of that untempted life presenting no disquieting problems, invested with an elementary moral beauty by the absolute straightforwardness of its appeal and by the singleness of its purpose.

The riding-light in the fore-rigging burned with a clear, untroubled, as if symbolic, flame, confident and bright in the mysterious shades of the night. Passing on my way aft along the other side of the ship, I observed that the rope side-ladder, put over, no doubt, for the master of the tug when he came to fetch away our letters, had not been hauled in as it should have been. I became annoyed at this, for exactitude in small matters is the very soul of discipline. Then I reflected that I had myself peremptorily dismissed my officers from duty, and by my own act had prevented the anchor-watch being formally set and things properly attended to. I asked myself whether it was wise ever to interfere with the established routine of duties even from the kindest of motives. My action might have made me appear eccentric. Goodness only knew how that absurdly whiskered mate would "account" for my conduct, and what the whole ship thought of that informality of their new captain. I was vexed with myself.

Not from compunction certainly, but, as it were mechanically, I proceeded to get the ladder in myself. Now a side-ladder of that sort is a light affair and comes in easily, yet my vigorous tug, which should have brought it flying on board, merely recoiled upon my body in a totally unexpected jerk. What the devil! ... I was so astounded by the immovableness of that ladder that I remained stock-still, trying to account for it to myself like that imbecile mate of mine. In the end, of course, I put my head over the rail.

The side of the ship made an opaque belt of shadow on the darkling glassy shimmer of the sea. But I saw at once something elongated and pale floating very close to the ladder. Before I could form a guess a faint flash of phosphorescent light, which seemed to issue suddenly from the naked body of a man, flickered in the sleeping water with the elusive, silent play of summer lightning in a night sky. With a gasp I saw revealed to my stare a pair of feet, the long legs, a broad livid back immersed right up to the neck in a greenish cadaverous glow. One hand, awash, clutched the bottom rung of the ladder. He was complete but for the head. A headless corpse! The cigar dropped out of my gaping mouth with a tiny plop and a short hiss quite audible in the absolute stillness of all things under heaven. At that I suppose he raised up his face, a dimly pale oval in the shadow of the ship's side. But even then I could only barely make out down there the shape of his black-haired head. However, it was enough for the horrid, frost-bound sensation which had gripped me about the chest to pass off. The moment of vain exclamations was past, too. I only climbed on the spare spar and leaned over the rail as far as I could, to bring my eyes nearer to that mystery floating alongside.

As he hung by the ladder, like a resting swimmer, the sea-lightning played about his limbs at every stir; and he appeared in it ghastly, silvery, fish-like. He remained as mute as a fish, too. He made no motion to get out of the water, either. It was inconceivable that he should not attempt to come on board, and strangely troubling to suspect that perhaps he did not want to. And my first words were prompted by just that troubled incertitude.

"What's the matter?" I asked in my ordinary tone, speaking down to the face upturned exactly under mine.

"Cramp," it answered, no louder. Then slightly anxious, "I say, no need to call any one."

"I was not going to," I said.

"Are you alone on deck?"

"Yes."

I had somehow the impression that he was on the point of letting go the ladder to swim away beyond my ken—mysterious as he came. But, for the moment, this being appearing as if he had risen from the bottom of the sea (it was certainly the nearest land to the ship) wanted only to know the time. I told him. And he, down there, tentatively:

"I suppose your captain's turned in?"

"I am sure he isn't," I said.

He seemed to struggle with himself, for I heard something like the low, bitter murmur of doubt.

"What's the good?" His next words came out with a hesitating effort.

"Look here, my man. Could you call him out quietly?"

I thought the time had come to declare myself.

"*I* am the captain."

I heard a "By Jove!" whispered at the level of the water. The phosphorescence flashed in the swirl of the water all about his limbs, his other hand seized the ladder.

"My name's Leggatt."

The voice was calm and resolute. A good voice. The self-possession of that man had somehow induced a corresponding state in myself. It was very quietly that I remarked:

"You must be a good swimmer."

"Yes. I've been in the water practically since nine o'clock. The question for me now is whether I am to let go this ladder and go on swimming till I sink from exhaustion, or—to come on board here."

I felt this was no mere formula of desperate speech, but a real alternative in the view of a strong soul. I should have gathered from this that he was young; indeed, it is only the young who are ever confronted by such clear issues. But at the time it was pure intuition on my part. A mysterious communication was established already between us two—in the face of that silent, darkened tropical sea. I was young, too; young enough to make no comment. The man in the water began suddenly to climb up the ladder, and I hastened away from the rail to fetch some clothes.

Before entering the cabin I stood still, listening in the lobby at the foot of the stairs. A faint snore came through the closed door of the chief mate's room. The second mate's door was on the hook, but the darkness in there was absolutely soundless. He, too, was young and could sleep like a stone. Remained the steward, but he was not likely to wake up before he was called. I got a sleeping-suit out of my room and, coming back on deck, saw the naked man from the sea sitting on the main-hatch, glimmering white in the darkness, his elbows on his knees and his head in his hands. In a moment he had concealed his damp body in a sleeping-suit of the same grey-stripe pattern as the one I was wearing and followed me like my double on the poop. Together we moved right aft, barefooted, silent.

"What is it?" I asked in a deadened voice, taking the lighted lamp out of the binnacle, and raising it to his face.

"An ugly business."

He had rather regular features; a good mouth; light eyes under somewhat heavy, dark eyebrows; a smooth, square forehead; no growth on his cheeks; a small, brown moustache, and a well-shaped, round chin. His expression was concentrated, meditative, under the inspecting light of the lamp I held up to his face; such as a man thinking hard in solitude might wear. My sleeping-suit was just right for his size. A well-knit young fellow of twenty-five at most. He caught his lower lip with the edge of white, even teeth.

"Yes," I said, replacing the lamp in the binnacle. The warm, heavy tropical night closed upon his head again.

"There's a ship over there," he murmured.

"Yes, I know. The *Sephora*. Did you know of us?"

"Hadn't the slightest idea. I am the mate of her——" He paused and corrected himself. "I should say I *was*."

"Aha! Something wrong?"

"Yes. Very wrong indeed. I've killed a man."

"What do you mean? Just now?"

"No, on the passage. Weeks ago. Thirty-nine south. When I say a man——"

"Fit of temper," I suggested, confidently.

The shadowy, dark head, like mine, seemed to nod imperceptibly above the ghostly grey of my sleeping-suit. It was, in the night, as though I had been faced by my own reflection in the depths of a sombre and immense mirror.

"A pretty thing to have to own up to for a *Conway* boy,"* murmured my double, distinctly.

"You're a *Conway* boy?"

"I am," he said, as if startled. Then, slowly ... "Perhaps you too——"

It was so; but being a couple of years older I had left before he joined. After a quick interchange of dates a silence fell; and I thought suddenly of my absurd mate with his terrific whiskers and the "Bless my soul—you don't say so" type of intellect. My double gave me an inkling of his thoughts by saying:

"My father's a parson* in Norfolk. Do you see me before a judge and jury on that charge? For myself I can't see the necessity. There are fellows that an angel from heaven——And I am not that. He was one of those creatures that are just simmering all the time with a silly sort of wickedness. Miserable devils that have no business to live at all. He wouldn't do his duty and wouldn't let anybody else do theirs.

But what's the good of talking! You know well enough the sort of ill-conditioned snarling cur——"

He appealed to me as if our experiences had been as identical as our clothes. And I knew well enough the pestiferous danger of such a character where there are no means of legal repression. And I knew well enough also that my double there was no homicidal ruffian. I did not think of asking him for details, and he told me the story roughly in brusque, disconnected sentences. I needed no more. I saw it all going on as though I were myself inside that other sleeping-suit.

"It happened while we were setting a reefed foresail, at dusk. Reefed foresail! You understand the sort of weather. The only sail we had left to keep the ship running; so you may guess what it had been like for days. Anxious sort of job, that. He gave me some of his cursed insolence at the sheet. I tell you I was overdone with this terrific weather that seemed to have no end to it. Terrific, I tell you— and a deep ship. I believe the fellow himself was half crazed with funk. It was no time for gentlemanly reproof, so I turned round and felled him like an ox. He up and at me. We closed just as an awful sea made for the ship. All hands saw it coming and took to the rigging, but I had him by the throat, and went on shaking him like a rat, the men above us yelling, 'Look out! look out!' Then a crash as if the sky had fallen on my head. They say that for over ten minutes hardly anything was to be seen of the ship—just the three masts and a bit of the forecastle head and of the poop all awash driving along in a smother of foam. It was a miracle that they found us, jammed together behind the forebitts. It's clear that I meant business, because I was holding him by the throat still when they picked us up. He was black in the face. It was too much for them. It seems they rushed us aft together, gripped as we were, screaming 'Murder!' like a lot of lunatics, and broke into the cuddy. And the ship running for her life, touch and go all the time, any minute her last in a sea fit to turn your hair grey only a-looking at it. I understand that the skipper, too, started raving like the rest of them. The man had been deprived of sleep for more than a week, and to have this sprung on him at the height of a furious gale nearly drove him out of his mind. I wonder they didn't fling me overboard after getting the carcass of their precious ship-mate out of my fingers. They had rather a job to separate us, I've been told. A sufficiently fierce story to make an old judge and a respectable jury sit up a bit. The first thing I heard when

I came to myself was the maddening howling of that endless gale, and on that the voice of the old man. He was hanging on to my bunk, staring into my face out of his sou'wester.

"'Mr. Leggatt, you have killed a man. You can act no longer as chief mate of this ship.'"

His care to subdue his voice made it sound monotonous. He rested a hand on the end of the skylight to steady himself with, and all that time did not stir a limb, so far as I could see. "Nice little tale for a quiet tea-party," he concluded in the same tone.

One of my hands, too, rested on the end of the skylight; neither did I stir a limb, so far as I knew. We stood less than a foot from each other. It occurred to me that if old "Bless my soul—you don't say so" were to put his head up the companion and catch sight of us, he would think he was seeing double, or imagine himself come upon a scene of weird witchcraft; the strange captain having a quiet confabulation by the wheel with his own grey ghost. I became very much concerned to prevent anything of the sort. I heard the other's soothing undertone.

"My father's a parson in Norfolk," it said. Evidently he had forgotten he had told me this important fact before. Truly a nice little tale.

"You had better slip down into my stateroom now," I said, moving off stealthily. My double followed my movements; our bare feet made no sound; I let him in, closed the door with care, and, after giving a call to the second mate, returned on deck for my relief.

"Not much sign of any wind yet," I remarked when he approached.

"No, sir. Not much," he assented, sleepily, in his hoarse voice, with just enough deference, no more, and barely suppressing a yawn.

"Well, that's all you have to look out for. You have got your orders."

"Yes, sir."

I paced a turn or two on the poop and saw him take up his position face forward with his elbow in the ratlines of the mizzen-rigging before I went below. The mate's faint snoring was still going on peacefully. The cuddy lamp was burning over the table on which stood a vase with flowers, a polite attention from the ship's provision merchant—the last flowers we should see for the next three months at the very least. Two bunches of bananas hung from the beam symmetrically, one on each side of the rudder-casing. Everything was as before in the ship—except that two of her captain's sleeping-suits were simultaneously in use, one motionless in the cuddy, the other keeping very still in the captain's stateroom.

It must be explained here that my cabin had the form of the capital letter L,* the door being within the angle and opening into the short part of the letter. A couch was to the left, the bed-place to the right; my writing-desk and the chronometers' table faced the door. But any one opening it, unless he stepped right inside, had no view of what I call the long (or vertical) part of the letter. It contained some lockers surmounted by a bookcase; and a few clothes, a thick jacket or two, caps, oilskin coat, and such like, hung on hooks. There was at the bottom of that part a door opening into my bath-room, which could be entered also directly from the saloon. But that way was never used.

The mysterious arrival had discovered the advantage of this particular shape. Entering my room, lighted strongly by a big bulkhead lamp swung on gimbals above my writing-desk, I did not see him anywhere till he stepped out quietly from behind the coats hung in the recessed part.

"I heard somebody moving about, and went in there at once," he whispered.

I, too, spoke under my breath.

"Nobody is likely to come in here without knocking and getting permission."

He nodded. His face was thin and the sunburn faded, as though he had been ill. And no wonder. He had been, I heard presently, kept under arrest in his cabin for nearly seven weeks. But there was nothing sickly in his eyes or in his expression. He was not a bit like me, really; yet, as we stood leaning over my bed-place, whispering side by side, with our dark heads together and our backs to the door, anybody bold enough to open it stealthily would have been treated to the uncanny sight of a double captain busy talking in whispers with his other self.

"But all this doesn't tell me how you came to hang on to our side-ladder," I inquired, in the hardly audible murmurs we used, after he had told me something more of the proceedings on board the *Sephora* once the bad weather was over.

"When we sighted Java Head I had had time to think all those matters out several times over. I had six weeks of doing nothing else, and with only an hour or so every evening for a tramp on the quarter-deck."

He whispered, his arms folded on the side of my bed-place, staring through the open port. And I could imagine perfectly the manner of this thinking out—a stubborn if not a steadfast operation; something of which I should have been perfectly incapable.

"I reckoned it would be dark before we closed with the land," he continued, so low that I had to strain my hearing, near as we were to each other, shoulder touching shoulder almost. "So I asked to speak to the old man. He always seemed very sick when he came to see me—as if he could not look me in the face. You know, that foresail saved the ship. She was too deep to have run long under bare poles. And it was I that managed to set it for him. Anyway, he came. When I had him in my cabin—he stood by the door looking at me as if I had the halter round my neck already—I asked him right away to leave my cabin door unlocked at night while the ship was going through Sunda Straits. There would be the Java coast within two or three miles, off Angier Point. I wanted nothing more. I've had a prize for swimming my second year in the *Conway*."

"I can believe it," I breathed out.

"God only knows why they locked me in every night. To see some of their faces you'd have thought they were afraid I'd go about at night strangling people. Am I a murdering brute? Do I look it? By Jove! if I had been he wouldn't have trusted himself like that into my room. You'll say I might have chucked him aside and bolted out, there and then—it was dark already. Well, no. And for the same reason I wouldn't think of trying to smash the door. There would have been a rush to stop me at the noise, and I did not mean to get into a confounded scrimmage. Somebody else might have got killed—for I would not have broken out only to get chucked back, and I did not want any more of that work. He refused, looking more sick than ever. He was afraid of the men, and also of that old second mate of his who had been sailing with him for years—a grey-headed old humbug; and his steward, too, had been with him devil knows how long—seventeen years or more—a dogmatic sort of loafer who hated me like poison, just because I was the chief mate. No chief mate ever made more than one voyage in the *Sephora*, you know.

Those two old chaps ran the ship. Devil only knows what the skipper wasn't afraid of (all his nerve went to pieces altogether in that hellish spell of bad weather we had)—of what the law would do to him—of his wife, perhaps. Oh, yes! she's on board.* Though I don't think she would have meddled. She would have been only too glad to have me out of the ship in any way. The 'brand of Cain' business,* don't you see. That's all right. I was ready enough to go off wandering on the face of the earth—and that was price enough to pay for an Abel of that sort. Anyhow, he wouldn't listen to me. 'This thing must take its course. I represent the law here.' He was shaking like a leaf. 'So you won't?' 'No!' 'Then I hope you will be able to sleep on that,' I said, and turned my back on him. 'I wonder that *you* can,' cries he, and locks the door.

"Well, after that, I couldn't. Not very well. That was three weeks ago. We have had a slow passage through the Java Sea; drifted about Carimata for ten days. When we anchored here they thought, I suppose, it was all right. The nearest land (and that's five miles) is the ship's destination; the consul would soon set about catching me; and there would have been no object in bolting to these islets there. I don't suppose there's a drop of water on them. I don't know how it was, but tonight that steward, after bringing me my supper, went out to let me eat it, and left the door unlocked. And I ate it—all there was, too. After I had finished I strolled out on the quarter-deck. I don't know that I meant to do anything. A breath of fresh air was all I wanted, I believe. Then a sudden temptation came over me. I kicked off my slippers and was in the water before I had made up my mind fairly. Somebody heard the splash and they raised an awful hullabaloo. 'He's gone! Lower the boats! He's committed suicide! No, he's swimming.' Certainly I was swimming. It's not so easy for a swimmer like me to commit suicide by drowning. I landed on the nearest islet before the boat left the ship's side. I heard them pulling about in the dark, hailing, and so on, but after a bit they gave up. Everything quieted down and the anchorage became as still as death. I sat down on a stone and began to think. I felt certain they would start searching for me at daylight. There was no place to hide on those stony things—and if there had been, what would have been the good? But now I was clear of that ship, I was not going back. So after a while I took off all my clothes, tied them up in a bundle with a stone inside, and dropped them in the deep water on the outer side of that islet.

That was suicide enough for me. Let them think what they liked, but I didn't mean to drown myself. I meant to swim till I sank—but that's not the same thing. I struck out for another of these little islands, and it was from that one that I first saw your riding-light. Something to swim for. I went on easily, and on the way I came upon a flat rock a foot or two above water. In the daytime, I dare say, you might make it out with a glass from your poop. I scrambled up on it and rested myself for a bit. Then I made another start. That last spell must have been over a mile."

His whisper was getting fainter and fainter, and all the time he stared straight out through the port-hole, in which there was not even a star to be seen. I had not interrupted him. There was something that made comment impossible in his narrative, or perhaps in himself; a sort of feeling, a quality, which I can't find a name for. And when he ceased, all I found was a futile whisper: "So you swam for our light?"

"Yes—straight for it. It was something to swim for. I couldn't see any stars low down because the coast was in the way, and I couldn't see the land, either. The water was like glass. One might have been swimming in a confounded thousand-feet deep cistern with no place for scrambling out anywhere; but what I didn't like was the notion of swimming round and round like a crazed bullock before I gave out; and as I didn't mean to go back . . . No. Do you see me being hauled back, stark naked, off one of these little islands by the scruff of the neck and fighting like a wild beast? Somebody would have got killed for certain, and I did not want any of that. So I went on. Then your ladder——"

"Why didn't you hail the ship?" I asked, a little louder.

He touched my shoulder lightly. Lazy footsteps came right over our heads and stopped. The second mate had crossed from the other side of the poop and might have been hanging over the rail, for all we knew.

"He couldn't hear us talking—could he?" My double breathed into my very ear, anxiously.

His anxiety was an answer, a sufficient answer, to the question I had put to him. An answer containing all the difficulty of that situation. I closed the port-hole quietly, to make sure. A louder word might have been overheard.

"Who's that?" he whispered then.

"My second mate. But I don't know much more of the fellow than you do."

And I told him a little about myself. I had been appointed to take charge while I least expected anything of the sort, not quite a fortnight ago. I didn't know either the ship or the people. Hadn't had the time in port to look about me or size anybody up. And as to the crew, all they knew was that I was appointed to take the ship home. For the rest, I was almost as much of a stranger on board as himself, I said. And at the moment I felt it most acutely. I felt that it would take very little to make me a suspect person in the eyes of the ship's company.

He had turned about meantime; and we, the two strangers in the ship, faced each other in identical attitudes.

"Your ladder——" he murmured, after a silence. "Who'd have thought of finding a ladder hanging over at night in a ship anchored out here! I felt just then a very unpleasant faintness. After the life I've been leading for nine weeks, anybody would have got out of condition. I wasn't capable of swimming round as far as your rudder-chains. And, lo and behold! there was a ladder to get hold of. After I gripped it I said to myself, 'What's the good?' When I saw a man's head looking over I thought I would swim away presently and leave him shouting—in whatever language it was. I didn't mind being looked at. I—I liked it. And then you speaking to me so quietly—as if you had expected me—made me hold on a little longer. It had been a confounded lonely time—I don't mean while swimming. I was glad to talk a little to somebody that didn't belong to the *Sephora*. As to asking for the captain, that was a mere impulse. It could have been no use, with all the ship knowing about me and the other people pretty certain to be round here in the morning. I don't know—I wanted to be seen, to talk with somebody, before I went on. I don't know what I would have said.... 'Fine night, isn't it?' or something of the sort."

"Do you think they will be round here presently?" I asked with some incredulity.

"Quite likely," he said, faintly.

He looked extremely haggard all of a sudden. His head rolled on his shoulders.

"H'm. We shall see then. Meantime get into that bed," I whispered. "Want help? There."

It was a rather high bed-place with a set of drawers underneath.

This amazing swimmer really needed the lift I gave him by seizing his leg. He tumbled in, rolled over on his back, and flung one arm across his eyes. And then, with his face nearly hidden, he must have looked exactly as I used to look in that bed. I gazed upon my other self for a while before drawing across carefully the two green serge curtains which ran on a brass rod. I thought for a moment of pinning them together for greater safety, but I sat down on the couch, and once there I felt unwilling to rise and hunt for a pin. I would do it in a moment. I was extremely tired, in a peculiarly intimate way, by the strain of stealthiness, by the effort of whispering and the general secrecy of this excitement. It was three o'clock by now and I had been on my feet since nine, but I was not sleepy; I could not have gone to sleep. I sat there, fagged out, looking at the curtains, trying to clear my mind of the confused sensation of being in two places at once, and greatly bothered by an exasperating knocking in my head. It was a relief to discover suddenly that it was not in my head at all, but on the outside of the door. Before I could collect myself the words "Come in" were out of my mouth, and the steward entered with a tray, bringing in my morning coffee. I had slept, after all, and I was so frightened that I shouted, "This way! I am here, steward," as though he had been miles away. He put down the tray on the table next the couch and only then said, very quietly, "I can see you are here, sir." I felt him give me a keen look, but I dared not meet his eyes just then. He must have wondered why I had drawn the curtains of my bed before going to sleep on the couch. He went out, hooking the door open as usual.

I heard the crew washing decks above me. I knew I would have been told at once if there had been any wind. Calm, I thought, and I was doubly vexed. Indeed, I felt dual more than ever. The steward reappeared suddenly in the doorway. I jumped up from the couch so quickly that he gave a start.

"What do you want here?"

"Close your port, sir—they are washing decks."

"It is closed," I said, reddening.

"Very well, sir." But he did not move from the doorway and returned my stare in an extraordinary, equivocal manner for a time. Then his eyes wavered, all his expression changed, and in a voice unusually gentle, almost coaxingly:

"May I come in to take the empty cup away, sir?"

"Of course!" I turned my back on him while he popped in and out. Then I unhooked and closed the door and even pushed the bolt. This sort of thing could not go on very long. The cabin was as hot as an oven, too. I took a peep at my double, and discovered that he had not moved, his arm was still over his eyes; but his chest heaved; his hair was wet; his chin glistened with perspiration. I reached over him and opened the port.

"I must show myself on deck," I reflected.

Of course, theoretically, I could do what I liked, with no one to say nay to me within the whole circle of the horizon; but to lock my cabin door and take the key away I did not dare. Directly I put my head out of the companion I saw the group of my two officers, the second mate barefooted, the chief mate in long india-rubber boots, near the break of the poop, and the steward half-way down the poop-ladder talking to them eagerly. He happened to catch sight of me and dived, the second ran down on the main-deck shouting some order or other, and the chief mate came to meet me, touching his cap.

There was a sort of curiosity in his eye that I did not like. I don't know whether the steward had told them that I was "queer" only, or downright drunk, but I know the man meant to have a good look at me. I watched him coming with a smile which, as he got into point-blank range, took effect and froze his very whiskers. I did not give him time to open his lips.

"Square the yards by lifts and braces before the hands go to breakfast."

It was the first particular order I had given on board that ship; and I stayed on deck to see it executed, too. I had felt the need of assert-ing myself without loss of time. That sneering young cub got taken down a peg or two on that occasion, and I also seized the opportunity of having a good look at the face of every foremast man as they filed past me to go to the after braces. At breakfast time, eating nothing myself, I presided with such frigid dignity that the two mates were only too glad to escape from the cabin as soon as decency permitted; and all the time the dual working of my mind distracted me almost to the point of insanity. I was constantly watching myself, my secret self, as dependent on my actions as my own personality, sleeping in that bed, behind that door which faced me as I sat at the head of the table. It was very much like being mad, only it was worse because one was aware of it.

I had to shake him for a solid minute, but when at last he opened his eyes it was in the full possession of his senses, with an inquiring look.

"All's well so far," I whispered. "Now you must vanish into the bath-room."

He did so, as noiseless as a ghost, and I then rang for the steward, and facing him boldly, directed him to tidy up my stateroom while I was having my bath—"and be quick about it." As my tone admitted of no excuses, he said, "Yes, sir," and ran off to fetch his dust-pan and brushes. I took a bath and did most of my dressing, splashing, and whistling softly for the steward's edification, while the secret sharer of my life stood drawn up bolt upright in that little space, his face looking very sunken in daylight, his eyelids lowered under the stern, dark line of his eyebrows drawn together by a slight frown.

When I left him there to go back to my room the steward was finishing dusting. I sent for the mate and engaged him in some insignificant conversation. It was, as it were, trifling with the terrific character of his whiskers; but my object was to give him an opportunity for a good look at my cabin. And then I could at last shut, with a clear conscience, the door of my stateroom and get my double back into the recessed part. There was nothing else for it. He had to sit still on a small folding stool, half smothered by the heavy coats hanging there. We listened to the steward going into the bath-room out of the saloon, filling the water-bottles there, scrubbing the bath, setting things to rights, whisk, bang, clatter—out again into the saloon—turn the key—click. Such was my scheme for keeping my second self invisible. Nothing better could be contrived under the circumstances. And there we sat; I at my writing-desk ready to appear busy with some papers, he behind me, out of sight of the door. It would not have been prudent to talk in daytime; and I could not have stood the excitement of that queer sense of whispering to myself. Now and then, glancing over my shoulder, I saw him far back there, sitting rigidly on the low stool, his bare feet close together, his arms folded, his head hanging on his breast—and perfectly still. Anybody would have taken him for me.

I was fascinated by it myself. Every moment I had to glance over my shoulder. I was looking at him when a voice outside the door said:

"Beg pardon, sir."

"Well!" . . . I kept my eyes on him, and so, when the voice outside the door announced, "There's a ship's boat coming our way, sir," I saw him give a start—the first movement he had made for hours. But he did not raise his bowed head.

"All right. Get the ladder over."

I hesitated. Should I whisper something to him? But what? His immobility seemed to have been never disturbed. What could I tell him he did not know already? . . . Finally I went on deck.

II

THE skipper of the *Sephora* had a thin red whisker all round his face, and the sort of complexion that goes with hair of that colour; also the particular, rather smeary shade of blue in the eyes. He was not exactly a showy figure; his shoulders were high, his stature but middling—one leg slightly more bandy than the other. He shook hands, looking vaguely around. A spiritless tenacity was his main characteristic, I judged. I behaved with a politeness which seemed to disconcert him. Perhaps he was shy. He mumbled to me as if he were ashamed of what he was saying; gave his name (it was something like Archbold—but at this distance of years I hardly am sure), his ship's name, and a few other particulars of that sort, in the manner of a criminal making a reluctant and doleful confession. He had had terrible weather on the passage out—terrible—terrible—wife aboard, too.

By this time we were seated in the cabin and the steward brought in a tray with a bottle and glasses. "Thanks! No." Never took liquor. Would have some water, though. He drank two tumblerfuls. Terrible thirsty work. Ever since daylight had been exploring the islands round his ship.

"What was that for—fun?" I asked, with an appearance of polite interest.

"No!" He sighed. "Painful duty."

As he persisted in his mumbling and I wanted my double to hear every word, I hit upon the notion of informing him that I regretted to say I was hard of hearing.

"Such a young man, too!" he nodded, keeping his smeary blue, unintelligent eyes fastened upon me. What was the cause of it—

some disease? he inquired, without the least sympathy and as if he thought that, if so, I'd got no more than I deserved.

"Yes; disease," I admitted in a cheerful tone which seemed to shock him. But my point was gained, because he had to raise his voice to give me his tale. It is not worth while to record that version. It was just over two months since all this had happened, and he had thought so much about it that he seemed completely muddled as to its bearings, but still immensely impressed.

"What would you think of such a thing happening on board your own ship? I've had the *Sephora* for these fifteen years. I am a well-known shipmaster."

He was densely distressed—and perhaps I should have sympathised with him if I had been able to detach my mental vision from the unsuspected sharer of my cabin as though he were my second self. There he was on the other side of the bulkhead, four or five feet from us, no more, as we sat in the saloon. I looked politely at Captain Archbold (if that was his name), but it was the other I saw, in a grey sleeping-suit, seated on a low stool, his bare feet close together, his arms folded, and every word said between us falling into the ears of his dark head bowed on his chest.

"I have been at sea now, man and boy, for seven-and-thirty years, and I've never heard of such a thing happening in an English ship. And that it should be my ship. Wife on board, too."

I was hardly listening to him.

"Don't you think," I said, "that the heavy sea which, you told me, came aboard just then might have killed the man? I have seen the sheer weight of a sea kill a man very neatly, by simply breaking his neck."

"Good God!" he uttered, impressively, fixing his smeary blue eyes on me. "The sea! No man killed by the sea ever looked like that." He seemed positively scandalised at my suggestion. And as I gazed at him, certainly not prepared for anything original on his part, he advanced his head close to mine and thrust his tongue out at me so suddenly that I couldn't help starting back.

After scoring over my calmness in this graphic way he nodded wisely. If I had seen the sight, he assured me, I would never forget it as long as I lived. The weather was too bad to give the corpse a proper sea burial. So next day at dawn they took it up on the poop, covering its face with a bit of bunting; he read a short prayer, and then, just as it was, in its oilskins and long boots, they launched it amongst those mountainous seas that seemed ready every moment to swallow up the ship herself and the terrified lives on board of her.

"That reefed foresail saved you," I threw in.

"Under God—it did," he exclaimed fervently. "It was by a special mercy, I firmly believe, that it stood some of those hurricane squalls."

"It was the setting of that sail which——" I began.

"God's own hand in it," he interrupted me. "Nothing less could have done it. I don't mind telling you that I hardly dared give the order. It seemed impossible that we could touch anything without losing it, and then our last hope would have been gone."

The terror of that gale was on him yet. I let him go on for a bit, then said, casually—as if returning to a minor subject:

"You were very anxious to give up your mate to the shore people, I believe?"

He was. To the law. His obscure tenacity on that point had in it something incomprehensible and a little awful; something, as it were, mystical, quite apart from his anxiety that he should not be suspected of "countenancing any doings of that sort." Seven-and-thirty virtuous years at sea, of which over twenty of immaculate command, and the last fifteen in the *Sephora*, seemed to have laid him under some pitiless obligation.

"And you know," he went on, groping shamefacedly amongst his feelings, "I did not engage that young fellow. His people had some interest with my owners. I was in a way forced to take him on. He looked very smart, very gentlemanly, and all that. But do you know—I never liked him, somehow. I am a plain man. You see, he wasn't exactly the sort for the chief mate of a ship like the *Sephora*."

I had become so connected in thoughts and impressions with the secret sharer of my cabin that I felt as if I, personally, were being given to understand that I, too, was not the sort that would have done for the chief mate of a ship like the *Sephora*. I had no doubt of it in my mind.

"Not at all the style of man. You understand," he insisted, superfluously, looking hard at me.

I smiled urbanely. He seemed at a loss for a while.

"I suppose I must report a suicide."

"Beg pardon?"

"Sui—cide! That's what I'll have to write to my owners directly I get in."

"Unless you manage to recover him before tomorrow," I assented, dispassionately. . . . "I mean, alive."

He mumbled something which I really did not catch, and I turned my ear to him in a puzzled manner. He fairly bawled:

"The land—I say, the mainland is at least seven miles off my anchorage."

"About that."

My lack of excitement, of curiosity, of surprise, of any sort of pronounced interest, began to arouse his distrust. But except for the felicitous pretence of deafness I had not tried to pretend anything. I had felt utterly incapable of playing the part of ignorance properly, and therefore was afraid to try. It is also certain that he had brought some ready-made suspicions with him, and that he viewed my politeness as a strange and unnatural phenomenon. And yet how else could I have received him? Not heartily! That was impossible for psychological reasons, which I need not state here. My only object was to keep off his inquiries. Surlily? Yes, but surliness might have provoked a point-blank question. From its novelty to him and from its nature, punctilious courtesy was the manner best calculated to restrain the man. But there was the danger of his breaking through my defence bluntly. I could not, I think, have met him by a direct lie, also for psychological (not moral) reasons. If he had only known how afraid I was of his putting my feeling of identity with the other to the test! But, strangely enough—(I thought of it only afterward)—I believe that he was not a little disconcerted by the reverse side of that weird situation, by something in me that reminded him of the man he was seeking—suggested a mysterious similitude to the young fellow he had distrusted and disliked from the first.

However that might have been, the silence was not very prolonged. He took another oblique step.

"I reckon I had no more than a two-mile pull to your ship. Not a bit more."

"And quite enough, too, in this awful heat," I said.

Another pause full of mistrust followed. Necessity, they say, is mother of invention, but fear, too, is not barren of ingenious suggestions. And I was afraid he would ask me point-blank for news of my other self.

"Nice little saloon, isn't it?" I remarked, as if noticing for the first time the way his eyes roamed from one closed door to the other. "And very well fitted out, too. Here, for instance," I continued, reaching over the back of my seat negligently and flinging the door open, "is my bath-room."

He made an eager movement, but hardly gave it a glance. I got up, shut the door of the bath-room, and invited him to have a look round, as if I were very proud of my accommodation. He had to rise and be shown round, but he went through the business without any raptures whatever.

"And now we'll have a look at my stateroom," I declared, in a voice as loud as I dared to make it, crossing the cabin to the starboard side with purposely heavy steps.

He followed me in and gazed around. My intelligent double had vanished. I played my part.

"Very convenient—isn't it?"

"Very nice. Very comf . . ." He didn't finish, and went out brusquely as if to escape from some unrighteous wiles of mine. But it was not to be. I had been too frightened not to feel vengeful; I felt I had him on the run, and I meant to keep him on the run. My polite insistence must have had something menacing in it, because he gave in suddenly. And I did not let him off a single item; mate's room, pantry, storerooms, the very sail-locker which was also under the poop—he had to look into them all. When at last I showed him out on the quarter-deck he drew a long, spiritless sigh, and mumbled dismally that he must really be going back to his ship now. I desired my mate, who had joined us, to see to the captain's boat.

The man of whiskers gave a blast on the whistle which he used to wear hanging round his neck, and yelled, "*Sephora*s away!"* My double down there in my cabin must have heard, and certainly could not feel more relieved than I. Four fellows came running out from somewhere forward and went over the side, while my own men, appearing on deck too, lined the rail. I escorted my visitor to the gangway ceremoniously, and nearly overdid it. He was a tenacious beast. On the very ladder he lingered, and in that unique, guiltily conscientious manner of sticking to the point:

"I say . . . you . . . you don't think that——"

I covered his voice loudly:

"Certainly not. . . . I am delighted. Goodbye."

I had an idea of what he meant to say, and just saved myself by the privilege of defective hearing. He was too shaken generally to insist, but my mate, close witness of that parting, looked mystified and his face took on a thoughtful cast. As I did not want to appear as if I wished to avoid all communication with my officers, he had the opportunity to address me.

"Seems a very nice man. His boat's crew told our chaps a very extraordinary story, if what I am told by the steward is true. I suppose you had it from the captain, sir?"

"Yes. I had a story from the captain."

"A very horrible affair—isn't it, sir?"

"It is."

"Beats all these tales we hear about murders in Yankee ships."*

"I don't think it beats them. I don't think it resembles them in the least."

"Bless my soul—you don't say so! But of course I've no acquaintance whatever with American ships, not I, so I couldn't go against your knowledge. It's horrible enough for me. . . . But the queerest part is that those fellows seemed to have some idea the man was hidden aboard here. They had really. Did you ever hear of such a thing?"

"Preposterous—isn't it?"

We were walking to and fro athwart the quarter-deck. No one of the crew forward could be seen (the day was Sunday), and the mate pursued:

"There was some little dispute about it. Our chaps took offence. 'As if we would harbour a thing like that,' they said. 'Wouldn't you like to look for him in our coal-hole?' Quite a tiff. But they made it up in the end. I suppose he did drown himself. Don't you, sir?"

"I don't suppose anything."

"You have no doubt in the matter, sir?"

"None whatever."

I left him suddenly. I felt I was producing a bad impression, but with my double down there it was most trying to be on deck. And it was almost as trying to be below. Altogether a nerve-trying situation. But on the whole I felt less torn in two when I was with him. There was no one in the whole ship whom I dared take into my confidence.

Since the hands had got to know his story, it would have been impossible to pass him off for any one else, and an accidental discovery was to be dreaded now more than ever. . . .

The steward being engaged in laying the table for dinner, we could talk only with our eyes when I first went down. Later in the afternoon we had a cautious try at whispering. The Sunday quietness of the ship was against us; the stillness of air and water around her was against us; the elements, the men were against us—everything was against us in our secret partnership; time itself—for this could not go on forever. The very trust in Providence was, I suppose, denied to his guilt. Shall I confess that this thought cast me down very much? And as to the chapter of accidents which counts for so much in the book of success, I could only hope that it was closed. For what favourable accident could be expected?

"Did you hear everything?" were my first words as soon as we took up our position side by side, leaning over my bed-place.

He had. And the proof of it was his earnest whisper, "The man told you he hardly dared to give the order."

I understood the reference to be to that saving foresail.

"Yes. He was afraid of it being lost in the setting."

"I assure you he never gave the order. He may think he did, but he never gave it. He stood there with me on the break of the poop after the maintopsail blew away, and whimpered about our last hope—positively whimpered about it and nothing else—and the night coming on! To hear one's skipper go on like that in such weather was enough to drive any fellow out of his mind. It worked me up into a sort of desperation. I just took it into my own hands and went away from him, boiling, and—— But what's the use telling you? *You* know! . . . Do you think that if I had not been pretty fierce with them I should have got the men to do anything? Not it! The bosun perhaps? Perhaps! It wasn't a heavy sea—it was a sea gone mad! I suppose the end of the world will be something like that; and a man may have the heart to see it coming once and be done with it—but to have to face it day after day—— I don't blame anybody. I was precious little better than the rest. Only—I was an officer of that old coal-waggon, anyhow——"

"I quite understand," I conveyed that sincere assurance into his ear. He was out of breath with whispering; I could hear him pant slightly. It was all very simple. The same strung-up force which had given twenty-four men a chance, at least, for their lives, had, in a sort of recoil, crushed an unworthy mutinous existence.

But I had no leisure to weigh the merits of the matter—footsteps in the saloon, a heavy knock. "There's enough wind to get under way with, sir." Here was the call of a new claim upon my thoughts and even upon my feelings.

"Turn the hands up," I cried through the door. "I'll be on deck directly."

I was going out to make the acquaintance of my ship. Before I left the cabin our eyes met—the eyes of the only two strangers on board. I pointed to the recessed part where the little camp-stool awaited him and laid my finger on my lips. He made a gesture—somewhat vague—a little mysterious, accompanied by a faint smile, as if of regret.

This is not the place to enlarge upon the sensations of a man who feels for the first time a ship move under his feet to his own independent word. In my case they were not unalloyed. I was not wholly alone with my command; for there was that stranger in my cabin. Or rather, I was not completely and wholly with her. Part of me was absent. That mental feeling of being in two places at once affected me physically as if the mood of secrecy had penetrated my very soul. Before an hour had elapsed since the ship had begun to move, having occasion to ask the mate (he stood by my side) to take a compass bearing of the Pagoda, I caught myself reaching up to his ear in whispers. I say I caught myself, but enough had escaped to startle the man. I can't describe it otherwise than by saying that he shied. A grave, preoccupied manner, as though he were in possession of some perplexing intelligence, did not leave him henceforth. A little later I moved away from the rail to look at the compass with such a stealthy gait that the helmsman noticed it—and I could not help noticing the unusual roundness of his eyes. These are trifling instances, though it's to no commander's advantage to be suspected of ludicrous eccentricities. But I was also more seriously affected. There are to a seaman certain words, gestures, that should in given conditions come as naturally, as instinctively as the winking of a menaced eye. A certain order should spring on to his lips without thinking; a certain sign should get itself made, so to speak, without reflection. But all unconscious alertness had abandoned me. I had to make an effort of will to recall myself back (from the cabin) to the conditions of the moment. I felt that I was appearing an irresolute commander to those people who were watching me more or less critically.

And, besides, there were the scares. On the second day out, for instance, coming off the deck in the afternoon (I had straw slippers on my bare feet) I stopped at the open pantry door and spoke to the steward. He was doing something there with his back to me. At the sound of my voice he nearly jumped out of his skin, as the saying is, and incidentally broke a cup.

"What on earth's the matter with you?" I asked, astonished.

He was extremely confused. "Beg your pardon, sir. I made sure you were in your cabin."

"You see I wasn't."

"No, sir. I could have sworn I had heard you moving in there not a moment ago. It's most extraordinary . . . very sorry, sir."

I passed on with an inward shudder. I was so identified with my secret double that I did not even mention the fact in those scanty, fearful whispers we exchanged. I suppose he had made some slight noise of some kind or other. It would have been miraculous if he hadn't at one time or another. And yet, haggard as he appeared, he looked always perfectly self-controlled, more than calm—almost invulnerable. On my suggestion he remained almost entirely in the bath-room, which, upon the whole, was the safest place. There could be really no shadow of an excuse for any one ever wanting to go in there, once the steward had done with it. It was a very tiny place. Sometimes he reclined on the floor, his legs bent, his head sustained on one elbow. At others I would find him on the camp-stool, sitting in his grey sleeping-suit and with his cropped dark hair like a patient, unmoved convict. At night I would smuggle him into my bed-place, and we would whisper together, with the regular footfalls of the officer of the watch passing and repassing over our heads. It was an infinitely miserable time. It was lucky that some tins of fine preserves were stowed in a locker in my stateroom; hard bread I could always get hold of; and so he lived on stewed chicken, pâté de foie gras, asparagus, cooked oysters, sardines—on all sorts of abominable sham delicacies out of tins. My early morning coffee he always drank; and it was all I dared do for him in that respect.

Every day there was the horrible manœuvring to go through so that my room and then the bath-room should be done in the usual way. I came to hate the sight of the steward, to abhor the voice of that harmless man. I felt that it was he who would bring on the disaster of discovery. It hung like a sword over our heads.*

The fourth day out, I think (we were then working down the east side of the Gulf of Siam, tack for tack, in light winds and smooth water)—the fourth day, I say, of this miserable juggling with the unavoidable, as we sat at our evening meal, that man, whose slightest movement I dreaded, after putting down the dishes ran up on deck busily. This could not be dangerous. Presently he came down again; and then it appeared that he had remembered a coat of mine which I had thrown over a rail to dry after having been wetted in a shower which had passed over the ship in the afternoon. Sitting stolidly at the head of the table I became terrified at the sight of the garment on his arm. Of course he made for my door. There was no time to lose.

"Steward," I thundered. My nerves were so shaken that I could not govern my voice and conceal my agitation. This was the sort of thing that made my terrifically whiskered mate tap his forehead with his forefinger. I had detected him using that gesture while talking on deck with a confidential air to the carpenter. It was too far to hear a word, but I had no doubt that this pantomime could only refer to the strange new captain.

"Yes, sir," the pale-faced steward turned resignedly to me. It was this maddening course of being shouted at, checked without rhyme or reason, arbitrarily chased out of my cabin, suddenly called into it, sent flying out of his pantry on incomprehensible errands, that accounted for the growing wretchedness of his expression.

"Where are you going with that coat?"

"To your room, sir."

"Is there another shower coming?"

"I'm sure I don't know, sir. Shall I go up again and see, sir?"

"No! never mind."

My object was attained, as of course my other self in there would have heard everything that passed. During this interlude my two officers never raised their eyes off their respective plates; but the lip of that confounded cub, the second mate, quivered visibly.

I expected the steward to hook my coat on and come out at once. He was very slow about it; but I dominated my nervousness sufficiently not to shout after him. Suddenly I became aware (it could be heard plainly enough) that the fellow for some reason or other was opening the door of the bath-room. It was the end. The place was literally not big enough to swing a cat in. My voice died in my throat and I went stony all over. I expected to hear a yell of surprise and terror, and made a movement, but had not the strength to get on my legs. Everything remained still. Had my second self taken the poor wretch by the throat? I don't know what I would have done next moment if I had not seen the steward come out of my room, close the door, and then stand quietly by the sideboard.

"Saved," I thought. "But, no! Lost! Gone! He was gone!"

I laid my knife and fork down and leaned back in my chair. My head swam. After a while, when sufficiently recovered to speak in a steady voice, I instructed my mate to put the ship round at eight o'clock himself.

"I won't come on deck," I went on. "I think I'll turn in, and unless the wind shifts I don't want to be disturbed before midnight. I feel a bit seedy."

"You did look middling bad a little while ago," the chief mate remarked without showing any great concern.

They both went out, and I stared at the steward clearing the table. There was nothing to be read on that wretched man's face. But why did he avoid my eyes, I asked myself. Then I thought I should like to hear the sound of his voice.

"Steward!"

"Sir!" Startled as usual.

"Where did you hang up that coat?"

"In the bath-room, sir." The usual anxious tone. "It's not quite dry yet, sir."

For some time longer I sat in the cuddy. Had my double vanished as he had come? But of his coming there was an explanation, whereas his disappearance would be inexplicable. . . . I went slowly into my dark room, shut the door, lighted the lamp, and for a time dared not turn round. When at last I did I saw him standing bolt-upright in the narrow recessed part. It would not be true to say I had a shock, but an irresistible doubt of his bodily existence flitted through my mind. Can it be, I asked myself, that he is not visible to other eyes than mine? It was like being haunted. Motionless, with a grave face, he raised his hands slightly at me in a gesture which meant clearly, "Heavens! what a narrow escape!" Narrow indeed. I think I had come creeping quietly as near insanity as any man who has not actually gone over the border. That gesture restrained me, so to speak.

The mate with the terrific whiskers was now putting the ship on the other tack. In the moment of profound silence which follows upon the hands going to their stations I heard on the poop his raised voice: "Hard alee!" and the distant shout of the order repeated on the maindeck. The sails, in that light breeze, made but a faint fluttering noise. It ceased. The ship was coming round slowly; I held my breath in the renewed stillness of expectation; one wouldn't have thought that there was a single living soul on her decks. A sudden brisk shout, "Mainsail haul!" broke the spell, and in the noisy cries and rush overhead of the men running away with the main-brace we two, down in my cabin, came together in our usual position by the bed-place.

He did not wait for my question. "I heard him fumbling here and just managed to squat myself down in the bath," he whispered to me. "The fellow only opened the door and put his arm in to hang the coat up. All the same——"

"I never thought of that," I whispered back, even more appalled than before at the closeness of the shave, and marvelling at that something unyielding in his character which was carrying him through so finely. There was no agitation in his whisper. Whoever was being driven distracted, it was not he. He was sane. And the proof of his sanity was continued when he took up the whispering again.

"It would never do for me to come to life again."

It was something that a ghost might have said. But what he was alluding to was his old captain's reluctant admission of the theory of suicide. It would obviously serve his turn—if I had understood at all the view which seemed to govern the unalterable purpose of his action.

"You must maroon me as soon as ever you can get amongst these islands off the Cambodian* shore," he went on.

"Maroon you! We are not living in a boy's adventure tale," I protested. His scornful whispering took me up.

"We aren't indeed! There's nothing of a boy's tale in this. But there's nothing else for it. I want no more. You don't suppose I am afraid of what can be done to me? Prison or gallows or whatever they may please. But you don't see me coming back to explain such things to an old fellow in a wig and twelve respectable tradesmen, do you? What can they know whether I am guilty or not—or of *what* I am guilty, either? That's my affair. What does the Bible say? 'Driven off the face of the earth.'* Very well. I am off the face of the earth now. As I came at night so I shall go."

"Impossible!" I murmured. "You can't."

"Can't? . . . Not naked like a soul on the Day of Judgment.* I shall freeze on to this sleeping-suit. The Last Day is not yet—and . . . you have understood thoroughly. Didn't you?"

I felt suddenly ashamed of myself. I may say truly that I understood—and my hesitation in letting that man swim away from my ship's side had been a mere sham sentiment, a sort of cowardice.

"It can't be done now till next night," I breathed out. "The ship is on the off-shore tack and the wind may fail us."

"As long as I know that you understand," he whispered. "But of course you do. It's a great satisfaction to have got somebody to understand. You seem to have been there on purpose." And in the same whisper, as if we two whenever we talked had to say things to each other which were not fit for the world to hear, he added, "It's very wonderful."

We remained side by side talking in our secret way—but sometimes silent or just exchanging a whispered word or two at long intervals. And as usual he stared through the port. A breath of wind came now and again into our faces. The ship might have been moored in dock, so gently and on an even keel she slipped through the water, that did not murmur even at our passage, shadowy and silent like a phantom sea.

At midnight I went on deck, and to my mate's great surprise put the ship round on the other tack. His terrible whiskers flitted round me in silent criticism. I certainly should not have done it if it had been only a question of getting out of that sleepy gulf as quickly as possible. I believe he told the second mate, who relieved him, that it was a great want of judgment. The other only yawned. That intolerable cub shuffled about so sleepily and lolled against the rails in such a slack, improper fashion that I came down on him sharply.

"Aren't you properly awake yet?"

"Yes, sir! I am awake."

"Well, then, be good enough to hold yourself as if you were. And keep a look-out. If there's any current we'll be closing with some islands before daylight."

The east side of the gulf is fringed with islands, some solitary, others in groups. On the blue background of the high coast they seem to float on silvery patches of calm water, arid and grey, or dark green and rounded like clumps of evergreen bushes, with the larger ones, a mile or two long, showing the outlines of ridges, ribs of grey rock under the dank mantle of matted leafage. Unknown to trade, to travel, almost to geography, the manner of life they harbour is an unsolved secret. There must be villages—settlements of fishermen at least—on the largest of them, and some communication with the world is probably kept up by native craft. But all that forenoon, as we headed for them, fanned along by the faintest of breezes, I saw no sign of man or canoe in the field of the telescope I kept on pointing at the scattered group.

At noon I gave no orders for a change of course, and the mate's whiskers became much concerned and seemed to be offering themselves unduly to my notice. At last I said:

"I am going to stand right in. Quite in—as far as I can take her."

The stare of extreme surprise imparted an air of ferocity also to his eyes, and he looked truly terrific for a moment.

"We're not doing well in the middle of the gulf," I continued, casually. "I am going to look for the land breezes tonight."

"Bless my soul! Do you mean, sir, in the dark amongst the lot of all them islands and reefs and shoals?"

"Well—if there are any regular land breezes at all on this coast one must get close inshore to find them, mustn't one?"

"Bless my soul!" he exclaimed again under his breath. All that afternoon he wore a dreamy, contemplative appearance which in him was a mark of perplexity. After dinner I went into my stateroom as if I meant to take some rest. There we two bent our dark heads over a half-unrolled chart lying on my bed.

"There," I said. "It's got to be Koh-ring.* I've been looking at it ever since sunrise. It has got two hills and a low point. It must be inhabited. And on the coast opposite there is what looks like the mouth of a biggish river—with some town, no doubt, not far up. It's the best chance for you that I can see."

"Anything. Koh-ring let it be."

He looked thoughtfully at the chart as if surveying chances and distances from a lofty height—and following with his eyes his own figure wandering on the blank land of Cochin-China, and then passing off that piece of paper clean out of sight into uncharted regions. And it was as if the ship had two captains to plan her course for her. I had been so worried and restless running up and down that I had not had the patience to dress that day. I had remained in my sleeping-suit, with straw slippers and a soft floppy hat. The closeness of the heat in the gulf had been most oppressive, and the crew were used to seeing me wandering in that airy attire.

"She will clear the south point as she heads now," I whispered into his ear. "Goodness only knows when, though, but certainly after dark. I'll edge her in to half a mile, as far as I may be able to judge in the dark——"

"Be careful," he murmured, warningly—and I realised suddenly that all my future, the only future for which I was fit, would perhaps go irretrievably to pieces in any mishap to my first command.

I could not stop a moment longer in the room. I motioned him to get out of sight and made my way on the poop. That unplayful cub had the watch. I walked up and down for a while thinking things out, then beckoned him over.

"Send a couple of hands to open the two quarter-deck ports," I said, mildly.

He actually had the impudence, or else so forgot himself in his wonder at such an incomprehensible order, as to repeat:

"Open the quarter-deck ports! What for, sir?"

"The only reason you need concern yourself about is because I tell you to do so. Have them open wide and fastened properly."

He reddened and went off, but I believe made some jeering remark to the carpenter as to the sensible practice of ventilating a ship's quarter-deck. I know he popped into the mate's cabin to impart the fact to him because the whiskers came on deck, as it were by chance, and stole glances at me from below—for signs of lunacy or drunkenness, I suppose.

A little before supper, feeling more restless than ever, I rejoined, for a moment, my second self. And to find him sitting so quietly was surprising, like something against nature, inhuman.

I developed my plan in a hurried whisper.

"I shall stand in as close as I dare and then put her round. I shall presently find means to smuggle you out of here into the sail-locker, which communicates with the lobby. But there is an opening, a sort of square for hauling the sails out, which gives straight on the quarter-deck and which is never closed in fine weather, so as to give air to the sails. When the ship's way is deadened in stays and all the hands are aft at the main-braces you shall have a clear road to slip out and get overboard through the open quarter-deck port. I've had them both fastened up. Use a rope's end to lower yourself into the water so as to avoid a splash—you know. It could be heard and cause some beastly complication."

He kept silent for a while, then whispered, "I understand."

"I won't be there to see you go," I began with an effort. "The rest . . . I only hope I have understood, too."

"You have. From first to last"—and for the first time there seemed to be a faltering, something strained in his whisper. He caught hold of my arm, but the ringing of the supper bell made me start. He didn't, though; he only released his grip.

After supper I didn't come below again till well past eight o'clock. The faint, steady breeze was loaded with dew; and the wet, darkened sails held all there was of propelling power in it. The night, clear and starry, sparkled darkly, and the opaque, lightless patches shifting slowly against the low stars were the drifting islets. On the port bow there was a big one more distant and shadowily imposing by the great space of sky it eclipsed.

On opening the door I had a back view of my very own self looking at a chart. He had come out of the recess and was standing near the table.

"Quite dark enough," I whispered.

He stepped back and leaned against my bed with a level, quiet glance. I sat on the couch. We had nothing to say to each other. Over our heads the officer of the watch moved here and there. Then I heard him move quickly. I knew what that meant. He was making for the companion; and presently his voice was outside my door.

"We are drawing in pretty fast, sir. Land looks rather close."

"Very well," I answered. "I am coming on deck directly."

I waited till he was gone out of the cuddy, then rose. My double moved too. The time had come to exchange our last whispers, for neither of us was ever to hear each other's natural voice.

"Look here!" I opened a drawer and took out three sovereigns. "Take this, anyhow. I've got six and I'd give you the lot, only I must keep a little money to buy some fruit and vegetables for the crew from native boats as we go through Sunda Straits."

He shook his head.

"Take it," I urged him, whispering desperately. "No one can tell what——"

He smiled and slapped meaningly the only pocket of the sleeping-jacket. It was not safe, certainly. But I produced a large old silk handkerchief of mine, and tying the three pieces of gold in a corner, pressed it on him. He was touched, I suppose, because he took it at last and tied it quickly round his waist under the jacket, on his bare skin.

Our eyes met; several seconds elapsed, till, our glances still mingled, I extended my hand and turned the lamp out. Then I passed through the cuddy, leaving the door of my room wide open. . . . "Steward!"

He was still lingering in the pantry in the greatness of his zeal, giving a rub-up to a plated cruet stand the last thing before going to bed. Being careful not to wake up the mate, whose room was opposite, I spoke in an undertone.

He looked round anxiously. "Sir!"

"Can you get me a little hot water from the galley?"

"I am afraid, sir, the galley fire's been out for some time now."

"Go and see."

He fled up the stairs.

"Now," I whispered, loudly, into the saloon—too loudly, perhaps, but I was afraid I couldn't make a sound. He was by my side in an instant—the double captain slipped past the stairs—through a tiny dark passage . . . a sliding door. We were in the sail-locker, scrambling on our knees over the sails. A sudden thought struck me. I saw myself wandering barefooted, bareheaded, the sun beating on my dark poll. I snatched off my floppy hat and tried hurriedly in the dark to ram it on my other self. He dodged and fended off silently. I wonder what he thought had come to me before he understood and suddenly desisted. Our hands met gropingly, lingered united in a steady, motionless clasp for a second. . . . No word was breathed by either of us when they separated.

I was standing quietly by the pantry door when the steward returned.

"Sorry, sir. Kettle barely warm. Shall I light the spirit-lamp?"

"Never mind."

I came out on deck slowly. It was now a matter of conscience to shave the land as close as possible—for now he must go overboard whenever the ship was put in stays. Must! There could be no going back for him. After a moment I walked over to leeward and my heart flew into my mouth at the nearness of the land on the bow. Under any other circumstances I would not have held on a minute longer. The second mate had followed me anxiously.

I looked on till I felt I could command my voice.

"She will weather,"* I said then in a quiet tone.

"Are you going to try that, sir?" he stammered out incredulously.

I took no notice of him and raised my tone just enough to be heard by the helmsman.

"Keep her good full."

"Good full, sir."

The wind fanned my cheek, the sails slept, the world was silent. The strain of watching the dark loom of the land grow bigger and denser was too much for me. I had shut my eyes—because the ship must go closer. She must! The stillness was intolerable. Were we standing still?

When I opened my eyes the second view started my heart with a thump. The black southern hill of Koh-ring seemed to hang right over the ship like a towering fragment of the everlasting night. On that enormous mass of blackness there was not a gleam to be seen, not a sound to be heard. It was gliding irresistibly toward us and yet seemed already within reach of the hand. I saw the vague figures of the watch grouped in the waist, gazing in awed silence.

"Are you going on, sir?" inquired an unsteady voice at my elbow.

I ignored it. I had to go on.

"Keep her full. Don't check her way. That won't do now," I said, warningly.

"I can't see the sails very well," the helmsman answered me, in strange, quavering tones.

Was she close enough? Already she was, I won't say in the shadow of the land, but in the very blackness of it, already swallowed up as it were, gone too close to be recalled, gone from me altogether.

"Give the mate a call," I said to the young man who stood at my elbow as still as death. "And turn all hands up."

My tone had a borrowed loudness reverberated from the height of the land. Several voices cried out together: "We are all on deck, sir."

Then stillness again, with the great shadow gliding closer, towering higher, without a light, without a sound. Such a hush had fallen on the ship that she might have been a bark of the dead floating in slowly under the very gate of Erebus.*

"My God! Where are we?"

It was the mate moaning at my elbow. He was thunderstruck, and as it were deprived of the moral support of his whiskers. He clapped his hands and absolutely cried out, "Lost!"

"Be quiet," I said, sternly.

He lowered his tone, but I saw the shadowy gesture of his despair. "What are we doing here?"

"Looking for the land wind."

He made as if to tear his hair, and addressed me recklessly.

"She will never get out. You have done it, sir. I knew it'd end in something like this. She will never weather, and you are too close now to stay. She'll drift ashore before she's round. O my God!"

I caught his arm as he was raising it to batter his poor devoted head, and shook it violently.

"She's ashore already," he wailed, trying to tear himself away.

"Is she? . . . Keep good full there!"

"Good full, sir," cried the helmsman in a frightened, thin, child-like voice.

I hadn't let go the mate's arm and went on shaking it. "Ready about, do you hear? You go forward"—shake—"and stop there"—shake—"and hold your noise"—shake—"and see these head-sheets properly overhauled"—shake, shake—shake.

And all the time I dared not look toward the land lest my heart should fail me. I released my grip at last and he ran forward as if fleeing for dear life.

I wondered what my double there in the sail-locker thought of this commotion. He was able to hear everything—and perhaps he was able to understand why, on my conscience, it had to be thus close—no less. My first order "Hard alee!" re-echoed ominously under the towering shadow of Koh-ring as if I had shouted in a mountain gorge. And then I watched the land intently. In that smooth water and light wind it was impossible to feel the ship coming-to. No! I could not feel her. And my second self was making now ready to slip out and lower himself overboard. Perhaps he was gone already . . . ?

The great black mass brooding over our very mastheads began to pivot away from the ship's side silently. And now I forgot the secret stranger ready to depart, and remembered only that I was a total stranger to the ship. I did not know her. Would she do it? How was she to be handled?

I swung the mainyard and waited helplessly. She was perhaps stopped, and her very fate hung in the balance, with the black mass of Koh-ring like the gate of the everlasting night towering over her taffrail. What would she do now? Had she way on her yet? I stepped to the side swiftly, and on the shadowy water I could see nothing except a faint phosphorescent flash revealing the glassy smoothness of the sleeping surface. It was impossible to tell—and I had not learned yet the feel of my ship. Was she moving? What I needed was something easily seen, a piece of paper, which I could throw overboard and watch. I had nothing on me. To run down for it I didn't dare. There was no time. All at once my strained, yearning stare distinguished a white object floating within a yard of the ship's side. White on the black water. A phosphorescent flash passed under it. What was that thing? . . . I recognised my own floppy hat. It must have fallen off his head . . . and he didn't bother. Now I had what I wanted—the saving mark for my eyes.* But I hardly thought of my other self, now gone from the ship, to be hidden forever from all friendly faces, to be a fugitive and a vagabond on the earth, with no brand of the curse* on his sane forehead to stay a slaying hand . . . too proud to explain.

And I watched the hat—the expression of my sudden pity for his mere flesh. It had been meant to save his homeless head from the dangers of the sun. And now—behold—it was saving the ship, by serving me for a mark to help out the ignorance of my strangeness. Ha! It was drifting forward, warning me just in time that the ship had gathered sternway.

"Shift the helm," I said in a low voice to the seaman standing still like a statue.

The man's eyes glistened wildly in the binnacle light as he jumped round to the other side and spun round the wheel.

I walked to the break of the poop. On the overshadowed deck all hands stood by the forebraces waiting for my order. The stars ahead seemed to be gliding from right to left. And all was so still in the world that I heard the quiet remark "She's round," passed in a tone of intense relief between two seamen.

"Let go and haul."

The foreyards ran round with a great noise, amidst cheery cries. And now the frightful whiskers made themselves heard giving various orders. Already the ship was drawing ahead. And I was alone with her. Nothing! no one in the world should stand now between us, throwing a shadow on the way of silent knowledge and mute affection, the perfect communion of a seaman with his first command.

Walking to the taffrail, I was in time to make out, on the very edge of a darkness thrown by a towering black mass like the very gateway of Erebus—yes, I was in time to catch an evanescent glimpse of my white hat left behind to mark the spot where the secret sharer of my cabin and of my thoughts, as though he were my second self, had lowered himself into the water to take his punishment: a free man, a proud swimmer striking out for a new destiny.

EXTRACT FROM THE
'AUTHOR'S NOTE' (1919)

[. . .] I had just finished writing "The End of the Tether," and was casting about for some subject which could be developed in a shorter form than the tales in the volume of *Youth*, when the instance of a steamship full of returning coolies from Singapore to some port in northern China occurred to my recollection. Years before I had heard it being talked about in the East as a recent occurrence. It was for us merely one subject of conversation amongst many others of the kind. Men earning their bread in any very specialised occupation will talk shop, not only because it is the most vital interest of their lives, but also because they have not much knowledge of other subjects. They have never had the time to get acquainted with them. Life, for most of us, is not so much a hard as an exacting taskmaster.

I never met anybody personally concerned in this affair, the interest of which for us was, of course, not the bad weather but the extraordinary complication brought into the ship's life at a moment of exceptional stress by the human element below her deck. Neither was the story itself ever enlarged upon in my hearing. In that company each of us could imagine easily what the whole thing was like. The financial difficulty of it, presenting also a human problem, was solved by a mind much too simple to be perplexed by anything in the world except men's idle talk for which it was not adapted.

From the first the mere anecdote, the mere statement I might say, that such a thing had happened on the high seas, appeared to me a sufficient subject for meditation. Yet it was but a bit of a sea yarn after all. I felt that to bring out its deeper significance which was quite apparent to me, something other, something more was required; a leading motive that would harmonise all these violent noises, and a point of view that would put all that elemental fury into its proper place.

What was needed of course was Captain MacWhirr. Directly I perceived him I could see that he was the man for the situation. I don't mean to say that I ever saw Captain MacWhirr in the flesh, or had ever come in contact with his literal mind and his dauntless temperament. MacWhirr is not an acquaintance of a few hours, or a few weeks, or a few months. He is the product of twenty years of life. My own life. Conscious invention had little to do with him. If it is true that Captain MacWhirr never walked and breathed on this earth (which I find for my part extremely difficult to believe), I can also assure my readers that he is perfectly authentic. I may venture to assert the same of every aspect of the story, while I confess that the particular typhoon of the tale was not a typhoon of my actual experience.

At its first appearance "Typhoon," the story, was classed by some critics as a deliberately intended storm-piece. Others picked out MacWhirr, in whom they perceived a definite symbolic intention. Neither was exclusively my intention. Both the typhoon and Captain MacWhirr presented themselves to me as the necessities of the deep conviction with which I approached the subject of the story. It was their opportunity. It was also my opportunity; and it would be vain to discourse about what I made of it in a handful of pages, since the pages themselves are here, between the covers of this volume, to speak for themselves.

This is a belated reflection. If it had occurred to me before it would have perhaps done away with the existence of this Author's Note; for, indeed, the same remark applies to every story in this volume. None of them are stories of experience in the absolute sense of the word. Experience in them is but the canvas of the attempted picture. Each of them has its more than one intention. With each the question is what the writer has done with his opportunity; and each answers the question for itself in words which, if I may say so without undue solemnity, were written with a conscientious regard for the truth of my own sensations. And each of those stories to mean something, must justify itself in its own way to the conscience of each successive reader.

"Falk"—the second story in the volume—offended the delicacy of one critic at least by certain peculiarities of its subject. But what is the subject of "Falk"? I personally do not feel so very certain about it. He who reads must find out for himself. My intention in writing "Falk" was not to shock anybody. As in most of my writings it is not the events that I am insisting on but their effect upon the persons in the tale. But in everything I have written there is always one invariable intention, and that is to capture the reader's attention, by securing his interest and enlisting his sympathies for the matter in hand, whatever it may be, within the limits of the visible world and within the boundaries of human emotions.

I may safely say that Falk is absolutely true to my experience of certain straightforward characters, combining a perfectly natural ruthlessness with a certain amount of moral delicacy. Falk obeys the law of self-preservation without the slightest misgivings as to his right, but at a crucial turn of that ruthlessly preserved life he will not condescend to dodge the truth. As he is presented as sensitive enough to be affected permanently by a certain unusual experience, that experience had to be set

by me before the reader vividly; but it is not the subject of the tale. If we
go by mere facts then the subject is Falk's attempt to get married; in which
the narrator of the tale finds himself unexpectedly involved both on its
ruthless and its delicate side.

Falk [*sic*] shares with one other of my stories ("The Return" in the *Tales
of Unrest* volume) the distinction of never having been serialised. I think
the copy was shown to the editor of some magazine, who rejected it
indignantly on the sole ground that "the girl never says anything." This is
perfectly true. From first to last Hermann's niece utters no word in the
tale—and it is not because she is dumb, but for the simple reason that
whenever she happens to come under the observation of the narrator she
has either no occasion or is too profoundly moved to speak. The editor,
who obviously had read the story, might have perceived that for himself.
Apparently he did not, and I refrained from pointing out the impossibility
to him because, since he did not venture to say that "the girl" did not live,
I felt no concern at his indignation [. . .]

                                                              J. C.
1919

EXPLANATORY NOTES

Nautical and foreign terms, and various place-names, are listed in the Glossary. In these notes, the following abbreviations are used:

AB   Andrzej Busza, 'Conrad's Polish Literary Background and Some Illustrations of the Influence of Polish Literature on his Work', *Antemurale*, 10 (Rome: Institutum Historicum Polonicum, 1966).

CEW   Norman Sherry, *Conrad's Eastern World* (London: Cambridge University Press, 1966).

JHS   John H. Stape: 'Topography in "The Secret Sharer"', *The Conradian*, 26 (2001), 1–16.

Letters Frederick R. Karl and Laurence Davies (eds.), *The Collected Letters of Joseph Conrad* (Cambridge: Cambridge University Press. vol. i, 1983; vol. ii, 1986; vol. iii, 1988).

LJ   Joseph Conrad, *Lord Jim: A Tale* (Edinburgh: Blackwood, 1900).

MOS   Joseph Conrad, *The Mirror of the Sea: Memories and Impressions* (London: Methuen, 1906).

NLL   Joseph Conrad, *Notes on Life and Letters* (London: Dent, 1921).

NN   Norman Sherry (ed.), Joseph Conrad, *The Nigger of the 'Narcissus', Typhoon, Falk and Other Stories* (London: Dent, 1974).

SL   Joseph Conrad, *The Shadow-Line: A Confession* (London: Dent, 1917).

TOS   Paul Kirschner (ed.), Joseph Conrad, *Typhoon and Other Stories* (London: Penguin, 1990; repr. with corrections, 1992).

Shakespeare quotations are from the 'Globe' edition: W. G. Clark and W. A. Wright (eds.), *The Works of William Shakespeare* (Cambridge: Macmillan, 1864).

Typhoon

3 *title*: before deciding on 'Typhoon', Conrad had considered 'Equitable Division' as a title.

   Nan-Shan: a steamer, the *Nan-Shan*, arrived in Singapore on 30 September 1887 with 546 Chinese on board, just as the *Vidar* (in which Conrad served as chief mate) was leaving for Berau (*CEW* 30 n.; *NN* 289 n.).

6 *Sigg and Son*: Jucker, Sigg and Co. were teak-merchants and ship-charterers in Bangkok (*CEW* 238).

7 *little straws. . . .*: i.e. 'little straws show which way the wind blows': small details may have large implications.

12 *Solomon says*: the biblical Solomon (who built a navy) was 'wiser than all men' (1 Kings 4: 31), and the famous 'judgement of Solomon' (initiated by his threat to divide in half a child whose maternity was disputed by two women) has a tenuous connection with MacWhirr's eventual decision to divide equally the disputed money.

17–18 *blanked ... blank ... condemned ... decayed ... gory ... crimson*: authorial euphemisms for the words 'blasted', 'blast', 'damned', 'rotten', 'bloody', and 'bleeding' (or 'bloody' again), which we impute to the engineer and which occasion MacWhirr's subsequent remark, 'A profane man'.

24 *the chapter on the storms*: the following extracts from a seamen's manual may explain both MacWhirr's perplexity and the *Nan-Shan*'s peril. The manual, by James Tait, Master Mariner, is *Tait's Seamanship* (3rd edition; Glasgow: Brown, 1902); I quote pp. 143–5:

Concise Rules for Revolving Storms.

1. Revolving storms are so named because the wind in these storms revolves round an area of low pressure situated in the centre. They have also local names, and are termed Hurricanes in the West Indies and South Pacific [...]; and Typhoons in the China Sea [...]

9. The indications of the approach of a revolving storm are (i) an unsteady barometer, or even a cessation in the diurnal range, which is constant in settled weather; (ii) a heavy swell not caused by the wind then blowing; (iii) an ugly, threatening appearance of the sky.

10. In order to judge what is the best way to act if there is reason to believe a storm is approaching, the seaman requires to know (a) in which direction the centre of the storm is situated; (b) in which semicircle the ship is situated.

11. As these points cannot be determined if a vessel is moving with any speed through the water, the first proceeding should be to 'stop' or 'heave to' [...]

12. If an observer faces the wind, the centre of the storm will be from 12 to 8 points on his right-hand in the northern hemisphere and on his left-hand in the southern hemisphere; 12 points when the storm begins; about 10 points when the barometer has fallen three-tenths of an inch, and about 8 points when it has fallen six-tenths of an inch or upwards.

13. If the wind shifts to the right the vessel is in the right-hand semicircle, if to the left in the left-hand semicircle, and, if the wind is steady in direction but increasing in force, she is in the direct path of the storm.

14. If the seaman has reason to think that his vessel is in the direct path of the storm he should run with the wind on the starboard quarter in the northern and on the port quarter in the southern hemisphere until the barometer has ceased falling. If she is in the right-hand semicircle in

the northern hemisphere she should remain hove to on the starboard tack [. . .]; if she is in the left-hand semicircle in the northern hemisphere she should run with the wind on the starboard quarter [. . .]

17. Should the centre of a storm pass over a vessel, the wind, after blowing furiously in one direction, ceases for a time, and then blows with equal fury from the opposite direction. This makes a confused pyramidal sea, which is especially dangerous.

(As the *Nan-Shan* is voyaging in the northern hemisphere, I have deleted some of the references to the southern hemisphere.) It will be seen that, in defiance of standard procedures (such as those of the Hydrographic Department cited here by Tait), MacWhirr directs his vessel through the centre of the typhoon.

25 *Melita*: the name of the vessel on which Conrad voyaged from Singapore to Bangkok in January 1888 to take command of the *Otago* (*CEW* 216–17).

33 *quietness in the enormous discord of noises*: the emphasis on a small but indomitable voice within the storm may recall the biblical 'still small voice' after the 'great and strong wind' (1 Kings 19: 11–12).

confident words on the last day: in the essay 'Henry James' (*NLL* 17), Conrad says that when the earth dies, 'if anybody, it will be the imaginative man who would be moved to speak on the eve of that day without tomorrow—whether in austere exhortation or in a phrase of sardonic comment, who can guess?'

when heavens fall, and justice is done: an echo of the Latin maxim, 'Fiat iustitia ruat caelum [*or* coelum]': 'Let justice be done, though the heavens fall'. Conrad had quoted this as 'fiat justicia ruat coelum' in March 1890 (*Letters*, i. 43), and Marlow broods on it in the penultimate paragraph of 'Heart of Darkness'.

47 *I can steer for ever . . . me*: in his heroic devotion to duty, Hackett resembles Singleton, the old helmsman in *The Nigger of the 'Narcissus'*. (The second mate, 'raging inwardly', resembles the resentful Donkin in that novel.)

51 *went on yelling the second*: one of Conrad's occasional lapses into unidiomatic, Gallicized word-order.

53 *as of girding the loins*: a biblical idiom, as in 'Gird up now thy loins like a man' (Job 38: 3). Thus, 'girding the loins' means 'preparing for brave action'.

62 *a slender hair holding a sword suspended over his head*: Damocles, flatterer of King Dionysius of Syracuse, was taught the insecurity of happiness by being made to sit through a feast while a sword was suspended above his head by a single hair. In *MOS* (106), Conrad says that once a seaman's ship has been imperilled, 'A man may be the better for it, but he will not be the same. Damocles has seen the sword suspended by a hair over his head [. . .]'

Falk

77 *Several of us, all more or less connected with the sea*: this 'transtextual' group clearly resembles the group described at the openings of 'Youth' and 'Heart of Darkness'. Conrad was recalling his Thames-side conversations (at such locations as the Lobster Tavern at Hole Haven, Canvey Island) with his friends Hope, Mears, and Keen, who were former seamen.

complained of hunger: together with the subsequent references ('primeval man', 'scorched lumps of flesh', 'tales of hunger and hunt—and of women', 'break-downs', the name *Arcadia*, and the cargo-steamer with its German couple), this phrase helps to give the tale a strongly proleptic opening: the 'inner' narrative is repeatedly foreshadowed by the 'outer' narrative.

78 *a man of over fifty*: later texts have 'a man of more than fifty'. This anonymous narrator resembles Marlow (who tells the story in 'Youth', 'Heart of Darkness', *Lord Jim*, and *Chance*) as well as the anonymous captain in 'The Secret Sharer', *The Shadow-Line*, and 'A Smile of Fortune'.

a certain Eastern seaport . . . kingdom: the kingdom is Siam (later Thailand); its capital is Bangkok; and the river is that often termed simply the Meinam or Menam (meaning 'River') but later the Chao Phraya.

my enemy Falk, and my friend Hermann: Norman Sherry opines that the name 'Falk' was suggested by the Bangkok firm of Falck and Beidek (though 'Falck's hotel' was also located there), and that the name 'Hermann' was suggested by a German steamer in Bangkok called *Hermann* (*CEW* 236–7).

80 *Diana not of Ephesus*: the classical goddess Diana (or Artemis) was usually depicted as a chaste, athletic huntress. 'Diana of Ephesus, although the patroness of chastity, was a fertility goddess; she wore a tight robe covered with animal heads, exposing her bosom of multiple breasts' (*TOS* 300).

83 *a man who had died suddenly*: the subsequent description of the narrator's predecessor in command tallies closely with that given in *The Shadow-Line*. There the former captain, who also plays the violin, resembles 'a wild boar somehow', and manages the ship irresponsibly. Nevertheless, his real-life counterpart, Captain John Snadden of the *Otago*, was apparently conscientious: according to Norman Sherry, 'far from being negligent, Snadden was extremely concerned about his ship' (*CEW* 226).

not been favoured by a scratch of the pen for the last eighteen months: in April 1888, one of the part-owners of the *Otago* complained to Conrad that Captain Snadden 'never favoured me with a scratch of the pen from the time of leaving Newcastle in August last [. . .]' (*CEW* 226).

The old mate . . . was not particularly pleased at my coming: in *The Shadow-Line*, the equivalent mate, Burns, 'expected to be confirmed in his temporary command' and was disappointed that a young newcomer gained the command instead (*SL* 105–6). His real-life counterpart, Charles Born of the *Otago*, is described in *MOS* (25–8) as pessimistic and reproachful.

Tottersen, or something like that: the second mate of the *Otago* on her return from Mauritius was F. Totterman, and 'Totterman' was the name used in the manuscript of 'Falk' (*CEW* 249 n.).

84 *the crew was sickly*: in *The Shadow-Line* the crew is stricken with 'tropical fever' and 'choleraic symptoms', though in that tale the mate is taken to hospital while the cook (Ransom) remains unaffected by the disease.

a certain Schomberg: the same character appears in *Lord Jim* and *Victory*. Norman Sherry says that the name may have been suggested by that of a German broker, Schomburgk [*sic*], who lived in Singapore (*CEW* 241–2).

audacious thief, and a first-class sprinter: Conrad is adapting an instance of theft from one of his crew. *CEW* 234 cites a report in the *Bangkok Times* dated 1 February 1888:

A chinese 'boy' employed on the barque *Otago* managed the other day to steal 15 gold mohurs from a sailor on board, and then to abscond. The captain and mate, however, met the juvenile thief a few hours afterwards in Mr Clarke's compound and arrested him. Whilst being conducted to the Bang Rak Police Station, he unfortunately managed to bolt and has not since been seen [. . .]

85 *trombone*: in the 1903 text the word was 'trump' (an archaic term for 'trumpet', as in 'the last trump': 1 Corinthians 15: 52); but Conrad later changed it to 'trombone' (*TOS* 38).

89 *his pound and a half of flesh*: thus Falk is, metaphorically, 50 per cent more extortionate than Shakespeare's Shylock; and the phrasing ironically beckons, for a moment, the tale's motif of cannibalism.

from early morn to dewy eve. In the last rays of the setting sun: Conrad is distantly echoing Milton's *Paradise Lost*, I, 742–5:

> from morn
> To noon he fell, from noon to dewy eve,
> A summer's day; and with the setting sun
> Dropped from the zenith like a falling star [. . .]

91 *great Buddhist Pagoda*: identified as 'the great Paknam pagoda' in 'The Secret Sharer'. 'Paknam' means 'river mouth'. The pagoda itself, with substructure, bell and spire, resembles a conical tower within the temple. In 1862, a traveller admired this 'temple all of purest white, its lofty spire, fantastic and gilded, flashing back the glory of the sun'. J. H. Stape comments that though the structure, now named Phra Samutchedi, still stands, 'its picturesque character has diminished' (JHS 6, 11).

93 *enough point in his behaviour to make me . . . wonder audibly what he might mean*: there are various instances of 'delayed decoding' in the tale. The fictional narrator is slow to perceive that Falk has been prompted by Hermann to regard him as a rival suitor; slow to recognize as consequences of the supposed rivalry both Falk's refusal to tow his ship and the bribery of Johnson; and slow to infer the reason for Falk's aversion to meat.

94 *tides in the affairs of men which taken at the flood . . . and so on*: Shakespeare, *Julius Caesar*, IV. iii. 216–19:

> There is a tide in the affairs of men,
> Which, taken at the flood, leads on to fortune:
> Omitted, all the voyage of their life
> Is bound in shallows and in miseries.

Kirschner (*TOS* 300) suggests that Conrad may be recalling Byron's *Don Juan*, VI, i: '"There is a tide in the affairs of men, | Which, taken at the flood,"—you know the rest'.

96 *his wife . . . her*: she reappears in *Victory*, with 'silk dress, long neck, ringlets, scared eyes, and silly grin—all complete'.

109 *Gambril*: he reappears as the elderly helmsman in *The Shadow-Line* (and survives the tropical illness).

116 *he didn't know any game.*: in the manuscript, this appears as 'he "didn't know any game".'; in the 1903 text, it is '"he didn't know any game."' In later editions, the phrasing changed to: '"he didn't know any card-games."'

117 *as his own idea of—let us say—"courting" seemed to consist*: the 1903 text reads: 'as his own idea of—let us say—courting, seemed to consist'. Removal of the ungrammatical comma creates an ambiguity which I dispel by adding the quotation-marks.

121 *peculiar domestic arrangements*: explained as a meatless cuisine.

123 *that Annihilation which is the worthy reward of us all*: Buddhists commend, as the best attainable state, Nirvana: the annihilation of individual existence and the attainment of transcendence.

129 *eaten man*: historic instances of cannibalism at sea include the controversial case of Thomas Dudley and Edwin Stephens. After a shipwreck in July 1884, three men and a ship's boy, Richard Parker, endured many days of thirst and starvation in an open boat. Eventually, two of the men, Dudley and Stephens, killed the boy, whose flesh was then eaten. The survivors were rescued and returned to England. At the subsequent trial, Dudley and Stephens (who had made no secret of their deed) were found guilty of murder; but their death-sentences were speedily commuted to sentences of six months' jail. In their defence, it was argued that 'there was an inevitable necessity that one life should be sacrificed in order that

the other three might be saved, and [. . .] they were justified in doing so in selecting the weakest' (*The Times*, 7 November 1884, p. 11). Paul Kirschner (*TOS* 301) notes that *The Times* for 25 September 1899, p. 7, refers to 'the arrest of Andersen and Thomassen, the Swedish survivors of the ship *Drot*, who are alleged to have committed acts of cannibalism on a raft after the wreck of that vessel'. Cannibalism at sea is depicted in Byron's *Don Juan*, Canto II, and is mooted in Wells's *The Island of Doctor Moreau*, ch. 1.

141 *the fable of The Flying Dutchman*: there are many versions of this legend, but their gist is that a Dutch sea-captain, Vanderdecken, commits blasphemy during a stormy voyage and is therefore condemned by the Almighty to sail the seas continually; his vessel, *The Flying Dutchman* itself, becomes a phantom ship with a spectral crew and imperils voyagers who encounter it. In Wagner's opera (*Der fliegende Holländer*, 1843), the Dutchman is redeemed by the self-sacrificial love of Senta, a sea-captain's daughter. Conrad certainly knew the novel by Captain Frederick Marryat, *The Phantom Ship* (1838–9). In this work, the blaspheming Dutchman kills a pilot, Schriften, whose spirit later impedes the endeavour of Philip, the Dutchman's son, to find his father and exorcize the curse. Philip loses his loving wife, but redeems his father after forgiving Schriften.

142 *an unerring and eternal principle*: 'Falk obeys the law of self-preservation without the slightest misgivings as to his right', says Conrad in the 'Author's Note' to *Typhoon and Other Stories*.

144 *Whereas if his niece went . . .*: Hermann's antipathy to Falk is vanquished largely by his aversion to paying for a second cabin.

Amy Foster

149 *title*: initially Conrad considered 'The Castaway' and 'A Husband' as titles for this piece.

the Ship Inn in Brenzett: the general location of 'Amy Foster' corresponds to south-east Kent (and the Kent–Sussex border) within a 13-mile radius of Dungeness. This area has its expanse of flat land, its long beaches of shingle, its Martello towers, and coastguard stations. The real village of Brenzett, however, lies more than 5 miles inland, unlike its fictional namesake, which was based on Dymchurch, with its Ship Inn and sea wall.

150 *brick cottage*: the 1903 text, and subsequent editions, had 'black cottage'; Paul Kirschner first restored the manuscript's 'brick cottage' (*TOS* 37–8).

152 *she ran out into the yard stopping her ears*: a proleptic irony, in view of Yanko's eventual fate.

German . . . thought: the claim 'Without phosphorus, no thought' is usually attributed to Jacob Moleschott of Heidelberg University, author of *Lehre der Nahrungsmittel* (1850). Moleschott, however, was born in the Netherlands and eventually took Italian nationality. William James, in *Principles of Psychology* (London: Macmillan, 1890), i. 101, says that *'Ohne Phosphor, kein Gedanke'* ('Without phosphorus, no thought') was 'a noted war-cry of the "materialists" during the excitement on that subject which filled Germany in the '60s [. . .]'

154 *castaway*: in the manuscript, following 'castaway;', there is a more personal passage, as Kirschner shows (*TOS* 298–9). This passage emphasizes the castaway's sense of strangeness among foreigners: 'your difference you feel creates a gulph—and there is no retreat'.

like an animal under a net: a major leitmotif in the tale. Related phrases include: 'a wild bird caught in a snare', 'as if the net of fate had been drawn closer round him', 'a wild creature under the net', 'a bird caught in a snare', and 'his fluttered air of a bird in a snare'. Ecclesiastes 9: 12 says: 'For man also knoweth not his time: as the fishes that are taken in an evil net, and as the birds that are caught in the snare; so *are* the sons of men snared in an evil time, when it falleth suddenly upon them.' Gaetano D'Elia has suggested that the tale exploits thematically the ambiguous term 'toil', which means both 'labour' and 'net or snare'. See 'Yanko, the Man Who Came from the Sea', in *Conradiana*, 11 (1979) 165–76.

155 *at the mouth of the Elbe*: this suggests Cuxhaven, but the port is later identified as Hamburg.

166 *Conceive you*: one of Conrad's occasional Gallicisms; this example appears in 'Heart of Darkness', too. (Instead of the English 'Can you imagine . . . ?', he gives a literal translation of the French 'Concevez-vous'.)

169 *Yanko . . . Goorall . . . surname*: 'Yanko' is a transliteration of the Polish 'Janko'; 'Goorall' corresponds to 'góral', the Polish word for 'highlander'.

174 *wicket gate*: the 1903 text, and subsequent editions, had 'wicker-gate'. Kirschner emended this as 'wicket-gate', noting that Conrad had pointed out the error to Doubleday's editor in 1915 but then failed to correct it when preparing the collected editions (*TOS* 38). The manuscript has 'wicket gate' (no hyphen).

The Secret Sharer

179 *title*: in the magazine text, the title was 'The Secret-Sharer', which means 'the sharer of a secret' and is therefore less appropriate than the unhyphenated version, which means 'the person who secretly shares'. The latter meaning is made explicit by the text in such phrases as 'the secret sharer of my cabin and of my thoughts' or 'the secret sharer of my life'. Alternative titles considered by Conrad were: 'The Secret Self', 'The Other Self', and 'The Second Self: An Episode from the Sea'.

fishing-stakes . . . eye could reach: JHS (5) cites a traveller's account of the mouth of the Meinam in 1892:

We make use of the floodtide to cross the bar, the half-muddy, half-sandy mass of which, during the low tide, shows, as far as the eye can see, a bamboo forest stuck into the soil, to which the Siamese and Annanite [i.e., Vietnamese] fishermen fix their huge conical nets [. . .]

To the left a group of barren islets . . . blockhouses: these correspond to the 'rocky islets [. . .] like the heaps of a cyclopean ruin' in 'Falk'. The location is again the Bight of Bangkok, at the north end of the Gulf of Siam.

181 *that ideal conception of one's own personality every man sets up for himself secretly*: attempted fidelity to one's ideal self is a major theme in Conrad's works, which so frequently deal with protagonists who have much to learn and are faced with crucial moral and psychological tests. Here the phrasing ('sets up for himself secretly') extends the meaning of the tale's title.

Sephora: in *Lord Jim*, ch. 13, Conrad attributed the same name to a ship which sank off the Spanish coast after a collision.

186 *a Conway boy*: the *Conway* was a training-ship for cadets, moored in the Mersey at Liverpool. Many of the cadets subsequently became naval officers; and the ex-*Conway* person could feel that (compared with the average seaman) he belonged to an élite. John Masefield's *The Conway* (London: Heinemann, 1933) makes clear that the trainees were encouraged to be loyal to each other in later life. (Conrad's 'Lord Jim' serves in a training-ship whose régime resembles that of the *Conway*.)

My father's a parson: this is one of several links between Leggatt and Lord Jim. Jim, too, is a parson's son, becomes a fugitive from a maritime scandal, and is sympathetically treated by a sailing ship's captain. Furthermore, in Chapter 19 of *Lord Jim* (*LJ* 213), that captain, Marlow, describes Jim's presence aboard his ship (during another voyage from Bangkok) in terms which partly anticipate features of 'The Secret Sharer':

Jim, for the most part, skulked down below as though he had been a stowaway. He infected me so that I avoided speaking on professional matters [. . .] For whole days we did not exchange a word; I felt extremely unwilling to give orders to my officers in his presence.

189 *capital letter L*: it becomes, literally, the L for Leggatt.

191 *Oh, yes! she's on board*: in *Nostromo* (Part 3, ch. 10), Captain Mitchell says: 'I was never married myself. A sailor should exercise self-denial.'

The 'brand of Cain' business: Cain slew his brother Abel and was condemned by God to be 'a fugitive and a vagabond in the earth'; but 'the LORD set a mark upon Cain, lest any finding him should kill him'. (See Genesis 4: 8–15.)

201 *"Sephoras away!"*: other editions give ' "*Sephoras* away!" ' and ' "*Sephora's* away!" ' As the sense is ' "*Sephora*-men, leave this vessel!" ', I do not italicize the final letter of *Sephoras* in the tale's text.

202 *murders in Yankee ships*: American vessels were notorious for harsh conditions. R. H. Dana's *Two Years before the Mast* (ch. 15) records the brutal floggings which the master of the brig *Pilgrim* inflicted on his crew; and, in *Round the Horn before the Mast* (London: Murray, 1902), 33–4, Basil Lubbock says:

> On some of the Yankee hell ships the things that go on are almost incredible, and the captains have to be skilled surgeons to cope with the work of destruction wrought by their mates.
>   Legs and arms broken were considered nothing, ribs stamped in by heavy sea-boots had to mend as best they could, faces smashed like rotten apples by iron belaying pins had to get well or fear worse treatment [. . .]
>   Thus the reputation of American ships has got so bad that none but a real tough citizen [. . .] will ship on them.

Lubbock claims that 'on board a British ship a sailor can get justice in port, and a captain or mate knows he will get heavy punishment for brutality' (p. 32).

206 *sword over our heads*: another reference to the legendary sword of Damocles: see note to p. 62.

208 *Cambodian*: the serial and the first book edition have 'Cambodje', a Gallicism, 'Cambodge' being French for Cambodia (later Kampuchea).

209 *'Driven off the face of the earth'*: 'And Cain said unto the LORD, [. . .] Behold, thou hast driven me out this day from the face of the earth [. . .]' (Genesis 4: 13–14).
     As I came at night so I shall go . . . Not naked like a soul on the Day of Judgment: cf. 'Naked came I out of my mother's womb, and naked shall I return thither' (Job 1: 21); 'As he came forth of his mother's womb, naked shall he return to go as he came' (Ecclesiastes 5: 15); and 'all things *are* naked and opened unto the eyes of him [God] with whom we have to do' (Hebrews 4: 13).

210 *Koh-ring*: in *The Shadow-Line*, this island on the eastern side of the Gulf of Siam, 'a great, black, upheaved ridge among a lot of tiny islets', is invested with apparently uncanny power: it 'seemed to be the centre of a fatal circle'. JHS (12–13) suggests that Conrad recalled the actual Koh Rin or Koh Ryn ('Koh' means 'Island'), which is 360 feet high.

214 *She will weather*: later editions have the more suspense-building version, 'She may weather'. The captain means: 'The ship will sail to windward of Koh-ring without needing to tack.' To help Leggatt by taking the ship close to the island, the captain purports to believe that she will safely

pass the south point of Koh-ring without changing course. Like the incredulous mate, he knows that she cannot do so.

The vessel's manœuvres are these. She has been pursuing a roughly south-easterly course down the Gulf of Siam. As the light winds oppose her direct route, the captain has proceeded by tacking, making a zigzag progress which captures the wind now on one side of the ship and now on the other. The latest tack, for twenty hours or so, has directed her mainly easterly, towards Koh-ring; and, in order to reduce the distance to be swum by Leggatt, the captain has let the vessel approach perilously close to the island's rocky coast. If she continues on this course, she will run aground; but, if he attempts to change tack, there is a danger— greatly increased by the darkness—that, on losing headway as she faces the wind, she will then drift backwards onto the rocks. (Initially, the ship is on a starboard tack, which means that the wind is coming over her starboard bow; therefore a sharp right turn, through the wind, is required so as to direct her on a port tack, southwards, away from the island.)

The captain tells the helmsman: 'Keep her good full': i.e. 'Keep the vessel moving with the maximum wind in her sails', so that she may have the necessary momentum to preserve headway during the subsequent turn; and, by that instruction, he deters the helmsman from modifying the course to aid a presumed weathering. At 'Are you going on, sir?', a questioner implies that weathering is now impossible. The warning 'Keep her full. Don't check her way. That won't do now' again restrains the helmsman. The captain orders all hands to be ready on deck, because they will be needed to reorientate the sails during the new manœuvre. They are apprehensive, and the mate begins to panic: 'She will never weather, and you are too close now to stay': he thinks that on her present course the vessel will run aground, and that it is too late to change tack. After giving the standard warning of the impending manœuvre, 'Ready about', the captain orders the mate to see that the headsheets are 'properly overhauled', thus initiating the procedure of variously slackening and hauling the ropes to reset the headsails. At the command 'Hard alee!', the helmsman turns the wheel so that the rudder is drawn to starboard, thus swinging the vessel to starboard; and the hands then re-angle the mainsail ('I swung the mainyard'). Now, however, the captain's situation is extremely perilous, because in the darkness he cannot tell whether the ship is progressing or, on the contrary, drifting backwards before the wind. If her motion were backwards, the rudder would have to be swung from starboard to port in order to maintain the intended turn (as, when a ship goes backwards, the effect of the rudder is reversed). The white hat in the water providentially shows him that the vessel has indeed 'gathered sternway', so he orders the helmsman to 'shift the helm' (i.e. turn the wheel so that the rudder is moved from starboard to port), and accordingly the ship's bows resume their swing in the desired direction. With the wind now blowing across the port bow, the order 'Let go and haul' follows: the foreyards (bearing the sails of the foremast) are

promptly hauled round to capture the wind, and the ship progresses
safely towards open water.

215 *bark of the dead ... Erebus*: in classical mythology, Charon ferries the
souls of the dead in his boat (or 'bark') across the river of the underworld.
(Charon is the son of Erebus, god of darkness, whose name is given to the
entrance to Hades.)

216 *the saving mark for my eyes*: in *So Long to Learn* (London: Heinemann,
1952; p. 71), John Masefield recalled that the *Conway*'s Seamanship
Instructor, Wallace Blair, taught the cadets that a white straw hat could be
used 'to *mark the sea*'.

a fugitive and a vagabond ... no brand of the curse: a further allusion to
Genesis 4: 12–15.

GLOSSARY

abaft behind, towards the vessel's stern

Ach's! cries of 'oh!'

Ach so! 'oh, indeed!'

affected (p. 8) made a show of preferring

aft, after- behind, towards the vessel's stern

after-hatch rearmost hatch in main deck

ahoy! traditional nautical cry to hail a ship or attract attention

Alsatian native of Alsatia (Alsace or Elsass), a border-region long contested by France and Germany

anchor-watch allocation of one man (or more) to keep watch while a vessel is at anchor

aneroid glass glass face of the maritime aneroid barometer, which can resemble a clock; its pointer, activated by a vacuum cylinder, registers changes in atmospheric pressure

arcadian felicity contentment like that attributed to the pastoral inhabitants of legendary Arcadia in ancient Greece

articles (p. 55) the contract between the master and the crew of a ship, specifying the conditions of employment and the duties of each member of the crew

ashore (as in 'put my ship ashore', p. 113) aground; in collision with shore, sandbank, or other obstacle

athwart across; at right-angles to the fore-and-aft line of a vessel

ballast heavy material used to steady a vessel; 'in ballast' laden with ballast only

bar (p. 91) shoal or bank of sand or mud opposite a river mouth or harbour entrance

bark small sailing ship

barque normally a relatively small three-masted ship, often square-sterned, with fore-and-aft rig on the mizzenmast but square rig on the foremast and mainmast

batten (noun) (*a*) slat of wood or metal which fits staples and thus secures a hatch-cover; (*b*) wooden slat nailed to a compartment-floor to retain objects

batten down fasten securely by means of battens

beam (*a*) broadest part of a vessel; (*b*) horizontal timber extending from side to side of a ship, supporting a deck

Bedlam asylum for the insane at London, named after the Priory of St Mary of Bethlehem which originally occupied the site

bend sails secure sails to spars

Bengal light firework yielding a sustained brilliance; used as a shipwreck signal-flare or to illuminate an area at night

bight (of bay) curve

billet (colloquial) post, occupation

binnacle stand containing the compass, its light, and its hood

black-squad men of the engine-room

block pulley; frame containing a roller over which a rope may run

boatswain naval foreman: petty officer on a merchant ship who immediately supervises the work-force and its tasks

bosun (colloquial) boatswain

bow, bows forward part of vessel, where it curves to the stem

bowsprit spar projecting forward from a vessel's stem

brace rope controlling the horizontal movement of the yards

brass-bound ornamented with gold braid

break of the poop front of the poop deck, where ladders lead down to the main deck

bridge platform from which the officer in command directs the vessel

bridge-screens panels to protect bridge-occupants from the weather

broached-to swung sideways to windward

bulkhead upright partition between compartments

bulwark ship's side above deck-level

bummer sponger or parasitic idler

bunker compartment for storing coal below decks

bunting thin material used for flags

burgomaster mayor

calotte soft round cap

capstan cylindrical device for heaving anchors or raising yards, rotated (if not by steam) by means of bars inserted into holes

Capuchin bearded monk of an austere branch of the Franciscan order

Carimata (subsequently Karimata) island off the south-west coast of Borneo, 1 degree 40 minutes south, 108 degrees 50 minutes east

Celestial familiar term for Chinaman (China being then 'the Celestial Empire')

centaur composite creature (in Greek mythology) with the head and torso of a man but the body and legs of a horse

chancery in a tight and uncomfortable grip

chit of a girl mere childish female

chock iron casting through which ropes or hawsers are guided; but 'rolling chocks on bilges' are keels on the curve of the hull below the waterline to resist the rolling motion of the vessel

chronometer very accurate maritime clock, often fitted with gimbals for stability; used for establishing longitude

chucked (p. 110) gave a friendly pat

chucker-out barman or doorkeeper ('bouncer') who ejects people deemed unwelcome

close-hauled under short canvas with sails reduced in area and hauled close (away from square), so that the ship bears as nearly against the wind as is consistent with retaining the wind's propulsive force

coal-trimmer man who stows the coal

coaming raised border, to repel water, round the edge of a hatch

cobble small fishing-boat with high bows and square stern, usually fitted with a lug-sail

Cochin-China region (later included in Vietnam) extending northwards from the Mekong Delta

coming-to coming to a stop by turning the bows towards the wind

companion (*a*) ladder or stairway; (*b*) entrance to a stairway; (*c*) skylight or window-frame admitting light to a lower deck or cabin

compass card rotating circular card displaying the main bearings; a pointer indicates the vessel's course

conceive you (Gallicism) just imagine; can you imagine?

Conway **boy** cadet or former cadet of the training-ship *Conway*, moored at Liverpool

coolies Chinese labourers

coram populo (Latin) in public

counter-scarp rising slope before a steep dip

country (as in 'country wife', 'country ship') indigenous; native, not European; local

crank arrested on the cant shaft-arm halted in a sloping position

cuddy in a small vessel (such as Falk's), a small cabin; in a larger vessel (like that in 'The Secret Sharer'), a saloon in which the officers take their meals. Hermann's cuddy, intermediate in size, resembles 'a farm kitchen'

cyclopean ancient and immense, built of irregular blocks or unhewn stone; in classical mythology, the Cyclopes were craftsmen credited with making fortifications

davits derricks by which a ship's boat is raised or lowered

deals (p. 142) fir or pine boards or planks

demurrage of the lighters compensation paid to a ship's charterer for undue delay in supplying or unloading her cargo

der verfluchte Kerl (German) the accursed fellow; the damned oaf

dodger canvas wind-shield for the ship's bridge

donkeyman man who tends an auxiliary engine

drawing nine feet aft requiring a water-depth of 9 feet (nearly 3 metres) towards the stern

draws over twenty feet has a depth in the water of more than 6 metres

dredging with the anchor down moving a vessel from one position to another by using a dropped anchor to guide or control its course downstream

Dumbarton Scottish town on the River Clyde, near Glasgow; then famed for its shipbuilding industry

Dutchmen (p. 95) obsolete colloquial term for Germans

Dutch Uncle (idiomatic) person who gives a severe reprimand or lengthy admonition

écarté card-game for two players in which each player may discard any or all of the cards dealt

Elbe German river that flows through Hamburg towards the North Sea via Cuxhaven

elevated (p. 172) elated by intoxication

enfilading view end-to-end view

Erebus name (meaning 'Darkness') of the gloomy cavern by which, according to classical mythology, the souls of the dead entered the underworld of Hades

fakir Indian ascetic, beggar, or magician, conventionally depicted as wearing only a loin-cloth

fall loose end of a rope used for raising or lowering (usually by means of a block); 'overhauled falls': ropes adjusted to separate their blocks

fiddle of the stokehold steel grating fitted over the hatch to the boiler-room

fishing-stakes bamboo poles to moor fishing-nets

Fo-kien a province (later called Fujian) in south-east China

forebitts pair of posts (at the foremast) to which cables are fastened

forebraces ropes used to change the setting of a foresail

forecastle (pronounced '*foke*-sul') forepart of the ship, including the crew's accommodation

forecastle head raised deck at the foremost part of the ship

forefoot foremost end of the keel, where it meets the stem

foremast front mast

fore-rigging ropes of the foremast and foresails

fore-royal brace rope of the fore-royal sail (the uppermost sail on the foremast)

foresail chief and lowest square sail on the foremast

foreyards spars supporting sails on the foremast

forward (on a ship) towards the vessel's bow

fracas noisy quarrel

friction winch hoisting machine (on which a rope is wound) fitted with a braking device

Fu-chau Chinese port (later Fuzhou) on the Formosa Strait (later Taiwan Strait)

funk (slang) fear

gamp (colloquial) umbrella, after Mrs Gamp's in Dickens's *Martin Chuzzlewit*

gasket canvas strap to fasten a sail to a yard or boom.

German Ocean North Sea

gharry small cab drawn by horse or pony

gig long, light boat

gimbals device for keeping an object level, often consisting of two concentric metal rings bearing at opposite points on knife-edges

gins pulleys for hoisting cargo

Good Hope the South African Cape

Gottverdamm! (German) God damn it!

grog-shop bar selling alcoholic liquors (grog being originally a mixture of rum and water)

gunny-bags jute sacks

Hades (*a*) the underworld; Hell; (*b*) the name of a god of the underworld

halyards ropes for hoisting yards and sails; 'signal halyards': cords for hoisting signal-flags

hard alee! 'Turn the wheel fully in a leeward direction!'

hawse pipe iron casting (in the bow) through which the anchor-chain runs

hawser rope or cable, often made of steel, by which a ship is anchored, towed, etc.

head-sheets ropes of the fore-and-aft sails in front of the foremast

helm steering apparatus, particularly the helmsman's wheel; 'shift the helm': turn the wheel

Himmel! Zwei und dreissig Pfund! (German) 'Good heavens! Thirty-two pounds!'

hooker mildly derogatory term for a vessel deemed clumsy or inadequate

Hussars cavalrymen

incontinently impetuously, immediately

inexpressibles facetious term for trousers

in extremis (Latin) at the point of death; in desperate circumstances

jalousie slatted shutter

Java Head the western tip of Java, where the Sunda Strait meets the Indian Ocean

jet (p. 69) black beading

Joss Chinese idol

jury rudder makeshift rudder

keelson (pronounced '*kel*-sun') ship's stringer or inner keel which fixes the floor-timbers to the outer keel

Kerl (German) fellow, oaf (cf. English 'churl')

Klings Indians (originating from south-east India and Sri Lanka) of Asian and Malaysian seaports

lacustrine lakeside

land breezes breezes which blow at night from land to sea (because the sea is then relatively warm)

lead-line line weighted with lead, used for measuring the depth of water

leeward (pronounced '*loo*-erd') towards the lee: the sheltered side (as opposed to 'windward', the side against which the wind blows)

let go and haul 'let go the sail-ropes on the windward side and pull the sail-ropes on the lee side': an order given during a tacking manœuvre when the wind has filled the rear sails and now the front sails need to be swung to capture the wind

light breeze on the Beaufort scale, number 2: windspeed of 4–6 knots

lighters open boats used for loading and unloading ships

limekilns furnaces in which chalk or limestone is reduced to quick-lime

Lower Hope Reach 4-mile stretch of the River Thames, extending northwards past East Tilbury

lug square sail on a yard that hangs obliquely to the mast

main-brace rope attached to the mainyard

main-deck uppermost of the decks which span the length and breadth of a ship

mainmast chief mast of a sailing-vessel with two or more masts: on a yawl or ketch, the foremast; on most other vessels, the second mast from the bow

mainsail largest and lowest sail on the mainmast

mainsail haul! 'adjust the ropes to change the angle of the largest sail!': an order given during the tacking manœuvre when the wind is nearly ahead; the mainyard is swung to capture the wind for the new stage of the ship's zigzag progress

maintopsail on the mainmast, the second sail up

mainyard lowest yard (horizontal spar) on the mainmast

manila line rope made from the fibre (Manila hemp) of the wild banana stalk

Martello tower circular fort resembling a squat tower; in south-eastern England, many such forts were erected in anticipation of a French invasion during the Napoleonic period

mastheads tops of masts

Meinam river (later called Chao Phraya) that flows through Bangkok (Krung Thep) into the Gulf of Siam (Gulf of Thailand)

mess money money for meals

mess together take meals together

midden refuse-heap, garbage-tip

mizzen-mast rear mast on a three-masted vessel

mizzen-rigging ropes of the mizzen-mast and of its spars

monachal monk-like, ascetic

mooring-bitts pair of posts to which mooring-ropes can be fastened

mountaineer mountain-dweller, highlander

nap (p. 38) the card-game 'Napoleon'

narrow seas seas offering numerous navigational hazards

nota bene (Latin) notice carefully

off-shore tack course heading away from shore during the zigzag manœuvres of tacking

olympian resembling a deity who, according to classical mythology, lives on Mount Olympus

pacific peaceful, calm

painter rope in the bow of a boat for securing or towing it

Paknam customs port on the Bight of Bangkok

pallet rudimentary bed; sometimes merely a straw mattress

P. & O. boat vessel of the Peninsular & Oriental Steamship Company

pâté de foie gras rich paste of fattened goose-liver

pepper-and-salt suit suit of mixed black and white material

pintles heavy pins or bolts on which the rudder swivels

pitch-pine pine-tree yielding pitch and timber

Platt-Deutsch (usually *Plattdeutsch*) Low German vernacular language

point division of the compass, being an arc of $11\frac{1}{4}$ degrees; 'four points off course': 45 degrees away from the intended course

pole-masts masts without yards and sails, as on steamers

polls heads

poop high deck at the rear of a ship

port (side of ship) left side, as one faces forward

ports (*a*) hinged porthole-covers; (*b*) covered openings for light and ventilation, e.g portholes; (*c*) rectangular sash-windows, each with several panes (as in Hermann's ship in 'Falk')

punkah large fan, often in the form of a flap raised and lowered manually by means of a pulley

quarter (of ship) either side of a ship abaft the beam

quarter-deck rear part of the main deck, between the poop and the mainmast

rack   contraption to torture victims by slowly stretching them; 'the working of the rack': the slow torment

ratlines   rope rungs to help seamen climb the rigging

rattan   cane made from a thin-stemmed climbing palm

ready about (p. 215)   an order to commence tacking

recrudescence   resurgence

reefed foresail   The foresail is reefed by being rolled up and secured; on the *Sephora* (p. 187), when the other sails have been blown away by the gale, the reefed foresail may suffice to enable the ship to be navigated instead of wallowing at the mercy of the winds

riding-light   white light, hanging in the rigging near the bows at night, when the vessel is riding at anchor

right-about   opposite direction; in drill, sometimes a turn preliminary to dismissal; hence, 'sent to the right-about' (p. 144): dismissed, rejected

River Plate   El Río de la Plata, the river which flows between Argentina and Uruguay

roads, roadstead   offshore expanse of water where ships may ride safely at anchor

rudder-chains   chains leading from the rudder to each of the two rear quarters of the vessel

runner   seaman engaged for a single short voyage

running gear   ropes which run through blocks or pulleys and are used to haul spars and sails

sampan   flat-bottomed oriental boat

scapulary   cloth with head-opening, worn round the neck as a sign of religious affiliation

scathless   (usually 'scatheless') unharmed

Sclavonia   (now-archaic form of) Slavonia, name of the region bounded by the Danube, Sava, and Drava

scow   flat-bottomed boat used for local transportation of goods

sheer against the helm   swerve away from the proper course

sheet   rope attached to the lower corner of a sail

siren (p. 142)   mythical sea-nymph, part woman and part bird, whose songs lured seamen to death

slice (noun)   hooked or bladed poker for removing cinders from the grate-bars of furnaces or for stowing coal

slop-made   ready-made

slush   grease and fat from cooking

slush-slingers   galley-hands

sou'wester (hat)   waterproof hat extending over the back of the neck

sovereign   British gold coin worth one pound in the values of that time

spars general term for the stout poles used as masts, yards, booms, etc., on a vessel

spliced to (slang) married to

spoken them (at sea) hailed them

square the yards by lifts and braces (p. 195) 'set the yards so that they are horizontal and at right-angles to the fore-and-aft line of the vessel; use lifts (ropes from each masthead to its yard-arms) and braces (ropes attached to the ends of the yard-arms) for the purpose'. Yards 'square by the lifts' are horizontal; yards 'square by the braces' are at right angles

stanchion upright post of wood or metal to support a rail, awning, or other object

stand right in sail very close to the coast

starboard (side of a ship) right side, as one faces forward.

stateroom private cabin

stay (verb) head into the wind in tacking. 'You are too close now to stay' (p. 215): 'you are too close to the land to be able to turn the vessel to windward in tacking'; 'put in stays' (p. 214): turned to windward in the tacking manœuvre

strop circle of rope used as a strap (for freight or rigging). 'Splicing a strop': joining two rope-ends by interweaving their strands so as to complete a strop

Sunda Straits channel between Java and Sumatra

Table Bay bay north of Cape Town in South Africa

table-d'hôte meal served at a set time and set rate in a hotel or restaurant

tack (verb) make a zigzag course (when the direct course is opposed to the wind) by angling the yards alternately for each oblique run. More specifically, a vessel 'tacks' when her bows are swung into and across the wind, thus changing the side exposed to it

taffrail aftermost rail of a vessel, following the curve of the stern

Talcahuano Chilean port on the Pacific

tam' pizness . . . tam' ropper 'damned business' . . . 'damned robber'

Taotai Chinese provincial officer in a *tao* (circuit or division)

tap-room public room in which beer is served directly from the cask

Teddington south-western suburb of London, beside the Thames

terra-cotta 'baked earth': a reddish-brown composition of clay and sand, hardened by fire

'thwart-ship across the ship, from side to side

tiffin light lunch

tinker's curse worthless oath

toils (of destiny) nets and snares

Tophet Hell. (Tophet was the name originally of a valley of human sacrifice near Jerusalem, and subsequently, as in Isaiah 30: 33, of the site of God's vengeance.)

towing chock iron casting at the bow through which a hawser is passed for towing the ship

treaty port port opened, by treaty, to foreign trade

trimming . . . the stokehold ventilators swivelling the ventilators to windward so as to increase the air-flow to the stokehold

trooper oaths swearing characteristic of a private cavalry soldier (proverbially fluent in swearing)

truck (p. 66) flat circular cap of wood at the top of a mast

trysail small fore-and-aft sail

turned-to (p. 74) set to work

'tween-deck area between decks, particularly between the main deck and the deck beneath

waist (of ship) middle part

warp (a ship) move a ship by hauling on a 'warp' (towing-rope)

watch (*a*) period of duty; (*b*) group of men allotted to a period of duty

waterman man who plies a boat for hire

way (p. 216) motion; progress through the water

way . . . deadened in stays progress arrested as the vessel faces the wind during tacking

weather (verb) sail to windward of an obstacle

weather-cloth protective tarpaulin

West Hartlepool coastal town in north-eastern England

whipping of the fore-royal brace (p. 80) binding of the rope of the fore-royal sail. The 'whipping' is the binding of twine round the end of a rope to prevent its fraying. The fore-royal sail is the uppermost sail on the foremast

whipping up (p. 16) hoisting by means of a 'whip', a rope passed through a block

windlass rotating cylinder used for raising or lowering the anchor

yard spar on a mast, to bear or extend a sail

The Oxford World's Classics Website

www.worldsclassics.co.uk

- Browse the full range of Oxford World's Classics online

- Sign up for our monthly e-alert to receive information on new titles

- Read extracts from the Introductions

- Listen to our editors and translators talk about the world's greatest literature with our Oxford World's Classics audio guides

- Join the conversation, follow us on Twitter at OWC_Oxford

- Teachers and lecturers can order inspection copies quickly and simply via our website

www.worldsclassics.co.uk

American Literature

British and Irish Literature

Children's Literature

Classics and Ancient Literature

Colonial Literature

Eastern Literature

European Literature

Gothic Literature

History

Medieval Literature

Oxford English Drama

Poetry

Philosophy

Politics

Religion

The Oxford Shakespeare

A complete list of Oxford World's Classics, including Authors in Context, Oxford English Drama, and the Oxford Shakespeare, is available in the UK from the Marketing Services Department, Oxford University Press, Great Clarendon Street, Oxford OX2 6DP, or visit the website at www.oup.com/uk/worldsclassics.

In the USA, visit www.oup.com/us/owc for a complete title list.

Oxford World's Classics are available from all good bookshops. In case of difficulty, customers in the UK should contact Oxford University Press Bookshop, 116 High Street, Oxford OX1 4BR.

GEORGE ELIOT	Daniel Deronda
	The Lifted Veil and Brother Jacob
	Middlemarch
	The Mill on the Floss
	Silas Marner
SUSAN FERRIER	Marriage
ELIZABETH GASKELL	Cranford
	The Life of Charlotte Brontë
	Mary Barton
	North and South
	Wives and Daughters
GEORGE GISSING	New Grub Street
	The Odd Woman
THOMAS HARDY	Far from the Madding Crowd
	Jude the Obscure
	The Mayor of Casterbridge
	The Return of the Native
	Tess of the d'Urbervilles
	The Woodlanders
WILLIAM HAZLITT	Selected Writings
JAMES HOGG	The Private Memoirs and Confessions of a Justified Sinner
JOHN KEATS	The Major Works
	Selected Letters
CHARLES MATURIN	Melmoth the Wanderer
WALTER SCOTT	The Antiquary
	Ivanhoe
	Rob Roy
MARY SHELLEY	Frankenstein
	The Last Man

TROLLOPE IN OXFORD WORLD'S CLASSICS

ANTHONY TROLLOPE

An Autobiography
The American Senator
Barchester Towers
Can You Forgive Her?
The Claverings
Cousin Henry
Doctor Thorne
The Duke's Children
The Eustace Diamonds
Framley Parsonage
He Knew He Was Right
Lady Anna
The Last Chronicle of Barset
Orley Farm
Phineas Finn
Phineas Redux
The Prime Minister
Rachel Ray
The Small House at Allington
The Warden
The Way We Live Now